By Force of Circumstance

By Force of Circumstance

Book 3 in The
Chosen Man Trilogy

J.G. Harlond

By Force of Circumstance by J.G. Harlond

Copyright © 2018 J.G Harlond

ISBN-13: 978-1-946409-(Paperback)
ISBN ——978-1-946409-68-3(e-book)

BISAC Subject Headings:
FIC002000 FICTION / Action & Adventure
FIC014000 FICTION / Historical
FIC027050 FICTION / Romance / Historical

Edit by C Wozny 14
Cover by The Book Cover Whisperer:
ProfessionalBookCoverDesign.com

Address all correspondence to:

Penmore Press LLC
920 N Javelina Pl
Tucson AZ 85748

Dedication

For Tony

"Take a good resolution and pursue it. Remember your own maxim,
that it is better to follow out a bad resolution than to change it so often."
Queen Henrietta Maria to her husband, Charles 1st, May 1642

Names marked with an * are recorded in history.

Pope Urban VIII* – Maffeo Barberini of Florence
Cardinal Barberini* – his nephew
Rogelio – a Vatican agent
Ludovico da Portovenere – Genoese silk and spice merchant
Leonora Gasca Figaroa – Ludo's wife
Maria (called Naomi) – their daughter
Ludovico (called Vico) – Naomi's twin brother
Father Gregory – English Jesuit priest
Archibald Guthrie – Scottish merchant ship captain employed by Ludo
Gifford Greenwood – a young Royalist
Marcos Alonso Almendro (Mark Almond) – Spanish merchant living in Plymouth
Joanna – his wife
Edward Beale – Marcos's father-in-law
Alina – Maria de Los Angeles, Baroness Metherall
Thomas Fulford of Crimphele – Baron Metherall
Tomás (Tommy) – Thomas and Alina's son, heir to Crimphele
Hetty (Henrietta) – Alina's daughter
John Hawthorne – ordained Catholic priest, tutor to Alina's son Tomás
Anne Villiers, Lady Dalkeith* – lady-in-waiting to Queen Henrietta Maria
Meg & Mercy – servants at Crimphele
Mrs Godwin (Bodkin) – Crimphele housekeeper
Agnes (Crookback Aggie) – cook at Crimphele

Cecil Cleverden – aide-de-camp to Prince Maurice
Prince Maurice* – Royalist general and nephew of King Charles
Percy – cousin of Thomas Fulford of Crimphele
Jim Hawkins – Crimphele boatman
Mrs Hawkins – Jim's wife
Queen Henrietta Maria* French-born wife of Charles 1st
Henry, Baron Jermyn* – Queen Henrietta Maria's chamberlain
Clothilde – inn-keeper's daughter at the sign of the Black Swan
Cristophe le Blanc – French sea-captain
Sir Piers Edgcumbe* – English Royalist
Prince Charles Stuart* – heir to the British Crown
Toxo (Tosho) – a Galician mariner, captain of the caravel Magdalena
Maria del Mar – wife of Toxo
Javi – Toxo's brother-in-law
Blanca – Toxo's daughter and Hetty's nurse
Dom Enrique Guzman da Costa y Clarendon-Greenwood, Marquis de Coimbra
Luisa de Guzmán y Sandoval, Duchess of Braganza, Queen of Portugal*
Duke of Braganza, King of Portugal*
Gerardo Ludo's Portuguese servant
Cinco – cabin boy
Laurent, a French mariner

Prologue

The Pope's nephew sat by his uncle's bed at his appointed time. Another ritual to be observed – the old man was taking his time to die.

"What news this day?" asked the Vicar of Christ.

"A letter from England. We are invited to purchase the English Crown Jewels."

The sick man started to laugh. It turned into a coughing fit that left a square of white linen stained with blood. "Orb and sceptre?" he finally gasped.

"Not the regalia: gewgaws. She's offering the Heretic's bastard's diamonds, though. Getting those would be a nice irony." The cardinal nephew paused then added quietly, "... and the Three Brethren."

The Pope's eyes opened. He struggled to sit up. "This requires our attention. This could help you a great deal."

"Me? How?"

"More votes in the enclave. A coup such as the Protestant's diamonds . . ." The Pope tried to clear his throat and started again. "Make it known that you have acquired Queen Bess's diamonds; it will impress."

Cardinal Barberini patted the silken coverlet and said, "Yes, Your Holiness, of course," keeping his true thoughts to himself.

"Acquire whatever you can. Let the *consistoria* know you have the gems – and more – you don't have to show them but a casket. And keep that hidden and safe until . . ." Pope Urban ran out of breath.

"Until?"

"Their war is over."

"Until their war is over and we return it to the next *Catholic* king as a meaningful gift?" The young cardinal began to laugh, "You old fox."

The Pope wheezed into his handkerchief then gasped out, "She's not to get a ducat in return. Promises, yes, give her anything in that line, but no money. She's had enough. We don't want her husband succeeding – not now. They had their chance and failed us. We need the boy, but with his mother's religion, and thanking us for our backing. Do you follow?"

"Yes, but she's asking us to *buy* the jewels to finance the Royalist cause – and many of them are Catholics."

The linen square was raised in a gesture of contempt: "Medici blood."

The cardinal watched the bald head settle back against a fat, tasselled pillow. He's not dying yet, he thought. There might be time to achieve this before the enclave.

"Always remember, the boy's grandmother is a Habsburg and Medici. Charles Stuart might be killed at any time – you need to be ready."

"Killed on or off the battle field: my intelligencers tell me Parliamentary Roundheads want him dead, not deposed. That can be precipitated."

"No. A step too far. Get to the heir. Tell him you have the baubles in safe keeping *for his reign*. That's the way. In safe keeping for his reign."

"So it's worth the effort – acquiring these jewels?"

"Yes!" A clawed hand came down on his arm. "Use Rogelio. He was in London with Henrietta Maria . . ."

"He failed us in the matter of the financial scandal in Holland. He cheated us over the Braganza funding."

The dying pope lifted the fleshless hand, tried and failed to speak. Cardinal Barberini waited, remembering the Genoese merchant who had outwitted Rogelio in both

Amsterdam and Lisbon, the wily Ludovico da Portovenere. If anyone could acquire the jewels without stealing or paying for them, or making awkward promises, he could. Rogelio wouldn't like it. The Genoese had cheated him by stealing a small fortune from Vatican coffers destined for the Braganza pretender. Proof, if proof was needed, of the so-called merchant's efficacy.

Cardinal Barberini smiled and sat back, musing on a strategy. Rogelio had been his uncle's creature. When he was pope he would draw modern, worldly men such as da Portovenere to him; establish his own network. The future lay with men of commerce, a fact Charles Stuart had ignored to his peril. The future was also with the Protestant Dutch and those travelling to far places to establish new trade routes. The Catholic Church should be with them, benefitting from them, not locked in a medieval feud. The English jewels would be a good excuse to bring the Genoese to his side. He relayed a shortened version of his thoughts to the master tactician in the curtained bed.

"You'll need a hold over him," was the reply.

"That is how you keep Rogelio's loyalty?"

"Rogelio owes us a debt for his survival as a child and promotion as a man." Pope Urban smiled for the first time in days. "Return tomorrow with a plan."

The cardinal nephew leant over the high bed to kiss the papal ring on the hand gripping the sodden linen square, as he did so the other hand grasped his hair and held his head to the jewel. "Let it be known you are bringing England back to Rome and the papacy is yours. Promise me *our* family will prevail when I am gone."

"I promise, Your Holiness."

Rogelio sat when instructed and wound his legs together under his black robe. Going to a shelf in a tall cabinet, Cardinal Barberini picked up a crucifix inlaid with silver and lapis lazuli. "Do you remember this?" he asked, returning to his desk and taking a seat.

The humourless agent, who had taken holy vows but was only ever addressed as Rogelio, gave his habitual sniff and said, "No, Your Eminence, I can't say I do."

"Perhaps you never saw it. It was a gift from a Spanish envoy."

"Ah, the Dutch debacle."

"I wouldn't call it that. His Holiness achieved what we – the Vatican – needed at the time."

"If you say so, Eminence."

Barberini gave the agent a sharp look. "We pay you for intelligence, not impertinence." Rogelio looked at the ceiling. Annoyed, the cardinal said, "Considering the current situation, you would do well to remember where your loyalties lie."

There was the briefest of reaction before Rogelio's sallow, beardless face resumed its habitual scowl. He said nothing.

"We are sending you back to the English queen," the cardinal continued. "She is planning to return to France, so make sure of her whereabouts before you set out. You are also to learn what Cardinal Mazarin is planning – for his future. I hear he has become somewhat *over ambitious*. That he would prefer to be wearing white."

"Him as well."

Barberini's eyes narrowed. "Find that Genoese rogue we used in the Dutch business."

"Da Portovenere? Him, why?"

Barberini looked at his agent, taking note of the change in his tone. It was not like Rogelio to betray emotion. "Is there something I should know?" he asked.

"It's personal."

"It is most unwise to let personal matters influence actions in your profession. Why is it 'personal'?"

"I have my reasons."

"Which I need to know before we go any further."

"Family reasons."

"Family!" It was a surprise. "I thought Ludovico da Portovenere was Agostino Doria's daughter's bastard by a corsair."

"He is."

"And that makes him 'family'. Interesting." Barberini raised his eyebrows and was about to ask for more details, then decided against it and moved on. "Going back to Mazarin, he has informers among us here. We cannot have the French thinking we are aiding England at this juncture. Lead them off the matter."

"Why am I really going back to the queen?"

"Henrietta Maria has been touting the English Crown Jewels around Europe trying to pawn them or sell them to raise money, but without much success. It would be convenient to have them here, and I *personally* want two items in particular."

Rogelio sniffed. "What's this to do with the Genoese? I don't want a repetition of Amsterdam or Lisbon. He made a fortune for himself each time. He'll cheat Henrietta if you're planning for him to do the selling."

"That is what I am hoping for. Can I also hope that you'll be fast enough to rescue at least two of the items before he does?" That silenced Rogelio's sarcasm. The cardinal, who was somewhat more intelligent than his overbearing uncle gave him credit for, continued, "Let me explain. I need him to acquire items Henrietta is offering for sale. He is to be instructed to act as her agent and make lucrative deals where he can. She'll be expecting him to pay her what he obtains for the jewels, minus a certain commission, one supposes."

"Commission, ha! He'll sell the lot for his own benefit."

"Not all of them, if you get what I tell you to. But yes, that is our general intention."

"Why da Portovenere? Can't someone else do the brokering?"

Cardinal Barberini tapped the encrusted crucifix then looked away, saying, "You yourself told me he has a way with women; our plan is that she entrusts the items to him as her agent – to sell them – and when he doesn't return her money nobody will be surprised. Events will dictate how we follow this through, thereafter."

"And I take – steal – your specific items *from him*, not her. That, Eminence, will be a pleasure."

The cardinal eyed the agent considering the implications of such open animosity. Under scrutiny Rogelio began unwinding and rewinding his long legs under his chair.

There was a brief silence. "Anything else?" Rogelio asked.

"Initially, you send me a coded list of what Henrietta Maria is selling. The two named items you are to acquire are a necklace known as 'Queen Bess's diamonds' and a brooch or clasp known as the 'Three Brethren'. There is also a gem that was given to the Isabella of Castile when she was named 'Catholic Queen' by the pope in her day, which she then gave to Catalina d'Aragon – we would like it back." Barberini paused, got to his feet and replaced the crucifix on its shelf, saying, "This Genoese – cousin, is he? – once you've found him make sure he doesn't wriggle out of it. But ..." he turned and looked Rogelio in the eye, "given the circumstances, you had better use Gregorio. Stay away from your dear cuz until he gets to France. Once he's got the jewels and you've got what I'm asking for, you can do what you like with him. How long will it take for Gregorio to locate him?"

"He's in Genoa according to reports. He's got a business in the East – Portuguese Goa – but he's back here now."

"You keep tabs on him."

Rogelio sniffed, "Usual sources. Goa is very Catholic."

Barberini nodded then continued. "Persuade – no, insist the queen entrusts all the jewels to him. Now get out, contrary to somebody's wishes I have an arms shipment to arrange. Come back tomorrow morning with your bags packed."

Part One
Genoa

Chapter 1

Genoa, early summer 1644

Ludo sat down in Leonora's much travelled cane chair in the gentle dark of their chamber, and rested his head, now greying at the temples, against her bright Indian cushions. "It was Vico," he said. "Nurse is with him. He was talking in his sleep. It feels strange for them, sleeping on dry land after so many months on a rolling ship." Ludo was referring to the small twins in the nursery along the passage. "You should go back to sleep as well," he said softly, noticing his wife's flushed face in the candlelight.

Leaning forward Ludo put a hand to her brow, she was sweating again: another bout of malaria, and in the final third of her pregnancy. He lifted a lemon-scented cloth from a bowl and dabbed her forehead. "Better?"

Hot fingers touched his. Leonora started to say something, then suddenly she was sitting bolt upright, clenching the sheets.

"Has it started?" he asked anxiously. "Surely, it is too soon."

"Yes – yes," the response was a twisted hiss. "Too soon."

"I'll fetch Nurse and send for the midwife."

As Ludo made his way back to the children's room there was a loud, insistent banging on the door below. Ignoring it, he raced to get the twins' nurse, who was already crossing the landing towards him. "Go to Donna Leonora," he said.

"Ludo!" Leonora screamed.

The battering below continued.

"I'm going for the midwife, *carina*. Here's Nurse." Ludo placed his large paw on the local woman's narrow shoulder. "Stay with my wife," he said urgently. "I'll send a servant up with water and fetch the midwife myself."

The small woman nodded and entered Leonora's chamber.

As Ludo reached the turn in the stairs one of their new maid-servants was reaching the front door. "Tell whoever it is to go away, we are not at home." Ludo stopped in his tracks, "No, don't, I'll go. You go for the midwife. You know these streets better than I do. Tell her to hurry!" The battering became more insistent. "Go on, run! I'll deal with this."

Whoever had come knocking at this time of night, and in such a manner, had an emergency of their own that no chit of a girl could deal with. Ludo pulled back the first bolt just as Leonora's second wail of pain rent the calm of their new home forever.

"What?" Ludo demanded, not looking at their visitor because he was staring back up the stairs. A rough hand pulled him out of the doorway.

Ludo was tall and broad-shouldered, but the brute manhandling him was bigger. A much shorter man flanked by two men-at-arms in fancy livery handed him a folded letter with one hand and brandished something like a rolled document in the other. "You are instructed to come with us," the letter-bearer stated.

Struggling to free himself, Ludo retorted, "Instruct who you please, I'm going nowhere. My wife is in childbed."

"That's no matter to us at present," the short man said. "Bind him!"

One of the men in livery flourished a length of rope from concealment and began winding it rapidly around Ludo's arms and body. The second magicked a thickly-knotted truncheon from nowhere, and the messenger stuffed a rag in his mouth.

"No!" Ludo's voice was a muffled scream. Then there was blackness.

Sometime later, he had no means of knowing how long, a slither of light showed Ludo he was in an extremely small space. Waking from an over-vivid dream of climbing waves and monstrous sea-serpents, he lay still, sweating and frightened. His mouth was dry yet sticky. He put a hand to his lips then his chest, the front of his cotton blouse was tacky. He assumed it was blood, but it was more like molasses or honey. He ran his tongue over his lips. They were sweet-tasting. Moving his hand across his chest, Ludo remembered he had been bound and gagged, but now he was not. He began to explore his confinement. He was lying on a narrow wooden pallet or shelf with his right shoulder shoved up against a stone wall. His feet touched another wall, his head touched a third. Turning onto his side, Ludo's next thought was not to his situation but what was happening to his wife. Had the midwife been found? Was Leonora all right? And their baby? How ironic, how appallingly ironic that she had survived sea-sickness and all the rigours of caring for two small children on a voyage half way around the globe to be caught by malaria in Genoa – and premature labour.

Ludo searched his memory for something resembling a prayer. Having never prayed except under duress as an adolescent he had no solace to grasp or employ.

The wall to his left moved, a door opened, a widening of the sliver of light brought a cup and plate then blackness returned. "Hey!" he called. No one replied.

A dull thud settled into his left temple – like the thuds on their door – thump, thump, thump. He pressed the heels of his hands against his forehead and drifted back to the nightmare at sea.

The next time the door opened a bucket was pushed in, allowing the smallest draught of enter, but the door was closed again before he could sit up. This time Ludo put his feet to the floor: his head threatened to explode but he stayed upright then tried to stand. His head cracked against wooden boards. His toes stubbed against the bucket. He was barefoot. He tried to remember what he had been wearing when he was taken: a loose blouse, thin pantaloons and Turkish slippers. It had been night time. His son had called out and his daughter had started to cry. He had gone to them. Anger pulsed through him as he reached across the black space and banged on the door. It made a hollow sound. Wooden planks. He tried to kick it open with his feet.

"You're wasting your time." A voice speaking English. Ludo sat still. English, here? Why? "Who are you?" he demanded. There was no reply.

Then the door opened, just wide enough to show an elderly priest standing in what appeared to be a large room. "Let him out," he said, addressing to two liveried men behind him.

Bent and aching, Ludo shuffled into a muted daylight. Thick curtains had been pulled across a window. He had no idea where he was or why, but the great brute that had manhandled him here was standing by the door with his arms crossed like the evil genie in an Arabic tale.

The cleric, a Jesuit from his robes, crossed to a desk and indicated Ludo was to stand before him. Lifting a document, he said in a thin but educated English voice, "Ludovico da Portovenere, you are hereby accused of conspiring with the devil in the practice of alchemy."

Ludo frowned. "What?"

"A crucible has been revealed in your warehouse."

"Yes. What has this to do with the church? There is no law against mixing spices, nor against melting metals. If there were, you'd have no swords or daggers – no dainty new forks to eat with." Despite the pain in his head he cast around for any such weapons. "And you can hardly call my crucible –"

"We can and shall call it what we choose. Sit," said the cleric, a spare man who matched his voice.

Seated, Ludo stretched his neck, trying to ease the pain across his shoulders where he had been coshed. As he moved, he took in the room again: a spartan chamber containing a plain desk bearing an ebony crucifix and a tiny brass bell. It was Indian in design. "This isn't anything to do with my metal experiment, is it?" he said.

"It can be – if you choose not to co-operate."

Ludo closed his eyes. "Tell me," he said.

"I have been instructed to convey an urgent message. Also a request, but that will come later."

"A message! About my wife? What? Is she all right? The child?" The Jesuit's eyes narrowed; he didn't understand. "My wife was in childbed when I was taken," Ludo snapped.

A moue of disgust escaped the priest. "Lamentable, but it has no bearing on this business. I am instructed by a cardinal at the behest of someone of very great importance..."

Ludo slumped in his chair. He had heard this before, almost the exact same wording, a life-time ago – ten years or thereabouts – from another English priest.

"... to return to England at the earliest opportunity."

"No."

"I was advised you might take this attitude." The Jesuit lifted the little bell and gave it a delicate shake.

The brute at the door crossed the room with frightening agility and bustled Ludo back towards the cupboard. Ludo shoved his arms against the opening and sighed, "All right. What is it you want?"

Taking the chair facing the Jesuit once more, Ludo silently vowed to agree to everything and get back to Leonora as fast as he could, having not the slightest intention of doing whatever the Church demanded of him. So he was surprised when the Jesuit said, "This is not entirely an ecclesiastical matter, *Signor* Ludovico. I am aware that you have, er... experienced some distress at the hands of a Vatican agent in the past. He somewhat overstepped his brief, perhaps, but given his role ... what can one say? Needs must when the devil drives."

Ludo stayed silent. The Jesuit was adopting a strategy similar to one he had often used himself – to his own advantage: wrap the listener in details that go nowhere, obfuscate and approach the target in a tangle of trivia. Ludo focused not on the words but their direction and watched the Jesuit's face as he stroked a finger over the dome of the bell until finally reaching his objective. "You are required to convey a valuable cargo of munitions to England as soon as possible."

"Bit difficult if I'm shut in a cupboard. Why have I been shut in a cupboard, by the way?"

"A precautionary measure. Having found you, I am not anxious to lose you again. You should also be aware that we are not to be underestimated. Our network guarantees that we can find you and put you in a cupboard in all manner of foreign places."

It was almost amusing but Ludo was not fool enough smile. Before he could say more, the Englishman was interrupted by a door opening. Ludo turned to see who was entering but no one actually came in. A tall, young man, judging by his physique, stood framed in the open doorway until a stockier, older man in a clerical robe pushed him out of the way. Catching sight of Ludo, the cleric rapidly closed the door again. Ludo's last glimpse was of a young man's fair, wavy hair that fell below shoulder length: another Englishman or a Dutch boy perhaps. What was he doing here with Jesuit priests? Storing the image, Ludo turned his attention back to his interlocutor. "Foreign places?" he queried.

The query was ignored so Ludo said, "My ship will sail for Plymouth the moment the war there has ended, that I can promise. Their internecine strife is costing me dear: I shan't need any particular inducement. However, the last time I tried to get into Plymouth we were turned away at gunpoint, so I am very wary about risking my vessel and crew again. May I go now? My wife needs me." Ludo started to get to his feet and intercepted a signal from the priest to the muscled brute blocking the exit. He resumed his seat.

The Jesuit now tapped the bell pensively then, choosing his words carefully, he said, "I carry a request from Her Majesty Queen Henrietta Maria. After you have conveyed the cargo to the new port of Falmouth – not Plymouth – she requires you to attend on her at your earliest convenience."

Ludo burst out laughing, "My earliest convenience being entirely in the hands of two warring factions. I am not walking or sailing into gunfire again so forget it. But tell me, out of curiosity, what is this *commedia* all about?"

The priest stared Ludo in the eye then said, "I was informed you would need persuasion and advised how best to obtain your consent."

By Rogelio, Ludo closed his eyes. He had been drugged and incarcerated on Rogelio's instructions: it had all the marks of *la Bicha*'s intervention. "Tell me what you want," he said drily.

"Her Majesty requires your skills. It is a matter of raising finance for the royal cause."

"*Requires!* She 'requires' that I raise money for her! What, to pay myself? I have sent her two entire chests of valuables – both containing silks and some very fine pearls and gemstones – and she has paid not a copper coin for them."

The priest inclined his head, "These are difficult times."

Ludo cocked his head to one side and tried a lighter tone. "Sorry, no. Under other circumstances perhaps, but I won't risk my vessel against English Parliament frigates."

The priest sat back, "I see." After a long pause, he said, "We *should* be able to protect you as you enter Falmouth. It is a small harbour I'm told. The garrison of Pendennis is nearby and that's safely under Royalist command. After you have unloaded you will then sail directly for Le Havre."

"France?" Ludo frowned then regretted it. "Will they purchase my spices and silks in Le Havre – assuming I can squeeze some in between your muskets and explosives? I have no argument against selling to the French if they'll pay my prices. Why Le Havre?"

"It is accessible for Paris, where Her Majesty will probably be residing."

"Then why in the name of all that's holy didn't you come to my office in the first place and ask me to sell my goods there, then? Forgive me, we have not been introduced and I regret our paths have never crossed."

"I am called Father Gregory."

Ludo waited for the man to say more, when he did not, he picked up a dropped word from something said earlier: 'probably'. "You mean you don't know where the Queen of England is, but I'm to go to her at my earliest convenience regardless." Ludo shook his head and regretted it again: his temple was bursting with pain. "One thing, if you know so much about me, you must also know I have a business partner and agent in Plymouth. As I said, the city was under siege when I tried to enter two years ago; has that changed?"

"I believe our Royalists failed to take the city, but they may have succeeded by now."

"*Our Royalists*? So the Vatican is aiding King Charles with weaponry. No surprise, but what's it to do with his wife? Or is she arranging supplies via the Holy See?" It was logical, he thought, given that she was an ardent Catholic intent on returning England, if not the entire Three Kingdoms, to the Catholic faith. It was good news at least for his friend Marcos and his family in Plymouth, if it could be achieved, but the way this Father Gregory was speaking suggested the other side was winning. He wanted to know more, was even ready to consider a proposal, but the more pressing matter was Leonora. "Look," he said, hoping to sound reasonable, "can we discuss this properly tomorrow? I need to get back to my wife."

Father Gregory stared through him. "I am instructed not to 'discuss' anything further until we have a signed statement that you will comply with our requirements."

Ludo sighed. "All right, in principle, yes. I hadn't intended to sell in France, but if you give me good reason, and a hefty reward for risking a new market, *I might risk* delivering your cargo. Genoese armaments first, I suppose."

He briefly let his mind evaluate sailing to England with such a hefty cargo then another attempt to get into Plymouth – and from there take a barge up the Tamar River to Crimphele, where the lovely but unattainable Alina lived. Then just as quickly dismissed it: Alina meant nothing to him anymore, not now he had Leonora and the twins. Another thought occurred to him. "Father Gregory, have you come all the way from England to deliver this message?"

"I was in Rome. I should also tell you I met with the Portuguese envoy to the Vatican while I was there."

Ludo closed his eyes. They'd got him. It had taken three years but they'd caught up with him for failing to assist the Portuguese pretender, the Duke of Braganza, as instructed – and stealing some of their gold and silver. Rogelio had been involved in that scheme; it was he who knew about his wife's family's religion, he who knew what the Spanish Count-Duke Olivares had asked him to do in Lisbon back in 1640; what he had and had not done. He looked up and caught Father Gregory staring at him as if he could hear every thought.

There was a taut silence. Furious at the time all this was taking and desperate to get back to Leonora, Ludo said, "Please, as a man of God, let me get back to my home and family. I'll return on the morrow and you can give me your instructions."

"Ah, yes, regarding your home and family, there is one thing more." The priest took a sheet of expensive parchment covered in tiny writing from a drawer.

"What now?" Ludo snapped.

"Apart from your recent dabbling in the dark arts, sir, we have received information regarding your wife's religion."

"So we are back to that. I thought as much. Well I have documents signed by the Conde-Duque de Olivares in Spain to show that my wife is a practising Christian."

"But not in your home, sir. We have been informed. Your daughter was baptised Maria, but you both call her Naomi, your wife's mother's name, whose religion follows the female line. We know all about it. You have been here in Genoa barely a month and we have all any Inquisitor needs to know. That, combined with your transmutation of metals –"

"I've been trying to make metal boxes! I have been trying to melt sheets of tin to form waterproof packaging. Since when was that a crime?"

"And the workshop in your new house?"

Ludo swallowed hard. They had placed an informer inside his house: who? He had been grinding turmeric roots and black peppercorns to go in more affordable commercial packaging, but they could twist it to say it was for the Tincture or the Philosopher's Stone. Calming his breathing, he said, "What happens if I choose not to fulfil your request?"

"I need only to obtain your guarantee that you will take the shipment to England then cross to France, where you will be instructed what is required of you."

"And the shipment, precisely what are we talking of here?"

"Weaponry: muskets, musket rests and other firearm material, and two hundred barrels of gunpowder."

Ludo took another deep breath, realising what was afoot: In the guise of a merchant vessel, *Tulip* would be carrying a cargo of explosives to run a Parliamentary blockade. If captured, the weapons would be traced back to Genoa. He and the ship had no links to the Vatican that anyone knew about. If he survived, he could then trot around France on a horse looking for a lost queen who already owed him a lot of money she was almost certainly not going to be able to pay. Was there a way out of this? Could he load *The Tulip* and take the cargo elsewhere? He'd get a good price in Salé, they could easily sell it on to... His thoughts were interrupted.

"Your experiments, of course, will be used against you. The Inquisition here, naturally, looks unfavourably on the dark arts. And as I said, we have documents relating to your wife for the Inquisitor General if you fail us. Added to which there is the dispute about the rightful ownership of your galleon –"

"I have documents from the Conde-Duque de Olivares about that as well."

"Which are meaningless. The Marqués de Carpio has taken on his uncle's responsibilities. Spain is the rightful owner of your ship, not you."

Ludo closed his eyes; he had gone to a good deal of trouble to hinder the Marqués de Carpio's ambitions a few years ago.

As if hearing his thoughts, the Englishman said, "Making such an enemy in Spain was unwise. You may go."

Furious, Ludo leapt to his feet and without a word raced barefoot down the narrow staircase of an insignificant house on the Genoa waterfront.

The door to his new rented house was open. Inside all was silent until he heard a small child call out, "I want my papa." It was Naomi. She and her brother were sitting on the top stair.

"I'm here," Ludo called, taking the wide stairs two at a time and gathering the little girl in his arms. "Where's Nurse?" he asked. The child pointed at her mother's door.

It was too quiet.

"I fell over," Vico whimpered. "Look." He pointed to a bruised knee.

Ludo kissed his son's head then shifted his daughter onto one arm and took the boy's hand. "Let's go back to your room and I'll get Nurse to find you something to eat." He had no idea what time of day it was but, like two young blackbirds, the twins were always hungry.

"Where are your shoes?" Naomi asked as he put her down on the nursery rug.

"Somewhere. Stay here and I'll be back directly." Then Ludo stopped. "Why is no one with you?"

The twins looked at him, bewildered. His blood ran cold. *Was their nurse the bad apple*? He had been taken at the worst possible time, and deliberately kept longer than necessary. Where were all the servants? Which of them was the informer? They were all recently hired and had no loyalty to Leonora, but surely they wouldn't all abandon her. Unless it was against their will, or they had been paid to do so.

Nurse was standing just inside their chamber, weeping, while two women in widow's weeds sponged down Leonora's face and body. A young girl was scrubbing the floor. There was a lingering smell of blood.

"And the baby?" Ludo demanded.

"A boy. He came too soon." The nurse indicated a wrapped bundle on the floor then put her hands to her face and muttered, "I tried my best."

So it isn't her, Ludo thought with relief. He went to the bedside. The widows covered Leonora's body to the chin and stepped aside. Dropping to his knees, Ludo took Leonora's hand. It was still warm. He pressed it to his cheek, staring at her gentle countenance – a truly beautiful woman, but past her childbearing years and they had both known it. He kissed her cheek and rested his forehead against the pillow. There was the softest flutter. Eyelashes. Ludo pulled away to see his wife staring at him.

"I'm sorry," she whispered.

"Sorry! No – you are alive and that is enough for me."

Chapter 2

Two days later, Ludo welcomed Archibald Guthrie his Scottish sea-captain into his new home. Guthrie was accompanied by a tall young man with flowing blond hair.

"Dom Ludovico," Guthrie began in the Portuguese manner to which he had become accustomed in Goa, then lapsing into English he said, "you sent for me?"

"I did. And this is?" Ludo gestured to the newcomer.

"Ah, yes: Mr Gifford Greenwood of England. Mr Greenwood wants to sign on with *The Tulip* for her next voyage."

"He does? In what capacity?" Ludo asked, giving the young man a critical stare.

"Well, not sure to be honest," gushed the would-be recruit. "I've acted as a midshipman in the royal fleet."

"Acted as a midshipman? Interesting. And that would be the English royal fleet? Or the French? Or the Swedish, perhaps?"

"Ah, yes, English. Finest navy in the world," Greenwood pronounced ingenuously.

"If you say so," Ludo drawled and glanced at Guthrie, who refused to catch his eye. Matters relating to crews were his captain's responsibility so he was suspicious as to why Guthrie had brought an English would-be midshipman to his notice when they had far more pressing business to attend, such as the loading of a consignment of gunpowder and weaponry. Pointedly leaving the young man standing at the door, Ludo said, "Take a seat, Guthrie."

As he lowered himself behind his Indian ebony desk, Ludo suddenly caught a glimpse of the blond-haired Englishman framed in the open doorway and remembered where he had seen him before. *And so it begins,* he thought, and tapped the desktop with his knuckles.

Taking this as a signal to start, Captain Guthrie said, "I would have come earlier, sir, but I feared to be an intrusion. The lady Leonora was a fine woman a fine, sir, a very fine . . ." The dry, unemotional Scot stumbled for words.

"And still is, Guthrie, I'm delighted to say."

Guthrie looked confused. "But I heard, erm ... otherwise, sir."

"Well you heard wrongly." Ludo was abrupt. Casting a quick glance at the door and the midshipman-spy, he said, "Shall we get to business? I need *Tulip* loaded and ready to sail with the material on the list I sent yesterday as soon as possible. Get her ship-shape then see if we can squeeze in any of my cargo from Goa. But that won't be unloaded in England; we're taking it to France." He raised his voice so their destinations carried across the chamber he had adopted as his office.

"Will you be travelling with us, sir? I thought you intended to stay in Genoa to start a new import business here. You've got a fine house and offices –"

"Circumstances have changed, Guthrie. Temporarily."

"But your family will stay here? You're not thinking to take the bairns back to sea?" *It's a miracle we got them here in one piece; you'll be tempting fate bringing them aboard again.*

"I don't see why, I grew up aboard ship. By the time I was eight I'd probably sailed on every type of Mediterranean vessel there is *and* 'acted' as crew. Besides, *Tulip* is a fine galleon."

"That is currently without a crew, sir. They were all signed off."

"Well, sign them on again! Word will have got around that you treated them well and I paid a bonus on reaching port."

"But, sir, your bairns ... they are but wee mites."

"They didn't slip through the scuppers getting here all the way from Goa, Guthrie, and they're bigger now. But stop fretting, they will be here with my wife – as soon as I have found someone safe and suitable to care for them all." Ludo paused, immediately regretting his words. How much of this had Gifford Greenwood heard? For undoubtedly, this was the same young man he'd seen in the priest's house.

Unaware of any of this, Guthrie looked about him, assuming the pause was related to the inappropriateness of two men discussing domestic and feminine matters. Quietly, he ventured, "I know you have a father in Salé, sir –"

"*Had*. The old devil who, if I remember rightly, put the wind right up your mizzen, is dead now." Ludo caught Guthrie's sympathetic look and smiled. "As it happens, he wasn't my father: a father figure only. Not that having a pirate king for a papa was a bad thing." Then he stopped again as an image of his mother sending him off with Murat Reis came into his mind. He didn't have a birth father – that he knew about – but he did have a true mother. Who had finally been located after he'd discovered she had left the Doria family castle in Portovenere. It had taken nearly a month, but his informers had told him where to find her that very morning. Perfect timing – he hoped. He hadn't seen her for a number of years but she was, he was informed, in good health, and with all her faculties intact. Could he risk visiting her? Could he contemplate leaving Leonora and the twins with her? More to the point, would Father Gregory's agents harass someone living in a house belonging to the influential Doria family, especially knowing she was the late Doge of Genoa's daughter?

Ludo ran the fingers of both hands through his thick black hair pushing it off his forehead then pulled a black ribbon from a drawer and tied it back. "I'm sorry, Guthrie, the last few days have turned my plans inside out. I was convinced returning to Genoa was right for my children; now I find it was a huge mistake. If you'll excuse me, apart from our new cargo I have matters to attend before the end of the day, regarding our firm in Goa."

Captain Guthrie got to his feet then paused, "You're not, by chance, thinking to sell the Gasca Figaroa business? It's a fine concern."

"It is." Ludo leaned back in his chair, frowning. "Do you want to discuss it?"

Guthrie hesitated for a moment then appeared to come to a decision. "I would, yes."

"Excellent, come with me." Ludo got to his feet and, placing a hand on Guthrie's back, marched him towards the door saying, "Let us discuss it as we walk. Mr Greenwood, do you think you can locate the good ship *Tulip* in the jungle of masts in the harbour?" As he spoke Ludo ushered Gifford Greenwood out of the door before them.

Taken a little by surprise the young man looked backwards. "Is this a sort of test, sir?"

"You could call it that. Off you go."

Gifford Greenwood, obliged to take the lead, pushed his way through the crowded narrow streets leading down to the harbour, stopping now and again like an obedient dog to see if his master was following. Ludo waited until the cobbled terraced streets got steeper and the blond hair was barely visible then with a smile of satisfaction picked up his conversation with his captain.

"I've been in two minds about Gasca Figaroa Spices. On the one hand I'd be happily rid of it and gladly never return to Goa. The climate is appalling, the pettiness of shore life is beyond tolerance, and as for the constant risk of the

Inquisitors knocking on our door ... but then again, it is a safe future for my son and it will provide an attractive dowry for Naomi." A round matron leading a diminutive donkey laden with fish-stuffed panniers came between them. As they re-joined, Ludo added, "Perhaps I should install a manager. But who could I trust to take it all on?"

"Me, sir."

"But you're *Tulip*'s captain. Don't tell me you're ready to settle ashore. Don't you have a wife in Scotland?"

"I did, sir, except she wasn't there when I returned last – and she didn't leave her new address."

"You didn't mention it."

"No – well – the fact is I've found what you might call solace, in Goa."

A smile crept about Ludo's lips. "Ah, I see. Well, I'm more than ready to trust you with the business, but who'll captain my galleon?"

"You yourself, sir, you have all the skills necessary. I've seen you in action often enough."

Ludo grabbed Guthrie's jacket before he stepped in a lump of ordure, and as they came close the Scotsman whispered, "May I ask what you're really planning to do, sir?"

Ludo's mouth gave an involuntary, one-dimpled twitch. Pulling Guthrie to the side of the alley he said, "The cargo is for the English Royalists from their friend St. Peter. Once delivered, I'm then supposed to sail on to find the English queen, who's French and might be in France, but who definitely owes me a fortune for goods received. And I'll bet a year's income your Mr Greenwood is coming aboard to report what I actually decide to do. 'Acted as a midshipman' – *Santa Maria*! I'll have him acting as a midshipman scrubbing the quarter deck, and may she alone help him if he starts spewing his guts."

Guthrie either didn't hear the latter comment or chose to ignore it for he continued, "She's the Scottish queen as well, remember. Henrietta Maria married Charles Stuart and the

Stuarts are Scots. But you're not taking it as an honour, sir? Why's that?"

"Prior experience, Guthrie. You may have forgotten that your precious Stuarts nearly did for me in Spain a few years back. As to what I am really going for, I still can't say. I'm assuming it's gun-running," Ludo huffed then, before Guthrie could respond, marched off to join Gifford Greenwood, who was now panting at the edge of quay and pointing at a dozen galleons – the spaniel had located its quarry. If he'd had a tail it would have wagged. Ludo swallowed a smile. "Well done, well done, but which exactly is *The Tulip*?"

Greenwood peered into the forest of masts and his metaphorical tail came to a halt. While they waited for him to find Ludo's ship, Guthrie took up their private discussion again sotto voce.

"So you'll be working for the Royalists. Are you sure that's the right thing to do? It grieves me to admit it, but word out is that it's not certain they'll win. Parliament and this man Cromwell they speak of – they're forging ahead."

"I know," Ludo replied. "But I'm under a certain pressure." He made no mention of the fears that had decided him to act as requested: that his eternal enemy had access to his new servants; that Leonora's miscarriage was not sheer misfortune, although how it had been provoked, via tampered food or drink, was unproven. No mention that the man he hated and feared most in the world knew where to find his children. He nodded in Greenwood's direction, "Later, you can tell me how this young puppy found you as well."

Then Ludo froze. Rogelio knew too much about him for the choice of Greenwood to be a coincidence: this young man been sent to ... he closed his eyes and took a deep breath at a painful memory ... to take the place of his cabin boy, José, the boy Rogelio had killed in Ibiza. It was no coincidence, either, that Greenwood had the same fair looks as a much younger Marcos of Sanlucar. Or was he being overly morbid and suspicious?

"Wait a minute," Ludo said putting a hand out to silence Guthrie, who was saying something. "Mr Greenwood, would you find someone to row us out to my ship."

Ludo waited until the boy was among the lightermen on the quay then said hastily, "What was I saying?"

"I was asking if could tell me what you are you *really* planning to do, sir?"

Ludo cocked his head to one side and closed a black-lashed eye. "To make the best of a bad situation, and hopefully regain at least in part that which is mine. The spices I sent for the Queen's household will be long gone, but I may be able to chase up the remains of two caskets of jewels. Some very fine pearls, uncut sapphires and Golconda diamonds were, if you remember, carefully conducted to the Palace of Whitehall on my behalf last year, and a similar consignment the year before. Both caskets remain unpaid. I shall also need to cover my costs, not to mention the inconvenience to my family and the risk it puts on my ship, which as you told me weeks ago, is badly in need of refurbishment." Ludo paused, Greenwood was returning. Raising a hand, Ludo called out, "One moment, Mr Greenwood. We'll be right with you in one moment."

Ludo gazed unseeing over the captain's head then he laughed and clapped Guthrie on the back with such gusto it nearly sent the stocky Scotsman over the quayside. "In the mean-time, I am more than happy to leave you to run Gasca Figaroa Spices, with instructions to make us a fortune in Goa in any way you can."

"Thank you, sir. But it occurs to me now that if you are intent on travelling north again, it might after all be advisable for the lady Leonora to return with me."

Ludo gave Guthrie a searching look. "Thank you, but no. I have job to see through, that is true, but I have every intention of returning to Genoa at the first available opportunity and resuming my original plan."

"To establish an import-export business here."

"That, and much more. To establish myself as a Doria, right here in the centre of Genoa. But for now ..." Ludo turned to survey the terraced skyline at his back and lost his thread. Guthrie coughed politely and he turned back, saying, "You asked what I am *really* planning, well I'll tell you, my friend. To make mischief! I'm planning to make *so much* mischief, the Vatican and all its connections will pay me to get out of their way. My wife nearly died because of them. An innocent boy in Ibiza was killed by a Vatican agent, and a harmless old friar called Friar Caritas has suffered greatly at their hands as well. I want a stop to it, and I want my revenge – on a creature named Rogelio, and on my Doria family, who have ignored me at their peril.

Chapter 3

While Guthrie arranged for *Tulip*'s voyage to England and France, keeping Greenwood with him as instructed, Ludo slipped away dressed as a fisherman and sailed down the Ligurian coast to the small fishing port of Lerici on his own.

He hadn't seen his mother for a long time, but she hadn't changed, judging from the glimpse he caught of her on a terrace as he climbed up from the tiny harbour. Pausing to catch his breath, he tried to identify who she was talking to with hands gesticulating at every phrase, but they both disappeared from view.

Thinking about how his visit might evolve, he took a more careful look at the location of her house and more importantly, its approaches. A narrow path marked in a steeply terraced incline led up to a tall gate in a rough stone wall. To one side of the path there was a sheer drop into the sea, to the other, dense Mediterranean scrub. By the time he reached the gate and had followed a nimble female servant up to the house, Gabriella Doria was lying on a shaded divan in the open porch. The girl disappeared from sight and Ludo stopped, slightly out of breath, to survey his mother's vast, wild garden. The low-roofed, white-washed dwelling with panoramic views was almost identical to Murat Reis's house in Algiers. He wondered if it was deliberate, and whether he dared ask her. Removing his wide straw hat, he wiped his forehead with his sleeve, then replaced the hat and mentally

22

prepared himself for the unpredictable with the volatile woman who had taught him to take risks.

"Ludo!" Gabriella Doria cried, rushing barefoot to the end of the marbled porch to greet him, where she stood blinking in the bright sunlight wearing only a plain shift under a vermilion tasselled shawl. The shawl fell to the floor as she lifted her arms like a child to be hugged. Ludo swung her off her feet. She hadn't changed: a little plumper around the face and shoulders, but still as animated and as delighted to see him as ever.

"My Ludo – at last!" she gasped when he returned her to the ground. Then, standing back she inspected his appearance, "My how picturesque. What are you today, fisherman or corsair?"

Ludo pulled the hat and colourful cloth from his head, laughing, and let her hug him again, taking in her familiar citrus scent.

"Oh, goodness, what a lovely surprise," she sighed, stooping to pick up her shawl.

As she drew it around her shoulders Ludo noticed it was almost threadbare. "Has your money run out?" he asked bluntly.

"Yes and no."

"How 'yes and no'?"

"My allowance ceased – a few years ago – I can't remember when, exactly."

"The allowance from your father's estate, why?"

Gabriella Doria looked at him and arched one perfectly shaped, black eyebrow. "Your uncles, of course."

"Ah," he said. "Word did get back from Spain then. I'm sorry, I should have anticipated that outcome."

"No, no! I think you did me a favour. They said ... here, come and sit with me." Gabriella pushed her son into a low chair by her divan, "They said you – we – had no right to use their name and told me to me to leave that dreadful dungeon in Portovenere. Which I did, gladly, before they could change their minds again! That's why I am here. For now, anyway."

Gabriella gave a cheerful smile and clapped her hands for a servant. As she moved Ludo noticed someone standing in the shade near the entrance to the house.

"It's all right, it's only Hassan. He followed you up from the gate but you didn't notice. Isn't he clever?" A Moroccan servant stepped forward and salaamed. "Hassan has been with me since I escaped that draughty castle. No prize for guessing who sent him."

Ludo smiled. Hassan was quite clearly a body-guard not a servant. "Poor Jan, he's dead you know."

"Yes, I heard."

Ludo studied his mother's features. She had been Jan Janszoon's mistress for years – Murat Reis as he became known – leader of the Salé corsairs, the Barbary Rovers.

The maid re-appeared. "Sherbet, please, Maria," Gabriella said.

When she had gone and Hassan had been dismissed with a not ungracious flick of the wrist, Gabriella settled herself back on her divan, exposing henna-painted feet.

Ludo grinned. "I hope your Hassan doesn't take that as an insult."

"What? Oh, my bare feet. On the contrary, Hassan's wife does them. She is so clever." Gabriella stretched out her legs and wiggled her toes. "Aren't they pretty?"

Ludo shook his head and chuckled: his mother was everything a respectable woman should not be.

"What?" Gabriella demanded again. "Don't tell me I embarrass you, you've seen more outrageous sights than my feet I'm sure. Where have you been this time, by the way?"

"Goa, in India. Six months sailing from here – on a good run. It can take longer."

"How exotic. Why have you come back?"

"I'm still a merchant. I trade in different ports. That hasn't changed."

"No, but something else has." Gabriella looked at him questioningly then seeing his discomfort she continued, "You don't trade in little old Lerici so you must have sent someone to find me, and you haven't come all the way from a strange place across the world just to see your mother."

Ludo bent his head. It was true and he felt ashamed. It crossed his mind that he was seeing – appreciating – his mother in a different way. Was it because Murat Reis had told him that she had kept him in Algiers, away from her dreadful family, destroying her reputation forever, but not, as he'd used to believe, because Murat had been his father? Or was it because he had a family of his own now?

The sherbet arrived, along with a salver of sugared almonds. Gabriella took her cup and sipped, staring at him over the painted rim, waiting.

Ludo sipped his own drink then looked out to sea. Across the calm water of the gulf was Portovenere. "Do you like it better here?" he asked.

"Being on my own, not being watched and reported on? I certainly do. My dear half-brothers must have been delighted when your step-father died. They could finally ignore me. Being a widow has definite compensations." There was a pause.

"Hassan tells me you have married."

"Hassan?" But yes, the word would have filtered down from Murat's house and crossed the Middle Sea.

"Tell me about it, about her. I assume it was a love match, you avoided marriage for long enough."

Ludo laughed and mimicking his mother's own earlier response he said, "Yes and no." Then told her how a beautiful young widow had neatly manoeuvred him into matrimony while he was trying to manoeuvre himself into ownership of her business, and how he had then come to love her. Then he told her about the twins, about the long voyage from Goa to Genoa and about the loss of the new baby.

"Oh, but that is so sad." Gabriella pressed her hands to her face then peeked out, "But I am a *nonna* at last. Send the twins to me quickly; I must spoil them while I still have breath to tease. Ah, but will Leonora approve? Perhaps not. Why did you really come back to Genoa, Ludo?" The question fell fast and sharp as a dart.

Ludo could not truthfully say why he had returned and brought his family, because his long-standing *vendetta* against his Doria uncles suddenly seemed foolish. His mother was glad to be rid of her Doria connection, so why was he hell-bent on re-establishing it? Could he confess that he wanted to be accepted into her family; and to do so he was increasing his wealth so they could no longer ignore him; that he intended to avenge the way they had treated her? He said nothing. Not least because Gabriella had accepted she was no longer one of them. She had been an outcast from the moment she had stepped back on Genoese soil after her sojourn in Algiers. She had done it all for him, but it had got them nothing but enforced exile in the spartan fortress on the Portovenere cliffside. "I wanted to come home," he said eventually, and bent to the cloying sherbet.

A gentle silence settled between them and Ludo came to a decision. Taking a deep breath, he said, "I need someone to take care of Leonora and the twins while I go to – away. She will need help with them. Especially Naomi – Naomi can be a handful." A thought crossed his mind and his mother caught his grin.

"Like her grandmother, is she?"

"Utterly."

"But, Ludo, there is no need to ask, of course they must come."

"I will arrange payments for their keep and –"

"Don't embarrass me."

"It is not a matter of embarrassment. There is another issue. They must have funds in case they have to leave in a hurry."

His mother shook her head knowingly, "What have you done?"

Ludo shrugged. "I have an enemy. Well, one or two. But this one is particularly venomous. I want to keep my family's whereabouts secret if I can."

"Not one of your uncles or cousins? They were *very* angry when they heard you had used their name to get preference in Spain."

Ludo opened his eyes wide. "Really? Good. But it's not any of them. It's someone from Rome, a Vatican agent."

Gabriella picked up her painted cup from the small wicker table then put it down without drinking. Sitting very straight, she folded her hands together and said in a hushed voice, "A priest from Rome . . ."

Ludo frowned. "A priest of sorts. An old friend of mine, a Franciscan friar, called him *la bicha*: the serpent. Let that suffice."

Gabriella nodded. "His name?"

"Rogelio – that is all I know."

"Rogelio," Gabriella repeated the name slowly, pronouncing each syllable.

"You know him? Has he been here – threatened you?"

"A venomous snake is a threat wherever it lurks."

Ludo wanted to ask more, but something cold, a sudden chill in the warm afternoon, advised him to wait. Deciding to approach on another tack, he said, "I went to see Murat Reis before he died."

"Dearest Jan." Tears welled in his mother's eyes. "I loved him. I should never have returned."

"Why did you?"

"Because of you and my inheritance." Gabriella gave a deep sigh. "All right, this part I will tell you. It is time. You have a family of your own now, so you will understand, I hope." She paused, gave Ludo a warning look then began, "Before I was captured, your grandfather Doria, who was in line to become the Doge of Genoa, had me legitimised. My mother was not his wife. She was, and had been, his mistress for many years. Anyway, after I was captured by the corsairs your grandfather's wife saw to it that my ransom was not paid. I was an embarrassment, of course. I have no proof of that, but what happened later with your uncles, my half-brothers, proved my suspicion."

"So they shut you away in Portovenere?"

"Yes – let me finish."

"When I returned to Genoa with you, your grandfather had been dead a number of years and they wouldn't have us anywhere near them. They assumed you were a pirate's bastard and sent their tedious poor second cousin Agostino to make an honest woman of me. The rest you know."

"And they insisted you live in Portovenere out of the public eye."

"With Agostino to keep me there. Now he is also dead and I am free of them all."

"But without any allowance."

"Yes."

"And the inheritance you mentioned?"

"I was named in my father's will: land and a portion of money should have come to me. My half-brothers took it and shared it between them."

"They cheated you; the richest family in Genoa and they took your inheritance? Why didn't you tell me this before, get a message to me?"

"Because...." Gabriella gave a slight shrug. "What could I expect? That I would be welcomed back from the Barbary Coast after spending over ten years with a corsair lover? We do not need them, Ludo: Jan made sure of that."

Ludo got to his feet and stared at the turquoise sea. Questions fought for supremacy, each related to his real father – not his grandfather or his uncles. Then a thought came to him about Rogelio; a terrible suspicion. "He's not a Doria, is he, this Rogelio?"

Gabriella tilted her head to one side and grimaced. "It's possible."

There was silence. A bird called from an olive tree. A dog barked from somewhere across the hillside. Ludo's head swam with an appalling suspicion. "He's not my..." He couldn't finish the words let alone the thought.

Gabriella looked at him. "Your what? Brother! No, indeed he is not! How can you even think it – he's much too old."

"Then who is he?"

"I can't tell you —because I don't know – for certain. There was a scandal to do with my youngest half-brother, a child was born and it was sent to a monastery. Rogelio could be this child."

"His mother was low born, I assume."

"Possibly."

"So if Rogelio is that child – man – and he knows you were legitimised but he wasn't, and knows that when you returned to Genoa after our time in Salé we were sent to the castle in Portovenere while he has never been accepted in any way, is that a reason to make my life hell?" Ludo got up, paced about and then sat down again. "That's twisted thinking even for a snake." For a few moments they were silent again then he asked quietly, "Was my father low-born? Not that it matters, but I am curious."

Ignoring the question, Gabriella continued on their previous track, "It may explain why he dislikes you, an absurd form of envy perhaps, if he thinks we benefited and he didn't. Or have you acted against him in another way?"

Ludo thought back to an interview in a Dutch lodging house with Rogelio representing a Vatican cardinal, and a fancy-garbed Spaniard who went by the self-styled name of 'the hawk'. "Well, for a start I had no idea there might be a family connection, and he certainly never mentioned it. I did once tell him a few home truths, though. At the time he was a faceless, nameless Vatican agent. If it's the same man." Ludo stopped then said sharply, "He's been here recently!"

"Yes, but I had no knowledge of your whereabouts at the time. There is no reason for him to return."

"He was asking about me?"

"Mmm."

Ludo got to his feet again and paced the terrace. Where could he send Leonora and the children to be safe from Rogelio? Not here: not now. The safest option was for them to return to Goa, but Leonora was a poor traveller in very poor health. He turned and stared unseeing at his mother's low roof. If he didn't send Leonora and the children back to Goa with Guthrie, and this house was no longer safe, what was the alternative? An element of panic entered his thinking and his mind went blank.

Returning to his mother's side, Ludo finally said, "Come with me to Genoa and meet your grandchildren."

Gabriella instantly scrambled off her divan. As she searched for her slippers Ludo said, "About your finances – do you know about Tellaro?" naming a tiny fishing village a few miles to the south of Lerici.

Gabriella lifted her head and gave a knowing smile. "Murat's treasure. Of course I know. It's my security. What a wonderful man he was, hiding treasure for my old age. Ah, but you know about it, too." She scrunched up her face in mock annoyance then became serious. "I don't want anyone else to know about it, Ludo. If they find out about whatever is up there in that abandoned village, they'll steal it from us. Let's leave it where it is until there is an emergency."

Ludo instinctively knew who 'they' were, and the reference to the abandoned village indicated she knew exactly where to find Murat's hoard, and wondered if she was right, or whether it was better to get the treasure right now and disappear back to the Barbary Coast where Rogelio couldn't get them.

While Gabriella shouted orders at her servants, he made a circuit of the house she had taken. Set on the hill near the old fortified castle, it could be reached from the small harbour by a winding donkey-track, or from along the spine of the hill by carriage, but it only had views out to sea. He strolled into the house and headed for the kitchen then a rear door, accessed through a long, dark dining chamber. Halfway down, he paused. A slight movement of air, a shush of soft footwear on marble tiles, told him he was being followed. He loosened the small dagger at his waist. Hassan might have *said* he was sent by Murat Reis, but that didn't mean it was true, or that he hadn't been bought since.

Ludo continued moving forward, slowly at first then at a rush. Reaching the far door, he tried to wrench it open but it was locked. He turned, dagger in the air. His arm was caught in a practised grip, the dagger fell to the floor with a clatter and a soft, rope-soled shoe pushed it aside. His arm was run up his back with expert ease as a voice whispered in his ear in the Arabic he had learned in Salé, "Relax, it is only Hassan. I come not to harm but to protect."

Released from the wiry Berber's grip, Ludo gulped for air. Hassan stepped past him and opened the door with a large key then, back-lit with outdoor daylight, he gave a gap-toothed smile. "You are out of practice, *signore*. Permit me to say that should be remedied."

"Why?"

"Because you have an enemy, who has you followed."

"He has been here, my mother said." Ludo gave a deep sigh. "Is she safe?"

"Safe enough. Hassan has a brother and cousin who are tired of the sea – they can come here and help protect her with me if you think necessary. They will require paying."

"Name your price and send for your brother and cousin."

Hassan put a hand on Ludo's shoulder and turned him so he could stare into his eyes. "And we can still trust you, Ludo, though you forget us?"

Ludo stared back; he had no memory of Hassan whatsoever. "Did you trust Murat Reis?" he asked.

"Never!" Hassan laughed. "But we had his measure."

"Then you have mine."

Hassan continued to stare, "His word was his bond – with us."

"As is mine in this respect. Family is sacred, is it not?"

Hassan touched his heart and bowed low. "And truly, you do not remember little Hassan who played with you at the water-front, younger brother to a big boy with red hair called Say'id, friends of the Moroccan fisherman Selim who –"

"Taught us to wrestle with grease on our arms! Now I do!"

Accompanied by Hassan and Gabriella, Ludo sailed back to Genoa. A maid opened the main door, bobbed a curtsey and scuttled off to the rear of the house. There was a silence, a fearful repetition of his previous return, then a high-pitched scream followed by a howl of pain and a small boy hurtled from a side door, pursued by a diminutive harridan. Seeing his father, the boy slithered to a stop on the chequered marble floor and scooted behind his legs. His pursuer, blind to all but her victim, careered straight into them.

Ludo bent down and extracted a long wooden spoon from her right hand. "What is going on?" he asked. Large, green-flecked hazel eyes examined his. "Papa?" she said, stepping backwards to survey his full appearance. "You look different. Are you my papa?"

"Yes, of course."

"Ah, papa, papa, papa," she sighed, hugging his white cotton-covered knees.

"He's my papa as well," whined a voice from behind them. "No, he's –"

"That's enough! Vico, Naomi," Ludo held out his wide, brown hands and each child grabbed a forefinger, "we have a special visitor. Behave nicely and say hello to your grandmother."

Gabriella made no move while the two children eyed her suspiciously. "You may call me Nonna," she said, smiling, waiting for them to come to her like timid animals. Not that the little girl looked remotely timid.

Before they had a chance to respond, however, Ludo asked, "Where is your mother?"

"In bed," Naomi huffed.

"*Again*," Vico added with a sigh, supplying a reason for his sister's annoyance.

Ludo turned to his mother and without speaking conveyed the twins to her charge then raced up the main staircase.

It was as before. Despite it still being daylight outdoors, the shutters and windows were closed, the room lit by a single beeswax candle. Above its sweet smell a cloying odour hung in the air. Leonora was lying against her pillow, drained of colour. The children's nurse was seated at her side next to a large bowl of water and a pile of torn linen cloths. There was a bucket at her feet, its content blood red.

But it was not as before. This time the room stank, reminding Ludo unpleasantly of upper deck carnage when a captain had refused to surrender his vessel and they had to board her.

"She is bleeding again, *signore*," ventured the nurse.

"The doctor – can he not give her something?"

The nurse shook her head.

"Ludo?" Leonora's voice was barely a whisper.

He went to the side of the bed and knelt down. "I'm here my love."

"Keep the children safe."

Ludo swallowed hard. Leonora had no knowledge of his fears; she was thinking only of their future.

Some hours later, after the priest had been and the undertaker sent for, Ludo went to find his mother and children. They were curled up together on a wide chair in the salon, fast asleep. Hassan was standing arms folded watching out of the window.

Between them, he and Hassan carried the little ones up to the nursery and tucked them into bed.

"I shall stay with them," Hassan said.

Ludo nodded, kissed each child's brow and went down to speak to his mother.

"May I see her?" Gabriella asked gently. "May I see the woman my son loved?"

Ludo returned to Leonora's chamber and stood back as his mother spoke some words into the dark.

After they had they exited the chamber and Ludo had closed the door behind them, Gabriella put a hand on his arm and said, "I have promised to look after her children. To keep them safe and make sure they get learning."

"But where?" Ludo choked and began to go downstairs ahead of her so she could not see his face. "They cannot go back to Goa without me and I cannot go anywhere until I have fulfilled a new mission. Leonora is gone so their threats to her are void, but they will come for my children – unless I take them with me or we go where we cannot be found – but where is that when the Church has spies in every town and village from here to the New World and Cathay?"

His mother stopped, "Who, Ludo? Who are you 'they'? Who are you afraid of?"

"It's a long story, but this Rogelio – I'm certain it's him – he's obliging me to do some sort of dirty work. The trouble is it's convenient to me. I could gain a good deal, and recover what is mine in the process.

"So you feel you must do whatever it is." Gabriella took a deep breath then tapped his shoulder, "Salé."

"Salé?"

"Yes. Let me take them to Jan's house. Hassan and his family can care for us there. Nobody will get to them or hurt them in that house. God help a meddling priest in Salé."

Ludo laughed despite himself. "Yes," he said. "And I will come to you as soon as I have completed my business." He paused, "Perhaps I should come with you and return to pirating."

"No!" Gabriella looked up at him. "No, that will not do. Build your business to rival your uncles' and cousins' empire, if that is what you want – then we can both thumb our noses at them."

"And in the process, I shall rid us of this odious Rogelio. He is to blame for what has happened to Leonora."

Gabriella frowned, "How?"

"He is to blame for me not being with Leonora when she needed me. He will suffer for this."

"That is not your way, Ludo," Gabriella said quietly. "You are angry, but violence is not in your nature. Jan told me that." She put a small hand on his sleeve and squeezed his arm. "Go if you must; your children will be protected at all times in Salé."

Neither of them mentioned what was to happen if he did not return.

J G Harlond

Part Two
England

Chapter 4

Crimphele, Cornwall, summer 1644

"Milady, there's an army coming!" Meg, maid-of-all-work, rushed into the Crimphele kitchen yard her freckled cheeks rosy with excitement. "There's a prince with them," she gasped, crossing the inner kitchen threshold. "One of the men said."

"A prince! Prince Charles – no it can't be, he's too young. It must be Rupert." Alina's own face flushed equally pink at the prospect of seeing the dashing Palatine prince again. He had been at Crimphele two years earlier; his presence had turned the entire house inside out and her into a simpering girl.

Wiping her hands hastily on her skirt, Alina straightened her bodice, checked the lacing then hastened through the great hall to the main courtyard. A small retinue of men on sweat-lathered horses were waiting as a humble covered-wagon rumbled under the stable block archway and came to a halt. As usual, the dogs were going berserk, snapping at fetlocks and running around in circles. "Quiet!" Alina screamed, and in that instant heard her late unlamented mother-in-law's voice. She paused, calmed her breathing, straightened her spine and became the Baroness Metherall again. It had been some time since she had played the role and she was a little rusty. Her husband had taken most of the men on the estate to fight with him for King Charles's Royalist cause and her household servants had had to take on many of their tasks, leaving her once again – the irony was not lost on her – to manage a fine house and extensive lands with insufficient staff or the money to pay them.

Smoothing her hands against the sprigged cotton of her daywear then holding them demurely at her waist, Alina waited to be addressed as custom required. A young Royalist soldier, no more than a boy, dismounted and came to her, shifting a terrier out of his way with an unnecessarily vicious kick. "Cecil Cleverden at your service, Baroness," he said, sweeping a dusty military cap to the cobbles.

Alina forced a smile and stepped forward to greet him with an extended hand. Close up, she could see scars on his face despite his youth. His leather coat was rent at the shoulder, his boots caked with dried mud.

"We beg your indulgence, Baroness, but we were advised you would give us shelter and help the Prince. We have met with much opposition since leaving Lyme – rather more than anticipated – and His Highness needs to rest. He is injured and we have had some trouble finding a safe haven."

"You have ridden far?"

"Since our last quartering, three days and nights with barely a stop. His Highness wanted to get into the far west as quickly as possible, so we cut up through Tavistock and came to you that way."

"Well you may rest here and welcome." Alina cast a look at the other men, some still mounted, some on the ground easing stiffened limbs or loosening saddle girths. They all had weapons at their waists, bandoliers for ammunition and bulging saddlebags. It dawned on her she would have to feed them. Her mind racing, she said calmly, "The Prince may have our best room, naturally, but I regret this house will not accommodate you all, unless you are willing to go into the servants' quarters. We have a vacant dormitory above the stables. How many are you?"

"Here, today, we are but thirty men. The Prince's troops number in the thousands, naturally, and we are to be joined by the King's own men, about which event I should not talk, but that will be near Bodmin, I believe, as things stand. Most of the Prince's men are marching there directly, although after Lyme I fear many will also have hung behind to rest or returned to their homes. But please do not concern yourself; they won't be coming onto your land. Although, I must repeat, that is as things stand. This is war and plans can be changed in an instant."

"I understand that," Alina said, aware she was being spoken down to and becoming annoyed.

Heedless, the young man continued, "When the Prince said he wanted to come here he decided keep our number to the minimum to avoid attention, in case you'd been – you know – occupied by the enemy, which would have been a nuisance."

"A nuisance!" Alina repeated angrily, then realised that of all her worries in the past two years she had never considered that Crimphele might be overrun by Roundheads. Nor had her husband, evidently, given that the only men he'd left behind were aged, infirm or downright simple.

Misunderstanding the look on Alina's face the young man added hastily, "It is all for His Majesty's cause."

"Yes, yes, forgive me. Well – perhaps we should help Prince Rupert first." Alina started walking towards the covered-wagon but a soldier sitting on the running board with the driver jumped to the ground to bar her way. She turned back to Cecil Cleverden for an explanation.

He nodded at the soldier then said, "It is Prince Maurice, Baroness. He has taken sick again and would prefer not to be seen. His surgeon should arrive within a day or two. In the meantime, His Highness needs absolute rest. Although I'm sure he will be most anxious to make your acquaintance when he is recovered."

Alina swallowed her disappointment. Prince Maurice, not the dashing Prince Rupert. She had heard unfavourable comments about Maurice. He was, so they said, nothing like the very tall, very elegant, very everything Rupert. Her thoughts came to an abrupt halt. What could the Prince – and Cecil Cleverden – not want her to see? "It's not smallpox, or the plague, is it? He hasn't got swelling and boils!"

"No, no. His Highness was injured and took a fever. It is a severe *grippe* only. But to be on the safe side . . ." Cleverden spoke hastily, endeavouring to cover the words of a soldier who Alina distinctly heard say, "He's already had that," at the mention of smallpox.

Alina looked at the young man then at the escort dubiously, unsure how to respond.

"Ah, I also have this letter for you," Cleverden added, pulling a small packet from a deep pocket.

"From my husband? Oh, thank you!" Alina's face lit up.

"Your husband? How it could it be from him? No, it is from Lady Dalkeith."

Confused, Alina said, "Lady Dalkeith? Do I know her?"

"You must do, ma'am, she is on her way here with her new charge. We have another new princess. Perhaps you have not heard? The Queen may have sailed for France already. This letter will explain it all, I'm sure."

As Cecil Cleverden spoke, his tired gelding spread its rear legs and moved onto the tip of its hooves. A fountain of yellow ammonia flooded the uneven cobbles. Alina jumped backwards to avoid the widening pool of equine urine and two of the men on horseback guffawed. Cleverden swung round to scold them, but in doing so he dropped Lady Dalkeith's letter in the lake beneath his mount. "You," he shouted pointing at one of the men, "dismount and pick that up!"

Alina looked at the much older, seasoned soldier and wondered who Cecil Cleverden was to command in such a manner then realised she'd still be expected to take possession of Lady Dalkeith's missive. Half-turning to see if Meg were nearby, she clicked her fingers in the Spanish way, forgetting it annoyed English servants and Meg came to her side. "Prepare our best chamber for Prince Maurice," she instructed, "quickly." Then, addressing Cecil Cleverden in her haughtiest manner, she said, "Bring the Prince into the great hall while we prepare his room."

As Alina spoke a large, heavily laden wagon trundled into the crowded courtyard and sent the terriers into another yapping frenzy. "More!" she gasped.

"Only our paddies, Baroness – our grooms and servants – they will not get in your way; they sleep with the horses."

It occurred to Alina there wasn't sufficient space in the Crimphele stables for the horses let alone their grooms, and as for fresh straw – she hadn't thought to have any delivered for weeks. The horses they used for her trap and to fetch supplies from Carlingford or Tavistock, now the barges had stopped coming up from Plymouth, were all out in the fields. She gave a meaningful huff of annoyance and strode back indoors.

As she re-entered the house, she noticed a plump girl hopping from foot to foot behind the door jamb, obviously trying to attract her attention. "Yes, what's the matter?" she asked sharply, making no attempt to conceal her ill humour.

The girl, one of the Crimphele boatman's many daughters, gulped and reeled off a message. "Mother says to tell you there's a fine lady arriving from across the river. She's got a baby with her. Two babies and a servant."

"Already!" The girl looked bewildered. "Oh, never mind," Alina responded tetchily. "Tell your mother to offer her some refreshments and I'll send ..." (Who could she send?) "...

someone to bring her up to the house. Is there much luggage; will your pony and trap be enough?"

"Can't say, milady."

Alina halted the flat of her hand in mid-air just in time. She had a courtyard full of fighting men, a sick nephew of the king – possibly carrying the *peste* or the smallpox – a royal lady-in-waiting was waiting on the landing stage with two babies, one of them in direct line to the throne, and they all had to be brought up to the house, where they scarcely had enough food to feed themselves on any given day.

That brought Alina to another unpleasant fact. "Meg!" she called and raced for the tower steps, taking them two at an unladylike time. "Wait! The princess will have to have the best room, she's more important than a Palatine prince. No. No, it's all right: the baby can go into the nursery. Prince Maurice can have my husband's room and Lady Dalkeith can go in Lady Marjorie's old suite."

Meg started pulling clean linen from a closet. "Can Mercy help me, milady? We'll do it quicker with two. And can you tell Mrs Bodkin to lend a hand as well, please."

"If you mean Mrs Godwin, then yes, of course. I always forget about Mrs Bodkin – Godwin. Why do you all call her Bodkin?"

"Cuz she hides in the sewing room all day," Meg muttered under her breath.

Not bothering to reprimand her, Alina raced down the servants' staircase to the kitchen.

"Has something happened?" asked Crook-back Aggie, the ancient cook, stirring something lumpy in a pot over the fire.

"It most certainly has, and it's still happening! Sit down, Agnes; you are not going to like this."

Charity Hawkins was sent back to the Crimphele landing stage with instructions to bring Lady Dalkeith along the river path to the rear gate, not into the main courtyard. When they finally arrived, Charity's mother was leading the family trap with its precious cargo up to the house. Trailing behind them walked a robust but sour-faced wet-nurse carrying another baby. Alina received them at the lower gate and led them on foot through the terraced rose garden to the south range door.

Alighting the cart, Lady Dalkeith, who was wan with tiredness, said, "Forgive the intrusion, Baroness, but Her Majesty was most insistent I seek you out, and to be honest, I also need help."

"The Queen sent you here? How wonderful. Does she want me to return to court?" Alina's eyes lit up. It was her greatest desire.

"I wish it were that simple. No my dear, she is thinking to travel to Spain to her sister for help, and ... oh, it's a long story."

Alina put a hand on Lady Dalkeith's arm. "Later. Let us get you settled; then you can tell me everything." Smiling, she peeked at the baby, a minute, monkey-featured bundle.

"I vowed to protect her with my life," Lady Dalkeith gushed as Alina struggled to find an apt compliment, "but truly it is proving most difficult. The men I hired in Exeter as bodyguards joined Her Majesty's men to sail to France as soon as we got to Falmouth. That left me with almost nobody except my personal maid, and even she has gone now."

"I don't understand: how could Her Majesty leave her daughter, and without a bodyguard?"

"I know. It is all so sad but Her Majesty was barely conscious. She is completely paralysed down one side and can scarce move on her own. I don't think she knew what she was saying, and we were in such a panic to get the other royal children onto the frigate that arrived for her ... The Chanel is full of Parliament ships. The whole thing was a compete nightmare." Lady Dalkeith caught her breath then continued, "No sooner had the Queen's vessel left the harbour Cromwell's ships fired on it. Imagine! Englishmen trying to kill their queen and heirs to the throne! I've been hiding our new princess since then. I bribed a boatman in Saltash and he managed to get us here unchallenged but ..." Lady Dalkeith gulped back tears.

The reality of the dangers the woman had experienced rushed in on Alina. "My poor dear," she said, putting a comforting hand on the woman's shoulder. "Come, let me show you to your chambers. Is it all right if we put both babies into our nursery with the nurse?"

The distressed lady-in-waiting nodded assent and, aided by dependable Meg who was always there when needed, Alina led the way to the upper south range and two large rooms facing the distant Tamar estuary.

Meg led the nurse and her baby into the nursery and Lady Dalkeith followed with the royal princess in her arms. Placing the tiny baby in a crib she said, "Can you put a guard on the door, please?"

Alina looked across at Meg, who raised her eyebrows and gave a very slight, silent shrug. Smoothing back her wayward hair, Alina made a quick review of her household: who could they ask to do that? Then she cried, "Ah, but there's no need! Prince Maurice and his retinue, or whatever you call them, are here. Although, he is sick, so we must make sure he doesn't come in to see his new cousin." She tried to smile but the very idea gave her palpitations: suppose he really did have the plague?

Lady Dalkeith's eyes opened wide. "Prince Maurice – here? Oh, no."

Alina frowned: Maurice was the King's sister's son and first cousin to the royal baby; how could it be undesirable?

Lady Dalkeith closed the nursery door and took Alina to one side. "I must be in the next chamber, is that possible?"

"Of course," Alina opened a connecting door to what had been her late mother-in-law's suite, "here you are, right next door, and you have an excellent view . . ."

Lady Dalkeith entered and walked over to the window. "Thank you. It's Maria de los Angeles, isn't it?"

"Yes, but even Her Majesty calls me Alina."

"I'm sorry, I returned to the Queen after you went to Spain for her and I don't think our paths have ever crossed at Whitehall or Somerset House. I am Anne Villiers. Please call me Anne."

Alina knew she ought to go through the usual pleasantries, but there was the distinct sound of men shouting below – inside the house – and she had a great deal to do. Before she excused herself though, she couldn't resist asking, "What exactly has happened to Her Majesty? Why has she had to leave with no lying-in period when she is unwell?"

Anne Villiers sighed. "It's a complicated tale: I don't know where to start. These are such trying and very strange times when a queen must deliver her baby in a bed not her own then rush from the country to avoid capture."

Alina opened her hands in a typically Spanish gesture, "But why didn't she take the child?"

"Because the wet-nurse refused to go! Can you believe that? It's a sign of the times when a servant refuses a royal command. The blessed woman disappeared as soon as she was told they were crossing to France. It was only by the grace of God that Mrs O'Dwyer," Anne Villiers indicated the nursery, "was found nearby. Her husband was killed in fighting, she said, although I think it may have been a tavern brawl, not a battle. He was a mercenary. She is Irish and a Catholic, but to be honest, I have my doubts about her, although Henriette is thriving, praise be."

"Oh, I have a Henrietta, except we call her Hetty." In precisely that moment the door to the passage swung open and the little girl named Hetty rushed into Alina's skirts. Peeping out from under a mass of black curls, she studied her mother's guest then crushed a grubby rag doll upside down to her chest as if the newcomer might steal it. Alina bent down, took the doll and gently smoothed its red flannel skirt over the lumpy wool-filled legs the right way up. As she did so, a much fairer, older boy arrived. "Mama, who are those men outside? Has Papa returned?" he demanded.

"Children, you may not go in there," scolded a slight man halting at the doorway. He could easily have passed for the boy's father, although he was, in fact, his tutor and an ordained Catholic priest. John Hawthorne nodded apologetically at Alina then spoke again to his charge, "Manners, young man: your mother is speaking with a lady."

The boy hesitated, but Alina smiled and beckoned him to her. "Come and meet Lady Dalkeith, Tomás. Lady Dalkeith is our guest and she has brought another very special guest with her –" She was about to say 'a royal baby' but only said "a tiny baby."

She was right to be cautious for Anne Villiers added, "But that is our secret," and put a finger to her lips.

"Why?" demanded the little girl half-emerging from Alina's skirts.

Tomás gave his mother a sideways look and Alina manoeuvred the two children to stand before her, saying, "Lady Dalkeith, allow me to introduce my son Tomás and a naughty girl called Henrietta, named after our queen." Then she gestured toward the slight man at the doorway, "And this is a special dear friend, Tomás's tutor, John Hawthorne."

As the formal introduction was concluded, a dumpy woman in a vast white apron tried to edge past the tutor into the chamber. "Beg pardon, milady," said the woman urgently, her eyes and head indicating behind her.

Alina glanced at Anne Villiers, "Forgive me; I have a number of matters to attend." Edging Mrs Godwin back into the passage, out of the embarrassing crush in the doorway, Alina hissed, "What? I hope this is important."

"I needs to know what we should do about putting decent linen in the servants' block, milady. Who gets the best sheets, these here in the nursery or him in your husband's chamber?"

"It's a bit of a pickle," Meg said joining them in the doorway with evident glee.

Furious, Alina glared at her. For numerous reasons to do with their shared past experiences and the absence of men they had spent two years on an informal footing in the house, but even so Meg was forgetting herself. Wafting a hand in annoyance, Alina physically pushed round Mrs Godwin and marched down the short corridor then stopped, knowing she was being watched. Turning, she smiled apologetically at Anne Villiers and said sweetly, "I'm so sorry. We live as one big family here I'm afraid. My servants and children are *all* forgetting their manners today."

Anne Villiers smiled back, "Oh, my dear, think not on it. As we have said, strange times. Could you send me a maid, please, and arrange for what little luggage I have to be brought up?"

"Naturally." Alina kept the smile on her face until the queen's lady-in-waiting was no longer at the door observing her, then pushed back past Mrs Godwin and Meg to grab John Hawthorne's arm. "A maid? A lady's maid? Who can do that here?"

"Fanny is still in the village, you could use her. Except –"

"Except what?"

"Well, her father is siding with Parliament and spouting Levellers' talk."

Alina sighed. She'd heard whispers in the kitchen and dairy, but didn't have a very clear idea what Levellers' talk meant. "Oh, Levellers," she said, "who bothers about them around here? Everyone works for the estate, don't they? Fanny's father is a cripple and they're living on Crimphele charity in a tied cottage: she must do as she's told. Fetch her for me, John. Fanny is a silly girl, but she can dress a noblewoman's hair when she has to. I gave her plenty of practice in Spain. And take these two with you."

Alina propelled her children forward then paused, gazing down at the large greenish eyes of her daughter, who was in turn gazing up at her nervously in the crush. Stooping to kiss her troubled forehead, Alina lifted the long black curls from her neck and said, "Would you like to spend a few days with Mrs Hawthorne at the farm, *Cielo*? She has got some nice little cows there. You could help her feed them." As she spoke, Alina made eye-contact with John. Then, speaking in Spanish, which he understood, and forgetting that her children did too, she said, "Take them to your mother, John. Keep them out of sight and safe, *please*. I hope it is only for a few days, but the courtyard will never be quiet and I fear they will be trampled by all those horses."

She didn't add that she feared Prince Maurice had brought the plague to them, but that was her principle reason – the reason she had to get Lady Dalkeith and the Queen's new baby out of the house as fast as possible.

John Hawthorne nodded, hearing the panic in her voice: they knew each other well. Taking Henrietta by the hand he said in English, "Come along pretty girl, let's go and find some little calves for you to play with. And you, Tomás."

"I'm staying here," the boy said, "to help Mama."

John turned to Alina, who shook her head. "I'll bring you back later, when your mother has got all the men outside organised," he said. It wasn't a lie. John Hawthorne was incapable of lying but it served the moment. Placing a surprisingly firm hand on the boy's neck, he swivelled him around to face the stairs and marched him out of the house.

As they went, Alina raised a hand, "They'll need a change of clothes."

"I'll get them when I bring Fanny back with me," John called.

Meg re-appeared at Alina's elbow. "What exactly is the problem, Meg?"

"It's about that bed linen for the soldiers, milady. There's officers – what do we do about their bedding?"

"Nothing at all," Alina snapped, remembering the rough appearance of the men and the way they had laughed at her discomfort when the horse urinated. "Let them shift for themselves, and don't on any account allow them indoors. Tell Agnes she isn't to feed them."

"But we'll take meals up to the prince, ma'am, won't we? And his servant? Oh, and he wants to know, the servant, if he can have his own room."

"*Diablos*! Clever Cecil, I'd forgotten about him." Alina looked this way and that trying to decide where to put him to be near Prince Maurice.

She started towards the linen cupboard and caught sight of Anne Villiers waving briskly from her doorway.

"Baroness, before you turn your household totally upside down, there are few things I should tell you about the Prince."

Alina looked at her and caught a knowing look. "Oh, dear," she sighed.

Chapter 5

Plymouth, England, Autumn, 1644

Mark Almond, as he was known in Plymouth, put down his knife, unable to chew another morsel of hard-boiled fowl.

"… best you get your haircut as well," his father-in-law was saying. "We don't want anyone thinking you've got Royalist sympathies. We don't want no-one sniffing round my business and getting wrong ideas. There's many a one here who'd be only too happy calling you out as a traitor. We all signed the covenant against they Royalists to save our city and we should be as one inside they great walls, but that doesn't mean much, now there's only a sliver of fish at every meal and barely a crust to be had."

It was a frequent topic at mealtimes and Edward Beale, father-in-law and business partner to Marcos Alonso Almendro, was wont to discourse at length without giving anyone else a chance to speak. Not that the two women at his table ever dared interrupt. Mother and daughter knew their places. But Marcos was increasingly riled, and on this occasion couldn't resist saying, "I didn't."

"Didn't what?"

"Sign the covenant to help protect Plymouth during the siege."

Edward Beale's jaw dropped, displaying a masticated gobbet of a hen past her laying days. "You did. They came to the house. I remember. I signed in this very room."

"You may have done, Father, but I didn't."

"Why ever not?"

Marcos shook his head. "Either because I was at *my* warehouse, or in *my* office, or perhaps up in the roof, stowing away our special supplies."

"Tsss!" Edward Beale hissed nodding at the door for fear his servants might overhear. When he was sure no one was listening he said, "T'is said, every man in Plymouth signed the covenant against the King."

"No, sorry, but I probably don't count anyway, not being English."

"Tsss!" Edward Beale nearly exploded. "D'you *want* to bring hell down on us? T'is bad enough you being a Spaniard and a Catholic without advertising it."

"You were Catholic when I married Joanna."

"That is enough!" Edward Beale slammed his knife to the table, sending his wife and daughter into tremors. Beale's temper was always on a short fuse but now, with the food restrictions, the eternal fighting and constant vigilance that no one might suspect them of being anything but loyal to the Protestant Parliamentary cause, he flared at the least excuse.

With a trembling hand, Mrs Beale rang a bell and a weary servant entered with a tray. Marcos got to his feet. "I'll not stay for dessert, Mother, thank you. I have things to do in my workshop. Please excuse me."

No one commented as he exited the dining room. Grabbing his hat to cover his growing locks, visible evidence he was not a 'roundhead', Marcos left the Beale's comfortable house in a quiet street off the Barbican and made his way down to the quayside and his all-but-empty warehouse. Pausing to look out into the harbour to see what vessels had managed to get past the Royalist blockade, he suddenly saw in his mind's eye another sea view: a clear blue sky reflected in the tidal waters of the Guadalquivir estuary. He closed his eyes and muttered a short, silent prayer for his parents then pulled a large key from a pocket and headed up an alley to his warehouse.

Opening the narrow side entrance, he was met with a waft of sweet sack and brandy fumes overlaid with a touch of cinnamon and clove spices. But of those all that remained were a few empty barrels, and some wicker chests impregnated with their botanical contents. The last pound of peppercorns had been moved to his father-in-law's attic for safe keeping. His mother-in-law had commandeered the last of the dried oranges, and more fool he for showing her how to use the citrus peel he imported for his gin, as his mother had done for her *mermelada.*

Thinking of marmalade made him turn to check that he had bolted the door behind him. The warehouse had escaped looting so far, but it was only a matter of time before desperate Parliamentarian soldiers got in. Soldiers who hadn't been paid or couldn't find enough to eat, or anyone else looking for loot in a city that had long since ceased trading with the outside world. He wondered if there was still a way to benefit from the siege. Could he risk selling the dusty crumbs of his nutmeg and cloves, or offer the remaining handful of cardamom seeds Ludo sent from India as pickling spices? That led him to wonder why Edward Beale had only given him permission to store the vastly profitable pepper in his attic and whether his father-in-law was really trying to get rid of him; having a Spanish Catholic in his house was, after all, a terrible liability.

Marcos sighed and climbed the steps to his still-room musing on ways to get Joanna to sail for Sanlucar with him. Each time he broached the subject she came over silly. Silly, and sillier by the day. The only thing truly keeping him in Plymouth now was his small daughter, Mary. Joanna had miscarried two sons and the way things were going Mary was going to be an only child.

The cool, high-ceilinged space was silent, the copper jugs dulled by dust; the bulbous gin still as lifeless as its name. Since his supply of botanicals, the grains of paradise, the cassia and even the juniper berries from the nearby moor had ceased, Marcos had shut it all down; another source of income lost. The ship bringing the sherry and brandy from Sanlucar, *La Magdalena* captained by Ludo's friend Toxo hadn't docked in Plymouth for over two years, and Ludo's galleon *The Tulip* had nearly been blown out of the water when she'd tried to get in.

Marcos took a cloth from a drawer and started to polish the belly of the still, then gave up, went to his desk and pulled out his ledger for 1644. It made sad reading. He put it away and retraced his steps, locking the warehouse carefully behind him, then wondered what he could do to avoid going back to Beale's transport yard – not that there was any transporting to do. Nobody had got in or out of the city gates since the Royalists arrived to add Plymouth to their West Country ports. In this, Edward Beale was right: the signing of a covenant to protect their homes had kept the city out of Royalist hands. It had kept them alive: but it was killing him.

Without any plan in mind, Marcos made his way to the Old Ship Inn, the one place he could sit for hours at the cost of occasional war-talk and speculation on whether Parliament would prevail. Eventually, however, he had to return home for the evening meal. Entering the dwelling, he was met by a silence as complete as that of his warehouse. Edward Beale and his womenfolk were in their family room, talking in whispers. The whispering stopped the instant Marcos entered.

"There you are!" said Edward Beale in an over-jovial tone.

"Here I am," responded Marcos, looking at his wife for a clue as to what was going on. She looked away then jumped to her feet muttering something about Mary's bedtime. As she left, Marcos intercepted a look between his in-laws and Mrs Beale followed her from the room.

"Now then," said Edward Beale, "sit yourself down, I've got a proposal I'd like you to consider. An assignment, you might call it."

Marcos sat down and placed his hands on his knees, convinced he was about to be sent back to Spain. "You want me to go," he said. "But if I go, Joanna comes with me."

"Ah, no. Don't let's be hasty, boy. We want you to go –"

"We? All of you?"

"Me and my business associates – wait – listen. What I was saying earlier about you being foreign and all that – well, we can put that to good use. I was talking with some fellows and we want you to go out and learn what's going on. You can do it, being Spanish, the King's men will take you in and tell you everything and then you come back to us and tell us, and we'll know what's what and where we need to defend ourselves better." Edward Beale gave a chuckle of self-appreciation. "How's that for a plan, eh?"

"You want me to be a spy?"

"Exactly."

"And once I've got what you need, I have to shave my head so you'll let me back into the city?"

"Eh?" Beale was flummoxed, but then saw what Marcos was getting at. "'Course we'll let you back in. That's what we're sending you out for."

Marcos studied his hands. He'd been in difficult, even dangerous situations before with Ludo. But Ludo had done the thinking. Not when he'd gone off to Antwerp in search of his father on his own and finished up in Dunkirk, that was true ... but he'd been full of cheek and confidence in those days. It had not gone well. He gave an inward shudder remembering what had happened in Dunkirk and how he'd been desperate to get back to Ludo and his tulip scandal. But what choice did he have now? Stay and be goaded for a coward by his father-in-law, punished in trivial ways by his girl-wife? Stay and go mad for want of something to do in a city without trade or enterprise?

Meeting Edward Beale's eye, Marcos said, "Tell me."

Four burly Roundhead merchants accompanied Marcos to the west gate. Two expressionless armed men opened it and pushed him out.

Standing under the wall alone Marcos felt defenceless and naked, as if he'd been locked in the stocks, trapped, awaiting the first foul missile. Except the missile in this case would be a lead ball from a Royalist musket. Frozen to the spot, he waited until the moon disappeared behind laden clouds then, doubled-over, ran towards the water. He needed a boat, and to get out into the blackness of Plymouth Sound as fast as possible because where he was now meant he could also be shot at from the city walls behind him. Edward Beale had wanted rid of him. Perhaps it was all an elaborate ruse.

"Halt! Who goes there?"

Who goes, who goes? Marcos hunkered down and shifted his satchel to the region of his chest. Who was asking: Roundhead or Royalist? If the former, would they know who he was? If the latter would they assume he was the former? His mind was a frenzy of doubt and options, then came a moment of utter, chilling calm. He'd been in a similar situation in Flanders: had wriggled through deep mud to find out if he was being challenged by Flemings loyal to Spain or Dutchmen who'd slit a Spaniard's throat like a slice of their greasy cheese. Being a Spaniard had proved a liability before; being a Spaniard in Drake's Plymouth had always been a hazard.

A rueful smile hovered over Marcos's lips. Slipping his satchel round to his back he lowered himself onto his belly and began to edge forward on his elbows the way they'd shown him in Flanders.

Chapter 6

Crimphele

Coming out of the estate office with a heavy iron box of coins under her arm, Alina heard shouts and laughter coming from the great hall. Cecil Cleverden had said the only men allowed into the house would be a senior officer, two lieutenants belonging to the Prince's lifeguard, and then only to confer with Prince Maurice. These voices did not sound as if they were conferring with a royal prince: far from it. There was a clanging noise. Alina suddenly knew exactly what was happening: they were raiding the swords and armour decorating the hall. Wedging the iron box under her left arm she loosened the small sharp knife she had taken from the same collection ten years ago and thereafter kept in her right-hand skirt pocket – even in Whitehall and with the Queen at Somerset House – and without giving a second thought to her personal safety or the contents of the iron box, she marched into the great hall.

Four men in tattered blue uniforms were stripping the wall around the fireplace; two other men had raided breast-plates from ancient suits of armour and rammed on half-helms. They were prancing about in mock battle with a rusty sword and a morning star.

"What do you think you are doing?" Alina shouted. "How dare you! That belongs to my husband's family. This is his property and my home. How dare you!"

Lost in their fun, the two men capered on until a private soldier tripped one up. They then struggled to remove the helmets causing more hilarity.

Scarlet with fury, Alina was about to explode when one of the men helping himself to a hefty Tudor sword stopped what he was doing and said, "Beg pardon ma'am, property of the Crown now. It's been requisitioned."

"By whom?"

The men looked from one to another then back at her. One winked and ran his tongue over his upper lip. Alina was beyond angry. "Stay there, don't move, *y no toquéis una cosa mas de esta casa.*" In her fury she had lost her English. The men exchanged glances again. Not caring a jot Alina pushed through them, the contents of her box giving a tell-tale jangle, and raced up the tower stairs to Prince Maurice's chamber.

Knocking but not waiting for an answer, she swung in and came face to face with a half-dressed man lounging in her husband's fireside chair. He had long, wavy brown hair – recently washed – and dark circles around his eyes. His right arm was in a sling. Was this what he hadn't wanted anyone to see? Agnes had treated his fever; she'd made no mention of a broken arm. Why?

"Your men – they may not have our old – old . . ." the word she needed evaded her in her hurry to say it.

"Old?" the prince raised a dark eyebrow in a pasty white face.

"*Armadura – armas . . .*"

Cecil Cleverden finished sanding a letter and got up from her husband's writing desk. "May I be of assistance, Baroness?"

"You said they wouldn't be allowed in the house. Your men – they are taking our food, killing our animals to cook on fires, cutting down trees without permission and now they are taking my husband's family..." The word still wouldn't come. Furious, Alina turned back to the prince, who in the past seven days had not left the room.

Clearly amused, he waved a hand at his aide-de-camp, "Go down, Cecil. Tell them to only take what looks serviceable. No point taking antiquities: serviceable blades only, and any armour that looks wearable."

Cecil Cleverden went back to the desk, turned the letter he was writing face down then, taking his time, went to the door and after a terse nod in Alina's direction shut it behind him.

Aware she was powerless and noting the heavy weight under her left arm, Alina shifted the money box to her other side. It gave a revealing rattle.

"For us? We thank you, Baroness." The prince finally got to his feet, but his initial rudeness was not lost on Alina. "Would you be so good as to put it on that little desk," he said.

Alina clutched the box tighter. "No, I will not be so good. This is to pay my staff and merchants. I was going to hide it. Your men are coming into the house, molesting my servants, taking food from our pantries, and goodness knows, we have little enough." She was about to mention Lady Dalkeith and the little princess in the nursery but something stopped her.

Prince Maurice pursed his cherub-like lips and Alina immediately saw the resemblance to his uncle the king. Should she let him have the money? And the arms? The Fulford family were staunch Royalists, duty bound to help save their monarch's nation from the rabble that called themselves Parliamentarians and were – for some reason that eluded her – commonly known as Roundheads. She took a deep breath and placed the box on the desk.

The prince inclined his head in acknowledgment and took her hand. "Forgive me, Baroness, I have been a most ungrateful guest, but I feared to leave the room until I could use my arm again."

Was that all? Alina cursed herself for not taking the time to question Agnes about the physic she had prepared. No doctor had been located and the prince's own physician had still not arrived. She searched the fair face for traces of smallpox blisters, which was misinterpreted, for the prince smiled into her eyes and raised an eyebrow. "Why?" she asked bluntly.

"Why? Why what, Baroness?"

"Did you not want to leave the room?"

A flash of annoyance crossed Prince Maurice's face. "I have a broken limb and I am troubled by ill-health. Perhaps you are not aware of the rules by which our ancient Teutonic leaders governed their men: that only a man wholly sound in mind and body is fit to lead."

"You fear your men will not follow you if they see you are – damaged?"

"Precisely."

Alina was not convinced. "But it is only a broken arm and a fever, or so your man said." Were they – he and Aggie – keeping something from her? She peered forward in the low light of the bedchamber for more serious symptoms. Again, her intentions were misinterpreted. Prince Maurice stepped closer and gave another smile, which Alina classified as a leer. She leaned back quickly, embarrassed but relieved that there were no apparent boils or pock marks. Apart from the dark circles under his eyes suggesting sleepless nights there was no blackness around the face at all; in fact, he looked remarkably healthy compared to his officers, who were all very thin, and despite their unpleasant antics, obviously weary. Nevertheless, there was something. Instinctively she did not like this prince. He was nothing like his brother, and in their brief exchange was already showing signs of the Stuart hypocrisy she had encountered at Whitehall.

No longer so pleased with her scrutiny, Prince Maurice said, "Take my chair, madam. Sit with me a while. Let us converse and get to know one another."

Alina reluctantly settled herself in her husband's favourite chair, while the prince remained standing. She gave an inward smile, knowing it was because she was taller than he. Smoothing her skirts, pleased that she had returned to wearing her better dresses – to remind their visitors of her rank and that she had been one of the Queen's ladies-in-waiting – she schooled her features and lifted her gaze ingenuously to her visitor.

Prince Maurice moved to stand directly before her. Staring down with another supposedly winning smile, he said, "My uncle the King will be most grateful for your contributions, madam. I will not conceal that we are in dire need of reinforcements, of armour, weapons and specie." From behind his words came the sound of men shouting again, but their tone was different to that of before, and it came from outdoors, not in. The shouting turned into a continuous roar interrupted by what sounded like an explosion.

Prince Maurice sauntered to a window that looked out on the fields. "Nothing to see," he said and wandered back across the chamber. "They could be testing some powder."

"Gun-powder! But, my horses and dogs!" gasped Alina. "They will be terrified."

"How sweet," Maurice gazed at her face. "Please do not fret, it may only mean more ammunition and powder kegs have arrived. They will only be testing a small amount. I doubt they'll waste it on shooting your pets."

At that moment there was the sound of musket fire followed by a trumpet call. Alina dashed to the window. As she opened the casement to lean out a round of grapeshot rattled off the wall just beneath her. There was another round of musket fire; voices called from the courtyard.

"What is it?" Prince Maurice demanded, pushing Alina aside. "Oh, dear God, no," he moaned, as they watched three dozen or more armed Roundheads race down Paddon Hill towards the house, followed by a motley bunch of locals bearing home-made pikes.

Alina watched in appalled confusion as a Royalist soldier on horseback galloped round the base of the old Tudor tower and jumped the low wall, right into a group of ragged pike-men. His horse screamed in agony as it landed chest down onto the end of a sharpened seven-foot stave. Another was buried in its rider's chest. Crimphele was under attack.

Alina hurtled from the room and down to the kitchen, screaming, "Lock the doors! Lock the doors!"

Meg was standing with her back to the kitchen door, her face drained of blood. "I – I was in the buttery," she stammered. "They'm coming down Paddon Hill – pike-men. Roundheads and –"

"I know! Stop talking, find Mrs Bodkin and bolt every door along the south range," Alina ordered, unhooking the bunch of keys she had taken to wearing at her waist. "I'll do the main doors and the chapel." She turned to the cook, "Put water on to boil, Agnes. Every pot you can."

Crook-back Aggie gave an intake of breath, "Oh, milady –"

"We'll have need of your skills today, I fear. Meg, go! These men must not get into the house. And stay out of sight, and if you see Mercy tell her to do the same, do you understand? Hurry!"

Leaving the kitchen, Alina rushed into the hall, half hoping the slovenly Royalist foot soldiers would still be there. They were not. She raced to the main door, locked it with one of her huge keys then dropped the wooden beam into place, offering silent thanks to her husband, who had made this one modification to their house when civil war became inevitable. Then she made for the chapel. The outside door had to be locked then the inner door between the chapel and the family room – just in case. If anyone got in, the last thing she needed was for them to see her Spanish crucifix or John Hawthorne's vestments. Coming back through the family room, Alina paused at the entrance to the great hall, wondering if she should go back up-stairs to the nursery to warn Anne Villiers, but opened the low door under the stairs instead. It led down to her late father-in-law's wine cellar. It was also where he had stored his usable weapons. Hanging on the back of the door was Alina's beloved longbow. Her quiver of arrows was on a nearby shelf.

Slinging the bow over one shoulder, the quiver over the other, she then grabbed a pistol and a bag of powder. The action brought her up short: she had been locking doors and was willing and able to defend her home, but she'd been assuming the royal princess was in it. Was Lady Dalkeith outdoors taking her daily walk instead? Another dreadful thought struck her. With so many men in Royalist garb in the yards it was hard to pretend nothing was happening, but could foolish Fanny – mean-minded Fanny, whom she had insisted come to Crimphele to attend the royal lady-in-waiting – have got word to her father about the baby princess? Did Crimphele now have enemies on the estate because they had an enemy who was inside of the house – who could unbolt doors and let them in?

Stuffing the pistol down her bodice, Alina hiked up her skirts and hared up the stairs once more. Prince Maurice was coming down. "Here," she said, "take this." Ignoring his injured arm, she pushed the pistol and powder into his chest. "Don't go out. Don't open any doors." It was evident who was in charge here. "Come with me. You have to protect the princess."

"I was just about to say the very same." Maurice was annoyed.

Alina ignored him. "Come," she said and grabbed his fine linen shirt, dragging him back upstairs then towards the nursery. "Hurry! I have to find Lady Dalkeith, and lock up her maid."

"Her maid?"

"Yes, Fanny, stupid, nasty Fanny. I have to lock her up!"

The fighting went on all day, but Alina did not dare open even the smallest window to see what was happening. As each hour passed she gave a prayer of thanks that the princess was safe in the house and that they still had not be been raided, and then another prayer that the house be not attacked during the night.

Fanny had been located and locked in the tower room, where Alina herself had once been confined. There was no way out save through a tiny window opening onto the closed kitchen yard.

Darkness fell. Crook-back Aggie served something passing as broth in the hall and the inhabitants of the house, Alina, her servants Meg and Mercy, Mrs Godwin the housekeeper, Lady Dalkeith holding the princess, the wet-nurse Mrs O'Dwyer holding her fat son, and Prince Maurice of the Palatine sat in silence together, barely daring to speak. If the familiarity disturbed her titled guests, Alina didn't care: she wanted everyone where she could see them. But her thoughts kept straying to her children and the inhabitants of John Hawthorne's family farm. Everyone in the local village knew John had gone to Spain to become a priest; everyone knew about his family and their close ties to the Fulfords of Crimphele. If the Roundheads had been tipped off by Fanny's Leveller father, or even recruited in nearby Carlingford or Tamstock they would have this information. Her spoon dropped to the table with a clatter. She willed herself not to cry. Not to show weakness. Then she raised her eyes and looked about her. Everyone was staring at the spoon. It had made a noise. They had heard it. The dreadful sound of men firing muskets, of horses screaming with fear and pain, had stopped. There was silence. Was it over?

Then there was a scrabbling noise. Crook-back Aggie's aged terrier, Perkin, yapped and waddled towards the kitchen. Aggie exchanged looks with her mistress and followed, her spine more twisted and bent than ever.

After a few moments, Aggie returned and beckoned. "There's someone at the kitchen door, milady."

"Don't open it!"

"But Perkin's wagging his tail, milady."

Prince Maurice pulled the pistol from his sling, but one-handed couldn't load it. Alina was about to help him but the knocking grew louder. Edging out of her seat she picked up her bow and cocked an arrow, then went to stand beside the heavy, bolted door. "Who is it?" she demanded, wondering if Perkin would wag his tail for Cecil Cleverden.

"It's me. Let me in, Aggie, for the love of all your fairies and spriggans, let me in." The voice was but a harsh whisper for the door was thick. Who would know about Aggie and her belief in Cornish spriggans? A wonderful thought occurred to Alina. "*Quien es*?" she demanded in Spanish.

"*Soy yo, tonta, abre la maldita puerta.*"

Alina pulled back the bolt and opened the door just wide enough for Marcos Alonso Almendro to fall in.

Next morning, Marcos, Anne Villiers and Alina sat together for a frugal breakfast in the family room. They were all bleary eyed with lack of sleep for Marcos had brought the information that Roundheads were now camped around the house. Crimphele was under siege.

As Alina cut the last of the bread, Prince Maurice joined them. "As soon as my men have finished their business with your local rag-tag Roundheads," he said, as if it were a tiresome interlude in his day's entertainment, "I shall continue with my original plan to move south-west to secure Falmouth. If you wish to evacuate the premises before we go,

I shall quite understand. I can offer you two or three men as escorts."

Marcos jumped to his feet and pulled out a chair for him to sit in. The prince took it without even a nod. He had removed his sling but was holding his wounded arm awkwardly, evidently in pain, and he had clearly had trouble dressing himself. The Fulford pistol, however, was now rammed into a wide belt over his military buff coat.

Alina made a mental note to ask for its return before he left then registered what he was saying. "Why might I wish to leave, Your Highness?" she asked. "This is my home."

"Well, your home or not," scoffed the prince, "you have to accept that you are no longer safe, especially given your personal circumstances." Alina heard the words and frowned, but before she could ask for more clarification the prince continued, "Someone informed a Roundhead commander of my whereabouts. This might have been a Tudor stronghold a hundred years ago, but it's hardly that any longer. We're trapped inside and it won't take long for them to set up heavy guns. They probably know my men have marched on further west and won't be dropping in to help us. Work it out for yourself, my dear."

"Do I assume you are troubled that Mr Cleverden has not returned, Your Highness?" Alina's voice was as acid as the turned milk in the jug before her.

A dark look crossed Prince Maurice's face. He was more concerned than he was going to admit, concerned and afraid. His men had been overcome by a rabble group of Roundhead soldiers and their local sympathisers, and his aide-de-camp, who wrote his correspondence and knew all his secrets, had not returned to the house.

Alina exchanged glances with Marcos. They had been so busy checking doors and windows and keeping watch over the princess she hadn't had a moment to find out how or why he had left Plymouth, or how he had come up river when merchant barges wouldn't risk it. Marcos gave her a look, inclining his head to one side to indicate he wanted to talk to her, but not in the present company.

Anne Villiers made a nervous gesture to gain Prince Maurice's attention, "And my charge, Your Highness? What do you propose if I cannot stay here and cannot leave the house either?"

"I hadn't forgotten my royal cousin, madam, she is my prime concern. We obviously must protect her. Given that this house is no longer safe I propose the Baroness forms a party to escort you and the princess back to Exeter."

"Will that be safe? Surely not," Anne Villiers was close to tears.

Ignoring her, Prince Maurice continued, "We must hope that the local rag-tags will respect the Baroness and her guests sufficiently let us leave the estate. *Her steward* will be accompanying you as well, of course...."

Alina looked from the prince to Marcos then realised the steward would be the prince in Marcos's clothing.

"... although two women and their children are hardly a threat, even to Parliamentarians. We'll be allowed safe passage, I'm sure. Travelling in a humble manner will also discourage other people from questioning our rank and status in the towns."

Alina pushed back her hair in an agony of a dilemma. She did not want to leave Crimphele, would never leave her children here or at John's farm, but nor could she let poor Anne Villiers, who had led a far more sheltered life than she, travel with only the dubious prince and the uncertain Mrs O'Dwyer for company. She looked at the queen's lady-in-waiting sitting next to her, giving her an opportunity to speak. There were tears in Anne Villiers' eyes now. The gentle woman shook her head, unable to speak.

Annoyed by the situation and the way she was being manoeuvred, Alina turned back to the prince, "Everything you say, Your Highness, makes sense, but surely it would be wiser for us all to stay here in the house. Most local men, those who remain on the estate, owe their livelihoods to us. I cannot believe they would do us harm. I also cannot believe it was anyone belonging to Crimphele who attacked your men. There simply aren't enough of them left. I think it will be safer to keep the princess here. How many even know she has been born? And if they do know she is here ... Ah, your Mr Cleverden ... but, surely, they have set up camp waiting to claim *you*, not her. Let's hope Mr Cleverden has said nothing. Let us think about why they are here. Perhaps Fanny is not responsible for telling her father about you and Lady Dalkeith. She says she isn't. That means they don't know about the princess; they only saw you crossing the bridge at Gunnislake in your uniforms *y ... han venido ...*" Alina's rambling thoughts came to an end as she lost her English in her distress.

Marcos came to her aid. "I think what the baroness is trying to say, Your Highness, is that she – *we* – don't think local men will try to harm us. Although going out among strangers could prove dangerous. None of the local men around here and on the estate can risk losing their homes. Baron Metherall would turn them out immediately. They all know he could make them suffer in the long run."

The round-faced prince stared at him. "Not if he's dead, he won't."

Alina froze: the prince's comment about her 'personal circumstances' suddenly made sense. She started to say something then stopped.

"Didn't you know? Haven't you been told?" Prince Maurice continued, reaching for some bread to avoid eye contact. "Your husband was killed weeks ago. An ammunition cart caught fire while we were camped outside Bristol. I do apologise most sincerely, what with my own illness and our battle at Lyme – I'd quite forgotten it."

"What happened?" Marcos asked quietly.

"Oh, he tried to help someone when a powder barrel on a cart exploded and got caught in the second blast. Body parts everywhere and we weren't even fighting."

Alina tried to swallow. Marcos put a hand out across the table but he could not reach her. Anne Villiers jumped to her feet and put her arms around her, glaring at the prince for his callous statement. There was a brief silence broken only when the prince's knife scraped up the last of the butter.

"Listen," Marcos said. "It has gone quiet again. Perhaps, Prince Maurice, it is safe for you to see how your troops are doing now."

"I haven't stayed indoors here because I am coward, you fool!" the prince retorted. "I have stayed with you to protect my small cousin and her guardian." Indignant, he got up and went to the window then stood on tiptoe to look out into the courtyard.

Marcos joined him, pressing his advantage, "I believe what Baroness Metherall says is true, sire. I have lived in this house and know the people. No one would harm her or those in her care while she is here."

"You overlook important details, sir: she is Spanish, a widow with no claim to this country, and the entire Fulford family are Catholics. Someone with a grudge or with something to gain might be – almost certainly will be, sooner or later – wanting this estate. That my aide has not returned to the house suggests there are more trained men camped in the vicinity than we'd like to think. I spoke of a local rabble to diminish the ladies' fears, but those who have attacked us and laid siege are *not* a bunch of local boys. Their manoeuvre and speed suggest Cromwell's new, so-called Model Army. These men have no love of popish Spaniards."

The insult, for that was how it was intended, was spat at Marcos by a frightened man. Overhearing him, Alina's thoughts went elsewhere. "Would Fanny do that?" she muttered.

"Maybe." Marcos turned to her, "Someone informed someone that Prince Maurice was here with very few men. Unless it's a coincidence." Marcos looked at her inquiringly. "Percy?"

"Percy, Thomas's cousin, of course. No, he joined Thomas to fight for the King. They went together. Except ..." Alina paused, put her hand to her mouth. "... he could have changed sides. He's the sort to do that. And he'd do anything to get his hands on Crimphele. If he knows Thomas is dead ... If he knows about Thomas ..." Alina bit her lip, unable to go on.

Marcos turned back to the prince. "I am concerned about why the baroness was not informed about her husband, Your Highness. Do you know who might have been charged with the message?"

"No idea. Messy business; drew attention to our position far too early as well. Fulford's nephew – cousin – whatever – was with him, though, that I do know, always trying to ingratiate himself. He might have sent the news. He's not the heir, is he?"

"No, Baron Metherall has a son," Marcos replied then got to his feet and went to the door of the wine cellar. He turned back, caught Alina's eye and made a hand gesture resembling a pistol. She nodded. They had already armed themselves but fetching more ammunition was a wise move.

Prince Maurice made a circuit of the table, presumably considering how to act, and Alina's mind returned to her one encounter with the odious Percy. He was exactly the sort to change sides for personal gain; he could have returned to the south west and recruited local men in Tavistock with obligations to his family there. She was about to join Marcos in the cellar to tell him to get every serviceable weapon he could find when Prince Maurice stopped beside Anne Villiers and said, "Prepare the baby in the nursery and stay there until I tell you."

"But I cannot go with her," Alina shouted, getting up so fast her chair toppled to one side. "My son is at our priest's – at a local farm. So is my daughter. I cannot go anywhere without them. We must stay here."

Maurice turned on his heel. "You are hysterical, madam." He turned back to Anne Villiers, "Do as I say –"

The words halted in mid-air as a gunshot rent the air and heavy boots began kicking at a door.

"The chapel!" Alina cried. "They're getting in through the chapel."

Within moments, feet began kicking at the door leading into the family room. A shot was fired through the lock. Anne Villiers and Alina screamed simultaneously and ran to hold each other. The prince – surprisingly – placed himself between them and the door just as it swung open.

For a moment nobody moved. There was silence but for the frantic yapping of an old dog in the distant kitchen. Then a youngish man with short cropped hair, wearing plain brown attire entered the Fulford family room, a man of an indeterminate age and exceedingly fair of face. A face that belied his nature.

"Ah, the voluptuous Arleen," he said, batting his eyes at Alina. "Greetings, Cousin, greetings. Apologies for the nature of our entry, I will arrange for repairs forthwith."

"Talk of the devil," muttered Alina.

Chapter 7

Staying where he was in the wine cellar, Marcos pulled the door to and in the remaining sliver of light groped around on a shelf for a pistol, which he stuffed down the back of breeches. He then scrabbled about for powder. Locating what felt like a full bandolier, he pulled off his woollen jerkin, tucked it over a shoulder then stuffed a second tinder box into his breeches' pocket. Then, after re-arranging his clothes, he selected a bottle of wine at random and re-emerged into the family room.

"And you are?" challenged the invader aiming a loaded handgun at him.

"Mark Almond, sir, milady's steward," Marcos said, making a show of blinking in the daylight then lowering his gaze to the floor in an attempt to look both surprised and humble.

"You sound foreign, another bloody Spaniard, I suppose."

Alina gasped and stepped forward but before she could speak Percy waved the gun at Lady Dalkeith. "Who's this, your sister?"

"No, this lady here is – Lady Dal ... Dalford," Alina replied. "She is visiting us."

Percy looked at Alina distrustfully then turned to the prince, who was now held firmly between two large men, one of whom Marcos thought he recognised as Jim Hawkins, the ferryman. The man met his eye, gave the slightest nod then inclined his head a fraction indicating they should talk elsewhere. Marcos responded with the merest acknowledgement. Jim Hawkins had played an important part in saving Crimphele when Ludo da Portovenere's corsairs had tried to ransack it, his role now with Percy was worrisome, but perhaps there was a reason for it. He turned his attention back to the intruder, trying to recall all he'd been told about the infamous Percy.

The handsome young man looked him in the eye, cocked his pistol and took aim, but then swung round to point it directly at Prince Maurice's head. Marcos swallowed hard. If this Percy was anything like the fervent Parliamentarians in Plymouth he was to be feared. And if – as was more likely – he'd turned coat to achieve an inheritance not rightly his, he was to be feared even more.

"Well, well, well," Percy said in a nasal whine, addressing Alina while keeping the barrel of his gun aimed at the prince, "I come to claim my late cousin's estate and find a royal bird in the nest. It ought to be perfectly splendid, and I know Cromwell and Essex will be delighted, but I have to say, just at this moment it's a trifle inconvenient." He smiled at Prince Maurice then back at Alina. "There are still dungeons here, I assume. I regret I didn't take more notice when I played tag with your late husband, not that he would have gone near them. Easily scared, poor dear Thomas, I expect they gave him the shivers."

Marcos switched his attention to Alina, who had straightened her spine and lifted her head, a warning sign if Percy did but know it.

"There are no dungeons here," she said. "There are storerooms beneath the kitchen, but I cannot put a royal prince in a storeroom. Think what will happen to you if you do when the King returns to London and the country is no longer at war."

"Ah, dear lady, that is *not* going to happen. Thousands of Parliament men march this way as I speak. There is to be one final battle and then it will be us in London and Oxford not that cheating, weakling Stuart. His days are most definitely numbered."

Marcos looked at Jim Hawkins, who nodded in confirmation. So that was why he was here: Hawkins had a large family to consider. And if true, both he and Alina were in serious danger, not only were they Spanish, Alina had been the Catholic Queen of England's lady-in-waiting. The thought brought him to the tiny princess in the nursery above and his mind raced for a way out of the situation, preferably a way that enabled Alina to stay at Crimphele. If she still wanted to? Perhaps she didn't. He looked at her for a clue.

Noting his gaze, Alina turned to Percy and said, "We have no dungeon, Cousin, but we do have a tower room that might serve. Mark, please check the room *Fanny is cleaning* is available, she should have finished by now. Tell her to return to the kitchen." She turned back to Percy, "It is a small chamber with no means of exit, and more suited to a man of Prince Maurice's standing than a storeroom. I will tell my housekeeper what is happening, shall I?" It was not a question for Alina, hand clamped down on her waist to keep her keys from jangling, was out of the family room and half way across the great hall before Percy could respond.

Lady Dalkeith's eyes flashed this way and that like a deer abandoned to the wolf. "Perhaps I should go with her," she said suddenly, and fled from the room.

"Mercy upon us," Percy muttered with a smile, "I must say this is proving easier than I anticipated. Still, having a hundred men posted around a house generally gives one the upper hand, don't you agree, Prince?" He waved the pistol at his henchmen, "Release him."

Prince Maurice grasped his injured arm as it was released from the Roundheads' grip, nearly fainting with pain.

"Clipped your wing, have you?" laughed Percy. "Let it be a warning, sir, it'll be more than a wing next time."

Marcos hesitated then said, "I will see if the chamber is ready, sir."

Percy narrowed his eyes, "If this is some sort of ruse, remember you're all prisoners in this house. There's no point trying to get out, if that's what you are planning. I wasn't exaggerating when I said I had a hundred men posted around the courtyards. There are, and they hate foreigners to a man."

Marcos bowed as a steward should, placed the dusty bottle of wine he was still holding on the sideboard then exited sedately. At the turn in the stairs he paused then entered the prince's chamber as if to collect personal possessions. As he did so he was grabbed from behind and pulled into a vice-like clinch. Barely able to move, Marcos could not see who it was. "I'm only the steward, sir," he grunted, as his throat was squeezed. "I'm no one." The pressure eased.

"Steward? There was no steward here when we arrived."

"Well I'm here now, sir." 'When we arrived' – was this one of the Prince's men? He took a chance, "The prince is being moved to a smaller chamber sir, a more secure room. I'm to take his clothes."

The pressure relaxed and Marcos looked down, taking in a pair of very expensive, once elegant but now mud and blood-stained boots. Torn blue ribbon dangled at the knee. Blue was the Royalist colour. The grip was loosened. He turned and faced a young man with a filthy face and torn shirt, who put a finger to his lips and pushed the door closed with a boot, then said, "If you're really the steward tell me who lives here."

"The lady Arleen," Marcos replied, slipping back to her old form of address. "Baroness Metherall, that is. I can tell you the names of the servants, if you wish."

The young man studied him much as Jim Hawkins had in the family room. "Hmm," he said. "Now, tell me what's happening?"

"Prince Maurice has – um – been taken prisoner, sir."

"The Roundheads have got in!"

"Yes, sir, but how did you get in?"

"Up the ivy, good old ivy." The Royalist went to the window. "But, damn it to hell, I should have stayed put! The princess – do they know she's here?"

"I can't say, sir. Perhaps not."

"Let's hope not." The young man blew through his cheeks. "All right, carry on, but not one word about me being here, all right? And make sure the prince's new room is left unlocked – and this room. No one is to come in. No servants – nobody."

Despite his knowing about the princess and the nature of his clothes, Marcos was still not sure about the young man, so, fearing to say too much, he said, "I expect Mr Percival will want to take this room, sir."

"Mr Percival?"

"He's the Roundhead leader, I believe, sir."

"Damn it to hell," the young man repeated. "Look, get me the key to the chamber the prince is going to. If there is one?"

Marcos wanted to ask why, who the young man was and what he planned to do but instead said, "Can I suggest you change your clothes, sir. You might go unnoticed if you appear to work here."

"What? Ah, yes. Good thinking."

"You'll find some of Sir Thomas's clothes in the press over there," Marcos pointed across the chamber then gathered some of the prince's belongings and hastened out of the room and up the stairs to where Fanny had been lodged.

Fanny, a silly female at the best of time, was exhausted from crying and disinclined to listen to Marcos's instructions. Eventually, though, he managed to bundle her down to the kitchen without undue attention, where Aggie sat her in a fireside chair and gave her a calming drink. Marcos then returned to the family room where Percy and the Palatine prince were seated facing each other in icy silence.

Bowing respectfully to Percy, he said, "The chamber is ready, sir, if you would like to follow me."

The prince was conducted to the chamber followed by the wily Percy, who locked the door and kept hold of the key.

Later that chaotic day, still playing his practised role as steward, Marcos slipped out of the house via the kitchen. Roughly dressed men in no recognisable uniform had been posted around the house but their rag-tag appearance made it relatively easy for him to pass unchallenged across the destruction that had once been Alina's precious rose terrace then down along a badger run through hawthorn bushes and ancient trees to the Crimphele landing stage. Three uniformed pike-men had been placed on guard: one was on the jetty looking up and down river; one was lounging against the wall of the boat house; the third was wandering along the lane leading to the Hawkins' cottage, paying more attention to his boots than what was going on around him. None of them appeared to be particularly alert, but it was a nuisance Marcos hadn't anticipated. Quickly, he pushed his way back into the undergrowth, snagging his jacket and breeches in the process then, more gradually, edged towards the back of the cottage built into the low hill. Once near enough, he stepped out of the bushes and wandered the final few yards along the cart track at a casual stroll, and ambled round to the back door past the privy.

One of the younger Hawkins was stacking kindling. Straightening up, he smiled an innocent welcome, although Marcos doubted very much if the lad was old enough to remember him.

"Is your ma home?" Marcos asked. The boy pointed at the back door and Marcos let himself in.

Mrs Hawkins blinked in surprise then pulled him into a hug. "I didn't know you were here, Mr Almond. Oh, 'tis a relief. Have you seen my Jim? Gert lummock thinks he's being clever joining they Roundheads – thinks he's being a spy. You be careful, I told him. Spies get hanged for treason, I said."

"Why? I mean, why is he with the Roundheads, Mrs Hawkins?"

Mrs Hawkins lowered her eyes, "Cuz I was saying as to how the Lady Arleen needed to be got away, in case they eejits from Tamstock took it into their thick heads to take over Crimphele – her being Spanish and all. And he jumps up and says, 'You're right, Ma," and rushes out without another word. "Mind you, there's more than they Levellers here now, aren't there? Jackie says there's proper soldiers come."

Marcos processed Mrs Hawkins' Cornish vocabulary and grasped the gist of what she was saying. "Yes. That's why I'm here. Did you know Lady Marjorie's nephew had come with the Roundheads?"

"Not that boy Percival! I seed him pull the head off a sparrow bird when he was no more 'n five. He's a nasty one that." She paused, "Ah, so that's what it's about then. He's come to get what he thinks is his. Oh, but no! That means the master is ... has Sir Thomas been killed?"

Marcos nodded and then began to relax a little. Mrs Hawkins had a bumble bee in her head most days but it didn't stop her thinking straight when need be. "Can you help us?" he asked.

"Can and will, don't you fret. But you got to get the Lady Arleen away, sir. She's not safe here. Nor her cheel, neither. They'll have her. The village was turning already 'spite they've only known her for a good person what has cared for them and even saved them from they Turks – with your help, of course, sir, and my Big Jim. But now they're saying as how she's a Catholic and protects Aggie, who everyone knows for a witch, and they're talking about how the Lady Marjorie passed away and ... well, Mr Almond, you'm not from here and the king looks to be losin' and now with this Mister Percival here, who's English and someone they'll have to please to keep their cottages and the like, I'm sorry to say it, but they'll have her, and you, one way or another."

"Yes, I know. The question is can you help us get away? There's guards on the jetty and down along the river, too."

Mrs Hawkins scrunched her wide brow. "You'll need a decent, fast boat. How many are you?"

Marcos did a rapid calculation: Lady Dalkeith and her royal charge, the nursemaid plus anonymous baby, Alina, her two children, and possibly John Hawthorne, who was as much at risk as any of them. "Five adults, two children and two babes in arms."

As Marcos spoke Jim Hawkins stepped into the kitchen. "We'll need the barge for that many, and I doubt we'll do it unseen. Not even in the night."

"I know," Marcos shook his head. "I wonder if Percy will let us go to be rid of the lady Arleen."

"T'is in his interest, sir." Jim Hawkins replied. "But he might want to keep young Master Thomas. It's what my missis was saying," Jim Hawkins acknowledged his wife with a nod, "Mister Percy will, like as not, want to keep the young master with him – in case they Royalists win this blessed war and we go back to being like before. But even so, with her good husband dead I do think as Milady should go back where she belongs, sir."

Marcos sighed, knowing he was right. "Give me a couple of hours and I'll come back to you. In the meantime, Jim, get your barge ready. No need to hide what you're doing; act like you're going for regular supplies the way you always did."

Jim Hawkins met Marcos's eye then nodded. "I'll get started right away."

Making no effort to conceal himself this time, Marcos wandered slowly back up to the big house lost in thought – musing partly on the fickle nature of the people who relied on the Crimphele estate for their livelihood, and partly on what Mrs Hawkins had said about Crook-back Aggie and the late Lady Marjorie's demise: something he had always suspected. Would they have to take Aggie as well? And what about poor Meg, married now to Toby who had gone off to fight in Bristol with Sir Thomas? Then he stopped in his tracks. Aggie was not ten paces away from him, bending over the ground, poking at something.

He coughed politely to let her know he was nearby. "Special herbs – for our supper?" he asked.

"Could be," the crooked old woman retorted.

"Or could it be for someone with a bellyache? Or better still," Marcos grinned, "to cause a belly ache?"

"What you suggestin', boy?" Aggie's squinty blue eyes glared at him and Marcos felt himself blush like a loon. "Kill or cure, is you askin'? But only if it's for Milady. I'll not do it for another soul."

"No, well, yes, erm ..." Marcos scrambled for words as random ideas flitted across his mind. "What you gave to Fanny to calm her down, but stronger, a sleeping draught but much, much stronger."

"Killin' him during his sleep won't do no good. Bring them all down on you proper that would," Aggie stated, cleaning the end of her special little knife. "But we could knock him out for a good while so as you can ..." she cocked her head to one side, "get Milady to safety."

"We need to take the children as well, and the Lady Arleen's visitors," Marcos said, deliberately using the name Aggie and Meg had been accustomed to when Alina first arrived at Crimphele, calling on their shared past as a moral binder.

"Bad belly ache and the trots might serve better – keep him distracted without rousing suspicion. Can't have they soldier boys thinkin' we've done for him, can we?" Aggie waved the knife to identify a pike-man walking directly towards them.

Marcos gave him a small salute as he approached and whispered hastily to Aggie, "Worst trots known to man, can you manage that?"

"Can I manage that?" Crookback Aggie rolled her beady eyes. "He'll have the squits so bad he won't dare bend over for a month."

Marcos laughed out loud despite the tension in his forehead. Then, becoming serious, "You'll come with us, won't you, Aggie?"

"Not me, Mr Almond. I growed here, I'll die here. I've already had more years than was given me. You and Milady get yourselves to safety and leave they two cheel with Meg and me. No harm will come to them with us."

Marcos wanted to gather the hideous little woman in his arms although he knew Alina would never agree to leaving her children behind. Instead, he turned on his heel and raced back to the ferryman's cottage, leaving the pike-man wondering who he ought to be watching, the local woman said to be a witch, or the estate steward.

Rushing back into the Hawkins' small dwelling, Marcos gasped out, "Mr Hawkins, are you to be trusted?"

"Until my family are threatened, yes."

"That I understand. Right, this is what I need you to do. Take the barge *upstream* as if you're going up to Gunnislake, and collect Mr Hawthorne and the Lady Arleen's children from the farm. Get them into the boat and stay out in the water until you see a signal. Then come alongside the trees here and wait until you hear me call out."

"I'll take my two eldest, they can handle the barge while I get milady's nippers aboard. What'll be the signal sir?"

"A fire, I regret to say."

Jim Hawkins stared at him and Marcos knew he had stopped listening; having said he'd take his eldest sons he was calculating the risk to his own family once Percy realised what his family had done. Marcos waited, wondering if he dare suggest that Percy would be delighted Alina and her children were out of his way. Except Percy was likely to want to keep Master Tomás with him, as Jim had suggested, in case the Royalists returned to power. Or worse, remembering the headless sparrow – to ensure the boy could never claim anything in the future. They had to get little Tomás away at all costs. He looked at the Hawkins youngsters standing around their parents. "Mrs Hawkins, how many children have you?"

"We got six for now, but we'd welcome two more and keep them as our own – until necessary," she said, knowingly.

Would it work? If the worst came to the worst and he had to get Alina away on her own. It was a possible solution. Leaving them with Aggie was too much of a risk, but Percy didn't know the Hawkins family.

"We'd welcome a new baby, too, come to that," Mrs Hawkins added, "'cept that sour-puss nursemaid won't fit in this little house with hers, as well."

Nearly choking with emotion, Marcos said, "I should tell you who that baby is."

Mrs Hawkins shook her head. "Best not, sir. What we don't know the village can't fret about – in case this lummock takes a cup or two more than he ought."

Marcos looked at Jim Hawkins and envied him his wife. "Tonight then?" he said to the ferryman. "Wait for us until you see the fire – and if it goes wrong, I'll get the children to you fast as I can."

"You can rely on us, Mr Almond," Jim Hawkins said, staring lovingly at his wife.

Returning to the big house for the second time that afternoon, legs weary from running and his stomach rumbling with hunger, Marcos passed through the kitchens where Meg and Mercy were peeling and chopping vegetables. Aggie was stirring what looked like a sauce in a copper pan, the nature of which he chose not to question. It was still at least an hour before supper and he needed to speak to Alina urgently, but he was waylaid by the surprising sight of Prince Maurice sitting opposite the foppish Percy at the long table in the great hall. Between them were various metal boxes containing Crimphele estate funds. Beside them were two other leather bags of coin with royal monograms. The young man who had been hiding in Prince Maurice's room was standing a yard or two behind his master with a travelling chest at his feet. A deal had been done. Percy was hedging his bets.

Chapter 8

Across the vaulted space of the great hall, the arched door to the courtyard was open and Marcos could hear the sound of horses. Percy looked up, noticed him and Marcos dropped his gaze, making as if to pass through the hall on some steward's errand.

"Ah, you," Percy said. "Not before time. Check Prince Maurice's carriage out there then go and fetch Lady Dalkeith and help her in." He spoke as master of the house.

Eliminating any expression of surprise, Marcos touched his forelock and hastened out of the door, hoping against hope that Alina was nearby.

She wasn't in the courtyard so he slipped up the back stairs to the south range gallery to speak to Lady Dalkeith. As he was hastening along the passage an arm shot out of an open doorway and yanked him inside.

"Don't say anything," Alina hissed. "Maurice has bribed his way out; told Percy that Anne Villiers is his mistress and the baby is his. Percy's letting them go. But I've got a plan for us."

"You have? What?"

Gabbling away in Spanish, Marcos explained what he had arranged with Crookback Aggie and Jim Hawkins, omitting only the fall-back arrangements for Alina's children.

Alina listened, biting her lip. "All right," she said. "But I start the fire, not you."

"As you wish, but find out from Aggie what she's preparing, in case you have to eat with Percy."

"I will. Give me an hour to get some things together."

"Only a bag, Alina, *por Dios,* we are escaping back to Spain not going to Whitehall palace."

"Ah, no, that is …" Alina started then stopped. "Never mind, I'll tell you later."

Marcos helped Prince Maurice's aide-de-camp push a travelling chest into the back of Crimphele's one remaining carriage then stood back politely as Alina spoke to Lady Dalkeith while the nursemaid and her baby were allocated space. Hasty words were whispered until Percy became suspicious and intervened.

Alina stepped back saying, "I will send word as soon as I can."

Percy grasped her arm, "Send word to whom from where, madam?" he demanded. "You'll be sending no word from this house to anyone."

Marcos wanted to grab him by the throat, but there were too many brown-coated Roundheads near. Clenching his fists, he wiped the anger from his face the way he learned from Ludo and watched the carriage trundle under the stable arch impassively. Cecil Cleverden followed on his horse without a word of farewell. Angry with Percy and furious at the prince's failure to support Alina, Marcos thought it wise to stay out of sight until it was time to help Meg serve supper in the family room.

Later, entering with the soup tureen behind Meg, the first thing he noticed was that Percy had made himself very much at home, then that Alina was present, dressed in finery and at her charming best. Head held high, spine rigid against the hard, wooden back of her chair, Alina's posture alone told Marcos that Cousin Percy was at risk. Did she too have fall-back plan in case Aggie's potion and the fire failed?

As the main course was served, a bluish-hued pigeon hacked in half and disguised in a pinkish paste, Marcos suddenly wondered how Alina was going to avoid eating it. Assuming she knew. She had to know. Had he mentioned it? His heart thumped in panic and he tried to catch her eye – had he missed that bit out? Unless Aggie's potion wasn't in the sauce at all ... he put his hands to his head. It felt like it was about to burst into flames. *Flames.* He had work to do.

As he left the room, Percy made a comment on Alina's appearance. Marcos stopped, then waited at the open door to see what would follow.

"Quite charming, Cousin, I see you have made an effort with your famous hair, as well."

"Famous?"

"Infamous, I should say. Lady Marjorie was appalled, and quite rightly. Your head should be covered. Not that it will matter as of tomorrow. No one will be seeing you." Percy focussed on his portion of pigeon for a moment then began outlining why Alina had no place at Crimphele, and what he planned to do with her. He was putting her under a form of house arrest, as his dear late aunt had done. She could go into the chamber she had recommended for the prince. He gave a whining laugh, which alone merited a hearty slap around the head. Marcos folded his hands behind his back and stayed where he was in case Alina needed him.

"Naturally, I shan't want to upset your children, but then again, naturally they cannot stay here – being illegitimate. The boy has no legal claim to either my cousin's land or my late uncle's title."

"They are not illegitimate! How dare you!"

"But they are, dear cuz. Your marriage was a travesty, a popish celebration, nothing more. It had no validity. It certainly won't be recognised by a Commonwealth court when we come to power, so there's no point contradicting me. Your son is a landless bastard – end of subject."

This was something Marcos hadn't considered: eliminating Percy, which he had considered, did not automatically ensure Alina's safety, or that her son would inherit his father's estate.

Percy pushed away his plate and served another measure of red wine from the now half empty decanter. As he filled his goblet Alina turned slightly, met Marcos's eye and gestured he was to leave with a tilt of her head. Marcos collected their plates, and placed them on the sideboard but stayed put. Meg appeared with a syllabub. Percy picked up his spoon and dug in with gusto. Alina picked up hers and played with the blotchy ochre froth around the edge of her glass dish. The spoon never touched her lips.

Percy gobbled down his portion then leaned over and said, "If you can't manage that, I can. I have a sweet tooth and this is quite delicious."

Alina pushed her dish across the table and smiled in the candlelight.

Percy didn't finish the second helping. Grabbing his stomach with both hands he yelled, "A close stool! Where's the nearest?" He was out of the door and racing, bent double across the great hall, before anyone could answer.

Alina held up a hand to Marcos, indicating they should wait. When Percy did not return after a few minutes she picked up a candle and sheltering it from drafts, walked sedately out of the room with a smile of satisfaction. Marcos followed her.

"A good plan my friend," Alina said as they reached the middle of the hall, then, looking around to see if they were observed, headed for the kitchen.

"Where are you going?"

Alina did not respond, just beckoned him to follow. In the kitchen she said, "Agnes, Meg, get some clothes together and wait for us out in the back courtyard."

Meg and Aggie stared at her as if she were mad. "We can't, we live here," Aggie stated flatly.

"But you can't live here any longer, it's not safe for you."

"We can. We must. We got nowhere else to go, neither of us. Meg's married to Toby but his folks b'ain't got nowhere for her in that ol' cottage."

"But, Agnes, people will remember what you did when … they'll remember your special skills."

"Oh, I know that. I've lived with it all my life. No, milady, you must go, that I can see, but we can't."

Marcos watched Alina's eyes fill with tears. "But Aggie I need you!"

Crookback Aggie took Alina's hands in her wrinkly fingers and squeezed them. "You'll be all right, milady. Don't you fret, you'm made of strong stuff and you'll be back here again one day. Your boy'll come back – maybe a grown gentleman by then – but he'll be back to claim his place. But first you've got to keep him safe. And that won't be anywhere near here for a good while the way things stand."

Alina took a deep breath and looked at Meg, who had her pinafore to her eyes. "She's right, milady," Meg mumbled.

"Very well," Alina said, then with a rustle of taffeta skirts she turned and started up the inner tower stairs.

Marcos hurried after her. "Alina, wait! Change into something darker, more modest; something that doesn't make a noise for heaven's sake."

Alina insisted on starting the fire in her husband's old room. Holding a lighted tallow candle to the hangings around his bed in the old tower she muttered to herself as she scorched a hole in the thickly embroidered fabric.

"What?" asked Marcos. "I didn't hear you."

"I embroidered these," she said, "when Thomas went to Oxford, after Tommy was born."

A flame lit up an exquisite bird, turning its feathers scarlet then black.

"Be careful!" Marcos warned. "That'll do. Come now."

Alina refused to move. The second drape began to smoulder then whooshed up in a tongue of smoking fire, and still she would not move.

"Alina!" Marcos grabbed her arm. "Move! We'll both die here if you don't come now."

Alina stared at the quilt burning on the high bed. "It's my marriage bed."

Horrified, Marcos knocked the candleholder from Alina's hand, grasped her around the waist and physically manhandled her down the back stairs to the kitchen.

"Meg," he said, "there's a fire in the tower; Sir Thomas's bed curtains are ..."

Before he could explain more Meg started to scream as she'd been instructed. The screams were genuine. She was terrified. He wanted to calm her but there was no time.

Mercy joined in, and knowing nothing of any scheme, did a sterling job of sending bewildered men rushing for the stable yard to douse straw and locate the outdoor wells. Mrs Godwin appeared and told them where to find more buckets. One of which was under Percy.

In the meantime, Alina and Marcos slipped out through the kitchen yard and made their way down to the river path through the trees in the dark. Tripping and tumbling over hidden roots, sometimes ankle deep in leaf-mould Marcos was convinced they were making enough noise to bring the Roundheads running after them, but the fire-trick worked its magic for they reached the riverbank rendezvous where John Hawthorne was waiting unchallenged.

Getting into Jim Hawkins' barge involved wading through mud, but it was a small inconvenience compared to the danger they had eluded. As the boat slid silently downstream, Alina stood in the prow with Hetty squirming in her arms, until she gave in and let the child have the run of the deck in the moonlight. John Hawthorne stood beside her, gazing back the way they had come twisting a small crucifix in his small hands.

Over-excitement soon drained the children of energy. Tomás curled up against John Hawthorne's chest in the cabin and Hetty fell asleep in a bundle on deck. Jim Hawkins wrapped her in a smelly blanket and went about his business. For a while Alina dozed, physically and emotionally exhausted. Marcos stayed at the prow, fearing there would be a Parliament boat at every turn in the old river to halt and question or board them. As they neared the estuary and the city wall of Plymouth loomed up on the port bow, the instinct for self-preservation sent Marcos into the middle of the barge to hunker down with his back pressed against the mast. Clutching the cold, slippery wood behind him, his mind leapt between the desire to return to his wife and child, and the regrettable wisdom of Percy's words: he was a risk to them. Jim Hawkins had turned his coat for his family, but Jim was a native Englishman: a Spaniard didn't have that choice, the Beale family would suffer if the Roundheads prevailed and he was still among them.

And now there was another family to consider: Alina and her children couldn't be left on their own. They had John Hawthorne, of course, but for all that he was a good man, John was not a man of action. No, he would have to stay with Alina at least until they reached the Spanish coast. Although how that was to be achieved was a mystery.

Alina must have been thinking along similar lines, for she came to him and said, "Sail with us. Wait until this madness is over, Marcos, then you can bring us back and return to your pretty Joanna."

Marcos stared at the horizon in the early morning sunlight and said, "We need to work out how we are going to get to Santander first. We can't expect Jim to cross the Narrow Sea, not in this boat. We need a proper ship to Spain."

"Ah, no," Alina put a hand on Marcos's shoulder, "that's what I was going to tell you before we left. We're going to France."

"France?"

"Yes," Alina's eyes glittered with excitement. "The Queen has sent for me. I was in two minds – not wanting to leave Crimphele – but well, circumstances are forcing me away now, so why not? We are to go to the Louvre Palace in Paris: isn't that wonderful?"

"And how precisely do you plan to get there?" Marcos demanded.

Alina touched his cheek with a finger and smiled then made her way aft to speak to Jim Hawkins. After a short time, she returned saying, "Mr Hawkins will take us round Cawsand to Porthferris. He says his cousin has got a fishing boat that can take us down to Falmouth, which is still Royalist as far as he knows. That's where the Queen sailed from, so we should be all right." She paused then said, "If you want to, you can leave me there and get a passage to Vigo."

"Toxo and Javi are in Vigo. They used to bring my wine from Sanlucar into Plymouth. That's where they live, Vigo." Marcos closed his eyes: 'that's where they live': the envy, the regret, the desire to have a proper home nearly unmanned him.

"Go to them, then." Alina's tone was tart.

"Maybe I will." But Marcos knew he wouldn't leave her.

As an apology, Alina leaned her head on his shoulder and he put his arms around her. "When shall I mourn him, Marcos?" she asked, her voice breaking in a whisper. "Thomas was my rock, he loved me, kept me safe and I … I loved him."

Marcos stroked her hair. "Seems we were both born for difficult lives," he sighed. "But we have children now, so we must look to the future not the past."

"That was my problem. I was always looking to the future – a better future – and failed to notice what a good present we had – until he went away to fight their stupid war. Then I missed him. And now I'll never see him again. Never know the comfort of his warmth at night. Poor Thomas, I should have been a better wife."

Quietly, Alina let her tears fall on Marcos's shoulder and he thought his heart would break with the love of her.

Chapter 9

Falmouth

Bringing *The Tulip* into Falmouth in a heavy squall had not
been easy. The new boatswain and scratch crew then
mismanaged the subsequent unloading, mixing the precious
rolls of vulnerable silk for France with the muskets and the
heavy wooden chests of swords in a downpour. The rain
entered the hold as a westerly slanting torrent while inexpert
mariners bungled hoisting the load up onto the deck then
slipped on the greasy companionway as if they were a circus
act. Stumbling around on the quayside, the boatswain swore
at them to move faster but it made no difference. Ludo
ground his teeth in anger seeing barrels of gunpowder left
unprotected on the quay in the driving rain while the swords
were loaded into the late-arriving carts. It was a nightmare
and he would have signed off the boatswain and half a dozen
of the crew there and then but one look at Falmouth told him
he was unlikely to find replacements. No more than a
collection of squat dwellings and ale houses seething with a
Royalist rabble and noticeably lacking a fishing fleet –
meaning fewer experienced seamen – Falmouth was a severe
disappointment to both captain and crew.

Apart from the visible bedraggled, motley and ale-sodden troopers wandering aimlessly from tavern to tavern, there were professional soldiers and volunteers belonging to King Charles' army garrisoned up in the castle on the hill. They were awaiting marching orders, or so Ludo was informed by a supply officer who appeared at Gifford Greenwood's side on the jetty. The two young men appeared to know each other well.

Once the unloading had been completed, a further delay kept Ludo out in the rain while relevant officers checked numbers against tally sheets and signed for the armaments. Accustomed to the haste with which cargoes of silks and spices could be loaded and unloaded in monsoon downpours or even Amsterdam cloudbursts, Ludo was impatient beyond words. Eventually, however, they got the hold closed and the Pendennis armaments began rolling uphill. Ludo was finally free to worry about where he was going to billet his crew and who he could trust to make sure his own lighter cargo was re-distributed ready to cross to Le Havre, knowing he was probably going to do it himself. The other concern was that while there was little chance of his men jumping ship, the presence of navy vessels signified press-gangs. The sooner *Tulip* left the Fal Estuary the better.

Ludo now needed somewhere to get a decent meal. He walked the full length of Falmouth then retraced his steps and settled, for want of choice, on the least raucous of the ale-houses. Exhausted, angry and heartily sick of Cornish rain, he hastened in to the fireside and set his pea-coat to steam on a vacant chair. Once seated and sipping thin French brandy, he mused on the role Greenwood had manoeuvred himself into and what he had seen of his behaviour in this grubby harbour, then gave a small chuckle of satisfaction knowing that for all his cleverness the young peacock had been soaked to the skin by the time he reported to whoever was his master. Then he stopped: had he played into the Englishman's hands? Was Mr Greenwood warming his shapely shins up at the castle with officers whose names he appeared to know – or with someone more significant? The carts had arrived after they had tied up, but uniformed men in the castle had been expecting the ship … A wench interrupted his thoughts, shoving a trencher of greasy bacon in front of him. She was gone before he could order a more palatable drink. The food did nothing to improve his humour.

While swilling down the last of the bread with the last of the brandy, Ludo turned his mind to the next stage of his voyage. He surveyed the crowded room looking for a local man who might give him some help about getting out into the sea roads for France, then became distracted by a tall woman of noble bearing in a good quality cloak ushering two children into the ale-house. She was followed by a slight, fair-haired man he had never expected to see again: the pestiferous English priest, John Hawthorne. Ludo blinked hard. The woman could not be his wife. She pushed back the hood of her cloak revealing her hair: thick, golden, wavy hair, which a woman of her age and status should have covered … It could only be Alina.

For a moment he lost sight of her among the press of men trying to get a drink. Then the door opened again and Marcos entered. Ludo slid down in his bentwood chair to watch. Part of him told him to get out unnoticed. But he knew he wouldn't do it. And just as certainly, he knew that by going to them he would be entering an emotional area he was in no condition to navigate. Alina had nearly done for him in Spain, physically and emotionally. He had all but died getting involved in the scheme she'd hatched up with her precious Queen Henrietta … except that it hadn't entirely been her scheme, and he was only cross, still cross, because the adventure had cost him dearly in a set of priceless pearls and a casket of sapphires, rubies and uncut Golconda diamonds.

Another thought edged in, unbidden: the main purpose of his trip to Spain – the effort of the tedious overland expedition, the risk he might be gaoled or worse – it had all been pointless. He had striven to win the confidence of the most important man in Spanish court, the Count-Duke Olivares; had convinced him he had his full support and would never act against him (again) in order that he would sign documents protecting Leonora – and now those documents were meaningless. The sad irony of it all compounded his general malaise.

So Ludo stayed hunched down and watched and waited.

There was no room at the inn. The woman and the man not her husband (or was he now?), and the priest and the two children turned around and pushed their way back through the crowd then disappeared into the street.

Ludo waited, still undecided. Finally, he slapped a coin into the serving girl's hand and left the inn. The rain had eased off but they were nowhere to be seen. Shrugging, for he knew that in such a small town, over-full with men in various arrangements of Royalist blues and reds, he was bound to see them again, Ludo pulled the brim of his black leather hat down over his eyes and headed for the quayside to be rowed back to his ship.

To his surprise, Gifford Greenwood was still on the quay: someone else he had to make a decision on. Greenwood whistled up *Tulip*'s lighter boys and once the youngsters had got their oars out to steady the boat on the choppy water, they climbed into the pinnace together. As the boat pulled away from the harbour steps, Ludo saw Marcos again. At least he thought it was Marcos. If it had been Marcos on his own, he would have instructed them to turn about and fetch him. But that wasn't the case, and Ludo was still undecided.

Ludo slept aboard in his cold stateroom in a none-too-clean but dry bed, and the next day, accompanied by Gifford

Greenwood, took the puddle-littered path up to Pendennis Castle. They were shown along a chilly passage into a labyrinth of connecting offices then led to an airless interior room where an officer of some description was seated at a desk writing a letter. Two younger men were seated at a trestle table against the far wall scratching entries in ledgers, in front of them lay an array of nailed squares overloaded with what looked like unpaid bills. On the floor around the bare walls were neat piles of folded pamphlets. The surface of a rough chest was crowded with used writing equipment.

As Greenwood entered behind Ludo, the officer got to his feet and saluted. He was older than Greenwood by many years; older and rotund, with lank, greasy brown hair and a moustache to match. Ludo mentally filed the salute and watched as the two men exchanged a meaningful glance. The supply officer went to the wooden chest and pushed the writing implements off with a sleeve. He then opened a padlock with a key from his uniform waistcoat and took out a bulging drawstring leather purse. Putting it on his desk, he said, "You have come to be paid, I suppose," as if Ludo had just delivered the milk.

Ludo nodded and they conducted their business. Despite the surroundings it proved very worthwhile, agreeable even, given the way he had been blackmailed into bringing the arms to England in the first place, not to mention the mysterious task he was yet to expedite in France. Ludo had been more than half-expecting to see no recompense whatsoever.

As they subsequently exited the offices, Gifford Greenwood took Ludo by the elbow and directed him through a side door onto a path leading not to the busy main gate, where a troop of horse were now mustered, but towards the curtain wall. Out of anyone's hearing he said, "I received news this morning that I must relay to you, sir."

"I'm listening," Ludo replied, noting the young man's new, superior tone, which matched the earlier salute and confirmed some if not all of his suspicions. Greenwood was clearly somebody, and/or in an important somebody's pay; he was certainly no aspiring maritime officer, acting or otherwise.

"Pope Urban has died," Greenwood said without preamble.

Surprised, for it was not remotely near to what he was expecting, Ludo looked at Greenwood then looked at the high stone wall ahead of them and said slowly, "Has he? Yes – well, that does probably change things, doesn't it?" He tucked the heavy purse under his left arm and held it tightly against his ribs. "Yes, thank you. I suppose that piece of information must affect me if you have taken the trouble to convey it." He paused and gave Greenwood a theatrical frown, "Has the black smoke informed you who his replacement is to be? A nephew, perchance?"

"Not a nephew. The new pope is a Pamphili; he is to be known as Innocent."

"Aren't they all," Ludo quipped cynically while his mind wandered through various possibilities as to how this would affect him directly. Rogelio was – had been – Pope Urban's creature, acting via one of the papal-cardinal nephews; how would this affect them? More importantly, would it give Rogelio a freer rein; more time and liberty to pursue a private vendetta? Or would he be too busy ingratiating himself with a new overlord?

A bugle boy emerged from a door behind them, realised he'd taken a wrong turn and after looking about him to get his bearings ran off towards the main gate. Greenwood took Ludo's elbow and directed him in the opposite direction over uneven cobbles slippery with stale rainwater. For a few paces the two men walked in silence: what Gifford Greenwood was thinking Ludo could not fathom, but the event in Rome affected his role, whatever that was, in some way, and Ludo dearly wanted to know how. He made a quick recount of what he did know: Gifford Greenwood knew who and what he was, and had not requested a place on *Tulip* by accident. Was the English priest in Genoa, Gregory, attached to Greenwood as well, though? Was the unpleasantness during Leonora's miscarriage all a terrible coincidence and nothing to do with Rogelio after all? Greenwood was known in this garrison by senior Royalist officers for a reason. Did that mean he was also close to the Catholic Queen of England? Very likely. Was he also working for Rogelio? Greenwood's next move would reveal much.

Ludo waited, mentally reciting a bit of ancient Chinese wisdom: 'keep your friends close: keep your enemies closer'. Then he halted and looked about him, not unlike the lost bugle boy. They were a good distance from the main gate now, getting closer to the high curtain wall. Archers were on watch on the battlements – looking inward at them. Ludo gave way to a shiver of foreboding, aware he might never leave: that he had brought them the arms and perhaps fulfilled his usefulness. France was just a ruse. Masking his disquiet, he adopted his old policy of positive action, turned his back on the archers and in a far brisker tone said, "Tell me, Mr Greenwood, does this sad news affect you – personally?"

"Affect me, sir? I regret I have never been to Rome, let alone met a pope."

"But you would like to go to Rome?"

Greenwood gave Ludo a suspicious glance. "I doubt I shall ever have the chance."

"Oh, but you might. Stick with me young man and you could find yourself anywhere in the world – in the old world that is. I am not drawn as yet to the New, but it's not beyond the realms of possibility. *The Tulip*, I'm sure, would cross that great ocean if I asked her, despite her age. But tell me, this news, it affects us how exactly? The orders for this shipment came from the Vatican, did they not? Pity they weren't waiting for us on the quay when we got here, my coat was soaked through, which reminds me, are you planning to jump ship here? You haven't said."

"Have I not? No, I...erm... no, I shan't be sailing with you again, I regret. I am headed for Oxford – to see how my family is doing. See if my pa needs me."

"Oxford?" Ludo queried then nearly choked. *Santos benditos!* Greenwood was with the royal household in Oxford. So who was this 'pa'? Instead of asking, he said lightly, "Oh, so you'll not be joining the King's men here?" and waved his right hand in the direction of the supply office. "I wondered if you'd be taking a commission – or perhaps already got one."

Greenwood gave an empty smile. "I know many of the men here of course; school, hunting, the usual round. This way, sir, the gate's over there."

Ludo was more curious than ever, but relief got the better of him and he trotted along behind Greenwood saying, "Change of roles for you now, Mr Greenwood, you being here on home territory and me being the one taking orders." He got no response so he blustered on, "Shame about you not coming with me: I'll need a new acting midshipman." Greenwood responded with another meaningless smile. "I need a cabin boy, too. I made shift coming here but I can't manage as captain and *patrón* and merchant again, not without help. Don't know anyone hereabouts, do you?"

"Not here, sorry. Ask in the taverns, that'll get you a pot boy willing to travel."

"Good idea."

They had reached the mustered troop of King's Horse at the main gate. The beasts were all prancing hocks and muscled rumps; chestnut and brown, dappled and grey flanks nudged and shoved each other as they got into a double file before the gate and portcullis. Tails lifted, horses farted. A man on the ground shouted orders and riders checked ammunition and side arms. It took some time and

Greenwood was obviously anxious to be elsewhere, although not as anxious as Ludo, who had no love of metal shod feet the size of dinner plates.

As they waited, Ludo rambled on conversationally, "By the way, I ought to say you've managed this business of the weaponry like clockwork. Letting them know *Tulip* had berthed like that – signal was it from the ship? I didn't see anything. Could have been the rain, of course, but well done, I hadn't given anyone an estimated time of arrival that I remember. Except you knew from start to finish what was expected of you, didn't you? Well done on that, shame about my crew, inept lot of amateurs, but there we are, and after you getting it all the cargo together in first place from different foundries and suppliers. Can't have been easy."

Somewhat lost, as Ludo had intended, Gifford Greenwood grappled with the main question tagged into the rigmarole and shook his head, "I was not involved in the initial arrangements for the arms."

"And yet you were informed personally about the Pope just now – why's that, Mr Greenwood?"

"Because it may not be good news for the Queen, and you are going to France, sir." Greenwood's voice had taken on an 'I know more than you' timbre.

"You have the Queen's ear, ah – I did wonder. Or are you speaking in general, from a Royalist perspective?"

"The latter, only, sir, but her secretary – chamberlain, I should say now – has informed me of ..." Greenwood halted and edged Ludo out of anyone's hearing, "how *you* have helped Her Majesty in the past. In fact, it's precisely your previous commission in Spain – albeit apparently unsuccessful at the time, I'm told, but to the benefit of Rome if not to the British people in their entirety – that has brought you here now. It is this, *I am told*, that has made you her chosen man once again."

"Is it really?" Ludo rewarded Greenwood with a generous smile. Feigning wide-eyed pleasure, he cocked his head to one side, indicating the young man should continue. "*Tell* me more!"

Less certain of himself now, Greenwood gave a small, embarrassed cough. "I understood you were aware of the task, sir. You are to – that is Her Majesty is expecting you to – to fulfil the task set you in Genoa. Or so Baron Jermyn informs me."

"And Baron Jermyn is?"

"Currently, Baron Jermyn is the Queen's secretary and chamberlain."

"*Da vera? Bene, bene*," Ludo lifted his eyebrows with theatrical appreciation although for the life of him he couldn't put a face to the name. Using his Genoese Italian to mark his distance from Jermyn, a French woman who was Queen of England and the Englishman at his side, he pushed on for what he needed to know. "*Alora*, seeing as you are in Her Majesty's and Baron Jermyn's confidence, can you just tell me, quickly, what new task I'm being expected to fulfil – as Her Majesty's 'chosen man'?"

"But you know, sir."

"Alas, I cannot recall."

Greenwood swallowed hard and tapped the wide pocket on his coat. "Well, the fact is, I have only been briefed to a certain extent. I fear what you are asking is not quite within my duties."

Ludo wanted to laugh but instead wiped all expression from his features and said, "Pity. Will you will be with me in France, perhaps not as my midshipman, but in another role?"

"Regrettably not."

"Shame, and I was just getting your measure. Our paths will cross again, no doubt."

"No doubt."

A rhythmic clattering of hooves announced the troop was moving off. "Oh, good, front door is open," Ludo said, clapping the young man on the back with his free hand then, raising his black leather hat in farewell, began to follow them.

"No, one moment, sir!" Greenwood's arm shot out to hold him back. "There's something I have to give you."

Greenwood pulled a folded letter with an elaborate seal from his jacket and handed it to Ludo.

"And this is . . .?"

"Your orders for France." The instant the missive was in Ludo's possession, Greenwood gave a small salute, turned on his heel and strode quick-march back into the castle.

Ludo watched him go, then studied the seal. Deciding he didn't recognise it, he pushed it into his own jacket pocket and sauntered through the gate unaccompanied.

Following in the horses' dung-littered wake, he descended the hill in good spirits: the letter could go in the sea if he didn't like it. He would admit to a seagull stealing it if pushed: "must have thought it was a hunk of bread..." The idea brought a smile to his lips and he let his mind wander. Changes in Rome meant Rogelio would be there convincing Pope Innocent of his usefulness to the throne of St Peter. That left him free from the hateful Vatican agent and supposed cousin, and now he was also free of young Mr Greenwood's spying eyes: meaning he could move forward as he chose.

Ludo returned to the harbour with the hefty purse of gold coins feeling more cheerful than he had since Leonora had died. It was time to cut and run. His children had been taken into safe-keeping by his resourceful mother; her body-guard Hassan had promised they would be watched night and day with the help of brothers and cousins with useful corsair skills. If *Tulip* weighed anchor, and he could get her back down the treacherous Portuguese coastline undamaged, he could be with them in three weeks – before he was even expected in Paris and before anyone could be informed that he had backed out of their dubious agreement. If he was nifty.

With a spring in his step, Ludo pushed through the crowd in the harbour. Reaching the quayside, he raised an arm for his pinnace and nearly knocked the blasted English priest head first into the water.

"Not you again!" he cried, grasping the slight Englishman to prevent him falling.

"Don Ludovico!" John Hawthorne replied, staggering somewhat from the blow. "Don Ludovico?"

"Yes, it's me. But let's pretend it isn't." Ludo sidestepped to the right to reach the steps, but without success.

"We need you, sir," John Hawthorne stated baldly, getting in his way. "It is a matter of great urgency. This is God's intervention indeed, for we have need of you."

"You're putting me and God in the same sentence, Mr Hawthorne? I never thought to hear that." Ludo sidestepped to the left now, but the priest responded with a parry he could not avoid.

"The Lady Arleen, the Baroness Metherall that is, has need of you."

"Of course, she does," Ludo sighed. Looking out across the water at his ship then back at the crowded jetty, he made a feeble attempt to come to a decision; but where Alina was concerned logical thinking was useless. It always had been. "Very well," he grunted, "lead on and let's see what mess I'm about to fall into this time."

Chapter 10

Alina was sitting on an upturned wooden crate holding a small girl tightly by the leading straps attached to her coat. The child in turn was hugging a rag doll with a vivid red skirt to her chest – exactly as Ludo was holding his bag of coin.

"Nooo," Alina was saying, "you stay here with me and don't you dare go anywhere on your own ever again."

Ludo stopped in his tracks. It was his daughter Naomi.

But that was impossible. And this girl was younger. She had the same mop of black hair, though, and the same chubby body, and precisely the same frown of determination. This little girl had a will of her own exactly like his Naomi; and each of them was the very image of his indomitable mother.

So this was why Alina had wanted to return to England in such haste after their stay in El Escorial. This changed everything.

Alina hadn't seen them approach, which Ludo played to his advantage. Standing slightly to her left so she would have to turn her head, he said, "My dear, if I promise to rescue you from the rabble on *this* quayside will you promise not to bite me."

Alina's entire upper body swivelled round, and in her surprise let go of the child, who immediately tried to run off. Ludo caught her and with a practised lift, swung her into his left arm. She kicked him hard in the stomach. "Oooh, strong girl! Ludo laughed.

The child stared straight into his eyes. "Who are you?" she demanded.

"Good question," Ludo replied, giving her a wink and a one-dimpled grin, which brought Alina to her feet and back to her old fighting self. Bouncing the child in his arms with the bag of coins, Ludo grinned and said, "I must say, milady, we do meet in the most picturesque circumstances. First among pirates, then in a palace and now..." he paused and surveyed the scene, "...what are you, homeless pilgrims in search of a cramped cabin and a crossing to a new life?" He had intended the words as a barb and was dismayed at their effect. Alina bit her lip and looked away, and Ludo's heart did something impossible in his chest. "*Que pasa?*" he asked quietly, and set the child on the ground. Handing a leading strap to Alina, he said softly, "What is it? Tell me."

Alina put a hand to her mouth and shook her head, tears welling in her eyes. He moved closer to put an arm around her shoulders but she leaned away.

"Who *are* you?" screeched the little harridan, pushing him away.

"A man with a ship," Ludo retorted in the same tone and turned back to Alina. "Where do you need to go? Back to Spain? I can take you; come."

"No," Alina shook her head and two loose ringlets fell from their pins. "I have to go to France – to Paris. I *want* to go to France." She spoke as if she was trying to convince herself.

Ludo stared at her then made sense of her words. "The Queen – Henrietta Maria – she's in Paris. Is that where you are going?" Marcos joined them as he spoke: "You too?" Ludo inquired, as if they'd been together all morning.

Marcos met Ludo's eye and gave a Latin gesture with his hands.

"*Va bene,*" Ludo muttered. "Here we go again."

*****

Later that night, once *Tulip* had weighed anchor and they were heading for France; after finding a dozen things to do beyond his normal duties as captain of his own ship, Ludo checked that his boatswain was sober and his crew had their orders, ensured that the priest and his charge, Alina's son Tomás, were all right on the officer's deck, then joined Marcos to catch up with what had been happening in Plymouth. What Marcos told him added greatly to his disquiet regarding Alina. Her sadness was evident and now he knew why. It made the interview he had been delaying all the more difficult.

Waiting a respectable time for Alina and her daughter to settle into their narrow, poop deck cabin, Ludo finally tapped at her door then ducked down to enter. He was struck first by the tranquillity of the scene. A shaded oil lamp was lit on the table, where Alina was seated, the little girl – he rapidly tried to calculate her age: two and a half, nearly three – was tucked up tightly on the bed with the head of her scruffy doll peering over the edge of her blanket. Controlling the urge to go to her, he took a chair at the small table. Alina looked at him, her face unreadable, then got up and went to the window.

"I wouldn't open it tonight," Ludo said quietly. "It's very cold and we'll be crossing the bar soon."

Alina shrugged, then stooped over the bed to adjust the blanket under the girl's chin and kiss her brow. An action he had seen Leonora make uncountable times. Realising where his thoughts had taken him, Ludo sat up straight.

Here we go again, he'd thought earlier, but this was not 'again'. Too many things had happened to him: Leonora had happened to him, and that made this situation infinitely more difficult.

Alina returned to the table and sat down. She adjusted the plain, somewhat grubby cotton at her neck then fidgeted with a sleeve, as ill-at-ease as he was. He gave a small sigh of relief, it was a minor comfort: at least she didn't have the upper hand this time.

"What?" Alina asked.

"What? About *what*?" Ludo queried.

"I didn't think I would ever see you again," Alina began.

"Likewise."

There was a silence. The ship groaned as it rode a wave. There would be a heavy storm before dawn. Ludo made a mental note to speak to his boatswain and first officer then, as the silence dragged on, wondered if Gifford Greenwood was sending Rogelio a message, and if so, what it said. Who was giving Greenwood his instructions? Thinking of the venomous *bicha* took him back to his mother. What had she not been telling him? Ludo's thoughts drifted back to Jan Janszoon's old house in Salé and how much easier life would have been if he'd stayed there – perhaps taken his role with the corsairs one day. He still could. There was still time to go up on deck and order a change of course ...

Interrupting his chain of thought, Alina said, "You're different."

"I'm older."

"No: you are different. Why?"

"Well, if I am – which I cannot judge – it is a long story." Ludo gave a half-smile, "There are wines and spirits in that cupboard, can I get you something?"

"A glass of Madeira would be pleasant."

Ludo lifted the oil lamp and examined the contents of a tiny cabinet then selected a square decanter. "Madeira, I think. Try it and tell me."

Alina accepted a tumbler and sipped while he poured a small measure for himself. "Don't know," she said. "Doesn't matter. So, tell me what you have been doing to become so – so – serious."

Ludo laughed and changed the subject. "Marcos told me about your husband. He says you have lost Crimphele."

"Lost? Yes, both of them. Except Crimphele is my son's birthright, I will not allow him to lose it forever: one day he will return to claim it."

"But for now? Where does this put you?"

"This puts me, Don Ludovico, exactly where I was ten years ago – only now instead of four small brothers I have two children of my own to care for." She looked about her and gave a rueful smile, "I am back in a ship, crossing the Narrow Sea again, with no home, no income, no clothes of my own, and nowhere to go for succour."

"You could go to your father in Santander."

"Hah! And return to being an unpaid housekeeper? No thank you."

"I'm here, let me help you."

"You were the first time I crossed this water and possibly – just possibly, I'm being generous here – you thought you were helping me when we landed in Plymouth. And look where that got me!" Alina's raised voice disturbed the child. She turned towards the bundle on the bed then looked back at Ludo. Catching him staring at the child, she said, "She is called Henrietta. We call her Hetty."

"I have a daughter very like her," Ludo said slowly, watching Alina's face.

"I said you were different," Alina countered. "A daughter: how charming."

"Also a son. They are twins."

"And the mother of these twins? Do you still see her?"

"I married her – before the children were conceived."

"Did you, indeed." Alina raised the tumbler to her lips. From behind the thick glass she said, "And this was Leonora in Goa, was it? Or someone else?"

"Leonora." Ludo's voice was barely a whisper. "How do you know her name?"

Alina gave a slight shrug. "I have a good memory. She was mentioned when we were in Spain." Alina sipped her drink then placed it softly on the polished walnut surface. "That explains it then. How you are different." Changing her tone, she said much more briskly, "I was not being entirely fair earlier. While there is a similarity to our first, unfortunate encounter, this time I do have somewhere to go."

"Yes, Marcos says you are to join the Queen of England – if you can find her."

"She is in Paris. At the Louvre Palace."

"Not yet, she isn't."

"How do you know that?"

"People tell me things. Wherever she is, I hope you find a new dress along the way, *carina*. This outfit is hardly fit for a queen. Perhaps you will allow me to offer a little money, as a loan, naturally. I don't see the French royal court letting you into the palace precincts let alone accepting your rank of baroness in that muddy outfit. Your sleeve is singed. How did that happen?"

Alina stamped her foot with annoyance and Ludo grinned. "The same but not the same. No matter. We are both at the mercy of fates far grander than our own."

"That is very profound, and a far cry from the individualistic instinct of Ludovico da Portovenere, I would say."

"I have spent much time at sea, but a voyage I made two years ago finally taught me to trim my sails according to the wind."

"And this wind – where is it blowing you now?"

Ludo drank down his Madeira – it had sugared with age, whatever it was – then rattled his large fingers upon the delicate table top and said, "The old pope is dead. The new one, who is not his nephew, has chosen to be named 'Innocent'."

Alina looked at him with surprise. "Are you working for the Pope?"

Ludo raised an exaggerated eyebrow. "Not anymore. In fact ..." he spread his arms out wide and the child woke up. Two large hazel eyes surveyed him in the dim warm gloom of the cabin and he gave a sigh so deep and full of mixed emotions he couldn't have explained it if he'd tried.

"In fact," prompted Alina then supplied her own answer, "you're up to no good as usual. That hasn't changed."

"Milady, you are too harsh."

"I doubt it. Why were you so willing to cross to France? Why were you in Falmouth anyway?"

"I was supplying your Royalists." Ludo went very still. "Listen," he said.

Alina made a show of listening. The child grunted, clutched the dirty rag doll to her then stuck a thumb in her mouth. Apart from the gentle slurping as the child sucked there was only the comforting sound of a ship at sea.

Eventually Alina said, "Listen to what?"

"The quiet. We have crossed the bar unopposed. Meaning we are en-route to Le Havre, unopposed. Six vessels chased the Queen of England out of the Fal and across to Brest, firing all the way, they say."

"*Madre mía,*" Alina swallowed and gaped at Ludo. "Were you – are you – expecting that to happen to us?"

"We are gun ready."

"But Parliament ships aren't interested in you. Why should they be? Unless they know what you brought into Falmouth."

"Exactly. It now occurs to me that my deserting 'acting midshipman' might have *two* masters."

"And whoever they might be is why Cromwell's ships haven't fired on us?"

"Possibly."

"Ludo, why are you taking me to France?"

"Didn't I tell you? I'm going to visit the Queen of England. She's in Rouen by the way."

"You were going anyway!"

"Happy coincidence, no?" Ludo got up to go. "Ah, I nearly forgot the reason for my visit: you are not sick with the *mal de mer,* are you?"

"Do I look it? I'm never ill. I love being at sea. That hasn't changed."

"Good." Ludo opened the door and ducked under the lintel without another word.

J G Harlond

Part Three
France

Chapter 11

France, Autumn, 1645

Prior to disembarking in Le Havre, Ludo showed Alina a few of his silks. She asked for three different lengths to be made into gowns for when she re-joined her queen. Realising it would be in his interest to have Alina back in Henrietta Maria's favour, Ludo agreed to wait in the port until a seamstress had created *one* decent garment. Meanwhile, he arranged storage for his precious cargo in a dry warehouse and visited merchants and a few other seamstresses, who might put him contact with agents for his luxury goods. Some of the spices were quickly disposed of, giving him useful local currency.

Despite this easy success, though, Ludo became irritable. Days were mounting up and winter would be setting in very soon, making his return trip to the Mediterranean via Salé before the New Year look more and more unlikely.

Before they could set off in the Seine River barge for Rouen, Alina requested more money to purchase winter clothing for her children. It meant a further delay. Seeing his expression, Alina said, "It is only a loan. I shall repay you as soon as I possibly can. I don't want to be in your debt and under your orders again."

Ludo gave an ironic laugh, "Under my orders! Since when have you ever done anything I have asked?" The jibe harped back to Alina's refusal to stay with him in Spain and he regretted making it. "Think of it as an investment," he sighed.

"An investment? Why are you investing in me?" she demanded, her eyes narrowing with suspicion.

"We are visiting your queen, it's to your benefit, not mine."

"Really?" Alina replied sarcastically. Then, to his surprise, she said quietly, "Thomas begrudged every penny I spent before I went to London; now he's dead and I can have anything I like. It's wrong. I shouldn't be thinking about pretty gowns at a time like this."

"Black can be very becoming, if worn well," John Hawthorne piped, coming to her side.

"Widows wear white in India," Ludo said.

John was shocked, "Oh, no, white might be misinterpreted as too young a colour, it being virginal, that is... erm, that as a wife and mother ..." He went pink, unable to continue.

"He's teasing, John!" Alina snapped.

"Oh, yes, of course." The timid priest moved away and stayed out of their way for the rest of the journey.

Alina watched him go then said, "The queen won't want a grieving widow at her side, whether she's in black or white. It'll be an unwelcome reminder of the dangers her own husband is facing. I have to please her, not cause disquiet. If I cannot be with her, where on earth do I go?"

Ludo cocked his head to one side, "Mm, tricky. Indigo is a serious colour and matronly."

"Matronly!" Alina retorted. "I don't look or act remotely matronly."

"Then perhaps you should start, my dear. A little gravitas may help us all in the coming weeks."

"You're angry," Alina said, catching his serious expression.

"Annoyed, not angry; I have matters to resolve, a cargo to sell, a commission to undertake and I want it all done in the greatest of haste."

"Why?"

Ludo waved a paw in the air, "None of your concern. But get a move on with your purchases, we have a long way to go and this dry weather won't last."

Henrietta Maria was not in Rouen as Ludo had been advised. It annoyed him greatly; not because Alina was right for insisting they were to go to Paris, but because it meant a much longer journey inland. Cursing to himself in various languages, he set about re-hiring the barge that had brought them to Rouen to take them further up the Seine. All out of his own pocket, naturally: Marcos had but ten English crowns with him and John Hawthorne said he had not a farthing to his name.

Before they left Rouen, Alina filled two large trunks with finery and acquired one small servant: a very small servant with no English and no Spanish, naturally, France and Spain having been sworn enemies for as long as anyone could remember. Space on the barge was cramped and Hetty refused to sit still in the cabin for more than two minutes at a time. Then she lost her precious rag doll. John finally located it under a bench but as they were disembarking on the steps of a riverside quay in Paris, she lost it again. There was a shrill scream and Alina raced to the side of the barge. Hetty was trying to scramble over the rail. Alina made a grab for the leading straps attached to the shoulders of her new coat but Ludo reached the child first and snatched her into his arms, only to have his black leather hat knocked off his head by an angry fist.

"Etta, Etta," screamed the little girl.

"What?" demanded Ludo, leaning back to see the child's face and interpret what she was saying.

"Etta is her doll," Alina explained, peering into the filthy water.

"It's here," said Tomás grumpily, coming up behind them with the rag poppet dangling by a torn arm. He heaved it at his sister saying, "She left it in the cabin."

Alina kissed his brow and took the rag poppet. As she smoothed down its red flannel skirt, she said to her daughter, "I'll keep Etta with me now, *cielo*, she can sleep in Mama's bag."

Hetty ignored her. She was staring adoringly into Ludo's face and stroking his beard. Ludo caught Alina's eye and cocked his head to one side with a grin. Alina flushed and turned away.

On their second day in Paris, staying in a suite of rooms in a flea-ridden hostel, Ludo set out for the Louvre and learned the Queen of England was not there either. She was taking the waters at a spa on the Marne.

Gossip gleaned in a servants' hall, where he sought a chamberlain or maitre for a name to add to his new list of spice outlets, told him the Queen of England might have been born in France but she wasn't welcome in Paris. Nobody knew precisely why. Other gossip told him she was seriously ill and likely to die.

"This puts weeks longer on my task," he moaned when he got back to their lodgings. "Weeks!"

"What task?" Alina asked.

"I am yet to find out. What's wrong here?" Ludo looked from Alina to Marcos, noting the tension in the air.

"This girl, my new maid, Marie is useless," Alina said, "– and dirty!"

"She's French," Ludo laughed and turned to Marcos for an explanation.

Marcos shook his head in mild despair. "Alina found her sifting through her small clothes and the girl's hands were filthy, apparently. See if you can sort it out, I don't understand a word Marie says."

Ludo frowned at Alina, "Can't you manage without a maid for once."

"And how will the Queen interpret that?" Alina retorted angrily. "Makes me look like a provincial nobody."

"And we can't have that, can we?" hissed Marcos, then muttered something about boats and gathered the children to take them down to the river.

"You've upset him again," Ludo sighed, watching him go. He turned back to reason with Alina. "Be nice to the girl. She's miles from home among strangers who don't even speak French."

"I am nice to her! I learned all about being among strangers a long time ago, remember."

"Well, at least find out if she was actually trying to steal anything. I've got work to do now, sort it out, *carina* and let's have no more antagonism, please."

Ludo went to the room he was sharing with Marcos to write down the names and details of his new contacts in Paris. The business with Henrietta Maria was a nuisance but he'd found two new clients for his Indian spices, one in the Louvre Palace itself – with a prospect of significant sales – so all was not lost. As he arranged his writing equipment and notebook, he heard Alina go to her room and lie on her creaking bed. The partitions were paper thin.

"Marie," Alina called, her voice as sugary as she could manage, "Mariiie!"

Ludo had pulled out the second layer of his writing casket before Alina called again.

"Marie!"

He scribbled down the names and spice requests in a journal. Noting prices agreed and delivery dates. There was silence. Checking to see he was not being observed but not bothering to close the door, Ludo then extracted three letters from the secret drawer of his casket. One bore the initials HM in the corner: it was the letter of commission for Ludo to send jewels from the East to the English Queen, who had dictated it to him herself in a Whitehall withdrawing room. It was in his hand, but Henrietta Maria had signed it with her flourish. His intention was to check the wording and write another very similar as soon as he had sourced suitable quality paper. The second folded letter he set to one side: that had been written by one of Charles Stuart's secretaries and signed by the monarch. It was his licence to obtain and provide the English royal court with 'luxuries and divers spices and tea' from the Orient. The third was a blank sheet of paper with only the carefully copied signature of the late Pope. That he slipped into an inner pocket.

John Hawthorne passed his open door without looking in and spoke to Alina. "She's gone I think."

"Marie, gone!" Alina howled.

Ludo tidied away his letters and replaced the second tier of the casket. Then he checked the lid on his ink pot, dried the pen on a rag and slipped it into its holder. Then, equally slowly and methodically, he re-buckled his leather-bound journal and returned that to his travelling chest. In the next room Alina was sobbing; it had all the makings of a full-blown spate and John Hawthorne was unlikely to calm the waters. Time to go out again.

Ludo returned to the main room for his hat and cloak, intending to remain in the city until everyone had retired for the night. Passing Alina's door, he noticed John Hawthorne was sitting on the side of her bed, stroking one of her hands. Feeling his presence perhaps, Hawthorne looked up and tried to smile. He too had been weeping. His pale eyes glistened, large and red-rimmed.

Ludo gave an embarrassed smile and moved away as Alina, unaware of his presence, said, "John, is it true that you and Thomas were brothers?" Her voice was softer then he had heard in a very long time.

"We never knew for sure." Hawthorne started to blow his nose. Ludo swung his cloak round his shoulders and took a while fastening the clasp, listening for other revelations. "My mother wouldn't speak of it, but not because she hated Thomas's father – far from it," Hawthorne continued.

"But you were very alike."

"In my heart, he is – was – my brother."

Alina murmured something and Hawthorne replied more strongly, "We need time to mourn Alina. We need time to examine our grief and our memories of a good man."

"I can't stop, John. That is all I do."

Hawthorne murmured something and Alina replied in snuffles, and Ludo hastened out of their lodgings, his ears red with shame. He had his own tragedy to deal with: a well of misery that would pull him down to the depths if he didn't keep active ... busy, busy, busy, it was the only way to stop worrying about the twins and his mother, and how he missed Leonora.

Shaking himself mentally, Ludo checked the small dagger at his waist for the city streets were not without danger, then shut the street door behind him, descended three worn steps and set off back to the Louvre Palace. His vague intention was to find out why Henrietta Maria was not welcome in the capital, and along the way see if you could guess what she might have in mind for him.

Obtaining entry earlier into the outer courtyards and kitchens of the Louvre Palace had been surprisingly easy; grocers and wine merchants came and went all day. Farmers brought in goods directly from the fields. Grubby urchins hurried in with messages and out with bags of leftovers or refuse. He had been just one tradesman among many. Getting into the offices occupied by secretaries and envoys attached to the royal household, however, proved a good deal trickier. A guard at a side entrance stuck out his hand for papers without a word. Ludo pulled the much-travelled, crumpled document he usually used in these circumstances from a pocket, this time blaming French rain for the splodged ink. It was in Latin.

"Ludovico Doria of the Abruzzi, merchant on business for the Kingdom of Naples," he said, hoping the guard knew the origins of one Guilio Raimundo Mazarini, otherwise known as Cardinal Mazarin. He obviously did; and Ludo gained access to the lower offices of the east wing.

The precise details Ludo needed to unearth were unlikely to be found in these dark passages and connecting chambers, but it was a start; a place to learn names and titles and responsibilities. Within a short time, he located three flunkies in conversation and by dint of eavesdropping learned that Cardinal Mazarin had recently returned from Rome and was "none-too-pleased, neither" for, according to one, "they'd elected the new pope before he could even get there."

Ludo wandered away and enquired innocently of another flunky in heavily accented Italianate French where he might find the English queen. He had a message for her from the new pope, Innocent – had he entered the wrong building? From there it was but relatively short work to find a scribe and then a secretary who informed him most politely that the King of France's aunt was at a chateau in Bourbon-l'Archembault, where she was taking the waters for ill-health.

About why she wanted him, he learned nothing.

The next morning Ludo hired a large carriage with a hopefully reliable driver and four sound horses. The morning after that they resumed their peregrination, this time along the bank of the River Marne.

When they arrived at the pretty spa town of Bourbon l'Archembault, they learned the English queen had moved on the Chateau-Thierry, to a house once occupied by the late Cardinal Richelieu. It involved another over-night stop in an uncomfortable hostel.

None of the adult occupants of the carriage were on speaking terms by the time they located Henrietta Maria's new residence. Relatively modest by royal French standards, the chateau had white stone walls, black slate turrets on rounded towers and was attractive in a folk-tale kind of way. It was also in disrepair; the drive overgrown, the gardens unattended.

Halfway down the drive Ludo called the coaches to a halt and retrieved a leather travelling bag from under his seat. It contained a sturdy oblong wooden box with ornate brass hinges. Inside the box was a pair of expensive long-barrelled pistols. He handed one to Marcos. "We may be walking into a trap. It's not impossible I have been sent on a wild goose chase deliberately. Someone could be after me. And I've been wondering if my enquiries in the Louvre might not have been relayed to … I don't know whom, but I have a bad feeling. *If there is a problem*, stay with Alina. The *cortijo* we visited near Sanlucar before we went to Holland is mine. Take her there."

"Do I have a say in this?" Alina demanded.

"No, but if at any time you are in a position to purchase the cortijo, I'll gladly sell." Ludo turned back to Marcos. "Do you know how to fire it?"

Marcos nodded, "I learned in Flanders with something similar."

"Good. Keep it with you – until I need it again, anyway."

"Have you ever used this pair?" Marcos's voice held a note of suspicion.

"Not yet, no."

There was no ambush and the coach drew up at the front of the residence unhindered, which in itself was suspicious. There was not an armed guard or liveried servant in sight.

The chateau may once have housed illustrious members of the royal family and the late First Minister of France, Richelieu, but its general aspect confirmed the neglect apparent in the grounds. Still fearing a trap, Ludo told them all to remain in the carriage and rang a huge bell somewhat tinged with verdigris.

The door was answered by an aging footman, who left him in the entrance to consult an elderly Frenchwoman; one of the Queen's oldest ladies-in-waiting. After what seemed an hour, Ludo was admitted. When he eventually re-appeared it was to beckon them inside.

Standing in the echoing reception hall waiting for an usher to attend them, Ludo caught Alina studying him. "You are suspicious as to why I am here," he whispered near her ear.

"Suspicious indeed," she replied, gripping her daughter's leading straps to stop her running off in pursuit of a cat that was sauntering across the hall as if it owned the place.

Which, Ludo thought, was not impossible.

Chapter 12

During the journey from Falmouth Alina's suspicions as to why Ludo was going to France had given way to very mixed feelings. There was no denying his help and financial support were a boon, but she had severe misgivings about arriving at the queen's residence in his company. Widowhood put her in considerable jeopardy where maintaining her social rank and good name were involved, so her heart sank when they were ushered into the queen's presence together. The aged footman then garbled their names, introducing them as Baron and Baroness da Portovenere.

Alina's annoyance as she endeavoured to correct the mistake, turned to panic the moment she caught sight of Henrietta Maria. Flanked by her faithful private secretary, Henry Jermyn, the exiled queen was seated in a wicker chair on wheels. She was looking out of a low window at the drive down which their carriage had arrived. Alina put a hand to her mouth, could they have seen Ludo retrieving his pistols from here?

Henrietta Maria, a tiny woman when she had first met her in Whitehall a few years ago, was now no more than a bundle of bones in mismatched satins. Alina sank into a curtsey. Behind her, Ludo stepped to one side and bowed low. Henrietta Maria turned her head and smiled at him. Baron Jermyn whispered in her ear and she gave a small clap of pleasure saying, "Oh, that is good." Then she looked up at

Jermyn and said something that sounded like, "You deal with it."

Remaining in her obeisance, Alina closed her eyes and muttered a prayer, fearing whatever was afoot and dreading dismissal when Ludo's business was concluded. When she opened them, she found the queen gazing at her kindly and signalling her to rise. Alina was so relieved she could have cried, for not only did the queen recognise her, she named her: "Baroness Metherall, what a pleasant surprise."

Fortunately, Ludo had the sense or good grace to stay where he was.

"How kind of you to visit," the queen continued, and beckoned her to the chair with a hand so small, the skin so taught and dry, it reminded Alina of a bird's claw.

"I came as soon as I received your summons, Your Majesty," Alina said.

Moving behind the queen, Baron Jermyn, a very straight man of middle years, glowered and shook his head: a warning Alina chose to ignore. It had taken weeks to get here and she had nowhere else to go: she wasn't about to be manoeuvred by a jumped-up secretary not matter how noble. A lot of people depended on this interview.

The queen raised her hand again to get Jermyn's attention: "Did I summon dear Alina, Baron Jermyn? I don't recall." Her voice was querulous and Alina moved a little closer to hear. "Did *you* ask her to come here?"

"No, ma'am," Henry Jermyn gave Alina another sharp look then said meaningfully, "perhaps you mentioned her while you were unwell, ma'am. I regret I wasn't present if you did."

Alina straightened her back to better face the opposition, but her right hand sneaked unbidden into her skirts to knead at the fabric. "Lady Dalkeith came to me at Crimphele, ma'am," she said. "Crimphele is my late husband's estate in Cornwall. She brought me your message, ma'am. That you wished me to travel with you to Spain as your interpreter."

"Lady Dalkeith? My message?" Henrietta Maria gazed up at Henry Jermyn, utterly reliant on her secretary. Jermyn bent to whisper her ear again. "Ah, yes. Oh, dear. It's all so very sad." The ailing queen dabbed her eyes with a fine handkerchief then took a deep breath as if gathering courage and said, "Lady Dalkeith, Anne Villiers, yes. And our daughter?"

Our? The royal 'we' or more? There had been rumours for years. Alina nodded her head and smiled. "A beautiful little girl."

"She fares well?"

"Small but lusty, ma'am. And in very good hands."

Henrietta Maria gave a brief sigh and looked back at Henry Jermyn for guidance. He nodded with a warm smile, suggesting to Alina that Henrietta Maria, whose determination in matters of state had brought Charles Stuart and the people of Britain into a civil war, had lost control over even personal affairs. An unfortunate circumstance given her own lack of security.

These fears were confirmed by the queen's apologetic tone as she said, "Well that must have been what I told Anne – take Minette to Cornwall." She paused then looked accusingly at Alina, "Why are you not there with them?"

Alina swallowed hard and gripped the fabric of her skirt, "Forgive me, ma'am, I understood I was to come to you in France and that we would then travel to Madrid to your sister."

"Madrid," Henrietta Maria gasped and burst into tears. A lady-in-waiting appeared from the other side of the room with another handkerchief at the ready.

As she did so, Henry Jermyn strode from the window embrasure towards Alina, saying, "Your Majesty, permit me to speak to Baroness Metherall for you." Taking Alina by the elbow he steered her into an adjoining ante room. Ludo bowed hastily and followed.

Jermyn closed the connecting door then said, "You do not appear to be aware that Her Majesty's sister in Spain has died, Baroness. In childbirth we are told. We have just received word, which, even if it were possible, means there will be no journey to Madrid or anywhere else for that matter."

"No, of course. I am sorry to hear it, Queen Isabel was ..." Alina lowered her eyes, determined not to give in to emotion, or be set aside so rapidly. "The Queen of Spain was kind to me when I was with her on Her Majesty's behalf a few years ago. Do *you* know of that, Baron Jermyn? It was Her Majesty's *special wish* that I visit her sister on her behalf. A difficult assignment as it turned out."

"And praise be that it failed or we'd all be in the Tower, madam, or worse. The British have no love of the Spanish, and no wish to return to the old religion, despite what Her Majesty believes. I am her staunchest of allies, naturally, but not in this matter." Henry Jermyn met Alina's eye and made a rapid movement with his mouth that could have passed for an apologetic smile had it been genuine. "Such a pity you are not able to stay, I'm sure Her Majesty would have enjoyed your company."

Alina shook her head, fighting for self-control then managed to say, "I have nowhere to go, Baron Jermyn. My home has been occupied by Roundheads. My husband has been killed." Distress got the better of her and she fumbled for her own handkerchief.

Jermyn closed his eyes, embarrassed at the show of emotion. "That is truly regrettable, Baroness. But the fact is that quite apart from Her Majesty's ill health and need for tranquillity we are in straightened circumstances here. The Queen is in no position to add you to her current retinue, however much she may wish to, for the simple reason that she has no allowance for personal attendants. It's hard enough maintaining a skeleton staff here: we can't consider housing and feeding your party as well. It would be most unfair of you to – how shall I say it – put pressure on Her Majesty; she is by no means well. We feared for her life at one time. The spa waters have helped but she still lacks the use of her left arm, and cannot walk unaided."

Alina was surprised by the genuine concern in Jermyn's voice and accepted that it would be unwise to fight him on this, but she was in dire straits of her own: staying with Henrietta Maria was her only option.

Ludo raised a hand and came to her aid. "Baron, I think perhaps you are unaware that it was Cardinal Mazarin who directed us here. He is expecting Baroness Metherall to remain in Chateau-Thierry while she is in the Queen of England's service. I was given to believe there will be a removal to Paris in the future, but for the time being she is to stay here at the Queen's side."

Alina bit her lip: could it be true? Ludo had been in the Louvre Palace: it wasn't impossible. But Jermyn, too, had his doubts. He eyed Ludo suspiciously then said abruptly, "And you are with the baroness because ...?"

Alina flushed and turned away, fearing what Ludo might say.

"Ah, I escorted Baroness Metherall from Falmouth as requested by King Charles' aide at Pendennis Castle, where I received my instructions as to where to find Her Majesty. Although I fear communication is not all that it should be. It may have been interrupted by enemy ships, of course. Getting here from England was not without its dangers for the baroness, as I'm sure you must appreciate. Nor myself, and I have travelled a good deal further. You did send for me did you not?"

Alina's mouth formed a perfect 'O' at Ludo's temerity – then realised what he was saying was true.

"We naturally paid our respects at the Louvre Palace. I must say I was surprised you weren't there," Ludo continued, "but the Cardinal hopes the matter of residency will soon be resolved. I promised to call in and see him on my return with news of Her Majesty. He is most concerned also about her poor health. Such a pity."

"Hmm," Jermyn said, arranging spectacles over his ears and shifting them on his nose for a better focus as if to detect a visible lie. Peering at Ludo, Jermyn was silent for a moment then he tapped his desk and spoke directly to Alina. "Well, now you are both here I can hardly turn you away like paupers. Who else is with you, Baroness? Quite a party by the looks of it. Have you abandoned your home entirely?"

His supercilious tone was the final straw. Alina flared with anger, "My husband, as I have just informed Her Majesty, sir, has been killed, our home overrun by Roundheads. My son is heir to the estate. I brought him here with me for his safety, along with his tutor. I also have a small daughter, Henrietta. My steward and – this gentleman," she waved a hand at Ludo, "who I believe has business with Her Majesty – accompanied me on the voyage and on the long journey from Le Havre, for our protection."

"So – a tutor and a steward? That could be useful." Jermyn turned back to Ludo, "And you go by the name of Ludo da Portovenere, correct? Somewhat picaresque for this day and age, what?"

Ludo bowed his head then said with his winning one-dimpled smile, "It is, I admit. You may have heard of my family, though, the Doria of Genoa."

That wiped the superciliousness from Jermyn's features. "You belong to the Genoese Doria ... do you, begad? I didn't know that. So *you* are the famous Ludo da Portovenere."

"You have heard of him!" Alina interrupted, astonished.

"Oh, yes. Her Majesty insisted on his coming to her. She often mentions him."

Ludo caught Alina's eye and raised a thick black eyebrow. She blinked hard trying to keep a straight face. Henry Jermyn moved out from behind his desk and began to circle them. Not unlike a round-eyed wolf, Alina thought:

immaculate in fine greys with a froth of white lace at the throat, a cruel jaw line.

"Perhaps there is a way to find you a more permanent place here after all," he said, pausing to look at her. "You mentioned a tutor?"

"Yes, Mr John Hawthorne, he is an ordained Catholic priest and my son's tutor."

"Excellent. We also have youngsters here; a tutor for the young princes will come in very handy. No children's nurse, by any chance?"

"No, I regret not."

"Never mind, you can do that."

"Me!"

"You have children, Baroness, you know about children, would it be too much to ask that you cared for the younger royals?"

Alina opened and closed her mouth then gave a small incline of the head. "Nothing would give me greater pleasure, sir."

"Splendid. As I said, we are in somewhat straightened circumstances as you will see, but if you are willing to lend a hand, I'm sure we'll battle through and return our precious queen to full health. Sorry to hear about your husband, by the way. I don't think I knew him, but a great loss to the Royalist cause I am sure."

Jermyn gave a low bow, putting his face in dangerous proximity to the flat of Alina's right hand rising rapidly from her skirt. He straightened and Alina placed her right hand firmly in her left for safety's sake.

Unaware of her volatile temper, Jermyn added in a stage-whisper said, "Send your steward to me later, Baroness, as well, will you? We could do with an extra footman to serve our meals."

Ludo gave a polite cough. "And my carriage, sir? Do you have stable hands to deal with my horses, or should I nip out now to speak to my driver?"

Jermyn laughed, "Quite. We do have grooms, but you might like to oversee arrangements yourself while they prepare your chamber."

Ludo inclined his head and the interview was over.

Chapter 13

Much later that day, after Alina and the English priest had been introduced in the royal nursery and Marcos taken to the housekeeping area of the chateau, Henry Jermyn conducted Ludo into a compact office on the ground floor. Day had given way to a dark, cloudy evening and candles flickered in wall sconces, a silver candelabra bearing three sweet beeswax candles had been placed on a cabinet carved with the French fleur-de-lis and acorns.

Jermyn went up to a wide desk and lifted a soft chamois leather cover from what should have been his writing pad but was now something quite different. Various rings, brooches, cloak clasps and hatbands had been set out on a green baize cloth. In the centre was a Turkish *cloisonné* bowl filled with giant, lustrous pearls. Ludo nodded in approval at the fitting nature of the receptacle: they were his pearls. Part of a consignment he had sent to Henrietta Maria, at her request, but for which he had never been paid. He cast an eye at the cabinet behind Jermyn to locate the lacquered box containing the uncut stones he had sent the previous year. It was not there.

"A fine display," Ludo said.

"For which we seek a fine price, sir."

So this was why he was here: not to receive payment or even returned goods, but as a purchaser. It was so absurd he nearly laughed. Schooling his features, he said, "All this is for sale? Or do you wish to raise money on it?"

"Pawning," Jermyn's tone was scathing then he too adopted a blander tone, "has proved somewhat problematic for Her Majesty to date."

Because she can't afford to redeem her goods or pay outstanding interest on loans, thought Ludo. "Well, if you are quite certain you wish to sell – I think I can arrange a good price for *some* of these items. To sell them all will require establishing a shop."

Jermyn gave him a sharp glance, "Is that mean to be amusing?"

"Not entirely, no."

If Jermyn knew how his queen had obtained the pearls, he said nothing. Determined to retrieve them, Ludo played his options carefully: "I regret I cannot purchase anything myself. I have my own suppliers and sources in India and the Oman for that. Nor can I set up a shop *or* offer loans on them, Baron. If this is what you are seeking, I fear you are talking to the wrong man."

"But you were named, sir, as the person to go to. And great deal of effort has gone into getting you here, or so I'm given to understand."

"Indeed it has. But I repeat, I have no interest in buying these gems, no matter how worthy the cause. It is quite beyond my budget for one thing. I trade in gems, I *sell* to jewellers, but I am not a jeweller."

"But you could arrange for their sale?"

"Well, as an intermediary, an agent – yes, that is a role I can fulfil."

Jermyn removed his steel-rimmed spectacles, polished them on a handkerchief and replaced them on his long nose. Eventually, he said, "You told me earlier you belonged to the House of Doria."

"I do, but financial matters of that nature, loans and the like, are quite separate to my business activities. I am a merchant, sir, not a banker. I actually have a Royal Warrant to provide spices and silks to the House of Stuart." It was something else Jermyn appeared not to know, but not wishing to alienate the Queen's secretary for there was much at stake, Ludo gave a winning smile and filtered pearls through his plump fingers. "I could act as a dealer in cut stones and precious gems if it will benefit Her Majesty, I suppose."

"And if I ask you to not advertise that fact, but to make your deals in as quiet and secret a manner as possible, would you do that?"

"Naturally," Ludo inclined his head.

"Hmm ..." Jermyn re-arranged items on his desk into a symmetrical pattern. "In that case, let me show what else we have."

"There is more? Good."

Jermyn frowned. "Good?"

Ludo shrugged as if the word were meaningless, secretly delighted he might be regaining more of his gems.

"There is more, and of a more valuable nature." Jermyn hesitated, started to say something else and then stopped.

Ludo tapped the fingers of his right hand against the hem of his jacket; choosing his words carefully, he said, "Baron, perhaps you should know that I arranged for the queen ... that is, at *my own expense*, I sent a lacquered box to Her Majesty last year, *and* the year before. What the Portuguese call a 'bizalho'. The last one contained pearls, uncut diamonds and sapphires in three separate compartments. I wondered if she still had them."

Jermyn frowned again. "She took a black lacquered box of sundries to The Hague. It was one of the few things to be sold, in fact. She may have pawned the other; I really cannot say. Does it matter?"

Ludo cocked his head to one side.

"You haven't been paid." Jermyn sighed. "That does rather shed a different light on this transaction." He fiddled with a jewel encrusted hatband on the desk before him, pushing it until it formed a perfect circle.

Ludo waited then said, "May ask, sir ... that is, it occurs to me that being in France, and the First Minister of France being a well-known connoisseur and collector of quality diamonds, that you might approach him. Or I could approach him on your behalf."

"Mazarin hasn't lifted a finger to help us – Her Majesty – that is. I don't know what his game is, but I do know this: I shall not be the first to approach him and if we are forced to beg for charity it will be directly with the Queen Regent – not a jumped-up Italian."

Ludo gave a wry smile at the irony and nodded, "I see."

"I doubt you do, sir. Suffice it to say the Queen of England, Daughter of France, does not stoop."

"No, quite." Ludo waited for Jermyn to control his anger and make the next move, and was not displeased when it came.

"I could offer you a significant commission on sales. Would that encourage you to act on the Queen's behalf? That, and our good intentions when she returns to London?"

Ludo inclined his head. "My percentage would have to be significant, sir. These are hardly baubles to be sold just anywhere."

"Quite and if I had my way, they wouldn't be sold at all." Jermyn sniffed with annoyance. "I feel bound to say, sir, that I have misgivings about this arrangement, somewhat compounded by your statement just now."

"You expect me to make off with the goods, or at least reclaim what is mine – or what I *say* is mine. You are wondering if I am to be trusted," Ludo said quietly. "Because," Ludo spaced his words, "you do not know me, and someone, perhaps someone with rather too much influence over Her Majesty has encouraged her to employ *my* skills – not yours." Jermyn flashed a look of surprise, confirming Ludo's suspicion. "A priest perhaps? A Vatican envoy?"

"You are well-informed, sir."

"An inspired guess based on experience. There is a priest named Rogelio – he was with Her Majesty in London when I first made her acquaintance," Ludo let the comment imply a relationship with the queen, hoping it would work in a positive direction and not alienate the humourless chamberlain further. "This priest, if it is the same man, is known to me. Although I do wonder how his situation may be affected by what is happening in Rome. A new Vicar of Christ, I hear."

Jermyn licked his lips then said diplomatically, "Yes, we have lost an ally. Pope Urban was most supportive of Her Majesty – but now ..." he opened his hands. "I plan to visit Paris in the next week or two, to meet the new papal envoy to the Louvre. I have been wondering if or when Father Rogelio will be replaced, but as yet we have received no word."

Jermyn sounded as though he would be glad to be rid of Rogelio and Ludo edged forward to fish for more information. "Father Rogelio has not been recalled to Rome, then? That must be a comfort to Her Majesty, especially with so many changes in her recent life. You will miss him, though, no doubt."

"Not I, sir. Far from it! Snooping around her ladies, asking questions he has no right to ask, pushing her to speak King Charles on this and that 'at the Pope's behest'. And look where it has got her: exile. Poverty. And if the war continues as it is, widowhood most likely. Britain will never return to Rome. She pushed too hard and now she's paying the price ... and why am I telling you this? What is your interest in this damned priest?"

"Me?" Ludo raised his eyebrows in surprise. "The man is of no importance to me, personally." It was both true and not true. But Ludo needed to know where the serpent was lurking. "Tell me, Baron Jermyn, you say he is close to Her Majesty – as her confessor should be, no doubt. Will she be anxious to keep him with her, if – when – you move to Paris? If he is free to do as she asks?"

"Ask him yourself, he's still here."

This was both good news and bad. Good, because the serpent was safely away from the twins: bad because Ludo had no wish to confront him. It also meant he would be in contact with John Hawthorne as the new royal tutor. Rogelio had unfinished business with the timid English priest he feared.

Ludo stared unseeing at the gems on the desk, wondering whether to warn John Hawthorne or not. Hawthorne was a nuisance, but he had disobeyed Rome and stayed in Cornwall to help Alina when she most needed it and deserved something for that. Falling deeper into speculation, Ludo was brought back to the present with a sharp click. Jermyn was opening a square jewel case containing a diamond and emerald necklace with a fat white pendant pearl and below that an emerald the size of a pigeon's egg. It was lovely and worth a fortune. Ludo perked up, Rogelio temporally forgotten.

"Charming," he said.

"One of the many items belonging to Queen Elizabeth. The emeralds came from the New World. It was made for her, so the story goes, from gems sourced by that rogue, Drake."

"A jewel with a story, how interesting. May I see?" The necklace was heavy but not garish or inelegant. Far from it. He picked it out of its bed of faded crimson satin and held it in his left hand, lifting it so the pendant emerald caught fire in the light from a candle. This he would take as part of his commission. He returned it to the box on the desk then said, "Delightful," and backtracked rapidly on the earlier conversation. "Regarding your misgivings on my reliability, sir, perhaps you should take into account that a *less* trustworthy man can sometimes achieve that which a more trustworthy person would not dare attempt."

Jermyn gave him the flicker of a smile. "Her Majesty suggested something along similar lines when she insisted on you as our – her – agent. Yes, agent, I think is the right term." He closed the jewel case and added, "How do you know Father Rogelio?"

"Our paths crossed in Whitehall." When I thought I was being clever tempting Henrietta Maria with pearls and precious gems from the exotic East, Ludo chided himself. But it wasn't all bad, he could make a small fortune with even one or two items on the table alone, and if there was more, and of greater value, he'd have the best of those as well. The commission could pay for a new home in a safe, secret haven. Somewhere permanent. On the Mediterranean coast, though, not back in India.

Henry Jermyn interrupted his thoughts. "I ought to tell you Her Majesty has already attempted to raise funds on some of these items with financiers in The Hague, who were very wary about taking them. In fact, they refused."

"If by 'financiers' you mean Dutch pawnbrokers I am not surprised. They'd be very cautious about helping a Habsburg not to mention the situation in England. Do I assume Her Majesty is also unable to redeem certain items?" Ludo eyes twinkled. "What a dilemma for the wily Dutch, but who can they sell such treasures to in the Low Countries? Calvinists are not permitted conspicuous spending, you know. No," Ludo paused then, indicating the emerald pendant necklace, he said, "glories such as these can only be sold outright. That is part of their appeal. An owner wants to revel in their *possession*, be they the woman wearing the jewel or the husband displaying his wealth. It's all about *possession*, Baron Jermyn. This is what drives men where land is concerned; and women, where jewels are involved. Or so I believe. There is more you say?"

Henry Jermyn pushed the gems on his desk to one side, moved the bowl onto the cabinet then took a key from his embroidered waistcoat opened the cabinet itself. From it he withdrew a sturdy, high-domed casket, which he set on the green baize cloth and opened with another key. The contents sparkled even in the poor light of the office, and it was only the top layer. Jermyn lifted it out to expose a second shelf crowded with ropes of pearls of varied hues. He selected one and set it out neatly beside the casket, then removed the second tray and set out two gold bracelets studded with pearls, a silk pouch with a silver ribbon and a garnet-studded hatband, then another small silk pouch. "The bracelets contain two hundred and two-hundred and fifty pearls each. This bag," he untied the drawstring, "contains a hundred pearl buttons. There is another hatband with two hundred pearls." He opened the palm of his hand and waved it over the desk, "These were all pawned back in '34 in Holland for seven thousand, five hundred pounds then redeemed. The Dutch have refused to lend on them a second time."

Ludo was unsure what he had been expecting, but this was more, far more than he anticipated. He stayed silent and watched as Jermyn pushed a pearl collar into shape. Ludo examined the arrangement of clustered pearls around alternate rubies and sapphires from across the desk. Jermyn caught his eye when he looked up, "It's in several of Queen Elizabeth's portraits; I believe it was made for her mother, Anne Boleyn. There's a diamond necklace that's hers, as well. It's known as Queen Bess's diamonds."

"This is pretty," Ludo said, trying to keep his voice flat and level. He turned a brooch to reveal its design, an anchor formed of diamonds and sapphires with seven pendant pearls on a thick blue ribbon.

"That collar," Jermyn pointed to another wide-spanned necklace designed to be worn like a ruff perhaps, "contains twenty diamonds. It's worth at least two thousand pounds. The brooch should be sold in the region of three thousand – more if you can get it. The pearl necklace with the pendant ruby arrangement – get what you can. The ruby alone is worth a king's ransom – if you follow me?"

Ludo looked up at the phrase and caught Jermyn's eye. "I do now, yes. Forgive me, Baron, I was a little slow in catching on. The queen needs funds for a very good reason – should the worst come to the worst."

"Which is why I can hardly oppose her. Although you will be selling items that belong to the English Crown Jewels," Jermyn touched a brooch as if it was a personal possession, "and that I am not happy about. Not at all."

"I will get what I can." Ludo was serious. It was a task he hadn't anticipated and it was not without major challenges – where, for a start, could he even offer these goods? But he was going to do it. And Alina would have the Empress Elizabeth's emeralds. They would look stunning with her golden hair.

Lost in speculation, Ludo watched wordlessly as Jermyn turned back to his cabinet and extracted a leather-bound box, which he set at a corner of his desk. He then took another, much smaller key from his doublet and opened it. Lying on deep blue velvet was what looked like an old-fashioned cloak clasp. "Here," he said passing it to Ludo.

It was a most unusual jewel. Ludo held it to the light: a triad of massive rose-tinted balas rubies and three pearls, set around what looked like a huge, wine-yellow pyramid diamond with a fourth, coloured drop pearl pendant. He swallowed hard and returned it to the box. "It looks very old."

"I'm surprised you don't know about it."

"Should I?"

"This, sir, is the Three Brethren. An inventory made ten years ago valued it at ten thousand pounds. Her Majesty had a buyer before we came to France – it is one of the principal reasons we are here – a Flemish gentleman. He has disappointed us. His offer was a fraction of the real value and he has so far failed to claim the jewel. You are a merchant, you bring jewels from India, and you are familiar with large sums of money, could you get a good price for this?"

Ludo put a hand to his chin and stroked his pointed beard, cunning ideas and devious thoughts forgotten. "Honestly, sir, I really don't know."

Jermyn gave him a questioning look. "It's not part of the regalia, but this piece is at the very heart of the Crown Jewels. I don't expect you can achieve what it's worth, but you should get an excellent price for it, taking into account your commission, of course."

Ludo stepped away from the table and stroked his neat beard again. He wanted to laugh, but he was all nerves. "This is not the Queen's private collection you are showing me, Baron. These are the Crown Jewels! You want me to try to sell the English Crown Jewels?"

Jermyn nodded, "If you can." He now poked at a diamond collar, keeping his eyes averted.

"*Maria Santissima,*" Ludo murmured "This changes matters."

There was only one place he could sell fabulous jewels such as these and that was to other royals. What other royals might be interested in...? Aha! Royals who had lost their own crown jewels to the usurping Spanish. New royals in Portugal. But were they sufficiently wealthy to purchase a new history? It meant going back to Lisbon: going back and facing up to his previous misdemeanours there. But hell's teeth, it was worth the risk. Keeping his expression under control, Ludo said more lightly, "So this is what you *do not* think I should be trusted with, Baron Jermyn."

"Not you, sir, nor anyone. They belong to the English monarchy. The actual regalia, crowns, orb and sceptre are in safe-keeping in London, I hope. Many nowadays would say they belong to the English people. This, for example," he lifted a heavy ruby necklace from the very bottom of the domed casket, "was made for Catherine of Aragon, mother of

Queen Mary. It's also – along with that rope of pearls –" he pointed across the table, "is in Queen Bess's first portrait as monarch. They are part of our national heritage. The problem is ..." the courtier shook his head, "I greatly fear that if they are returned to London, and if Cromwell prevails, they will be scattered, sold, broken up and re-used willy-nilly. So I am forced to accept that they might as well be sold to finance the war to *prevent* the Roundheads ever getting them. But where on earth," Jermyn turned to Ludo accusatively, "can someone like you actually sell them?"

Somewhat taken aback by the fervour in the man's voice and the truth of the question, Ludo said, "Well, for a start, I can't sell them all. A few items, yes. I have someone in mind for the Three Brethren, and very likely for the Spanish queen's necklace. They are spinels – balas rubies – in the cloak clasp, I think. Rare and very valuable, as you say."

"And very antique."

"There are two people who will be thrilled to obtain some of this, I think; I doubt very much they could afford more than a small portion, but I suspect the lady in question will take the ruby necklace once she knows its history. Tell me about the Brethren."

"It was made as a cloak clasp for John the Fearless, Duke of Burgundy, some years before his murder in 1467, or so I believe. It then passed into the hands of the Fuggers – bankers to Burgundy, and elsewhere of course. Some say they sold it to Edward the Sixth, others that it came to the second Henry Tudor, possibly as a wedding gift. It is certainly painted into his daughter Elizabeth's ermine portrait. It also appears in portraits of our present king's royal father, James."

"So it should definitely stay in royal hands."

"That would be of some comfort." Jermyn started to replace the cloak clasp in its box, giving Ludo a little time to pace beside the window and examine the idea of going to

Lisbon. Jermyn eventually seated himself at his desk and indicated the chair in front of him. Ludo sat down and waited. There was a brief silence then Jermyn took an itemised list from a drawer and said, "We shall need you to sign for everything, naturally."

"I'll sign for what I take, but it cannot be all this, Baron. Let me have a few of the items and do my best with them first."

"And will you do 'your best' for Her Majesty?" Jermyn asked.

"I will." And not just for the queen, Ludo added silently.

"In that case," Jermyn said, taking a Portuguese *bizalho* box from a deep drawer at the side of his desk, "you may have this."

Ludo felt a warm irrational sense of satisfaction at regaining something that had cost him dear in effort. Jermyn had not the slightest understanding of the dangers of a voyage from the East. Ludo's mind then ranged over the next problem: how to transport it all without a body-guard, for he most definitely did not want a body-guard reporting on his whereabouts.

Jermyn picked up the box and put it back in the drawer. "We naturally require something as security – given the enormous value of what you will be acquiring, so I will keep this until you return to us."

Furious, Ludo's hands flew up of their own accord. "We agreed I should be your agent." Ludo stated. "I will arrange sales, and take a commission for my efforts and to cover my costs; the rest will come back to Her Majesty." *Eventually, one way or another, in part.*

Jermyn leaned forward, "Did you honestly expect to take the goods with without leaving any form of security?"

Ludo frowned: was Jermyn now giving him a reason to refuse to do as the Queen requested? Was he trying to prevent him actually taking the jewels so he could tell his precious Henrietta that he'd tried to persuade the Genoese merchant to help her and the man had refused?

Ludo gave an audible sigh and got to his feet, saying, "We seem to have wasted each other's time, Baron. I regret also to disappoint Her Majesty."

"You said you were a Doria, sir. Doria are bankers, do they not require some form of security in their transactions?"

"Regrettably, I am the black sheep of the family so I have no idea how their arrangements work." Ludo surprised himself in a moment of truth.

Baron Jermyn pursed his thin lips and tapped his fingernails on the edge of his desk. "We can't risk you taking anything just like that," he snapped the fingers in the air. "Imagine if you were robbed. Even with a trained bodyguard, roads are treacherous, taverns full of highwaymen and ships always at the mercy of pirates."

"Perils at every turn. I could offer you shares in my spice business in Goa."

"A commercial enterprise." The words were a sneer.

Ludo took a deep breath. The arrogant English Royalists deserved to lose their civil war; the future was in commerce with the new entrepreneur. He'd told someone that ten years ago in Spanish cortijo and had been proved right at the time. So it would be again. In those three words Baron Jermyn had sealed the fate of the famous Three Brethren, Queen Bess's diamonds and emeralds, and the rope made for the Spanish Catalina, plus a few other choice gems belonging to his precious queen and country. They'd be sold at amazing prices, but she'd never know that because of the difficulties he was going to encounter finding buyers – it would take years, simply years for him to conclude transactions.

Ludo pointed at the casket. "I will take that and certain items and sell them, then convey the proceeds to Her Majesty – wherever she may be. If you wish, you can make a new list. I will take the Three Brethren clasp; Queen Bess's diamond necklace, the emerald pendant necklace, the diamond collar and the bags of pearls." He pointed at the dish of his own Hormuz pearls. "I'll take those as well."

Before Jermyn could reply, he jumped to his feet as the Queen was wheeled into the office in her wicker chair. A fluffy, lop-eared dog was perched on the rug over her lap. "Has everything been settled, gentlemen?" she asked as they bowed.

"Yes, ma'am," they replied in unison.

"Oh, good," she clapped her small hands, sending the creature into a yapping frenzy. When it quietened, she said brightly, "We have been learning to make bread! One has to make the dough the afternoon before it is cooked, isn't that amusing?"

"Indeed, ma'am." Ludo turned to Jermyn and gave him an enquiring look.

"Come back in an hour," Jermyn snapped. "I'll have everything ready for you. Bring the warrants you hold to supply the palace; I'll take them into safe keeping for you. I shall also want more details about your enterprise in the East."

The Queen pointed at the bowl of pearls on the cabinet, "I was going to have those threaded in London." She gave a small, dramatic sigh and looked up at him. "They are the Hormuz pearls, aren't they? You sent them to us."

Ludo smiled and Jermyn bent to whisper in her ear.

"Oh dear," she said. "What a nuisance. Still if he can sell them ..." Her hands fluttered in the air then she said in more serious tone, "Signor Ludovico, we charge you with finding a good home for our pearls and other jewels that we might send the proceeds to King Charles in England. Between us we will finance this war and fight on. We *shall* prevail and our Catholic faith will be celebrated in provincial towns once more." Her voice was reed thin, but not lacking the least determination.

"Yes, ma'am, I will do my best."

"Excellent, very well, carry on."

Ludo extended a leg and arm behind him and bowed from the waist. As he did so, a side door opened a fraction and an elongated form in clerical black insinuate itself into a shadowy corner of Jermyn's office.

Keeping his eyes lowered Ludo backed from the room, noting as he exited the absence of a lock on the door. Then he hastened to his room to pack everything that would fit into two saddle bags. He was leaving with his loot at first light, and without a body-guard.

Chapter 14

The chamber Alina was allotted had a high ceiling, thin cotton curtains and barely any furniture apart from a canopied bed and two chairs. Unable to sleep soundly for the greater part of the night, a noise awoke her sometime towards dawn. A door along the passageway opened or closed. She wondered if it might be a child, but there was a nursemaid with them and her eyelids closed again before the thought was completed.

Waking again later, remembering the sound of the door and worried that her children would be unsettled in their barrack-like nursery, she pulled a skirt and shawl over her night shift, put on her only pair of indoor shoes and crossed the ice-cold chamber to the connecting door.

The eldest princess had her own room, but the younger princes, James and Henry and their sister Elizabeth were still tucked up together and fast asleep. As were her own two children in truckle beds by the window and the nursemaid in an adjoining cubicle. Hetty's rag doll had fallen to the floor. She picked it up and bits of lamb's wool caught on her fingers from loose stitching down the back of the upper body. I ought to re-make it and refill the limbs, she thought, tucking it under Hetty's chin.

Alina surveyed the room in the poor light and the action brought her up short: she was checking on the well-being of royal children. She was lucky to have a useful role in a royal household; lucky to have a roof such as this over her head.

Restless and hungry, and unwilling to return to bed, she left the nursery by the main door and crossed the gallery to a window embrasure overlooking the courtyard. Apart from a scurrying cloud, backlit by the first rays of reluctant sunlight, pink and orange, nothing moved. Except no, there was the distinct sound of feet coming from her left, then descending the servants' stairs. A skivvy going down to light fires most likely. Who else from the servants' attic rooms might be up and about at this hour? Marcos might be up there, now he was a footman or steward. Could it be Marcos? Was he angry at his treatment? Was he getting away, leaving her to manage on her own? Or was it Ludo? Or both of them? Colour rising to her cheeks, Alina turned and followed.

The figure reached the ground floor well before her. Medium height, slightly built – not Ludo – but he was unsure of his surrounding because he was standing still, wondering which way to go. Alina halted at the bottom of the staircase, feeling very nervous, for she had the distinct sensation that someone was following her now. It would have been amusing, had the chateau not been quite so eerie.

Marcos – it had to be Marcos – set off to the left, down a corridor that led through a still-room and pantry area into a servants' hall and finally to an outside door. Waiting until he had exited then pausing again at the door leading to an inner courtyard, Alina strained to hear if there really was someone behind her. Perhaps she had imagined it. The only sound was the patter of rainwater from broken guttering. She waited a moment more, deciding where Marcos could have gone from here: the stables most likely. It then occurred to her that he hadn't been wearing a cape or carrying anything.

More curious than frightened, Alina lifted her skirt and tried to step between the puddles in the uneven cobbles. She managed to save her skirt, but by the time she reached the stable block her soft red slippers were soaked through. Keeping her skirts gathered around her knees now to avoid dirty straw, Alina moved into the alley between the horses' stalls, then stopped in a panic. Supposing it wasn't Marcos; could she be trailing someone else? Who? Who from the chambers occupied by the royal footmen might be here? Two lovers in a secret tryst? Or worse, lovers of different ranks? How embarrassing! Alina turned to retrace her steps, but there was a glow from an oil lamp half way down the left-hand row of stalls and the murmur of voices. Curiosity got the better of her. Treading on tip-toe she advanced past the mostly empty stalls until a sleeping beast detected her presence and with a groan struggled to its feet. The voices stopped and Marcos appeared in front of her.

"What are you doing here?" he demanded in a whisper.

"What are *you* doing here?" Alina countered.

"Well, whatever you are doing, you are not coming with me – either of you," Ludo said, edging round Marcos to pick up heavy saddlebags leaning against the partition wall.

"Oh, I might have guessed it would be you," Alina huffed. "Who else goes sneaking around at night? I suppose you are leaving without saying farewell – again." A sense of betrayal she knew too well lodged itself under her left ribs. Recalling the pain of being abandoned at Crimphele so many years ago, she spoke now with genuine anger. "Why do you do this?"

"Because my life is my life, and I can." Ludo pushed at a black wooden box. It rattled as he shoved it deeper into a saddlebag and he hastily he pulled the top flap over it then closed the buckles.

"He won't tell me where he's going, or why I can't go with him." Marcos touched her arm then added quietly, "See if he'll tell you."

"*Va bene,*" Ludo huffed and went around the other side of his horse to tighten the girth. Speaking over the beast's flank said, "I'll tell you why you can't – shouldn't – come with me. Firstly, because you both have a great opportunity here with the little queen – while she lasts. Alina, you have somewhere to live and you are in her confidence; your children are in the royal nursery –"

"And I'm a nurse maid!" Alina hissed.

"As I was saying: a great opportunity for your ambitious career at court."

Alina gaped at him, "As a glorified servant? Are you mad?"

"No, I am reminded of the Countess-Duchess of Olivares in Spain, who is or was in charge of a royal nursery. Remember the power that lady wields."

Alina remembered. Ludo was right, which only served to make her angrier. Before she could say anything, however, he turned to Marcos saying, "As for you, you shouldn't go back to England until the Stuarts return to London, for your own safety. I heard at supper that the Roundhead garrison across the river from Plymouth has been put to the sword. Jermyn was cock-a-hoop. Report has it that five hundred men died in Saltash *in one night*. I don't reckon the chances of any Royalist on his own within a hundred miles of Plymouth after this. So, as far as you are concerned, returning to your little wifey is not an option, it will only jeopardise your family. You do know this."

"I know this. But I can't stay here as a footman. I'm a merchant. I have a business to consider the same as you."

"Yes, and that's *your* future. You've got a Royal Warrant for heaven sake. I made a point of not surrendering my warrants yesterday as Jermyn demanded. But you can go to him, tell him who and what you are, tell him you're my associate and there has been some misunderstanding and go from there. Negotiate some new role – as the Queen's steward if necessary – but stay here. Apart from anything else you'll get all the information you need to know when it is safe to return to England. Or tie your colours to the elder princes, and when they cross the channel to help their papa let me know. Let me know, too, if you hear there is to be a new king. Your time here could be very beneficial to both of us."

Marcos started to say something then hesitated. Alina looked from one to the other. They had a friendship, a camaraderie she was not part of. She hadn't asked Marcos about his business, not once, let alone his wife and child.

"Take the main chance, you fool," Ludo continued, speaking insistently to Marcos. We have warrants to supply palaces, use your skills. You were sharp enough in Holland to make something of yourself, don't lose the advantage here. Find a way to the son and heir."

"He's in England," Alina interrupted. The two men looked at her as if they had forgotten who she was. "Prince Charles is part of the war. He's got his own men and he's fighting – he's not here."

"There's the other boy – boys," Ludo snapped. "The queen will be in Paris before winter's out anyway and then you'll have all of the French court to –"

"*Aprovechar*," Alina interrupted sarcastically, "that's what you're telling him, isn't it? Take advantage of them – any of them."

"Oh, and they aren't doing that to you, milady? Forgive my cynicism, but you'll have the time of your life in Paris."

"I am a widow," Alina stamped her foot.

"All the better, you can find a new husband in the Louvre Palace and climb the social ranks here as well." Ludo moved around the horse to stand in front of her. "Being the daughter of a Spanish grandee might be a bit tricky, of course. France is always at war with Spain, but I'm sure you'll charm your way out of that inconvenience; the Queen Regent of France is Spanish after all."

Ludo pulled a rolled parchment from the front his inner cloak pocket and waggled it at Marcos then walked him out of the stall saying, "If you really don't want to stay in France, go to your parents in Sanlucar. You can take charge of cortijo there, the way I suggested before. This is a copy of the deeds." He pushed the parchment into the younger man's chest. "I've kept it with me for a variety of reasons, fortunately. This wasn't one of them, but take it anyway. Go there and start making wine not selling it. Listen, Marcos, seriously, you've lost your trade in England, possibly forever if Parliament wins. My estate in Sanlucar produces wine, I still bring spices and silks from the East and the Levant, but we'll both need a new market if Cromwell wins. Keep your ear to the ground and let me know the minute the war is decided one way or the other. You can get messages to me through Toxo in Vigo the usual way. Think about it – there are juniper berries in Spain as well. Take your gin-making skills home and begin again there."

Marcos took the rolled parchment and started to reply, but Ludo placed a hand on the small of his back and ushered him further down the line of stalls. "I haven't finished. You can do any or all of that, but I'd prefer you to stay with Alina and her children for as long as you can."

"Why, is she in jeopardy?" Marcos asked, concerned.

"Possibly. The Vatican agent Rogelio is here."

"What's that to do with me?" Alina asked coming up behind them.

Turning slowly, Ludo took a deep breath and in the low light from the small lamp looked her in the eye. "This Rogelio has reason to dislike me. He also appears to know more about me than I know myself, and that's not an exaggeration. I don't know why, but he will strike out at anyone close to me. You may not remember my cabin boy José or the friar in Holland –"

"Brother Caritas?" Marcos asked.

Ludo nodded. "I do not want what has happened to them to happen here. Remember El Escorial."

"Alina – in the lake: that was him?" Marcos gasped.

"I thought you knew." Ludo frowned and said, "Almost certainly. He will lash out at anyone close to me, which is another reason I'm not happy about leaving you all here, but hopefully he won't harm you while you have the queen's favour. It's bad enough worrying about my children."

"Then why don't you do something about it?" Alina demanded. "Get rid of him, for instance?" She spoke hastily recalling what had happened in El Escorial when someone had pushed her in a lake in the dark. She had nearly drowned.

Ludo rubbed his chin. "I may have to one day."

"But – if he did what he did in Spain because he thought I meant something to you," Alina's words were sharp, "you don't have to worry. He must know you are nothing to me now. We went our separate ways. What has this to do with *my* children anyway?" she added.

"Because, milady, I too have a small daughter with black hair and hazel eyes and enough character to command a ship of corsairs." Ludo's voice was low and flat, matter-of-fact.

Alina bit her lip. "They are alike?" Her voice cracked in a whisper.

"Two peas in a pod," Ludo cocked his head and gave her a wry grin.

And that was the end of the conversation. Ludo slipped the horse's bridle over its head and led it from its stall, causing Marcos to comment, "That's a fine horse. It's not one we used for the carriages from Le Havre."

"Is it not? Oh, dear," Ludo replied, and swung himself into the saddle.

Chapter 15

The tall, high-stepping black horse was well-bred and elegant, as Marcos had noted, but it was unused to carrying heavy saddlebags fore and aft. Not the most skilled rider, Ludo was jogged and jolted for several miles before the beast settled into a walk. By which time they were both already tired. Nevertheless, Ludo pushed on, going west, aiming for the city of Paris then a Seine barge to Le Havre and the relative comfort of his cabin aboard *The Tulip*.

By the afternoon the horse had thrown a shoe. Giving up the day for lost Ludo located a farrier at the nearest village then left the animal in a livery stable for the night. He managed to secure a single room in a hostel then ate well, slept well, albeit somewhat constrained in the narrow cot, wearing all his clothes with their many pockets and pouches and clutching the smelly saddle bags. Setting off the next morning he was in a much better frame of mind, but it was short-lived, for heavy rain set in and the road along the Marne Valley became a quagmire. The horse didn't like mud, either. Giving up another day as lost, Ludo sought shelter in a monastery and slept in a freezing cell.

The third and fourth days were overcast and his cloak and clothes were permanently damp from repeated soakings, but he pressed on, focussed on his ship, a gilded barque on a golden sea. Approaching the outlying villages of Paris, Ludo's spirits lifted. He could sell the horse – it was still in reasonably good condition, which was more than he could say for himself – and find a barge to Le Havre. On the fifth day, on the outskirts of Paris itself, and with the sale of the horse in mind, and needing to find a barge-master, he sought out a well-established inn.

The inn-keeper of The Leaping Trout, a jovial, fat man as inn-keepers should be, assured him he had a fine single room available, "But you'll have trouble getting a barge this week, sir. Harvests are long over, there'll only be merchant trade on the river now. Crews do still come in, though. You may find a berth if you're lucky." Ludo groaned out loud. "Not to worry, sir. I got your room ready. Single as requested, you won't have to share with no one – for tonight at least."

His French being limited to the cursing and banter of Mediterranean seaports, Ludo took little notice of the inn-keeper's wording and followed him up a rickety staircase to the second floor and a spacious, well-appointed chamber.

"Best in the house apart from the other two," the inn-keeper muttered, allowing Ludo to squeeze past him and enter alone then descending far faster than he came up.

There was a carved wooden press along the right-hand wall and a large four-poster bed with a fancy quilt and thick drapes hooked up at each corner that looked very inviting. A padded chair and footstool had been placed next to a blazing fire. It was cosy and inviting, especially the bed, but he needed a warm bath first. Dropping his old leather hat and saddlebags onto the press and the other bag onto the chair, Ludo untied his cape, hung it behind the door and went to the fire to warm his hands. Turning to warm his derriere he surveyed the room for a tub. A log in the grate sent up a shower of sparks. They caught the glint of metal from a primed flintlock pistol. It was pointing at him from the open doorway.

Who had followed him – with a gun? A felon who'd registered his fine horse and saddlebags earlier in the journey? Slowly, Ludo opened the palms of his hands at his sides. "I carry no weapon," he said in bad French.

"Then you should, sir," replied a voice in English. "No need to unpack. I'll take your bags from here."

Ludo lifted an eyebrow, "Could be tricky if you're aiming a pistol at me. I was beginning to regret not bringing someone with me – for the purpose of carrying."

"I have someone below."

"The inn keeper?" Ludo sighed: 'I got your room ready' suddenly making sense.

"Not the inn keeper." The voice was muffled under a swathe of dark coloured scarf but seemed familiar.

"Ah, well," Ludo shrugged as if it were a matter of no importance, "what can an unarmed merchant do in the circumstances?" He moved away from the fire towards the bed, "help yourself or whistle up your porter. I'm in no position to put up a fight."

The Englishman, a youngish-looking man with a wide-brimmed hat very much like Ludo's own pulled at a rakish angle over his right eye, and a wide scarf wound round his chin, was evidently well accustomed to armed robbery, for he held the pistol with a steady grip. Just like a soldier, in fact.

"There it is," Ludo gestured to the saddlebags on the press by the door. "Although why you let me get all the way here from Chateau Thierry, intrigues me. Why didn't you rob me on the road like a common highwayman? This method of extraction suggests you are not doing it for yourself. Working for England, are you? Royalist or Roundhead?" As he was speaking Ludo edged closer to the bed. "Or does Baron Jermyn want it all back? That's a possibility." Ludo took another step and leant against one of the posts at the foot of the bed. "Frankly, I wish you'd claimed it earlier, I've got saddle sores that'll last for months. I'm not a good horseman, never have been." There were two lumpy pillows on the quilt. Ludo smiled and cocked his head to one side, "Aren't you supposed to say 'your money or your life', by the way? I thought that's what robbers always said."

Ignoring him, the young man yelled, "Up here, damn you!" Then, keeping the pistol aimed at Ludo, he lifted the saddlebags from the press with his free hand.

"That's got my smalls in it," Ludo said, petulantly. "Do let me keep them. I prefer not to wear dirty clothing, unlike the French. If you're looking for trinkets to sell, you'll find them in that one." He pointed at the chair with one hand and unhooked one of the bed hangings with the other.

"They are not for sale."

"What aren't? My smalls? I should hope not. Ah, my trinkets! Really? That's interesting." Ludo leaned across the tall bed as if to converse and tugged at a pillow in the process.

"Leave it!"

"What? Leave what!" Ludo stood back in mock surprise, the pillow clasped to his chest.

The second man arrived at the door. Similar age, similar garb, but hatless and shorn-headed. The Englishman with the hat nodded at the other set of saddlebags. "Take that, there's nothing else that I can see, but check what he brought in with the inn-keeper downstairs before you pay him the remainder."

Shorn-head came into the room. Ludo peered at him, Rakish Hat was familiar in some way – what about this one? This one had a badly pock-marked face, but was otherwise the sort of young man you'd expect to see behind a shop counter or in a warehouse: ordinary. Not doing anything ordinary now, though. He grabbed the stuffed saddlebag, the one that unfortunately rattled, and hastened down the stairs.

Ludo edged closer to the corner of the bed and unhooked a second bed hanging from the post. As he moved, he said, "Oh, come on! Let's be decent about this. I'll let you run off with my loot if you'll let me keep a few bits and bobs that are actually mine. I do need to pay my hotel bills."

"That's your look out," the Englishman said, casting an eye around the room for more bags, giving Ludo just enough time to bring the two moth-eaten bed hangings to his sides.

"Tell me," Ludo said conversationally, "have we met before? I seem to know your voice but can't put a face to you under that hat."

"Can't you?" the English soldier sneered. "I must be improving."

It was exactly the sort of comment Ludo would have made himself and it unnerved him. "You're a soldier, I can see that. Good with a gun; experienced are you?"

"A lot more than you might think." The young man eased the weightier of the saddlebags over his free shoulder and backed towards the open door, keeping the gun trained on Ludo's chest.

His accomplice thumped back up the stairs and hissed, "Come on, let's get out of here."

It was a split second of distraction and Ludo grabbed it. "Hah," he laughed holding the pillow to his chest with one hand like a craven coward and taking hold of the edge of a curtain with the other, "like a London a play, this is. Before you leave, boys, satisfy a gullible traveller's curiosity: whose side are you on? I assume you have come for the jewels, but are you saving them for a future king or taking them to raise extra cash – or taking them for ... I don't know ... to help pay for a republic with no monarch? Just curious."

The young man with no hat and shorn hair pushed Ludo's other saddle bag over his left shoulder and pulled a pistol from his belt. "Does he know who we are?" he demanded.

"No!" shouted his companion.

"Shoot him anyway."

"He'll never find us again – leave him. Let's go, he's not putting up a fight."

Fat chance, Ludo thought. Staying exactly where he was, he looked around the chamber towards the window then back at the door. There was nowhere he could escape, no means of avoiding a lead ball from a flintlock pistol save a length of balding curtain and a feather-filled pillow: of course he wasn't putting up a fight. But he was losing a change of clothing, a bag of Hormuz pearls and far too many of his uncut diamonds and sapphires. He made one last attempt: "If you are aiming for the best price, and I'm assuming you know what I'm carrying, I am the *one* man able to help you." Rakish Hat– who now reminded Ludo of acting midshipman Greenwood – gave him a sharp glance. "Selling them as a job lot won't work, you see." He had their full attention now. "You'll need to select one piece at a time and pretend it belonged to your grandmother. Or – for example – you could say your land has been ruined in the fighting, assuming you're going back to England – or you've lost your house. Whatever you say, you'll have to sell well below true value; otherwise you'll arouse suspicion."

"They're not for sale." It *was* Greenwood.

"I do know you," Ludo smiled amiably.

Shorn-head hissed something at Greenwood.

"Shut up, fool!" Greenwood spat out the words and pushed his companion out of the door, as he did so Ludo wrenched the curtain from its rail and wrapped himself into it with the cushion.

The movement attracted attention and there was an explosion of noise. A hefty thud against his left shoulder. Ludo slumped to the floor.

He waited as long as he could. He waited until dust threatened to choke him and he began to cough, setting off an excruciating, searing pain in his shoulder. "Not dead yet, then," he said to himself, wincing.

Waiting again until he was as sure as he could be that he was alone, Ludo managed to free his right arm enough to pass a hand into his damp, padded leather travel jerkin, which he'd wisely stuffed with feathers from a chateau pillow. He felt inside it to check the straps of two small, canvas shoulder bags, then to the inner pocket of his cambric shirt where he always kept a ruby next to his heart. Touching the protective stone for luck, he then checked the left-hand pocket of his jerkin. The cloak clasp was still there: three balas rubies arranged around a giant diamond. The action made him gasp. The impact of the lead ball in his shoulder – safely above his heart and protective, talisman ruby, but exactly where he'd been stabbed in Spain – was hampering his breathing. The thick curtain, plus the layers of cushion and his padded jerkin had worked like a shield, but the dust the skirmish had raised was suffocating him now.

Struggling against pain, he shifted onto hands and knees then crawled out from under years of bad housekeeping until he bumped into a wall, which was not a wall but the base of the window seat. He used it to pull himself upright. It had gone dark outside. It was night time in a place he did not know, but injured or not he had to get away, immediately. If they really knew what he was carrying they'd be back, especially if they were working for Jermyn, which seemed most likely. He'd been set up and played ... By Gifford Greenwood, acting for Jermyn? Who was not in favour of his queen's wishes and had not wanted him to take the jewels – or who had wanted him to take the jewels so that they could be stolen from him? The loss then easily attributed to a most unreliable agent: "I did warn Your Majesty", he'd say.

So Greenwood had got him to France to lift the jewels – for Jermyn? And if they'd planned it this far, what was going to happen when they realised they hadn't got any of the best pieces? Once they realised that, he was done for – because his pockets and the small shoulder bags under his jerkin were still stuffed with all the most valuable items.

"Help!" Ludo called feebly in English then Genoese and Spanish. What the hell was 'I've been shot' in French?

Chapter 16

Having slept badly yet again, Alina rose fuzzy-headed and ill-tempered and set about her duties. She had established a routine by collecting the older prince, James, and her son from their breakfast and escorting them up to John Hawthorne in the school room for their morning Latin, calligraphy and arithmetic. Princess Mary had begged to be allowed to study with them, to which John Hawthorne made no objection, leaving Alina with nine-year-old Elizabeth, four-year-old Henry and her toddler Hetty.

On her first day in the royal nursery Alina had racked her brain what to do to keep the younger children entertained and decided on her own routine at Crimphele: a morning constitutional could be justified as a 'nature walk' to recognise plants and trees and name birds. It was a good excuse to be outdoors while real servants cleaned their rooms, and it delayed the tedium of the rest of the day.

Putting on coats and the little ones' protective pudding hats took a while, but as soon as they were outdoors Alina encouraged the children to run ahead and use up their energy. It also gave her a brief time to think: she had decisions to make today. Her mind a-whirl with possibilities and obstacles, she dropped Hetty's leading straps then immediately regretted it as the small girl, clutching Etta the poppet to her chest, immediately followed the older children straight to the lake. Its dull green waters were not inviting but Henry and Elizabeth soon invented a game with twigs and dead flower heads.

Choosing a bench out of the wind, Alina sat down to keep watch then got up again to collect Hetty, who had begun paddling her hands in the water. After a brief, noisy protest, Hetty arranged Etta the rag doll in a sitting position on the bench then stood back to admire her. Alina looked at the rag doll, now perfectly balanced at a right angle and smiled. The poppet was made of stitched linen and flannel, with ragged yellow wool for hair, but sitting on the bench, plump around the middle, her arms stuck out stiffly at her side, she looked almost life like. Nothing like the floppy creature that had been dragged through mud and floor dust from Crimphele.

"Piensas que Etta le gusta estar aquí?" Alina asked her daughter, smiling. "She's getting fatter."

Hetty scrunched up her chin and shrugged, then sat on the ground to examine a snail.

"No lo metes en la boca," Alina warned. The little girl shook her black curls, threw the snail away and struggled to her feet, intent on reaching the water again.

Alina stood up caught her by a leading strap attached to the shoulders of her coat and shouted to the children by the lake, *"Niños, ven!"*

Sensing someone behind her, Alina wheeled around to see who it was. There was nobody there – then there was. A tall man in black. Gripped by a sudden panic, she scooped Hetty into her arms.

The person came up behind her: "It's all right, Baroness. I'm sorry if I surprised you."

"Baron Jermyn," Alina gasped, trying to calm her breathing. *"Que susto!"* Hetty struggled to be put down and Alina said, "Please, one moment," and returned to the bench to settle the child there.

Baron Jermyn waited and gestured for her to sit as well. An awkward silence followed. Hetty slithered to the ground and rediscovered her snail. Alina prized it from her pudgy saying, "No, *Cielo no, no,*" in the Spanish way.

"You speak with your children in Spanish, madam." Jermyn said, blandly. It was not a question.

Alina looked at him. "Yes, I suppose so. It's my language, so I suppose I do. They understand perfectly."

"I'm sure they do. But you also speak with the royal children in Spanish, madam, and *that* will not do. That will not do at all."

Alina flushed bright red. Jermyn ruled the queen's household in exile, acting as secretary and chamberlain and, it was gossiped, far more. She couldn't afford to upset him, but she hadn't realised he was watching her, nor that she had been speaking Spanish either. "I'm sorry," she said. "I forgot they have no Spanish."

"Nor need they have. Do you understand, Baroness? You would be doing them a kindness if you spoke only in French like Her Majesty from here on."

"Oh, but my French is not –" Alina bit her lip and rephrased her response: "I never seem to remember. I must, mustn't I?" She gave the chamberlain her most winning smile.

He responded with a hardened stare. "You *must*, madam. If you are to remain with us until we leave for Paris."

"Paris?"

"Yes, finally. I received a letter from Cardinal Mazarin yesterday: our removal to the Palace of the Louvre is imminent. The Queen Regent now welcomes Her Majesty in the capital – the *royal* children will join the *royal* nursery there, of course."

Alina was about to enquire who exactly would be included in the 'removal' but Hetty chose that moment to make another dash for the lake. Once retrieved and once her squirming had body quietened, Jermyn said, "That child should still be with a nurse, she's too young to be with the princes."

It was true: what could she say? Alina extracted a few twigs from Hetty's black curls then a thought occurred to her: "Oh, but, the Queen of France is Spanish. I'm sure the King Louis must speak his mother's tongue. My son does."

It was a foolish thing to say. Baron Jermyn glowered. "No one, no one, I can assure you, speaks Spanish in France. The country is aligned with the Dutch against Spain. We must be most careful, madam. Her Majesty is very anxious to secure the future of her children, and the way things are unfolding in England, well ... Need I say more?"

Alina lowered her gaze, "Yes. No. Of course. I am out of touch with current affairs."

Jermyn looked out across the lake, making no comment, then with the merest bow of the head bade a silent farewell and returned the way he had come.

Alina watched him go, then, taking her daughter's leading straps firmly in one hand, she ushered the royal children back indoors, where she delivered the Stuart children to the schoolroom. John Hawthorne took one look at her face and came to her aid.

"Find them something to do, John, please. I've as good as been dismissed and I need to talk to Marcos to warn him not to use Spanish. We're being watched."

Alina scoured the chateau with Hetty in her arms clutching the poppet Etta. Marcos was impossible to locate and it wasn't until after the evening meal that she was free again to look for him. She finally located him in the stables, where he was paying their carriage driver his retainer from money supplied by Ludo.

"Oh, good. We might need him soon." Marcos gave her a questioning look. She shook her head, "Not here," she said.

As they walked around the rear of the chateau towards the servants' entrance, where they could speak without being overheard, it occurred to Alina that Marcos might be planning to get away. Innocently, she asked, "If you have to leave, Marcos where will you go? Back to England?"

"Too dangerous."

"So you'll go to Sanlucar and take over Ludo's estate?"

Marcos gave a deep sigh. "It might be best – for me anyway. I can't go back to England and to be honest, Alina, I can't stay here."

"Nor you, nor me. The queen is to be lodged in the Louvre Palace, where our services will not be required. We Spanish are not welcome in France."

"*Gracias a Dios*," Marcos said. "How soon are they going?"

"Too soon for me. Having my children in the royal nursery is my – and their – salvation."

"You could come with me."

"To do what exactly? Be your housekeeper?"

"No, well, something will come up."

"Will it?" Alina snorted, then said, "I'm sorry, I ... I ... never mind. I have to get back. Time to make sure the older ones have settled in for the night."

Before she could leave, though, Marcos grabbed her arm. "What Ludo was saying about the cleric, Rogelio –"

"You mean Her Majesty's spiritual advisor?"

"Is that what he is? Ludo said he's a Vatican agent."

"Maybe he is, but things have changed in Rome, haven't they? Everything's changing everywhere, it seems to me. Perhaps he'll get his marching orders as well, when they go to Paris. Sorry, what were you going to say? I *am* avoiding him, if that's what all this is about?"

"No, I was going to ask what you knew about him."

"Me? Nothing, except he apparently tried to drown me, which I have never understood."

Marcos shook his head. "It's something to do with a feud with Ludo. Or with Ludo's past. He was in Amsterdam during that tulip business as well."

"What tulip business?"

"Oh, one of Ludo's merchant ventures; he was selling tulip bulbs if you remember?"

"Vaguely. But how do you get from tulip bulbs to attempted murder?"

"Ha! If you knew the half of it ..." Marcos paused and changed his tone. Surveying Alina, he said. "You're very calm about all this. I'd be terrified if I knew I was in close proximity to someone who'd tried to drown me."

"I wasn't this morning. I nearly had heart failure when I realised somebody was behind me near the lake. It was Jermyn, and the outcome was little better. As to Ludo's bête noir – he may not even know I was the woman in El Escorial – either way, I'm hoping my role in the nursery means he won't risk offending the queen. Jermyn will have me turned off like a lazy maidservant if he can, though."

Marcos stared at her in the gathering winter dusk. "I wasn't planning to leave without you, Alina, if that's what you think. Not like that anyway. I assumed you'd stay with the queen – not want to come with me."

Alina was humbled. Leaning forward she gave him a kiss on the cheek. "Marcos, Marcos, how would I ever manage without you?"

He put his hands on her shoulders and looked her directly in the eyes. "Alina, I have loved you since we met among corsairs on a Santander quay – since you kicked me off your carriage going to Crimphele, since ... always. You know that, don't you?"

"Yes, I know that, but ..."

"But your husband has died and I am still married and we are in a right royal situation here in France."

Alina put a finger to his lips. "Enough," she whispered and turned to go.

Later that evening, as Alina was kneeling on the floor returning a scattered array of wooden horses and soldiers to the nursery toy box, John Hawthorne found her. "I have been summoned to speak the Baron Jermyn," he said.

Alina straightened up, tugging at the bodice of her second dress. "Don't say anything before he does, John. Let him speak first and tell you what is happening in case they are going to keep you on."

"Keep me on? What is happening?"

"They are moving on to Paris and we are surplus to requirements. Although you are useful; they may want to keep you as a tutor for the princes."

"I doubt it," John frowned at her.

Alina gave him a weak smile, "Come to my room and talk to me when you've seen him. Oh, and John, listen: try to find out what will be happening to the queen's confessor from Rome. I need to know if he'll be going with them – that's really important, do you understand?"

"Er, no."

"Well, find out what you can and I'll explain later."

John was back within half an hour. "I have some news," he said. "You may not like it, but I have no choice but to accept."

"Accept what."

"To remain as the princes' tutor and travel to Paris with them – as you suggested. I am to coach them in English grammar and maintain their conversational skills – for the future – in English."

Alina's hands grabbed fistfuls of skirt, "So my children and I will be homeless, and now friendless."

"No, not exactly. Jermyn wants Thomas to stay with the princes. I said he was a studious boy and a good influence on them."

"And he can speak *only English* with them and forget his mother is the daughter of a Spanish grandee, of course, how better to insult us?"

"Alina, calm down. This is not altogether a bad thing. Your son will be the friend and schoolroom companion of the second and third in line to the throne. Think about it!"

Alina collapsed on a chair. "I am thinking about it," she sighed. "I'm thinking I will lose my son, possibly forever, and as you say, I have no choice but to accept."

There was a silence between them, then John said, "I shall look after him – it will be like when you went to be with Her Majesty in London – a temporary separation."

Alina closed her eyes, remembering an earlier separation, when her son, as a new-born baby, had been wrested from her at Crimphele by his so very English grandmother. The thought made her shiver.

John touched her elbow. "I will be like a father to him."

"You always have been. What of Father Rogelio, though? Will he be with you in Paris?"

"I can't say. There was no opportunity to ask. I try to keep away from that man – given that he was in charge of the business I was supposed to expedite with Ludo when we he and I first met, and the fact that I failed to return to Rome as instructed. Father Rogelio has either not made the connection, or it doesn't matter anymore, but either way he repels me."

"Protect Tomás from him, John."

John looked at her sideways. "Of course. As I say, I have reasons of my own to keep a distance from him. I disobeyed his orders. Well, Cardinal Barberini's orders, ultimately. But, Alina, what will you do? You have little Hetty to think of."

Alina looked away, her hands kneading the fabric of her skirt. Swallowing hard she managed to say, "I shall take her to my father's house in Santander. He won't be there I expect, but his wife will, and," she gave a small shrug, "I might come to like her."

John reached out a hand. "That is good news, my dear. I shall be happy to know you are with your family again."

Alina nodded but could not return his smile. John was the only person who knew her full history for she had never told her husband, and Marcos and Ludo only knew portions.

John's blessing meant a lot. She began to relax for the first time in weeks. Suddenly convinced returning to Spain was the right decision, she said, "I must find Marcos, ask him to escort us to Le Havre, at least. We might be able to get a ship for Spain together and then he can go on to Cadiz."

Within days the queen's French ladies were in a dither of excitement – they were going to Paris at last. Jermyn ordered Alina to pack the children's belongings and before she could spend any time with her son, Tomás was squeezed into a coach with John and the younger princes and a lady-in-waiting.

Pushing attendants and servants aside, Alina hastened to the carriage and pulled open the door. She wanted to take her boy in her arms, hug him; tell him she loved him and that they would be together again soon, but she had no way of knowing that, and the expression on his face halted any demonstration of motherly love whatsoever.

Tomás was so obviously terrified she would embarrass him Alina stepped back in surprise and straightened her shoulders, speaking to John instead, she said, "I shall be in Pamanes, near Santander. I will send word when I arrive. Send me word of how you fare in return." She looked meaningfully at her son, who smiled angelically. Fighting back tears, Alina gushed: "We can arrange to go back to England – to Crimphele – when..." When? She had no idea when or even *if* they would see Crimphele again.

Before she could say anything more a footman slammed the door of the coach and the driver set the horses at a brisk walk down the unkempt gravel drive. A pain lodged itself under Alina's left ribs. The scene around her became a blur, but it wasn't tears threatening to escape her, it was a full-blown scream. A hand tapped her shoulder, bringing her back to the moment; reminding her she was being watched.

It was Baron Jermyn. "Madam, come with me," he ordered.

Alina followed him silently, drained of energy, and climbed the stairs to the nursery. Jermyn opened the door and ushered her in. Spread across the rug in the play area were what seemed like a hundred small beads, part of a broken necklace, and various rings. Hetty was sitting beyond the rug on the cold floor, hugging her broken poppet and sobbing. A large female servant was standing over her like a prison guard, arms folded across a formidable bosom.

"Wherever have all these beads come from?" Alina asked, crossing the room to pick up her daughter.

"Beads, madam? Is that what you call them?" Jermyn's voice was dry and sarcastic.

Alina bent down to comfort Hetty. "Etta broken," Hetty sobbed.

Alina took the poppet. Its red felt skirt was torn, an arm almost wrenched from the body, but the greatest damage was a gaping hole in the back of the white cambric body. She examined the torn stitching and touched something very small and hard. A piece of grit? No, a sharp-edged stone. She looked at Jermyn, then at the servant. "What has happened?"

"Tell her," Jermyn ordered the servant.

The servant gabbled something in her native tongue and Alina looked at Jermyn for translation.

Jermyn nodded then said, "Leave us," to the servant and waited until she had gone before he continued. "She says she tried to pack the poppet with the other toys for removal to Paris. Your daughter grabbed it and pulled so hard that the doll came apart. This," he indicated the beads on the rug, "is what fell out."

"My God, she could have choked!" Alina gasped. "What sort of joke is this?"

"A very bad one, madam – for you."

"But ..." Alina went down on her knees and picked up what looked like a small fancy brooch, then realised it was a pendant from a necklace. The size of a large coin, it was an arrangement of pearls set in a crucifix with a central ruby. She reached out and touched what she had taken for beads. "But these are gemstones," she said, scooping up a handful of pearls, "and pearls. Real, beautiful, beautiful pearls."

"The pendant forms part of a necklace given to Her Majesty on her marriage," Jermyn stated flatly.

"But, how did all this get into my daughter's rag doll? She's never separated from it. How on earth...?" But as Alina formed the question, she suspected the answer. Ludo had stolen the queen's jewels and stuffed them inside the rag doll – for Hetty's future.

Sour-faced, Jermyn watched Alina get to her feet and pull the child in her arms. "What I must decide now is whether to inform Her Majesty or whether the news that Baroness Metherall is a thief will be too distressing for her."

Alina stood ramrod straight. "That is a lie, sir. I have no idea how this has happened." It suddenly dawned on her that it had nothing to do with Ludo – Jermyn had arranged it to disgrace and get rid of her. She gave a deep, resigned sigh. "Do as you please, Baron."

Jermyn glared at her, his cold, humourless eyes searching her face. "You are telling the truth," he said at last.

"I am the only daughter of the Condé de Pamanes, a grandee of Spain, sir, I have no need to tell petty fibs."

Jermyn continued his stare. "I was not aware of this."

"I think you were, sir. I tried to tell you myself. Her Majesty, if you remember, sent me to Spain a few years ago precisely because of it."

"Yes. Yes. Forgive me, I may have been hasty. My duties are many and I have been most concerned about Her Majesty's health. I ..., perhaps I have been over-hasty. My apologies if I have offended you, madam."

The change in Jermyn's tone was too sudden. Alina glared at him. "I shall leave within the hour," she said, "with my steward. We have a carriage."

Jermyn raised a hand. "Baroness, I will investigate this matter," he extended the hand to indicate the rug. The jewels were entrusted to – someone. It's possible they may have been taken from him without his knowing. Your steward is –"

"Entirely trustworthy."

Jermyn pursed his thin lips and turned to leave. At the door he paused and said, "You may want to say farewell to Her Majesty. She will be leaving early tomorrow. And madam," he attempted his vulpine smile, "I am aware we may be in need – the queen – may be in need of her late sister's family in Madrid one day, if you follow me? It is possible, that is, not impossible that she may call on you again one day. I should not wish there to be animosity between us."

Alina stared at him coldly then with the briefest incline of her head she said, "It never does to alienate friends, Baron Jermyn. Now, if you will excuse me, I have to pack."

Pushing through the adjoining door to her chamber with Hetty and the rag doll in her arms, Alina kicked it none too gently closed with the heel of her shoe. Leaning back against it, she sighed, "Can things get any worse?"

"Yes," replied Hetty, giving her a big kiss on the nose. Alina didn't know whether to laugh or cry, but she did think she ought to gather at least some of the scattered jewels on the rug before the servant returned.

Chapter 17

"You have become predictable," Rogelio said, "I knew you would be by the river. All I had to do was ask for a foreigner in a black leather hat with cockerel feathers."

"The tail feathers of a rare Indian pheasant, actually."

Ludo pushed his platter of quail aside and drank some wine, grimaced and called for brandy. "Are you here to gloat or to offer me another of your dubious enterprises? You set me up to fail very nicely on this occasion, I must say."

Rogelio made no response, but took a chair and sat down at Ludo's table. Ludo leaned back at exaggerated ease. "So, what brings you to these delightful parts?" he asked. "Not the climate, nor, I regret, the cuisine of this establishment. I'm intrigued; what have you up your soutane for me this time?"

"I'm considering giving it up." Rogelio's mouth twitched but Ludo was unsure if it was meant to be a smile. "The soutane, my calling. Not that it ever was my calling; I was given no choice of careers."

Ludo snapped his fingers for service then said, "I would have thought your role with the Vatican is eminently suited to your skills."

"Perhaps it was – once."

"Ah, I see, you no longer have that role. A new Vicar of Christ with his own team of ... what do they call men such as you in Rome?"

"Useful. Necessary."

"But not as in 'humble man of God succouring the poor and needy' or bringing spiritual ease to the troubled?"

Rogelio's mouth twitched again. "No."

Ludo raised an eyebrow. "Oh, come on tell me why you're here. You have dogged my steps for years, arranged the deaths of innocent people around me, threatened my immediate family. You must be aware that my toleration of your proximity is being sorely tested. Despite being somewhat handicapped," he lifted his left arm in its sling, "my right hand remains strong and I am struggling to stay civil."

"I have come about the jewels."

"Of course you have. What about them?"

Rogelio looked about him then said, "Jermyn and *she whom he cares for* expect you to return to them with the proceeds of the sale or sales you make. Correct?"

"Correct."

Rogelio paused, selecting words. "Cardinal Barberini intended that they should be used to raise money to augment that which Rome has provided the lady in question to ... succeed in the matter she instigated on her marriage in England. There are two items, however, which are of special interest to him and should not be sold under any circumstances. Jermyn erred in including them on his list. I am here to collect them and to make you a certain offer ..." Rogelio paused and looked about him again then said slowly, "What did you mean, I 'set you up to fail'?"

Ludo cocked his head to one side, "Finish what you were saying and I'll see if it still applies. I may have been hasty. But do remember, it was you who found me, and persuaded me in such a forceful manner to come to the lady's aid."

"Me?"

"Father Gregory, then, but you were behind it. He as good as told me so."

The serving girl came with a plate of quail in a sticky orange-coloured sauce and a tumbler of local wine.

"And more brandy," Ludo demanded. "Bring me the flask."

Rogelio began dissecting the tiny fleshless skeleton on his plate with his own knife. Eventually, he said, "You are right in part: I was commissioned to expedite a certain arrangement. 'Plan' if you like. But then I discovered – confirmed – something of a family nature while I was in Genoa, and then, of course, we have had the tragic loss of Pope Urban. Both of which changed matters for me."

Ludo drummed the fingers of his right hand on the table and waited. When Rogelio didn't resume speaking, he said, "And what you learned in Genoa – was it before or after you created the conditions to kill my wife?"

"Your Jewess is dead? I didn't know that."

"She was a good Christian, as was her mother before her."

"*Marranos*! Portuguese converts are never 'good Christians'," Rogelio hissed.

Ludo got to his feet but Rogelio leaned across the board and pulled on his leather jerkin. "Let me finish, please."

"Please?" Astonished, Ludo sat down and gulped the brandy that had that moment been placed before him.

"We are cousins," Rogelio said.

Ludo burst out laughing. "Go on," he said, gesturing with his free hand to hear the rest.

"Actually, I suspected it after the debacle in Amsterdam, when I started investigating your background. I didn't know then about your home in Salé and your time with the corsairs."

Ludo felt a chill crawl up his spine: *the serpent knows where my children are.*

"Then, when you started calling yourself a Doria in Spain, I learned more."

"Go on, let's get it over with."

"We have a mutual grandfather: Agostino Doria, late Doge of Genoa. Our grandfather sent *me* away because I was an embarrassment: my existence would have prevented the betrothal of his wayward son, my father, to a most suitable wife. When I was in Genoa this time, I made a few more personal inquiries."

Ludo swigged down his brandy, gasped and waited, remembering what his mother had told him: Grandfather Agostino had sent an illegitimate grandson to a monastery, and the boy's father had never made any attempt to find him. Knowing that must have been galling, even more so upon learning that the other illegitimate grandson had returned to Genoa with his disgraced mother, who had *chosen* to live with a corsair, and had been housed in the Doria castle at Portovenere. The interpretation suggested a far rosier situation than what had actually happened in Portovenere, but Rogelio could not know that. So it all boiled down to jealousy – exactly as Gabriella had suggested.

"You think you were treated unfairly," Ludo said.

"Think? I know damned well I was. I was sent to a monastery to survive or not on gruel and beatings..." Words fell from Rogelio's mouth so fast Ludo could barely decipher them. "... until one kindly priest took me to Rome and ..." He paused for breath and slurped his wine. "*Your mother* was named in grandfather Agostino's will. She was left land and money."

"Was she? I don't think she knows that, but it explains why her husband took her on." Ludo shook his head. "We never saw a ducat, if there was any money, and as to land –" Ludo stopped: was Rogelio trying to trick him into some other revelation? What? He couldn't possibly know about the hoard Jan Janszoon had hidden above Tellaro – could he?

"As to me," he began again in a lighter tone, "all I have belonged to my late wife, who died because you kept me holed up in a wardrobe. Forgive me if I do not welcome news of our consanguinity. Blame your church not me, you stigmatise the illegitimate ... All that Christian morality, pah! Speaking of which, I hope this is not leading up to a Cain and Abel scenario. Perhaps not – I was not raised among Catholics so my knowledge of the Bible is haphazard." Ludo got to his feet, "I'll bid you good day, Cousin, we have nothing to say to each other of a pleasant nature and I'm sure you are needed elsewhere. I am all but recovered and ready to move on, and you have a very satisfactory career as a confessor to a queen to pursue."

"No, wait! That's why I'm here."

"To check on the lady's jewels, I suppose, except they aren't hers at all, are they? They actually belong to the English, or maybe their king, or the heir to the English crown. Tell me fast or I'm going," Ludo huffed and sat down a second time.

The inn-keeper of the Black Swan, a hostelry along the lines of his previous ill-chosen accommodation, brushed his belly against their table and paused to enquire what they else they would like. "Nothing more, thank you. Make up my bill and add this to it," Ludo instructed.

The inn-keeper lingered within ear-shot until his wife screeched at him from the kitchen and his bulk was edged sideways with Ludo's half-eaten meal through a narrow doorway. Ludo felt a moment of remorse; they had been kind to him here; served him meals in his room until he was strong enough to come down to the common room and risk being seen with a sling. He had no reason to be surly with them, but he was desperate to get away, desperate to get as far from Rogelio as he could. "Well?" he demanded, turning back to *la Bicha*.

"I have a proposal. You have a very considerable fortune with you. It is to be sold and I understand you will be taking a commission, which is as it should be. But I need two named pieces, which cannot be sold."

"So you will be rewarded by the new pope, who will re-instate you into whatever post you have lost to the incoming regime and ... Is there an 'and'?"

"No, listen. You make your sales while I take the two pieces to Rome, and keep the proceeds. Then we use this money to establish ourselves as we should be in Genoa." Rogelio's voice was silky with anticipated success. "We have a number of valuable skills between us. My role with," Rogelio dropped his voice, "the Holy Alliance has given me access to many useful contacts and secrets that can be of value to us, not to mention my network of informers, who could be put to good use. Your spice and silk business could be just the surface of what we are actually trading in."

"A commercial enterprise," Ludo mimicked Jermyn's sneer.

Ignoring him, Rogelio continued, "And together we undermine our legitimate cousins and uncles. Destroy their business if we can."

"An interesting proposition," Ludo said. "One that I set in motion ten years ago as it happens, and can manage perfectly well alone. Why do you think I came back from Goa? To set up shop exactly as you suggest." Ludo rubbed his chin, unsure how to proceed then said, "Apart from not wanting to work with you, cousin, there is also a very big flaw in your plan."

"Flaw?"

"I no longer have the jewels."

Rogelio's eyes widened in his sallow face; his mouth opened and closed.

"Oh, come now," Ludo said, "don't pretend you are surprised. It was you who sent two young men to steal them."

Rogelio shook his head.

"No?" Ludo queried. "Really? Perhaps it was Jermyn. He was very much against the transaction. Perhaps that's why he insisted on making a list of what I was supposed to take – so he'd know what was going into safe-keeping away from his mistress's greedy fingers until their war is resolved." Except as Ludo spoke the words, he knew this was not the case: if Jermyn had been behind the extraction Gifford or partner would have come racing back to collect the missing items. Jermyn would know exactly what was missing and send them back to get it. Ludo placed a hand over the bullet wound in his shoulder – if they managed to find him again, he planned to swear the missing jewels had been taken from his clothes while he lay injured on the floor.

The inn-keeper's eager daughter, Clothilde, had tended his wounds. He could blame her. He'd managed to keep her close like a watch dog *and* avoid any intimacy – her unwashed body repelled him. Clothilde had served him well and he felt somewhat guilty about his ulterior motives. That awareness reminded Ludo that he really had to move on. Not least because of the collateral risk that the wench might actually have found his loot during her ministrations and would be happy to sell the information, once she knew he'd betrayed her affections.

The inn-keeper's other daughter simpered to their table with a jug and spilled a pool of acidic grape juice on their table as she missed Rogelio's glass. Ludo grabbed her pinafore to mop it up. "Quick, before it corrodes the wood!" he laughed. Getting to his feet he whispered something in her ear, making her flush as red as the liquid she was serving and scuttle away with a giggle. Then he turned back to his enemy and newfound cousin. "Shame about the baubles: I can see you might have benefitted quite well. Still, I'm sure someone as resourceful as you with informers in so many useful places will find a means to curry favour with *Papa* Innocent. Farewell, I must be off."

Rogelio flung out a long arm again. "Wait! We could find the jewels together and start that way."

"Father Rogelio," Ludo's voice was a harsh, menacing whisper, "I would not join forces with you if we were shipwrecked and alone on a desert island. You personally killed my cabin boy, José."

"He got himself killed. I didn't touch him."

"You didn't try to save or protect him, either. You also tried to drown Alina – a Spanish noblewoman – in Spain. What was the purpose of that anyway; to cause me pain – suffering? And now, my wife. Do you honestly think I could ever forgive or forget that? Plus, I don't need you."

Rogelio's hooded eyes became a serpent's slits. "It's the other way around, isn't it?" he hissed. "You're lying. You are the one who has set me up to fail! I have to go back to that meddling woman and tolerate her snivelling while you enjoy the spoils of the English Crown Jewels – because she'll never see a single coin, will she?"

"Not if I've got nothing to sell, no."

"Ah, but you have. You can't fool me like that. Oh, no, I'll tell her how you're cheating her, and I'll tell them in Rome, and someone will come for you. Remember I have *very* influential contacts in the Vatican. You can tout your body round every wench from here to India, but you'll not sleep easy in any of their beds, be sure of that. I'll not be set aside like this," Rogelio hissed. "You haven't seen the back of me, *Cousin*, nor your precious mother and children!"

Rising to his feet to look Ludo in the eye, Rogelio rounded off his threats and promises with a curse worthy of a children's fairy tale then insinuated his thin frame through the crowded hostel and disappeared.

Ludo watched him go. "*E allora, la vita è piena di brutte sorprese*," he muttered to himself. Life is full of nasty surprises.

Chapter 18

Le Havre, France, Winter 1644

"This is a foolish undertaking," Marcos said.

Alina wasn't listening, or couldn't hear. Holding her daughter tucked into her cape, she had her head down to avoid the searing off-shore wind. Marcos stopped and Alina bumped into him, causing the child to call out. Marcos took Hetty in his arms; she grew heavier by the day but Alina wouldn't risk letting her walk in the crowded streets for fear of losing her.

Humping the protesting child a little higher in his left arm, he said, "Look at the pretty ships, which one is for us, do you think?"

"That one!" Hetty thrust out a fur-mittened fist, barely missing a grocer's boy carrying a tray of eggs.

"Come on then," Marcos said. "Let's find someone who'll take us to Spain."

They'd tried two taverns already and no crew was risking the bad weather. They shouldn't be risking the bad weather either, he knew, but what choice did they have?

The next tavern was less crowded and more expensive in its decor with polished settles and ladder-back chairs, a blazing fire and a quieter clientele. Passing Hetty back to her mother, Marcos headed for the bar searching his memory for Dutch words and phrases: the Spanish weren't welcome here and being English might attract the wrong kind of attention.

His plan was to find a ship sailing for Lisbon or Marseille and hope whoever took them aboard would listen to their plea to be landed in Santander. Alina said she'd go into a phantom premature labour in the Bay of Biscay if necessary. The Bay of Biscay in mid-winter – it was madness.

As he questioned the inn-keeper a dapper sea-captain-looking man with a recently barbered beard showing patches of white where the sun had not reached addressed him in English. "I'm returning to the Antilles in the New Year. If you are looking for a comfortable berth, a cabin if you can pay for it, with adequate rations and a place at the captain's table for meals, look no further. If you are thinking of warmer climes sooner, that gentleman over there is Henri Tours, he's sailing for Louisiana after Christmas – the man on his right is going up to the St Lawrence."

The place names meant nothing to Marcos, but something made him want to continue the conversation. He had seen pilgrims leaving Plymouth to hazard the voyage across the Atlantic but it had never occurred to him to join them having a healthy business to attend. Now he suddenly wondered if this could be the answer to his personal dilemma: whether to continue punishing himself by staying with Alina or set off on his own and make a completely new start. He bit his lip: dare he escape from here – from France – and leave Alina on her own? Did he really never want to see Plymouth, Joanna and his daughter again?

His head a muddle of conflicting options and emotions, Marcos pulled himself together and asked, "Are there other ships' captains here?" He studied the clients grouped in pairs and quartets, talking in low tones.

"A lot of business goes on in here, my friend. If you're interested in expanding an enterprise or importing tobacco and sugar ..." The dapper sea-captain was fishing and Marcos let him for he had questions of his own.

"As it happens, I am. I have a spice import business in Plymouth."

"Plymouth?" The captain raised an eyebrow.

"Long story," Marcos replied, giving a slight, amiable shrug.

The captain gave him a searching look, then nodded and said, "Life carries us across unexpected oceans: we all have our stories." He shook Marcos's hand in the French manner and introduced himself as Cristophe le Blanc.

Relieved, Marcos let himself relax as le Blanc indicated a group at a round table, saying, "If it's spices you're after, they may let you in if they like the look of you, and if you can offer them good prices or a reason to include you in their transactions. They are setting up an expedition to the West Indies. Fertile lands there. Some say the climate is right to grow Eastern spices." His voice dropped to a conspiratorial whisper and he turned so nobody could see him speak but Marcos, "*Nutmeg* trees."

Nutmeg was the most expensive of all spices, and the most difficult to obtain. As far as Marcos knew it only came from two islands many weeks' voyage beyond India.

"Not without dangers of course," le Blanc continued. "Not an easy enterprise; natives are not welcoming, but a great opportunity for a young man with capital, especially someone seeking a new future."

Marcos turned at his words and met the man's eye. "Thank you," he said, earnestly. "I may consider the idea, but for now I must find a berth for Lisbon."

"You can sail for Brazil from there but New France is a better prospect. If it's Lisbon you want, though, buy me a brandy and I'll ask my friends. Come back this evening and I'll tell you."

Marcos bought the brandy then led Alina back into the cold. Wandering back along the main quay of Le Havre, watching gulls bank away in the driving wind, Marcos's mind wouldn't let go of the trans-Atlantic possibilities. How long would the voyage take? Was it more or less dangerous than Ludo's voyages to India? He stared at the forest of masts in the harbour, each stripped of canvas and clinking frantically in the wind. Could such small vessels really travel so far?

Noticing a bigger vessel, he pointed and said, "That galleon reminds me of Ludo's *Tulip*," but his words whisked away before anyone could catch them. The ship's ornate prow, facing the quay on a receding tide, was indeed very like *The Tulip*. Could it be, he wondered? It wasn't impossible. Ludo had left Chateau Thierry well over a week before them; if he, too, had been delayed by bad weather ... Supposing it was *The Tulip* – where would he be?

Moving closer to Alina, Marcos shouted, "Take Hetty back to the lodging house and get warm. I'll manage better without you."

Alina nodded inside her hood and let Hetty down to the ground, then, holding the straps attached to the child's shoulders tightly, set off down a narrow side street out of the wind. Something told Marcos to retrace his steps. It wasn't impossible Ludo had been in one of the taverns they'd visited – and it wasn't impossible he'd pretended not to see them. Perhaps Ludo had been in the last place, where he'd let himself become distracted by the idea of another sort of life in New France or Brazil.

"Right the first time," Marcos told himself, after returning to the well-appointed hostel and making a stealthy circuit of the tables. Ludo was in a chair by the fire. "Contemplating the fires of hell or just staying warm?" Marcos inquired, taking the bentwood chair next to him.

"Warm? I've forgotten the meaning of the word."

"I thought I saw *Tulip* in the harbour."

"You did. We sail the moment the wind drops. I said that last week, and the week before. Bad planning being here in winter, worse planning getting through the Bay of Biscay before the New Year."

"I know. You'll take us to Santander, though, won't you?"

"As destiny ordains," Ludo sighed.

"You haven't told us your plans," Alina said, speaking to Ludo across the supper table in their Le Havre lodgings.

"And I don't intend to," he replied.

"You do realise I'm only here because you set me up as a thief by stuffing Hetty's doll with stolen jewels." Alina's voice was shrill with tension.

"They *were not* stolen! Those gems and pearls are all mine. Not the rings, I admit. I hope you've still got them."

"What were you thinking? She could have choked to death!"

"I was thinking to provide a little security for you both. Forgive my charity: it won't happen again. Have you sold them yet?"

"No, the poppet came apart and Jermyn took them."

Marcos watched as the spoon in Ludo's hand halted in the air. Custard desert plopped back into his dish. There was silence. Even Hetty, sitting on a plumped-up cushion, remained quiet.

"All of them?" Ludo's voice was an icy whisper.

Alina looked away. "Most of them. They fell out on the nursery floor in front of Jermyn. I managed to – erm – rescue some of the gems, and the pearls, and there were still two rings stuffed in the poppet's legs. I had to give up most of it though, to convince him I wasn't stealing."

Marcos tried to redirect the conversation. "Are you going back to Genoa, Ludo?"

"By way of Lisbon. If I survive the Costa de Muerte."

"For your spice business?"

"Indirectly. I plan to visit the new Lusitanian monarchs, the Duke and Duchess of Braganza."

"Why?" demanded Alina, causing Marcos to wince.

"I have something of interest for them, something special," Ludo rallied.

Leaning back in his chair Ludo gave Alina one of his mischievous one-dimpled grins and Marcos spoke without thinking: "You've got the Crown Jewels. You're going to sell them the queen's jewels."

"How do you know that?" Ludo leaned forward, peering at him histrionically through narrowed eyes. "Who told you that?"

"No one: I was a footman, remember? Footmen have ears."

Ludo laughed. "And did these ears pick up that said jewels were taken from me at the sign of the Leaping Trout near Paris?"

"No, what happened?"

Before Ludo could explain anything, Alina said, "He's bluffing. If they'd been stolen he wouldn't be going to Lisbon, would he?"

Ludo turned to look at Alina. "Actually, it is true. My entire baggage was stolen."

"But you wouldn't have had the most valuable items in a saddle bag. Not the most valuable; they'd be in one of your special pockets. You forget, I know all about your secret pockets," Alina retorted.

"Indeed, you do, *madonna*," Ludo's eyes twinkled and Alina flushed scarlet. "Your mother is too clever by half," he said to Hetty, tickling her under the chin. The little girl chuckled and waved a laden spoon, sprinkling the tablecloth liberally with the last of her custard.

Ignoring the mess, Alina said, "I'm coming with you."

"With me! To do what?" Marcos could see Ludo was struggling to keep his temper.

"To make sure the price you get is appropriate, and then to take the money back to Queen Henrietta Maria. If I do that, she'll know that I wasn't a thief, and it'll help Tomás's chances of getting Crimphele back. She'll tell the King I have helped her and the King will restore Crimphele to us as soon as the war is over."

Marcos gazed at Alina. "Have you just contrived that plan? Just like that?" He snapped his fingers, causing Hetty to laugh again and copy him.

While he and Hetty played snap-the-fingers, Ludo and Alina were locked in a table top battle of wills. Marcos tried to ignore them with the pretty black-haired girl, so very different from his little daughter Mary, tried not to let his mind drift back to playing finger games with Mary sitting on his lap, then sat up straight, noticing the atmosphere had changed.

"That might work," Ludo was saying, "as long as you are willing to masquerade as my wife."

"Ah, no. That is going too far. I am a widow, and a widow who needs to re-marry quite soon if she is to secure a new home. I have to be practical – realistic – the Royalists may be defeated, we may lose Crimphele altogether."

"And you think hooking a Portuguese nobleman in Lisbon is a realistic plan?"

Alina's chin shot up. "As realistic as you selling the Crown Jewels."

"Hush!" Ludo looked about them but the common room was empty of other diners and no servants hovered in view.

Alina suddenly clapped her hands, the way both the Queen and Hetty did when they were pleased or excited. Then, placing a hand on Marcos's sleeve, she said, "Change of plans. We don't need a ship to Santander after all." Making no comment, Marcos got to his feet. "Where are you going?" she asked.

"First, I shall put Hetty to bed then, while you two concoct your *strategy*, I am going out to see a man about a berth."

"But we don't need one, we've got *The Tulip*," Alina insisted.

"You may have," Marcos replied, hoisting Hetty over his shoulder, "but I'm going elsewhere."

"Where?"

"Back to England to ask Joanna a question then, depending on her answer, I – or we – will join a ship to cross the Atlantic for my spice business."

"You can't go back to Plymouth; that's madness!" Alina cried.

"I can and I must," Marcos replied, suddenly absolutely certain he was doing the right thing. It was time to escape Alina's thrall, time – not a good time, admittedly – to get back to having a life of his own without Ludo and Alina deciding it for him.

Marcos had been in bed an hour or so when there was a knock at his door. Wide awake, he stared into the dark: had Alina come to beg him not to go? Was it possible? He sighed, angry with himself. This was exactly why he had to go his own way.

"Come in," he called.

The door opened. It was Ludo. Marcos started to light his stub of tallow but Ludo said there was no need, grown men could talk without candles.

"Now what?" Marcos asked, sitting up.

"Like that is it? You're angry," Ludo replied.

Marcos huffed and lay back on his pillow. "Yes, I'm angry, but not just at you. What are you here for? What can't be said in front of milady?"

Ludo was silent. Marcos, genuinely surprised, said, "It's something personal. That can only be told in the safety of darkness. What is it, Ludo? What do you need me to do?"

"You – nothing. I came to give you this."

There was a dull thump on the blanket beside him. Marcos located a soft leather purse full of hard coins. "Money?" he asked.

"Pieces of eight, various other coins including English sovereigns and a few Dutch florins. You'll be needing it."

"Yes – thank you." Marcos felt guilty about accepting it. "Why?"

"Why am I giving it to you? Oh, because you were once a pimply youth begging to be my servant. Because you helped me in Holland, and in London and Spain."

"You owe me nothing, Ludo. I learned a lot along the way."

"And now it's time to move on."

"Yes, I know; I agree. It is for me, as well." Ludo moved to the tiny, thick-paned window and stared into the night.

"Are we being watched? Followed?" Marcos asked.

"I am, almost certainly."

"By?"

"A man with contacts in every church in every village from Saxony to Sicily and beyond – all the way to Goa in the East Indies."

"Rogelio. Can't you buy him off? What's he got over you that ...? You're afraid of him, aren't you? I've never known you to be afraid: why?"

"I think he knows where my children are."

"Oh, dear God," Marcos felt himself go cold. After a while he said, "You have two possibilities, as I see it."

"Yes, I know: do what he wants or kill the devil, with my own hands, to be sure he's dead." Ludo crossed to the door. Before he opened it, he said, "Aren't you going to ask about Alina? You're angry with her – with both of us – for a reason."

Marcos closed his eyes. "It's a foolish question, but I need to know –"

"What are my intentions?"

"She's vulnerable. She has no husband no home –"

"I know all that," Ludo's voice cut through the chill winter night. "And I understand. She's not the only one with a personal tragedy. We'll have to find a way through it. Making ourselves some money, having a bit fun in the process. If you come up with a better alternative, send me a letter. Speaking of which, a letter can still get to me via Toxo in Vigo. So can you yourself, if push comes to shove in Merry Old England."

The door opened. The door closed. Marcos huddled back under the blanket, clutching the bulging purse of money to his chin like Hetty's poppet. But he did not sleep.

J G Harlond

PartFour
England, Spain and Portugal

Chapter 19

Plymouth, England, mid-winter 1644

Getting into Plymouth on a French fishing vessel was easier than Marcos anticipated. All the sea approaches were guarded night and day, but the skipper slipped between Royalist vessels in the dark, lowering the sails as they passed alongside hulls and under prows until, if challenged, they could admit to being just another fishing village vessel from along the Devon coast, anxious for a catch on a winter's night. Paid, and prepared to make a run for the nearest, safest stretch of coast if they were threatened, the dour Frenchman steered his boat into Sutton Harbour in the early morning light, unchecked.

"You've done this before," Marcos remarked.

"More money in brandy than fish, my friend, but this time I bring in mackerel and onions to keep you safe."

Humbled, Marcos tried to give his thanks, but the skipper was busy for before they had even tied up a crowd of women with empty baskets were gathering on the quay, squawking like the gulls above, each angling for scraps. Not that there would be any scraps from this boat, every morsel would make a broth. The goodwives needed to feed starving children.

The sight of the women's faces, their hollow-eyed desperation, frightened Marcos. He scrambled onto the quay then, hoping his knitted French hat and wispy beard would serve to avoid recognition, he headed for his old warehouse. From across the street it appeared untouched, but then he noticed the side door was open a fraction.

Crossing the uneven cobbles, he stepped inside, expecting to see the warehouse looted down to dust. It was empty and yet full. There was a dull noise like the rumble of men's voices and a smell he couldn't name – an unpleasant smell. As his eyes became accustomed to the gloom, he started to make out shapes, the angular shapes of haggard men and scarecrow boys crouched on the floor, cleaning weapons. The glorious aroma of his distillery, his botanicals, the dried citrus peel and cinnamon bark, the juniper berries and cardamom seeds had been replaced by the stink of humanity. It was worse, far worse than he feared.

He turned back onto the street and set off for Edward Beale's house then stopped at a tavern, deciding it would be better if he had unbiased news of recent events before he confronted his father-in-law, who would spin any tale to be rid of him. The tavern was empty except for two men hunched by a meagre fire. One looked up and nudged the other. The second man stared at him just long enough for Marcos to notice that, despite a heavily pock-marked face he looked healthier, a lot healthier than his companion. Feeling nervous under the man's gaze, Marcos retraced his steps and made haste along the narrow street, then turned uphill from the quay. The two men followed.

As he approached the Beale's fine house with its tall windows and patterned brickwork Marcos wondered if he should walk on past. How many remembered Joanna Beale's husband was a Spanish Catholic? How many assumed he was a traitor? What might Edward Beale have put about to explain his son-in-law's prolonged absence?

Marcos walked on by but as he looked back, he bumped into Edward Beale himself.

"Beg pardon," said the man who had once welcomed him as a replacement for his only son, who had died too young, as a replacement heir for his business. Beale's sense of enterprise had helped finance his first jaunt to London, to obtain a Royal Warrant to supply palaces with wines and spices.

"Father?" Marcos said, giving Beale the chance to deny him and go on his way.

Beale did not deny him. Instead, he placed a finger on his lips, took him by the arm, and led him through the stable yard gates.

As Marcos turned to close the gates, he caught sight of the two men from the tavern: would-be robbers ready to take advantage of a solitary man, or spies for any number of causes. The skin on the back of his neck prickled.

Edward Beale pointed at the door to the transport yard office, where a mild-mannered foreman with one leg shorter than the other had once checked orders and kept tabs on which drays were needed where and when. Marcos tried to remember the foreman's real name; everyone referred to him as Hobble. As he crossed the threshold to the now-empty office, Beale took his arm again, pulled him in and bolted the door behind them.

Everything was the same but different, here, too. Ledgers, musty relics of a prosperous past, were propped between bricks on a shelf. The desk itself had a layer of dust and straw as thick as a horse blanket.

Ignoring the surroundings and standing with his back to the door, Beale said, "I should welcome you back lad, but you'll regret coming."

"As long as *you* don't regret my coming," Marcos replied warily, loosening the strings of his cape over his woollen jacket then removing his hat.

Beale sniffed. "I do and I don't. For a good while I feared you wouldn't – for Joanna's sake – now for the same reason I do. You were a good lad so I thought you'd be back, but then

I hoped you wouldn't be. Getting you out was for all our sakes, you know that don't you?"

"Yes. But I never was a spy."

"No, course you weren't."

There was a silence. Beale chewed his inner cheek nervously then said, "We've had it hard here, boy. And it's getting worse. Traitors are giving us away now, getting out and making it easier for the King's men to get in. Two of them were caught this week. They were put to the rack – *tortured* for information then ... You can guess the rest. There's a General living among us here now from Cromwell's army, a real bastard."

Marcos heard the warning in his father-in-law's voice. "I heard Parliament was winning. I heard ..." he stopped in time. Saying where he'd been in France and who he'd been with was a death sentence in Plymouth.

"You'll want to see Joanna," Beale said, lost in his own thoughts

"Of course. And Mary, how is she?" Marcos couldn't keep the excitement from his voice.

Beale shook his head. "We lost her, poor little mite. Got a cough and cold and then a fever and...."

Marcos felt the ground under him shift. He put a hand out to steady himself – little Mary, gone. A lump rose in his throat and he clenched his fists as tears welled in his eyes. "Was it peaceful? Did she suffer much?" he asked, but Beale wasn't listening.

"... we had a physic made up by the 'pothecary but ... then my goodwife caught it. They went within a day of each other. It's just Joanna and me now, and an empty house and an empty yard and no business, and, dear God, I wish it were all over for me as well."

Marcos stared at the old man, for that was how he now saw him. Beale had lost his swagger, his florid cheeks and his certainty; his clothes hung from bony shoulders. If this had happened to Edward Beale, what might his pretty wife be like? "And Joanna?" he asked.

"She'll be in the kitchen. We've no maidservants. No food here, so there's no gossiping time-wasters in pinafores, neither."

"May I go to her?"

"No." Beale moved against the door. "There's no point. You won't be stopping, and you'll only go making her unhappy again with foolish words. I can't have you here, boy, you must see that, 'specially not with talk of traitors and betrayal everywhere. You'll have to go back where you've come from, and God help you if you say you've been here."

"But ..." Marcos remembered the two men who'd followed him from the tavern and said no more.

"Listen, Mark," Beale's voice was cold, insistent, "now your little Mary has gone from us there's nothing to show there ever was a marriage, you understand me? You have no claim over my Joanna anymore."

Marcos felt a lump rise in his throat again and swallowed hard. He raised a hand but no words came.

"Here," Beale said, crossing the small office and thrusting a canvas bag containing something bulky into Marcos's chest. "This belongs to you. It'll serve to show why you visited me if you're stopped, which you will be in that fancy cape."

Marcos clutched the bag. "Joanna and I were married in church," he said, grappling for a reason to stay.

"Wasn't legal, wasn't binding. You're a Catholic."

"So were you and all your family at the time."

"No, we weren't." Edward Beale's eyes glittered in the feeble light from a filthy window.

Marcos knew he was beaten. He gave the bag a shake, "What is it?" he asked.

"The last of your precious spices. The end of our partnership. You owe me nothing: I owe you nothing."

"And our Royal Warrant to serve the Crown?"

"What crown – where? Cromwell will win this fight. Parliament will rule the entire country soon and there'll be no special warrants ever again. Quite right, too." Beale unbolted the door and strode towards the gate.

Marcos started to follow him then made a dash for the house and the kitchen. At first he was confused, Beale had said they no longer had servants but there was a girl wiping a copper milk pan in the scullery. It wasn't Joanna, she was too thin and far too dowdy; Joanna had loved her frills and ribbons. The girl turned around and Marcos took an audible gasp: hair scraped up under a cotton cap, a plain white collar over a homespun brown dress, this Joanna was no one he knew.

Joanna too took an audible gasp, but not of pleasure. "What you doin' here?" she snapped. "Go away!"

"Jojo," he murmured, "what's happened?" It was a foolish question, it was obvious what had happened, Beale and his daughter had adopted Puritan garb and attitudes to survive. And he was a liability to them. Despite this – or because of it – he said, "Come with me, Jojo. I've come to ask you if you'll travel with me to the New World. To New France, if you like, there are islands with spice trees and good land," the words fell from him in a jumble. "Or we can go to my home and live in a *cortijo* – it is very big and I can make wine and we can live well. We can be rich, you can have lovely clothes again and ... and your father can come. We'll make a new life there. My mother –"

"You mazed in the head, boy?" Joanna interrupted, snapping at him. "How'm I to go to Spain? It's full of foreign people that don't speak my language."

"But you could learn Spanish – from me."

"I don't want to learn. I'm a good girl, I'm loyal to my father and to Parliament and I don't want you near me ever again."

"But Jojo ..."

"Get out!" The milk pan flew across the kitchen and crashed into the dresser. Marcos watched it fall to the stone floor, hoping the dent would act as a reminder of their one-time happy marriage whenever Joanna used it.

Turning to leave, he noticed his father-in-law in the doorway. Beale nodded at his daughter in approval and stood aside to let Marcos pass without a word.

Chapter 20

Marcos wandered in a daze back down to the quay. The French fishing boat was still there but there was nobody aboard so he sat on the steps to wait. The three man crew would be back for the next tide. An icy wind burnt his ears. He stuffed the canvas bag Beale had given him into the wide inner pocket of his cloak, pulled the woollen cap down over his ears, then wrapped himself in the thick woollen cloak more tightly and stared unseeing at the choppy green water. Something nudged him from behind. He started to topple forward into the harbour then was pulled backwards as his head was covered in a rough sack. Grain dust got up his nose making him sneeze and choke. He tried to get his arms free from the folds of his cloak but he was being manhandled forward onto a boat. First, there was the sound of oars in rowlocks, then the sound and rhythm of a small boat being rowed out to sea.

The sack was removed under a ship's towering hull. Two men in homespun browns were pointing expensive pistols at his chest, while two other men steadied the boat with their oars, then manoeuvred it until they reached a rope ladder.

"Up," said one of the men with pistols.

Marcos climbed the ladder, tripping awkwardly on the front of his cloak, and swung himself onto the deck. A man in a naval pea-coat was waiting for him. Another in Royalist colours stood beside him. One of the homespun brothers, the one with a badly pock-marked face reached the deck behind and pushed Marcos forward as the Royalist led the way to a narrow cabin. Marcos was shoved inside the cupboard-like space and the door was bolted from the outside.

Leaning against the wood, Marcos tried to distinguish voices. He lay down on the narrow bunk and tried to pretend whatever was happening didn't matter. "I am nobody now," he said out loud. "I wanted to be *un hidalgo*, and I became a servant. I wanted to be a wealthy merchant, and I became a steward and then a nameless footman. I am nobody. Nothing matters anymore."

Except as the hours went by and the gentle roll of the ship became a steeper rise and dip, he let his mind remember a little girl called Mary with yellow hair and pudgy fingers. And he realised that if he felt this strongly about his lost daughter it explained why his own mother had tried to keep him so close. And that meant he had failed her, too. If he escaped – *if* he escaped – he would go home to Sanlucar and stay there forever.

The bolt was drawn; a bowl of broth and a beaker of wine were set on the floor by a cabin boy. Then he was alone again until the next morning when the ship berthed.

There were no pistols this time and he was treated with courtesy. But he was a prisoner, of that there was no doubt. First, he was escorted to a blockhouse fortification overlooking Plymouth Sound, from there he was escorted by a soldier in Royalist colours to a vast Tudor-style mansion.

"Where am I?" he asked the soldier.

"Mount Edgcumbe, sir. Home of Sir Piers Edgcumbe."

Marcos tried to get more information but the soldier went deaf, evidently regretting the little he'd already imparted. It meant nothing to Marcos. Nothing until he was escorted by a liveried footman into a palatial drawing room and left there on his own, save for the footman, until two new men entered. One was very young, very dark, very tall and very handsome. He was not introduced. The other man, elegant in yards of lace and in his thirties at least, appeared to be the host. They were joined by a third man, who addressed the first as Your Highness. Was this Prince Charles? He had his mother's Medici hair and eyes – but twice his father's height. Marcos held himself taller, waiting to hear why on earth they had taken him at gunpoint and brought him to meet a future king.

But the future king had more pressing matters. "You deal with it, Greenwood," he said to the third man and left the room, followed by the man Marcos assumed to be Sir Piers Edgcumbe.

Suddenly aware that he was still wearing his woollen hat, Marcos pulled it off his head and felt himself starting to sway. He put out a hand to steady himself: he had not slept for two days, and apart from the broth and wine, he'd barely eaten anything since they left France.

Greenwood said, "Are you all right, sir? I do apologise, we have been remiss. Please, take off your cloak and sit down." He nodded to the footman who retrieved the cloak, but not before Marcos removed the spice casket.

Taking a seat on a brocade chair, and placing the canvas bag that had miraculously remained with him, on his lap, Marcos looked at his interlocutor. A man somewhere in his twenties with a youthful appearance, but used to responsibility, and on personal terms with the heir to the throne.

"Gifford Greenwood," he said, introducing himself. "Forgive the cloak and dagger treatment, finding you was by way of serendipity and we couldn't risk you returning to France." He paused and studied Marcos's weary face. "You look exhausted, can I get you something? I'd prefer it if you didn't faint." He rang a small bell. Another footman appeared then disappeared.

A few minutes later, as Marcos ate a piece of chicken breast and sipped small beer, Greenwood started to explain how and why he was at Mount Edgcumbe. "We've had quite a time trying to locate you, Mr Almond. I didn't know about your being in France as well until it was too late and you were crossing back to England or I would have sent for you there. Luckily, my men got into Plymouth before you. And luckily, we've got both you and them out again. Tricky business that." He smiled.

Marcos tried to smile back but he was so confused he ended up blinking. He wanted to ask how 'they' even knew he existed.

Greenwood intercepted his question. "You want to know how I know about you, of course you do. We get information and messages, you know, and your being in France with the queen brings me neatly to the matter I need to discuss. It's regarding some items of special value." He looked meaningfully at the bag placed on a small table at Marcos's side.

Marcos frowned. "It has got nutmeg in it, I think, by the smell. I haven't opened it."

"Really? Well, now might be a good moment, don't you think."

Inside the bag was a small casket. The casket was locked. Marcos didn't have the key. He felt a complete fool.

"Not to worry," said Greenwood. "It doesn't look a very strong a lock, have a go at it with your knife."

Marcos did as he was bid, prizing the eating knife under the lip of the casket and wrenching it up – to reveal a bundle of cotton pouches.

"Aha!" laughed Greenwood.

Marcos opened the first pouch: nutmeg, as he'd thought. He passed the pouch across to Greenwood. His face registered disappointment.

The second pouch contained cloves, the third, cardamom seeds."... I'm a spice merchant – or was," Marcos said. "I had a Royal Warrant to supply Whitehall."

"Did you? What interesting people you two are."

"Two? Mr Beale is –"

"Not Mr Beale. I speak of one Ludo da Portovenere."

"Ah, I see."

"Do you? That's good. He has something – various things belonging to the King, to England really, and Prince Charles feels very strongly that these items should be returned to us forthwith."

Marcos waited, a tactic he'd learned from Ludo. Gifford Greenwood got up and paced the fine carpet, staring at its blue and gold design then started again in a more conciliatory tone. "There was a misunderstanding in France. Her Majesty believes it necessary to sell her jewels to raise money for her husband, but His Highness the Prince of Wales doesn't believe such a drastic..." Greenwood searched for an appropriate word, "...measure is actually necessary. We have retrieved some of them – the jewels – but now I learn the most valuable and the most antique and historic ... that your friend or partner, whatever you choose to call him – still has them."

"Ludo da Portovenere? He was my partner in an enterprise, yes, at one time. Originally, he was my supplier; he arranged shipments of these spices to Plymouth for me." Marcos tapped the spice box, wondering how far the truth would get him into trouble. "We had a business arrangement before the war – as I did with Mr Beale – but it's over now – with both of them. Mr Beale is in Plymouth ... Don Ludovico is ... wherever he is. We went our separate ways some time ago. Ludo has a business in Goa, in the East Indies, he may have returned there."

The 'Don Ludovico' had slipped out but Greenwood caught it. "Of course, you're Spanish, aren't you? Taking a double risk returning to Plymouth, I must say. That took guts." Marcos could feel Greenwood watching him for a reaction. "Or perhaps not. Perhaps you are welcome in Plymouth. Your wife and father-in-law are there, after all."

Marcos closed his eyes. "I'm not a spy, Mr Greenwood. Do you honestly think a Spanish Catholic is welcome in Plymouth?"

"Your looks belie your nationality. You are fair, and speak fluent Dutch, I am told."

Marcos looked up, frowning, "Yes, so?"

"The Dutch have been fighting to rid themselves of the Spanish yoke for years, and yet you lived there."

"Your informer could have told you how we had to get out of Amsterdam. We were not welcome; and I for one shall never return."

"We – are we are back to your Don Ludovico? What were you doing there, by the way?"

"Selling tulip bulbs."

Gifford Greenwood burst out laughing. "That's so ridiculous it might even be true." He turned on his heel and snapped, "And in Plymouth – what have you been doing there in the past twenty-four hours?"

"Personal matters: I needed to see my wife."

"Naturally. How touching." Greenwood raised an eyebrow inquiringly "And she ...?"

"If you must know, she couldn't get rid of me fast enough." Marcos kept his voice flat but the admission raised a lump in his throat.

"That is good to hear. Does that mean we can rely on you? That you won't be going back there?"

"No, I won't be going back there. Why?"

"Because I need to ask you a serious question, which, superficially, is naïve but will help me to make a decision."

Marcos shrugged. "Ask your question."

"Where do your loyalties lie, Mr Almond, or should I say Don Marcos?"

Now Marcos burst out laughing. "Yes," he said, "Don Marcos will do very nicely, as you English say." He paused, then said, "My loyalties – good question. Actually, this is what it is all about, my coming back to Plymouth."

Gifford nodded his head as if understanding. "Go on."

Looking ahead of him, avoiding eye contact, Marcos said, "Ten years ago, my mother allowed me to sail with Ludo da Portovenere as his servant. We went to Amsterdam, where he enabled me to participate in selling tulip bulbs. He helped me get quite rich, showed me how to make money out of money, then helped me get out of speculation before I lost it all. Later, he helped me get my spice import business going, and against my wishes set us up with a Royal Warrant. I suppose I should be loyal to him, if I am loyal to anyone. But nowadays, fortunately or unfortunately, we do not always see eye to eye."

Greenwood sat down and elbows on knees leaned forward. "I should tell you I do know your Ludo. I have sailed with him in fact."

Marcos looked up, surprised, then not surprised. Greenwood looked like a dandy youth, but he was trusted by a monarch and apparently worked directly for the Prince of Wales.

"Let's say I am aware that Ludo's own concept of loyalty is – flexible," Greenwood added.

"If you know that what are you asking me, Mr Greenwood? What do you want?"

"We are looking for someone who will take risks, and know when to stop taking risks as well, a brave man, but not a fool. Someone who will do as we request and not be tempted to betray us because of a private sense of duty. Would *you* be prepared to cross back to the continent and retrieve what belongs to a king who rules by divine right – as do your monarchs in Spain?"

Marcos leaned back in his chair. He was being asked to go after Ludo to get whatever it was Ludo had thought valuable enough to keep out of his saddlebags. He was being asked to steal from Ludo. The only way out was to agree to do it then disappear. He looked across at the window, catching a glimpse of a clear sky, knowing the open sea was out there and that once aboard a vessel he could slip into any port and change ships and disappear. "It would be difficult, but I believe he was sailing for Lisbon," he said.

A smile spread across Greenwood's fair features. "Difficult perhaps, but that is good news. We have a strong relationship with Portugal, and a very effective agent – ally – there to boot. I shall contact him directly and ask him to keep an eye open for our mutual friend. You are not afraid to go to Portugal, are you, being Spanish? I must say your nationality is proving a burden to you. Perhaps you should change it."

"Mmm," Marcos replied, missing the innuendo in the final phrase so he was caught off guard when Greenwood surprised him with an offer he couldn't resist.

Taking the murmur for assent, Greenwood said, "In that case, I am instructed by the Prince of Wales to tell you, that should he, sadly, attain the throne sooner rather than later – I'm paraphrasing here, of course – that you will be welcome not only to live on English territory in perpetuity, but would be given a house and lands."

Marcos's eyes opened wide.

Greenwood's wide, blond moustache twitched with genuine good humour, "There might even be a knighthood, you know."

Un hidalgo, with an estate and crest: a coat of arms. At last. A scene flashed before Marcos's eyes: he was sitting at the dining table in the Crimphele family room with Alina, Meg was serving them food and addressing him as 'milord'. Not Crimphele itself of course, that was the Fulford property, but somewhere very nearby.

"Tell me more," Marcos said, trying not to grin.

Chapter 21

Vigo, Spain, New Year, 1645

An inner voice insisted Ludo put into to Vigo before sailing on to Lisbon. The crew he'd scraped together in Le Havre were mostly other captains' rejects and those so desperate for pay they'd risk the Bay of Biscay in winter seas, and from what he'd seen of them so far, he'd need local mariners to get any further round the Galician Costa da Morte then into Lisbon in one piece.

Ludo was ill at ease and out of sorts. Seeing little Hetty every day only served to remind him that two other young lives depended on him in Salé, if they were still there. If they had even arrived. He'd given Captain Guthrie clear instructions how to get into port safely, but even with Salé natives aboard there were all manner of dangers involved. To compound his worries, nobody knew where he was so nobody could send him any messages, except via Toxo in Vigo, which was another reason it was expedient to head there now. The only good thing about the voyage so far was that acting as his own captain and getting *Tulip* safely around the perilous coastline was a full-time undertaking. He needed to be on deck as much as he possibly could – thus avoiding Alina and re-starting the argument about her joining him in Lisbon.

He understood Marcos's need to return to England; he understood why he was torn between moving to the New World and starting again or returning to Sanlucar and living on the *finca* there: Marcos's ultimate decision would make sense to him, but Alina's determination that she should be part of his enterprise in Lisbon made him very nervous.

Alina kept to her cabin except when entertaining Hetty on deck, who needed a watchful eye at all times. The very image of his impish mother Gabriella, Hetty was a small person to be reckoned with and despite his duties, Ludo found an excuse to spend time with her every day. Before they left Le Havre, he would take her with him while making arrangements for *The Tulip* – while Alina was with her dressmaker. As the daughter of a Spanish grandee and about to meet the Duchess of Braganza, now the Queen of Portugal, Alina needed to look the part ... although quite which part Ludo had yet to decide.

Alina had persuaded him that in the matter of the jewels her presence was to his benefit, which was possibly true. She was a baroness with links to the royal court in England in her own right; her son was being educated with the Stuart princes in the Palace of the Louvre. Alina could make the necessary transaction with the Duchess of Braganza on her own – if he let her.

But the warning voice whispering in his ear about the voyage was also nagging him about Lisbon. He could be accused of theft the moment he arrived for what he had perpetrated during his visit there four years ago. He could deny it perfectly, saying he had never seen the contents of the chests and caskets he'd been employed to take from Lisbon to Oporto, so how could he know anything was missing? Then there was the manner of how he had acquired *The Tulip* in the first place – from under the harbour-master's nose in Lisbon a few years before that. It wasn't an auspicious start to the transaction of a lifetime, the one final deal before he took his gains and settled down somewhere safe from self-proclaimed cousins and belligerent Royalists once and for all.

They celebrated Christmas on board and arrived in Vigo the day before 'Reyes', the Spanish Twelfth Night festivity. Ludo sent a boy to the quayside and Toxo returned with him to pilot *Tulip* into a sheltered berth. Then, somewhat embarrassed at his new role as host, Toxo invited Ludo and Alina to stay at his new house.

A solid, square, stone-built edifice, Toxo's house stood a short distance from the busy harbour on a hillside. As they approached in a covered cart, Ludo studied the roof above the high hedgerow and said, "You've done well, Toxo."

"Thanks to you, *Patrón,*" the wiry Galician responded. "You saved us, Javi and me and our families – once you'd stopped trying to kill us in colanders. We were just about done for that first time in Lisbon before we met you; we thought we'd lost everything. Then we damned near lost our lives!" Toxo barked out something approaching a laugh.

Ludo nodded at the memory. He had put them at very grave risk, testing the sea-worthiness of an ancient caravel in the Tagus Estuary. The vessel didn't sink but they'd been fired on by cannon, almost certainly at Rogelio's command. Setting the memory aside he said, "So, you've grown land-legs at last. You'll not be returning to the East Indies with *La Magdalena* for another cargo?"

"No. Nor to Plymouth, neither, not while the English war goes on, and maybe then not ever. Is Marcos safe, do you know?"

"He's just gone back there."

Toxo crossed himself and said, "He should go back south to Sanlucar where he belongs, do the same as Javi and me. It's time to stay home now and enjoy what we've got, not take more risks."

"Wise words," Ludo sighed, knowing he should heed them.

They drove on in silence save for the scratching sound of bare hedges along the sides of the cart and Hetty fell asleep on Alina's lap with the rhythm of the pony's steady trot. After a while, Toxo turned into an even narrower lane and the normally taciturn mariner started the conversation anew. "When my eldest girl got married, we set them up with a fishing boat. Javi's done the same for his eldest."

Ludo smiled, "Living off the younger generation now then."

"Don't see why not, we done enough to help them."

Toxo drew the cart to a halt at a low iron fence and a small boy with a large catapult appeared from around the side of the house to open the gate. As he did so a crowd of clucking russet hens scrambled out to root along the hedgerow. Hetty woke with a start and started to cry, then caught sight of the hens and clapped her hands. "Hetty kickens!" she shouted and tried to climb out of the cart to join them.

Ludo got out before her and swung her into the air, joining in her excitement, but then caught the expression on Alina's face; she had gone white. A gaggle of matronly geese with ample grey bosoms and starched white wings hove into view. Another awkward memory. A flock of geese had contributed to the obstacles preventing him from taking Alina away with him when he'd gone to fetch her at Crimphele, after the Amsterdam business. He'd wondered for years whether she'd really have been grateful if he'd tried harder – let his cut-throat corsairs get her. If they could have had a happy life together after all.

Ludo set the child into the crook of an arm, making sure her repaired rag doll Etta was safe from falling into the mud and strode towards the open front door, leaving Alina to deal with her past on her own, as she deserved.

Alerted to their arrival by the geese, Toxo's wife and offspring emerged from the house in order of age or height, the tallest first. There were seven children between marriage age and five or so; then two more young women appeared with babes of their own in their arms. Ludo tried to catch Toxo's eye, but he kept his head down except to introduce Mrs Toxo as Maria del Mar, who everyone called Maree. A square shouldered, square faced woman designed to match her house with abundant, scraped-back white hair stuffed under into a no-nonsense cotton cap, Maree barely reached Ludo's chest. She leaned back in an attitude of wonder to study him – for she had no doubt heard a great deal about him – then flushed beetroot red and gabbled a greeting in Gallego. Standing on the tips of her wooden patens she tried to kiss him on the cheek, then fell back in confusion and began pointing at her brood, racing through their names, of which Ludo caught about one in three: Santiago, Carmiña, Victoria, Rosario, Jaunito, Blanca, Jorge ... and various others. Mrs Toxo then noticed Alina, who was still sitting in the cart because, Ludo realised, nobody had come to help her out.

Groaning with annoyance, for this was not the time or place to play the great lady, Ludo set Hetty among the younger children and returned to the cart. Standing to attention like a footman, he ceremoniously extended a hand. Alina inclined her head graciously and got to her feet, but before she reached the ground Ludo hissed, "I owe this family much, do me the favour of some generosity of spirit."

Alina gave him a superior look then, surveying the muddy track, lifted her considerable skirts and walked towards the house, ignoring his offered hand. Behind her, Ludo raced through alternative ways to introduce her, including the temptation to tell them she was his floozy. Not that he had to, because Toxo, who had known Leonora in Goa and was as perceptive as he was taciturn, had steadfastly refrained from even looking at her.

Expressionless, Alina paused in front of the dumpy Mrs Toxo and waited. Giving an inward sigh, Ludo said, "Doña Maria del Mar, permit me to introduce the *la Baronesa* Metherall."

Toxo's boys gaped; the girls dropped in various attempts at a curtsey; and Mrs Toxo patted her chest in a fluster. There was a collective kerfuffle as the children broke ranks as fast as they could, each of the older offspring finding a plausible excuse to be elsewhere. A smaller boy and girl, not understanding the concept of a *baronesa*, took the opportunity to get some free time away from their chores by each taking one of Hetty's hands and wandering away. Ludo followed their progress to the side of the house with his eyes, straining to hear whether Hetty was in for the delights of a henhouse or a pond. Toxo disappeared in another direction with his pony and cart. That left Alina alone, towering above the goodwife. *There you are*, Ludo thought, *and serves you right.*

Then Alina confounded him by taking Mrs Toxo's hand, smiling into her eyes and chattering away at her in Cantabrian Spanish. Mrs Toxo instantly fell in love and they were led into the house as long-lost members of the family.

They stayed in Vigo for the next week, shut indoors by a rare, persistent storm of driving snow. Toxo and the older boys finally ventured out on foot with two handcarts for food and fuel, and Ludo, who was desperate for the open air, joined them.

They walked in single file between walls of snow, following in Toxo's footsteps except where he disappeared up to his waist. Despite chilling parts he would have preferred to keep warm, Ludo felt his spirits lift and began to sing a bawdy sea shanty. Picking up the chorus very quickly, the boys joined in with grins as wide as summer-sliced melons, and in this way they pushed on until they reached the town's maze of slippery alleys and the rutted, filth-strewn main street. Shopkeepers had spread wood shavings but it made little difference. Ludo took shelter in a tavern, which was entirely empty save for the inn-keeper's wife and daughter, while Toxo went to find his brother-in-law, Javi. The boys were detailed off for supplies.

When Toxo arrived back at the inn an hour or so later he was accompanied by his brother-in-law, the faithful Javi, and a third man. Standing at the door to shake snow from his cloak, the third man was revealed to be a priest.

"Don Ludovico?" he asked, as they joined Ludo beside the fireplace.

Ludo, standing with his back to the blaze still warming his nether regions, looked from Toxo to Javi, who ignored his annoyance. "Yes," he said, it being pointless to deny it.

"I have a message for you." The priest reached into a pocket and extracted a folded letter.

"A message?" Ludo enquired. "Have we met? I have been in Vigo before but forgive me, I don't know you and I don't attend Mass."

"No, no, I am Padre Ramon. I know of you from – erm – well, from asking." He pushed the letter out as if it were burning his blue-tipped fingers. "It comes from France. All the way from France," he added as if by explanation, then looked about furtively. Mentioning France in Vigo was unwise; local mariners and *tertios* sailing out for the Low Countries risked French guns along their voyage.

Ludo took the small square of folded paper. The priest stood back and waited. "Oh, you want me to open it." Ludo kept his voice light and did what was expected, turning only slightly, so the contents were not visible.

I am informed that not all the goods were stolen. Return with what you have to the Palace of the Louvre and the matter will be concluded without penalty or sanction. If you fail to do so before Ascension Day, we shall locate your family to ensure you have understood our message and what is required of you. R

Had there been a previous message? Or was this confirmation of Rogelio's verbal threat in the hostel on the banks of the Marne? Ludo looked at the priest and enquired, "When is Ascension Day?"

"Fortieth Sunday after Easter."

"And that's in March or April this year?"

"Resurrection Sunday is April sixteenth, I believe."

"Ah, good, that should just about give me time." Ludo read the note a second time and threw it into the flames.

The priest watched the paper catch fire and gave an embarrassed cough, then said in Castilian Spanish, "The letter, this letter – that is – I have to say when and how it was delivered and that I delivered it by hand, from my own hand to your hand, Don Ludovico."

"Well you have and you can." Ludo clapped the priest on the shoulder and called for drinks.

"Yes, but a reply is expected. Is there no reply?"

"Not that I can think of."

The priest, a man in premature middle-age, balding and weary from tending a flock always at the mercy of the elements, took a deep breath. Ludo understood his dilemma but there was nothing he could do, apart from write a meaningless reply, which would be misinterpreted as the odious Rogelio saw fit. He put a hand on the priest's shoulder, more gently this time. "Tell your messenger that I will return my compliments to the author of this note when I have something to report."

The priest gave an audible sigh of relief and said in a dramatic whisper, "You report also. I see. I *understand*."

Ludo gave him a conspiratorial wink and Padre Ramon accepted a clay beaker of wine from a proffered tray a happier man. Ludo reached for his more slowly, wondering how fast he could get to Lisbon, and whether to continue with his original plan. Then, to what extent Alina and Hetty were also at risk: Rogelio had a mortal way with innocents.

On the way back to the house, Ludo found a stretch where he could walk beside Toxo. "I need to take *Tulip* into Lisbon," he said. "Much sooner than I wanted."

"Bad weather for that."

"I know. Can you find me a good local pilot? Someone who knows the coast like you do? I need deck hands, too. Local boys, if possible."

"Javi can pilot you; I'll do boatswain's duties."

"I thought you two had retired."

"Not all the time, we're not," Toxo huffed.

"Excellent. That makes you *Tulip*'s new captain. Thank you."

That evening there was a grand dinner in the Toxo household with fresh food instead of the endless salted cod they'd been consuming. Outdoors, the snow drifted softly across frosted window panes. Indoors, there was warmth and jollity and a sense of safety, and Ludo knew it was madness, but he had to leave as soon as possible. As the main course came to an end, he tapped his good crystal goblet and announced his travel plans.

The family were sitting in order of height on two sides of a long dining table, with Ludo at one end and Alina at the other. Hetty was next to her favourite, a serious girl called Blanca, who never tired of retrieving Etta from wherever she had been abandoned. All eyes turned on him with a combination of surprise and horror.

"You can't go nowhere in weather like this!" Mrs Toxo exclaimed. "It's madness."

"Oh, I agree. My own thoughts exactly," Ludo replied. "But needs must, I'm afraid."

"I suppose he's going with you," Mrs Toxo said, indicating her husband, who became intent on scraping his plate clean with a crust of bread. Neither Ludo nor Toxo replied.

"Thought so." Mrs Toxo sniffed and with the wind in her sails went on, "Putting out in this weather, no thought for wives and mothers and little ones who need a papa. You men!"

On the contrary, Ludo murmured to himself. He looked at Alina, wondering what was going through her mind: whether the woman's words would convince her to stay here where it was safe and warm. Alina's face was the picture of sadness. Was she thinking of her one-time family at Crimphele? Was this reminder of family life the last straw in her own battle against grief?

Mrs Toxo began giving orders for the table to be cleared and dessert served. Dessert was followed by throat-burning *aguardiente* for Ludo and Toxo and the older boys, while the women and girls collected the china plates and silverware. Blanca, kind and wise beyond her years, took the sleeping Hetty and Etta to bed without being asked. The older males moved their conversation to the parlour fireside.

Ludo made an excuse and went to find Alina. Placing a hand on her elbow, he led her to a dark corner.

Somewhat tipsy from too much wine, Alina's said, "Is this going to be another of our secrets?"

"Yes and no."

"You never, never, never give a straight answer," she sighed.

"Well here's a straight question for once. Could you stay here for a month or two longer? Could you see the winter out with Toxo's family? You'd be warm and safe. Hetty would have friends and ..."

Alina was shaking her head. "You promised I could make some money with you."

"I didn't promise that."

"But, I have to take what we get for the jewels to the queen so I can get my place back."

"We!"

"Yes, we."

"How about if I go ahead to Lisbon and make the transaction, then I come back and give you the proceeds, and maybe a little extra for your journey, and –"

"Why don't I trust you to do that?" Alina's voice was low but sharp.

Ludo stepped back as if slapped. "Alina, I don't want to put you and Hetty in harm's way," he said.

"We've had worse snow than this in England."

"I wasn't referring to the weather."

Alina came to his room that night wearing a soft, white woollen robe over very little else. Ludo was sitting by the remains of his fire, warming cold feet on a footstool – the stone floor was freezing. As she entered, he looked at her feet, which were hidden in sheepskin boots.

"Planning a night-time get-away?" he asked.

"That's what I came to see if *you* were doing. You won't go without me, will you? You won't just disappear and ..."

"Leave only an emerald on your pillow?" Ludo shook his head. "Dare I admit that I do not feel strong enough right now to bear the agony of leaving you again?"

Alina looked at him in surprise. "But you're always fighting me," she said.

"You mistake fighting for self-defence, *madonna*."

Alina bit her lip and joined him at the fireside. He opened his arms and she sat in his lap, snuggling under his chin. They were silent together, watching the dying embers of the fire until Alina whispered, "Will it always be like this between us?"

"Isn't this what you wanted, excitement not commitment?"

"I've never ever said that. I was given commitment and it was taken from me."

They were silent together again, Ludo aware that he had touched a raw nerve: Thomas Fulford had given her commitment; a safe, boring man, whose death left her homeless, at least while the war in England continued. "I'm sorry," he said quietly. "I didn't mean to upset you."

"I loved him, Ludo. I'm so sad he died and yet here I am in your arms. What sort of awful woman am I?"

Ludo kissed the top of her head, "Not awful, *carina*, just natural. You are a *natural* woman."

Alina ignored his words, lost in her own recriminations. "When you found me – saved me in Santander – yes, I was anxious for some sort of excitement, I suppose, to escape my chores, those endless days looking after my brothers. And I hated you for selling me to the Fulfords. You sold me, didn't you? You told them a story and accepted payment for it. And condemned me to exile in a country where I spoke not one word of the language and had no wish to stay."

Ludo swallowed hard but said nothing for it was true.

Alina didn't need a response, though. "I loved you," she whispered, "and that was how you repaid me. Then you came back to me at Crimphele and betrayed me again. So I tried to hate you. Then I came to love Thomas, but in a different way. And I still love you both, and that will always be wrong."

"And if I tell you, I understand perfectly because I too have – had – a wife whom I loved, would that help us?"

"What happened to her? You have never said."

"She died – last year."

"Did you really love her?" Alina sat up and looked him in the eye.

Ludo closed his eyes, trying to control his emotion. "Yes, I loved her and I shall never forgive myself for what happened in Genoa. For letting myself be ..." he stopped speaking. Alina didn't need to know what had happened in Genoa. Nor did he want this conversation to go where it was leading. Words would be said that would either anger or alienate Alina, or worse, that would lead her to her pity him. He did not want to bind her to him in that way. In fact, right at this moment he didn't want to bind her to him in any way – it would only put her at greater risk from Rogelio. She had problems enough without knowing she could be attacked by Rogelio again.

"For letting yourself do what?" Alina asked.

"No, nothing."

"Tell me."

Instead of telling her anything, Ludo kissed her, long and deep, then edged her off his lap and carried her to the bed.

He had no idea what time of night they were disturbed, their love-making was over and they were both sleeping. A heart-rending call for Mama broke their unity.

"Mama!" Hetty screamed again and Alina was off the bed, wrapping the robe around her nakedness and leaving the room barefoot before he had sat upright.

"Mama!" the child was in the passageway. There was a mumble of female voices and the hysterically sobbing child was lifted into her mother's arms.

The voices died away. A draught from the open door relit a dying ember, illuminating a length of feminine muslin draped across his bedcovers. Ludo lifted it to his nose, took in its scent, then for a reason he dared not name, tucked it under his pillow with a few other very precious objects.

Chapter 22

Lisbon, Portugal, February 1645

Rogelio arrived in Portugal overland via Spain battered, bruised and much poorer for the experience. Bribing his way over the battle-torn frontier had cost him dear, despite his clerical robes. Along the way he had picked up two giant-size brutes: one in a town, begging alms but well-fed nonetheless; the other was a simpleton purchased from a widowed mother, who needed him for digging turnips but dared not refuse a priest.

With these two walking behind his hired nag as bodyguards, Rogelio made his way directly to the great monastery in the Belem district of the Lisbon, where he was awarded a reasonable guest room. The horse was stabled and the two brutes were sent to find beds in a harbourside hostel in the Alfama district. They were also instructed to enquire about a ship called *The Tulip*.

The monastery was an ideal location, on the waterfront and within walking distance of the palace. Priests, and just about anyone else with a reasonable excuse, were in and out of the Braganza Palace, Rogelio learned, like dogs at a fair. Donning a long soutane and carrying his old Bible, he set off on the second day along the sea wall, aiming for the Terreiro do Paço, the palace courtyard. When he was half way between the tower housing the Casa da India and the city he stopped, turned his back on the water and surveyed the scene. Coming to Lisbon had been a gamble based on likelihoods extracted from what Baron Jermyn could remember of his conversations with Ludovico.

If Ludovico was not here with the English jewels, to secure his continuing role as agent for Cardinal Barberini – or Barberini's replacement – he would have to take advantage of the journey in other ways. That meant he needed to build on his previous relationship with the new monarchs, a relationship that had been seriously undermined when Ludovico had stolen half of the funds the Vatican had provided help finance Portugal's separation from Spain, and he, Rogelio had organised. Three times Ludo had cheated him, now, if you counted how he'd failed to engineer the total disaster in Holland the way Barberini had wanted. Three times too many.

He walked on, musing on how and why Pope Urban had quietly supported the Braganza claim to the Portuguese throne. That would gain him access to the duchess, but he hadn't been in contact with her since she had discovered the loss of the money sent to Oporto. The Duchess of Braganza, now queen of Portugal, would require delicate handling, not least because she was a big woman with a loud voice and a hasty temper.

Reaching the palace courtyard, Rogelio stopped and looked up. The palace was modest, by French and English standards, plain as an artisan's dwelling compared to St Peter's. What kind of court did it house: formal or more casual? What sort people surrounded the Braganza couple now? Who could be cultivated, put to good use? If he couldn't return to Rome because he couldn't obtain the two jewels Barberini wanted, or if his role in Rome no longer existed, he'd need to secure a strong alternative. A new monarchy was a good place to start: they'd have need of his skills. Perhaps the Braganza would be interested in paying for exactly the same service he rendered the Vatican. Musing on this possibility, the idea of recruiting agents and developing a secret service for Portugal began to appeal to him more than working for Cardinal Barberini and enduring his perpetual insults.

The palace courtyard was crowded. A small child interrupted his thoughts, barrelling into his long skirts with a well-padded, winter pudding hat. He bent down to move him or her away from his legs with a shudder. An older girl saved him the bother, running up and grabbing the child's leading straps, then hoisting her – it was a she – into her arms.

"*Lo siento, disculpad*," mumbled the pasty-faced girl in accented Spanish.

He managed a smile and began to walk away, but not before hearing the girl rattle off something else to the child. Curious, he turned to see where they were going. The girl carried her charge back to a tall, hatless woman with an abundance of golden hair leaking from its pins. "*Madonna mia!*" Rogelio gasped, could it be? Pulling the brim of his clerical hat over his eyes, he gave the woman a long searching second look. It was *her* – the Spanish vixen Ludovico had taken up with in France; the one who'd been with him at Whitehall, as well.

The child was having a tantrum now, tearing off her hat to reveal a pile of black curls: the child had been in Chateau Thierry. Ludovico's love-child – it had to be.

Rogelio crushed his old Bible to his bony chest as a new plan came to him, perfectly formed. All he needed to do was kidnap the child, demand the jewels from Ludovico and return to Rome.

He would exchange one worthless girl-child for Three Brethren and Queen Bess's necklace and keep his reputation if not his old post in Rome. Two birds with a few stones.

Chapter 23

The house Ludo rented in Lisbon looked out from a series of single windows arranged higgledy-piggledy, one above another in a street barely wide enough for a donkey cart. Being conveniently located between the harbour and the palace there were a lot of donkeys in the street, also many mules and numerous fine horses belonging to dashing young men eager to be seen. Ludo wanted to be in the city and unseen for at least a week, possibly two, possibly more – to decide on a strategy, he said. Alina knew he was up to something, but was in no position to complain; he had given her money to acquire two servants – more would not fit in the dwelling – and adjust her wardrobe again, as necessary, to the latest Lisbon fashions. One servant was to occupy herself with the house; the other with Alina's hair. Hair was a serious matter in Lisbon this winter, she said, judging from her perambulations around the crowded palace courtyard.

Alina was instructed to put her trips to haberdashers and elsewhere to good use and gather gossip. Having Hetty with her proved a boon. Expecting to have to leave her daughter with her nurse, Toxo's daughter Blanca, Alina soon learned that aristocratic mothers might accompany smaller children in parks and even in the crowded, noisy palace courtyard. This was where anyone who wanted to be someone gathered daily to eye up their peers and rivals, and keep abreast of events. The wide, treeless courtyard reminded Alina of

Whitehall, where commoners might wander in from the city and observe their betters.

The courtyard was approached along the sea wall, either from the direction of the city or from the huge monastery on the bank of the Tagus. Coaches entering or departing would halt so their respective occupants could chat. Sturdy but sleek and elegant bay and black horses pulled carriages in ornate bridles, or danced pirouettes at the twinge of a spur so their riders could show off. Children played hoops and tag, shouting and laughing under boot-blackened hooves, causing Alina and Blanca to hold their breath and Hetty to clap her podgy hands with glee. The whole area spoke of familiarity and a disregard for safety. It was chaotic and very noisy as people on foot shouted above the howling wind with a complete absence of the restraint and good manners that characterised the confines of English palaces.

Gregarious by nature, little Hetty soon instigated numerous new acquaintanceships. She slipped Blanca's hold to join in games uninvited or wandered up to complete strangers because she liked their hat or the fabric of their skirts. Dogs were another matter, though. Despite growing up at Crimphele with its domestic pack of terriers and sheep dogs, Hetty did not like dogs, and there were always dozens of sleek, long-nosed hounds racing around barking at horses and each other in the palace yard.

It was in this way, when Hetty expertly twisted her leading straps from Blanca's hands then fell under the feet of an elegant courtier, that Alina first met Dom Enrique Guzman da Costa, a distant cousin of the Duchess of Braganza, the Spanish born queen. Or so he said. There was something about the charming Dom Enrique that made Alina instantly wary. But it was a start, and she encouraged it because Dom Enrique was not in the palace courtyard to see and be seen, he was entering the building because he lived there.

The following day, quite by chance, at the same hour and location, Dom Enrique paused to greet Alina and engage her in conversation. This presented Alina with a major problem: her status. During the short but hazardous voyage from Vigo, she had happily welcomed Ludo into her cabin each night. Peril, the restricted size of the bed and the motion of the ship made their lovemaking intense and joyful; the wild seas around them eliminating reality, detaching her from the adversities and sorrows that had entered her home with a sour-minded Palatine prince and the odious Percy.

One night she had even put it into words. Edging to one side, for the bed was short and narrow and Ludo filled most of it, she said, "Do you ever think about going back and starting again?"

"Going back where?"

"Not literally – well yes, perhaps: I mean going back to a moment in time *before* something happened and willing it to be otherwise."

Ludo turned his head on the sweaty ticking of the pillow. Tracing a finger down her nose he said, "Regret is pointless. It can only lead to further regret – which leads to remorse, which, I fear, has no remedy. The only way is forward." With that he kissed her forehead and retired to his own cabin.

Ludo's words stayed with Alina for days to come, ironically bringing her back to a sad reality. When they reached Lisbon and circumstances forced her into sharing his rented house she insisted on separate rooms. She had to move forward, and that meant avoiding another pregnancy at all costs.

Despite this, Ludo was all for presenting themselves as husband and wife. In his scenario Alina remained a lady-in-waiting to the Queen of England (nearly true) and he had a business arrangement the Stuarts were exploiting in the East (more or less true) and an arrangement that might be of interest to Portugal (which was actually true).

The second meeting with Dom Enrique forced Alina to confront her awkward and embarrassing circumstance. As a widow with no income she was compelled to accept charity in any form, but what Ludo was offering was an obstacle to improving her situation – possibly with Dom Enrique, who had mentioned no wife as he told her about his living quarters in the palace.

That evening, after the second encounter with Dom Enrique, Alina waited until she and Ludo were alone at supper to open a difficult conversation. She began by mentioning her new friendship with the Portuguese courtier then went on to say, "I'm sure he will introduce me to the duchess, she's his cousin."

Ludo cocked his head thoughtfully to one side and raised a warning hand, "Don't rush things, *carina*."

"I'm not rushing," Alina retorted, reluctantly seeing her enthusiasm for Dom Enrique in darker tones.

"I know I said we need to make ourselves known and be invited here and there before we start anything serious, but don't look too eager," Ludo continued. "I'd rather take it more slowly. There's just about time –"

"Time? Is there a time limit? Who set you a time limit? Jermyn?"

Ludo ignored her and continued, "If push comes to shove, I can engage in card games and lose until I am forced to pledge a gem to cover my debts. That will attract attention and give me a means of presenting the booty. I've kept a couple of stones back in case."

"Back from what? You mean you've taken Hetty's stones from my bag?"

"No! Good heavens no. Stop talking and listen. I – we, if you still insist on sharing the profit – don't want it to look as if we're anxious to sell. It will not only bring the prices down, it will destroy my opportunities with the duchess. The time limit is that I absolutely need to get rid of the stuff and get out of Lisbon before Palm Sunday, but we'll do it my way, please."

"And your way is …?"

"That I present myself to the duchess and offer her two of the most important jewels, which she can purchase from me, and then – at my suggestion – use as dowry for her daughter. She can have other items for herself, or tell her ladies and let them buy from me as well."

"What two special items?" Alina queried. "What exactly are we selling?"

"I'll show you in a minute," Ludo held up his hand again. "For now, wait and listen. Tell your Dom Enrique that you have been with Henrietta Maria and when it's right, mention that she has entrusted you with jewels to sell, to raise money for the Royalist cause – which you think is very sad because they are valuable antiques – treasures. Tell him some things are actually priceless because of their history, except we're putting a price on them, of course. The key words are all related to exclusivity. This, hopefully, will filter back to the duchess – if he's really her cousin – and she'll think she's getting something that is not only exclusive but full of English history, and that'll play into my gambit."

"And is she – getting something exclusive and full of history? Or is this one of your lines? Sounds like it to me."

Ludo smiled, stood up and straightened his long, embroidered gold damask waistcoat saying, "As I think I mentioned, Baron Jermyn arranged for the return of Henrietta's jewels before I got out of France. Naturally, I wasn't stupid enough to put anything of major value in my saddle bags." He tapped the large patch-pockets on the skirts of his waistcoat meaningfully. "I have always paid attention to the form and nature of pockets, you know. Never liked the loose ones you tie round the waist – jiggling about inside your breeches, poking at your delicate bits – but pockets in shirts and jackets, they're another thing." Ludo pulled a white bundle from his right-hand waistcoat pocket. It was a handkerchief knotted to form a bag. Putting it on the table, he continued, "My leather travel jerkin has lots of pockets, inside and out. Got an ugly hole in the shoulder where a lead ball lodged itself now, unfortunately, but this one," he began opening his embroidered waistcoat, "is still in good order and has just the sort of pockets I like: deep, spacious and with a secret inner button to prevent contents falling out."

Reaching into an inner pocket he pulled out two objects also wrapped in lawn handkerchiefs and dropped them on the table. "This," he said, undoing one of the handkerchiefs, "is called The Three Brethren. These stones," he separated the gems from around a central pyramid diamond, "are spinels, otherwise known as balas rubies. Exquisite examples of the purple or rose-hued spinel, in fact. As far as I know. Rare and very precious."

Alina poked the pearls into shape. "What is it? A brooch?"

"Cloak clasp – or it was. It's in Queen Elizabeth's portrait as a brooch, though. Apparently."

Alina eyed him suspiciously. "Really? In a royal portrait?"

"On my honour. Baron Jermyn told me."

"I didn't trust him either," Alina huffed. "And this?" she undid the other handkerchief to reveal a set of lustrous small pearls arranged as a necklace for an enormous, old-fashioned square-cut pendant ruby encased in dull gold. Leaning forward, Alina examined the stones, "there are hundreds of pearls here with alternate sapphires and rubies, or are they garnets?"

"Garnets! I should hope not. This belonged to Catalina d'Aragon, given to her when she went to England to marry the Prince of Wales; later it went to her daughter, Queen Mary. I'm going to offer this one to the duchess *for its history*. Let's hope she sees the irony."

"Giving something that belonged to Spain to her daughter when she marries an English prince?" Alina laughed. "She should jump at it."

"Let's hope so. Now, what about these, Baroness?" Ludo whisked a chamois pouch from a pocket in his breeches and teased out a long strand of bright stones. "These are Queen Bess's diamonds."

Alina gasped and picked them up. Putting them to her neck she said, "They're warm."

"And so they should be, considering where I have to keep them."

"Are these for me, then?" Alina's eyes sparkled like the stones in the candle light; she was only half-joking. "Or are you going to offer them to the Duchess of Braganza as well?"

"I am, but despite what I was saying earlier about dealing only with the her, there is a fly in the ointment."

"What sort of fly?"

"I hear the new king is a frugal man. Except when it comes to horses and hounds, he won't spend money on anything. The income they get from taxing the spice ships goes to paying his army to keep Portugal out of Spanish hands. My interpretation is that he doesn't like spending money because he's not interested in raising it or dealing with the corruption in his civil service. Ah, but no, if your Dom Enrique can bring you to his wife's attention. We can bypass him."

Ludo paused and looked at Alina so intensely she could visualise the cogs and wheels of his machinations.

"You are both daughters of Spanish grandees, start with that. If this Dom Enrique is who he says he is –"

"Why shouldn't he be?" Alina snapped.

"*Madonna*, this is a tiny new monarchy with an empty palace to fill. All manner of people could be claiming consanguinity. Long lost cousins are all over the place these days, and not just in Lisbon, I can tell you. Actually," Ludo paused again and studied Alina's face, "I don't suppose your august father the Conde de Pamanes has any relatives here?"

"I very much doubt it, and I'm not going to ask, either."

"Pity. So, we focus on the wife, for wives can find ways around husbands better than anyone else, or so I'm told. The duchess will be the one buying the goods, and I'll lay a hefty bet she'll do it *without* her husband's permission. Are you still with me?"

"I'm not a fool, Ludo," Alina huffed.

Ludo gave her his one-dimpled, wry grin, "No you are not."

"Go on: what is this plan?"

"The duchess is ambitious beyond words. Having attained sovereignty, she'll now want to marry her offspring into royal households. Spain is closed to them, obviously, and she not a Habsburg; the Dutch are mostly Protestants, but the younger Stuarts are half-Catholic, if not rather more. If she acquires the English jewels she can then, as I said, return them to the Stuarts as part of a dowry when one of the Stuart princes marries one of her daughters. What better way to curry favour than to buy them, knowing the money will be used to safeguard the monarchy in London, an ally against Spain, then return the stuff as a gift to its 'rightful owners'."

"It's brilliant – will it work?" Alina gazed at him. "How do you know so much about the duchess?"

"I visit places where one hears what matters. I also acted on her behalf a few years ago." Ludo grimaced, "More or less."

Alina's shoulders slumped, "Oh, no, you didn't cheat her."

"Not her, her suppliers. The ... some people who were providing funds to help pay for their revolution and enable them to reclaim the throne from the Spanish. It didn't go quite according to their plan, although, looking back, providence was with me because I left Lisbon without actually meeting her face to face."

"But you were up to no good."

"On the contrary, I was up to a lot of good; I was fulfilling conflicting orders. No mean feat, though I say it myself."

"And from which you benefitted handsomely."

"Of course! Why else would I put myself at risk?"

Alina gave a sigh combining annoyance with despair. Then perked up: this was as good a reason as she needed to distance herself from Ludo. Their relationship as a couple had always been doomed: she needed him on her side but he was the last person she should truly rely on, and this was why. Taking a deep breath, she said, "I can't be your wife."

Ludo eyes widened in genuine surprise, "Santa Maria, when did I ask you?"

"Your plan, the way we are sharing this house; it's what you said you wanted people to think – that we are ... Your strategy – whatever you choose to call it – I can't do it. I have to be who I am: a widow and lady-in-waiting to the exiled Queen of England." Alina arranged a fold of fine lace around her left hand then wafted her right hand in the air and repeated, "I have to be who I am."

"Because it is more convenient for you to be a widow than ..." Ludo wafted a mimicking hand in the air. "Ah, Dom Enrique – you have met someone interested in your status, and, in the long term, that may be of more benefit to you than running back to your tricksy little queen with her loose change. I see."

Alina wanted to smack him. Why was he always so perceptive, and so annoyingly straightforward when it suited him?

"Yes." Her voice cracked with tension. She had walked into a stupid situation by staying under the same roof as Ludo. And now he was entangling her in a business for which she had no skills and no experience. On top of it all, she was going to be trapped as a 'fallen woman' as well if she wasn't very careful. "I have to leave," she stated baldly.

"All right," Ludo replied and gathered the jewels together, wrapping each one carefully and stowing them out of sight.

The new servant, a wide-hipped girl with a moustache, entered and placed a tureen of something fishy on the table then returned with a bowl of the New World roots called potatoes. Alina served the stew from the tureen and they ate in silence. Neither of them touched the potatoes.

"You're not helping," Alina sighed, putting down her spoon.

"What can I do? What can I say? Leaving this house makes sense to your good name: I agree. To the world beyond this door you are either my wife or my whore. You could try being a cousin but that sends your rank as the only daughter of a Spanish grandee straight out of the window. I can see that as the widow of an English nobleman – given that England has helped Portugal regain its independence – is a sound choice. But will it help you achieve what you said you wanted, to return to the English queen's favour?"

They put down their spoons simultaneously and stared at each other. Before Alina could say anything, though, Ludo pulled another soft chamois pouch from a pocket and shuffled out the contents: another necklace with a pendant stone, but designed to be worn as a collar.

Alina picked it up and examined it in the candlelight. Clusters of pearls and diamonds were arranged around tiny emeralds. Facets caught fire in the light from candles around the room. "It's beautiful," she sighed, fingering the large pendant emerald.

"And worth a king's ransom."

"Henrietta Maria showed me this – or one very similar – when I was dressing her for a ball in Whitehall. This one belonged to Queen Bess as well." Alina traced her fingers through the setting.

"Would you like it?" Ludo asked.

"*Would I,*" Alina whispered longingly.

"You might like these more." Ludo took a larger chamois pouch from inside his fine white shirt. "I keep my favourite gems here with my special ruby," he said, patting the region of his heart.

"With your ruby," Alina laughed. "Do you still wear it?"

"That ruby has seen me safely through numerous long and dangerous voyages. But these," he undid the pouch and revealed a number of large, irregular pearls, "will see me safely to a house in a location of my choosing, where I may stay for a very long time. These are mine. I bought them in Hormuz for your English queen and was never paid."

The misshapen pearls, soft pink, cream and smoky grey, were glorious. "You have no intention of returning any money to the Queen for the Stuart cause, have you?" Alina said quietly, picking up one of the largest pearls between finger and thumb and holding it to a candle.

"Well, for a start, these beauties were mine in the first place, for which I have never received a single coin. And the other stuff," he tapped his waistcoat pockets again, "was stolen from me on Jermyn's orders – or so I believe."

"Ludo ..." Alina didn't know how to respond.

"If you are going to be paraded at court, you'd better have this – for now," Ludo said, picking up the pendant necklace.

To Alina's surprise and delight he stood up and fitted it around her neck. She lifted her hands, caressing each cluster then the large pendant emerald hanging below a perfectly round white pearl at her throat.

"It's called 'Elizabeth's Emerald' or the 'Empress Emerald' or some such name," Ludo said, closing the clasp with deft fingers. "This is the card to play, Baroness. Wear this and be who you are: a once wealthy noblewoman now a grieving noblewoman, whose eldest son is with the English heirs to the throne. Will this help your morale, do you think?"

Alina's face flushed. "Yes," she whispered. "I'm sorry, Ludo, I just know ..." Afraid to turn around and let him see her eyes, she moved her right hand behind her neck. Ludo took it gently in his and stroked the cushion beneath her thumb.

"Would you like me to arrange for a suite of rooms for you?"

"Please."

"Then I shall," he murmured, and kissed the palm of her hand.

Alina controlled her response. She didn't want a suite of rooms away from him; she wanted to be with him all the time and forever, but there was no security in that, and as always, her thoughts returned to her children. She needed to provide for them in case Crimphele was lost altogether.

Ludo gathered up his pearls, tucked them into their pouch and started to leave the room. "I have to go out for a while," he said.

"Where? It's dark and cold outside. You can't go out with all those jewels on you. What happens if you are attacked by robbers?"

"True. Keep these under your pillow, will you?" Ludo tossed the pouch of pearls from the door.

"What about the other jewels?"

"Might need them," he said and disappeared.

A moment later Ludo popped his head back around the door and said, "Don't forget to hire a chaperone."

Alina stamped her foot – another dratted expense. And where was she to find an old biddy that was decent enough to pass muster and circumspect enough not to pass comment?

The servant entered and removed their plates. "Is there anything you'd like, *señora*?" she asked in Spanish.

"Yes: somewhere to live with peace of mind."

Chapter 24

Alina was delighted with her new lodgings. They were dirty, but everything in Lisbon was grubby and most people stank to high heaven. The rooms were spacious and looked out onto a wide, terraced street leading down to the harbour. Ludo helped arrange for her trunks to be moved and provided her with more money with which to employ a new skivvy and improve the furnishings. She had taken this purse in guilty silence. The guilt was somewhat allayed by knowing why he was helping her so much, and the knowledge that in moving she was also setting him free.

On the first afternoon, after Hetty and Blanca were settled in their new room, Alina made her way down to the palace courtyard unaccompanied. If questioned she would tell the truth; she was looking for a suitable chaperone. It took two circuits of the crowded location before she located Dom Enrique, but once *he* noticed *her*, he was at her side in a trice.

"Dona Maria de los Angeles: what a pleasure," the Portuguese courtier said, sweeping his hat to the ground and bowing over her extended right hand. "Enrique Guzman da Costa y Clarendon-Greenwood, Marquis de Coimbra, at your service once more."

Alina inclined her head in acknowledgement, tempted to list her father's title and eight family surnames as well, but knowing that would be unwise given Portugal's continuing war with Spain. Instead, she stuck to her British husband's title. The momentary tension made her stand to her full height, chin high and she was delighted to see that Dom Enrique was taller than her. Then she noticed his hair for the first time. It was silvery grey. Their previous meetings had required him to remove his hat, but she hadn't realised he was quite so old. How old was he? Older than his exquisite apparel suggested, that was for sure. Setting the minor disappointment aside, Alina graciously allowed him to invite her to a banquet that evening in the palace. He would send a carriage for her, he said.

"Oh, but Dom Enrique, I have yet to find a suitable lady as my chaperone," she said.

Dom Enrique gave her a reassuring smile under his moustache, which was also silvery grey now that Alina was being more observant. "I may be able to help you in that matter. She may not be available this evening, however. Would you risk your reputation at my side for one evening?"

Alina gave him her sweetest confiding smile.

Some hours later, Dom Enrique helped her into his carriage and they set off downhill towards the palace for a banquet.

Dom Enrique was in every way an ideal partner for the evening. He knew everyone worth knowing. He was also, despite or because of the mane of silver hair, the most handsome man present.

The banquet was being held in an elaborate vault with a decorated ceiling and heavy, hanging candelabra illuminating exquisite designs on the walls, which Alina realised were tiled. She looked about her, taking in the glamour and splendour of the occasion. Conversation across the board distracted her. Someone asked her where she was from. She could follow bits of Portuguese but was forced to answer in Spanish. "*Inglaterra*," she said. Fortunately, nobody appeared to mind, many of them being in the duchess's situation of having been born in Spain and married into Portugal.

Alina touched the stones at her neck, adjusted the emerald at her throat, then ran a finger along the fine white Viseu lace around her midnight blue bodice. Leaning back, she gave the merest sigh of satisfaction. Then sat up straight and blinked. Ludo was sitting virtually opposite her. He caught her eye and winked. She snapped open her new fan and pretended he wasn't there.

As the evening wore on – numerous courses of somewhat coarse fare for a royal banquet, including wild boar charcuterie, partridge in a sauce worthy of Crook-back Aggie's worst intentions, then venison that required healthy teeth – she allowed herself to relax again and drank rather more than she should. Dom Enrique remained charming; his table manners were agreeable but his conversation, as he drank rather too much fortified wine, became somewhat worrisome.

"... and then my wife died so I do understand your circumstances, Dona Alina, and the sadness that may accompany it. Although of course, not all arranged marriages result in contentment."

"Arranged marriages, Dom Enrique?"

"Were you lucky to have a love-match? Forgive me, I assumed, you being the daughter of a grandee, resident more often than not in the royal court at Madrid, that naturally your father had chosen for you. I find it curious that your late husband was an Englishman."

Alina picked up her goblet to hide her discomfort, wondering how he had obtained her history, and what was he hinting at. "Have you been a widower long, Dom Enrique?" she asked.

"Four years. Four long years."

But not without female company, Alina thought. So here is a man who can choose any woman he likes from among the highest born of his country – but hasn't. Why? Why is he interested in me, an outsider? Or has Ludo been his source of information? She glanced at Ludo, but he was no longer in his seat; he was sitting beside the duchess. Alina was reminded of a banquet in Spain, when Ludo had made his way directly to the late Queen Isabel's side, thanks to her father's intervention.

Dom Enrique interrupted her thoughts and she chided herself; she should be paying attention to him, not remembering a Genoese merchant's tricky antics. Dom Enrique was paying court to her, and *he* was a marquis, meaning apart from his palace suite he would have a grand mansion and liveried footmen and... and there was something she had overlooked. What? Lost in thought once more, she didn't notice that he had left her side until she looked around, then up towards the royal end of the table. He was leaning over his cousin's shoulder, and the Duchess of Braganza's face suggested he wasn't telling a joke. Ludo was back in his place.

Alina tried to clear her head. The room had started to swim. Snapping her fan open, she wafted it this way and that to cool her cheeks, surveying the other diners over its stiff lace. There was a youngish man farther down the table who looked like Marcos. Poor Marcos, would he ever be happy again? He deserved to be happy – if it wasn't for Marcos she wouldn't even be here now.

Evidently noticing that she was looking at him, the young man returned her gaze. It wasn't Marcos. Pink and jittery with embarrassment she jumped, as Dom Enrique resumed his place at her side. He started to say something but a neighbour grabbed his attention. A species of dessert landed in front of her. It looked like common or garden flan made of maize and eggs. It was ordinary housewife's flan. Alina put down her spoon and sipped more sweet wine to remove the cloying taste, remembering Crook-back Aggie's terrible flans and the special dessert she'd made to keep Cousin Percy on the pot while they got away from Crimphele. She wanted to cry.

"Excuse me," she said, getting to her feet and heading for where she hoped the ladies' retiring room would be.

Later, as Dom Enrique's Lusitano geldings clattered up the streets he said, "I was speaking with the duchess, we are to make a party and visit my house in Coimbra. I have had word that its renovations are nearing completion."

Alina took a deep breath, unsure whether she was being invited or informed of his forthcoming absence. She stared out of the open square in the carriage door at passing blackness and tried not to give way to despair. Enrique took her hand and squeezed it gently. "Would you like to come and see my house?"

Alina bit her lip hard. "Thank you, but I... I still haven't found a chaperone to accompany me on outings, save for my daughter's nurse."

"Oh, that is what I meant to tell you. My younger sons' tutor has a mother, she is of no particular use to anyone, but you can have her. I'll have her put in the coach to travel with you."

Alina bit her lip again: that was the question she had forgotten to ask: did he have children, and if so, how many? But instead of asking, she blurted out, "Dom Enrique, you need to know why I am here – without a chaperone. I've come to sell the Duchess of Braganza some jewels."

Dom Enrique patted her hand. "You are a widow in distressed circumstances: I am aware my dear."

"No, they belong to Queen Henrietta Maria. She wanted us – me – to sell them to raise funds for her husband. Can you help me?"

Alina couldn't see Dom Enrique's expression in the dark interior of his carriage, but she noticed him shift in his seat. The atmosphere between them changed.

"Should you be telling me this?" he asked quietly.

The answer was 'no'; that it was the wine talking and that she had blundered. Alina struggled to find a response but before she could say anything, he filled the awkward silence by saying, "My English ancestor met his wife at the wedding of Philip the Second to Mary Tudor." Alina failed to see the connection, but then he added, "My connection to the English monarchy goes back many generations so I follow what is happening in England with interest. In fact, I have close contacts with the Royalist cause. I attended King Charles, briefly, when he was in Madrid as suitor to the Infanta. That was over twenty years ago now, of course, but old loyalties remain. Queen Henrietta Maria often wore a pearl necklace with a pendant ruby that was given to Catalina, the daughter of Isabel *la Católica*, when the poor girl was sent to England. My ancestors were in her train. You don't have that, I suppose?"

Alina's mouth went dry. "I – I'm not sure. No, that is ... no." She shook her head and regretted it.

"Pity. Ah, here we are. I will send Dona Dolores to you tomorrow."

The postilion opened the door and helped Alina alight the carriage. Enrique joined her in the narrow doorway of her new lodgings. Over his shoulder in the moonlight, Alina caught the pinched features of a street child. Poor boy was freezing cold and probably hungry. The distraction enabled Dom Enrique to move closer to her. His proximity, her fuddled head and the sight of a homeless child completed her anxiety to be in her own room – on her own. Making a fuss of gathering her cloak around her then offering her hand, she said, "Thank you for a most pleasant evening," and rapped on the door sharply for Blanca to let her in.

As she finally settled into bed and adjusted the pillow to reduce the effect of the spinning bed, Alina came to a reluctant realisation: she was out of her depth. She had no idea how to go about selling the queen's jewels and, more importantly, she didn't want to, even if it meant she would never return to Henrietta Maria as a lady-in-waiting or anything else. If there was a future with Dom Enrique, he would have to take her as Thomas's widow with nothing – for that was who she was.

Chapter 25

Less than twenty-four hours after his arrival in Lisbon, following instructions, Marcos sought out a Portuguese nobleman, the Marquis de Coimbra. He was shown into a dowdy back room of the royal palace. An elegant man wearing various shades of grey with whitish hair and a sculpted silver beard was seated beside an octagonal oriental table. He was eating a dainty pastry and flapped a crumpled napkin to indicate Marcos was to sit down.

"Would you care for a cup of coffee?" the nobleman asked, speaking English like a native. "I always enjoy coffee at this hour. It boosts the spirits, especially when one has a long day ahead."

Marcos shook his head. He had tasted coffee in Holland but he had never taken to it. It was far too expensive, anyway.

"Pour wine for my guest," the marquis instructed a footman.

The fortified wine the Portuguese favoured was sweet and pleasant but Marcos sipped it slowly; he needed his wits about him. The footman was dismissed and they were alone. The white-haired nobleman poured himself another cup of coffee. Marcos studied the design on the silver pot. Expensive and very pretty. If this didn't work out, he'd go back to his plan for the New World and get into the coffee business somewhere.

The marquis finished his pastry and wiped his mouth then said, "Your information was only partly correct."

"I'm sorry; I did warn Mr Greenwood I might not –"

"Tch – no names. Except I should warn you that I do know yours, and, this being a small world I also know where your parents reside in Andalucía. I too have relatives in the Province of Cadiz. My intelligencers are fast and efficient. They have to be or they are of no use."

Marcos inclined his head and said bravely, "Then you will know, sir, that I am no 'intelligencer' merely a wine and spice merchant, and that I am here under duress."

"I know exactly why you are here, and how you got here. What *you* should know is that you are watched night and day by my men, and one or two women when required. We are also watching your previous travelling companions."

Marcos frowned: could they really have been tracking him in France as well?

As if in answer the marquis said, "New arrivals require servants; new servants are easily bought – having no loyalties."

Marcos wanted to get up and walk out: move the hand on the clock of time backwards so he could return to his mother's hostel and get on with his chores. Instead, he said, "If my orders are the same as I was given in England then I can tell you that I plan to get the items tonight. Do you want me to give them to you directly, or do I take them back myself, as arranged?"

"Your friend says he doesn't have them anymore. He says they were stolen from him in France. Do you know if there is any truth in that?"

Marcos laughed. "No." Then he paused, remembering what Ludo had told him and wondering to what extent he was prepared to betray his friend. Taking the items the English wanted from Ludo was one thing, knowing he'd only sell them for his own benefit anyway, but actively betraying confidences, that was something else. Weighing up his alternatives, and aware he needed to cover his back very carefully, Marcos said, "However, if I find it is true, could you relay that to your contact in England? I would be most grateful. It would mean I could return to Sanlúcar directly, my business for England being null and void."

The Marquis of Coimbra gave him a long stare then, switching to Castellano Spanish, said, "My illustrious uncle, when he was still *valido* to the King of Spain, made over an entire *cortijo* in Sanlucar to Don Ludovico, did you know that?"

Marcos tried not to smile. *Did he know all about the cortijo?* Of course, he did: he was there at the time. What he didn't know and was anxious to find out, was where the comment was heading.

In England, the arrangement had been straightforward: he would acquire the items on Greenwood's list and return with them to Falmouth. He hadn't bargained on an interfering Portuguese go-between. And why was he being told he was being watched? They knew who he was, where he came from, where he was going. He could change that of course, and disappear. Perhaps they feared he'd disappear with the jewels. A memory flashed past: 'Where are you going?' 'To disappear.' Ludo knew they were being followed in France. Had they done anything unobserved? He hoped whoever the bloodhounds were, they had been sea-sick on the various Channel crossings.

"Baroness Metherall has the jewels now. Did you know that?" the marquis enquired.

Wrenched from his private thoughts, Marcos said, "Baroness Metherall?"

"You know the lady. You were her steward at one time, or so I am told. You will have to obtain them from her now. Although it could be that she has only a few. Whether they are the better or the lesser of the items I cannot say, yet."

"She is here in Lisbon?" Marcos stalled, wondering what he could do to avoid this. "I didn't know that. It will take time to find her –" A square of paper was pushed between a cup and plate. Marcos picked it up and read an address. "I see. Thank you." He lifted his gaze from the paper and looked the nobleman in the eye: "May I ask why, if you know far more than I do and you have 'operatives' who include women, why you don't you arrange for one of them to acquire the jewels for you? If the baroness has servants who are spies, why can't they take them?"

The marquis leaned back against his chair and arranged his hands primly in his lap. "Good question. My orders come also from England, so I am reluctant to make changes. If I had known about the jewels and been trusted with the extraction in the first place, we could have saved you a journey. As it is," he folded the napkin on his knees and placed it on the small table, "you are expected to play the retriever. You will receive a reward, I assume. If this is not the case, let me know and we'll go about it my way."

Marcos was tempted to let him do it his way, but said nothing.

The marquis studied his expression. "Not very good at hiding your feelings, are you? Before you decide, perhaps you should consider why you were sent."

Marcos was lost. "Why I was sent?"

"Yes: why you have been chosen to save some very valuable jewels for a most important person, an entire nation, if you like."

It was a question Marcos had been asking himself since he left Mount Edgcumbe. Among the many things his apprenticeship with Ludo in Holland had taught him, though, was when not to speak, when to listen and not to talk.

The Portuguese nobleman warmed to his theme, ignoring his earlier stricture to name no names. "The heir to the throne is eager to bind different orders of men to him in

England, eager to find loyal subjects of different degrees and walks of life who will benefit from his rule when he returns to London, men who will benefit from establishing mutual obligations. That's the key word here, 'mutual'. You have warrants to supply the royal palaces, do you not? You'll want to keep them, I expect, renew them after this sad war is over. That is probably why you were chosen – being beholden in some way."

Marcos looked at his hands. "I hadn't thought about it like that."

"No, well, affairs of state, even clandestine matters such as this often boil down to obtaining or securing loyalty. Do you still want to do it? I can send a message saying you couldn't fulfil your mission."

Was this what he wanted? Marcos sipped his wine. He had been 'chosen' but he was out of his depth. This world was not for him, despite its many attractions. He was sorely tempted to accept the release then he remembered the comment about the *cortijo* in Sanlucar. If he did obtain favour with the Prince of Wales and continued to supply the royal palaces in England, those vineyards and fields would be useful. If the Royalists lost, and he chose not to go to the New World for any reason, he could still go there – unhindered – to continue his wine business as Ludo had suggested, when *he* had gifted it to him. Either way, as long as he carried out what Greenwood wanted successfully, he'd keep the *cortijo* – and either way he was going to need it because the promised house in England (and possible knighthood) wouldn't materialise until the English war was won. Securing the Royal Warrants was paramount: they guaranteed his future as a merchant.

His head buzzing with jumbled reasoning, Marcos said, "I'll fulfil the task and take the items back to England myself as I promised."

"Excellent. But one favour. I would very much like to see these jewels. Call it an old man's curiosity – could you bring them here to me as soon as you have them, just for a peek?"

Marcos was immediately suspicious. He inclined his head as if in agreement, and said nothing.

The marquis gave him an empty smile and added conversationally, "Ah, by the way, Baroness Metherall will be one of a party visiting Coimbra tomorrow and staying overnight. The party will include the Duchess of Braganza, our new queen. I suspect Dona Alina intends to offer the gems to the duchess while we are there, so we should assume she will bring the items you seek with her. If you are to make the extraction, it must be tonight, before she has access to the duchess."

"I understand."

The marquis smiled again and picked up a silver bell to ring for a footman.

Later, wandering along the sea wall, Marcos studied the ships and re-assessed his options. Despite the appalling weather and the winds off the Atlantic, ships were being loaded for Brazil. Did he really want to go to Brazil? He could sign on as crew right here and now ... but, no. That sort of escape wasn't what he was looking for. Not yet. He should go back to Sanlucar first to tell his mother his plans at the very least, and to do that unhindered he needed to be seen to have acquired the jewels from Alina – or Ludo – or both.

"Ah, but no!" Marcos stopped in his tracks, causing two mariners to bump into him, cursing in different languages. "I don't need to steal anything!" he shouted at them.

He *and* Alina could return the jewels to England together. That would confirm his loyalty and hers as well. He'd get his title and she could secure Crimphele for the future. Not that she need live there, for if he had a title in his own right she surely wouldn't refuse him again. It meant jeopardising her relationship with Henrietta Maria, but if they were loyal to the queen's son – and that son was to become king in the near future – well, then *their* future was safe, and Alina couldn't refuse him!

Marcos pulled the slip of paper with her address from his pocket and headed for the Belem district of the city.

Chapter 26

"Marcos! What are you doing here?" Alina fussed about him, taking his cloak herself and stuffing it into the arms of her servant.

Marcos wanted to say there and then, "Get rid of her, she's a spy," but he didn't. Instead he waited until he was in Alina's drawing room and whispered, "Send the maid on an errand."

Alina frowned then left the room. When she returned, she said, "How did you find me? Have you seen Ludo?"

Marcos touched the square of thick paper in his jacket pocket then decided not to mention it. "Let me speak first," he said, "I have a lot to tell you. Then you can ask questions. I need to tell you what has been happening and what will happen if..." he paused and turned around. Alina's grumpy-looking servant in a stained pinafore had returned to the door. "Get rid of her," Marcos hissed.

Alina got up, spoke to the girl again then followed her to the kitchen area. When she returned, she closed the door and said, "Marcos, it's so good to see you, but what is all this about?" Not giving him time to respond she lowered her voice in a dramatic whisper, "How did you get here from France, though? How on earth did you find us?"

"It's a bit complicated – I'll tell you about my journey later. For now, listen: there's a way we can get back to England and it'll help you return to Crimphele, to keep it –

or at least keep it for Tommy. All we have to do is take the jewels back to Falmouth."

Alina narrowed her eyes suspiciously. "What jewels?"

"The ones Ludo took from Chateau Thierry, unless you've got them all now."

"Take a chair. Let me pour some wine," Alina said innocently.

When he was settled by the fireside with a fine goblet in his hand, she sat beside him and said, "Now, start from the beginning. From when you left for Plymouth."

Marcos began to relate what had happened to him in Plymouth, skirting around Edward Beale and moving on to being taken to Mount Edgcumbe. More slowly, he then told Alina about the fine offer made there, watching her face for a sign of joy; her realisation that not only had he come to her rescue but that he could now offer her all she wanted. About his future marriage plans and the nobleman he'd visited in the Braganza palace he made no mention.

"That's wonderful," Alina said. Exactly as he hoped she would. "But why do you think my servant isn't to be trusted?"

"I've been warned – erm – that people are watching us."

"Us? Me as well? Ah, because of Ludo. I knew it! That's why I ..."

Marcos looked at Alina questioningly, but refrained from comment. "We have to be careful," he said. "Especially now you have the jewels."

"But I don't. Where did you get that idea? I only have a few loose gemstones and this ring," she proffered a hand bearing one of the rings from Hetty's rag doll, "and a necklace. Ludo has got the special brooch and Queen Bess's necklace and all the other old stuff."

Marcos felt his heart thump out of rhythm. Concerned, Alina leaned over to him, "Marcos, you've gone white. Are you all right?" Her concern was genuine and he started to feel better.

"Never mind, between us we can get them off him." Marcos pressed on, explaining what he'd been told by Gifford Greenwood, why it was necessary to recover what Henrietta Maria wanted Ludo to sell, repeating the promises they had made him at Mount Edgcumbe. Then it dawned on him that, in Alina's eyes, he was still married to Joanna. He stopped talking and gave a deep sigh. "It won't work, will it?"

"No, because he keeps them on him all the time."

They were talking at cross purposes. She hadn't registered his news about a house and land and title in England; she was entirely taken up with Ludo da Portovenere – as always. Giving up his fine plans for lost, Marcos nevertheless ploughed on with what Greenwood in England wanted him to do. "I'll get into Ludo's lodgings when he's asleep and go through his clothes," he said. "I'll get them that way."

"Not if he sleeps with them under his pillow, you won't."

"Does he?" Marcos asked, not wanting to know how she knew.

"Yes. I'll have to come with you."

"No! It will tarnish your name, being in his lodging at night with two men and no chaperone." It was a cheap barb but he couldn't resist it.

Alina wasn't listening; she was creating a plan of her own. "This is what we'll do," she said. "We'll wait until midnight – the monastery bell for Matins will tell us when – then we'll go to his house and I'll distract him. You go into his room, get the jewels you need – all of them if you want ..." She drew breath, apparently considering different scenarios. "Then I'll stay with him and you leave. That way he won't know what's been taken until he dresses in the morning, and by that time, with a bit of luck, I'll be gone as well."

"Alina, you can't do this. It will ruin your reputation."

"Too late for that! According to Ludo, I was ruined on a Santander quay during a corsair raid, if you remember?"

Marcos did not want to get into past quarrels or discussions involving the man she obviously still adored so he downed his wine and got to his feet. "I'll go back to my lodgings and change my clothes. I'm not wandering these streets in fancy gear after midnight."

"Come back and have supper with me. We can scandalize Hetty's nurse and my new maid, by sending them off to bed while you're still here. Hetty will be thrilled to see you, too."

Thoroughly subdued, Marcos descended the worn, uneven stairs from Alina's rented rooms tugging his cloak about him then set off for his own lodging nearer the harbour. As he exited the hallway a gaunt figure in clerical black crossed the hall and exited behind him. There was something familiar about him. Marcos swung around but in the time it took to turn and raise a hand in greeting the figure had disappeared into the busy street.

Each dressed in black, cloaked and hooded, Marcos and Alina strode purposefully along the narrow street to Ludo's rented house. The clamour of the bells gave way to the laden silence of a city at night. Above them a feeble moon peeped out of threatening clouds, making the irregular cobbles shiny in places and unpredictable in others. Uneven and slippery from the perpetual dampness off the Tagus estuary, the streets of Lisbon were always hazardous; in the dark they were perilous. Alina stumbled badly, falling forward. Marcos grabbed the back of her skirt, which sent them both into giggles. It was nervous laughter and at Ludo's doorway Alina had to stop and pull herself together. Marcos realised he hadn't asked her what she was going to say. He would have to improvise. In the old days back in Amsterdam he'd been good at improvising, now it produced a knot in his stomach.

He rapped the knocker, a brass cockerel's head. They waited. Eventually a tousled man in a short night gown and holding a stub of candle opened the door. The wind blew out the flame.

"We're here for Dom Ludovico," Alina announced, pushing her way into the black hole before he could speak.

Marcos paused, trying to see the servant's face that he could commit it to memory. Then he followed, tripping on the first stair and praying to God Ludo was alone in bed. He couldn't face how the scene would play out if not.

Alina opened the door to a drawing room, then shut it and climbed another flight of stairs. Marcos followed. The stairs being far too narrow for anyone to get past her, the servant had no alternative but to follow.

She opened another door, "*Cariño!*" she called, which would upset any possible bedfellow – "*Cariño*, look who's here!"

A flint box rattled: a candle flickered. Ludo swung his legs out of bed. "I wondered who was making all that racket. Not thieves, obviously." He pulled a dressing gown around his shoulders and stood up. "Gerardo, for God's sake take them down to the drawing room, and bring them *more* wine."

"Do you want us to go down?" Alina asked, prancing to the window like a child and opening it. "It's awfully stuffy in here! How can you breathe? Ah, that's better." Wind raced in and tore around the room, extinguishing Ludo's candle in the process. "Ooh, it's all gone dark," she called, and began groping around with her arms before her. Marcos knew it was his cue to get to the bed and grab whatever was under the pillows but he simply couldn't do it.

"Shut the window!" Ludo ordered. The candle was relit; then, pushing Alina none too chivalrously before him, he led the way down to the drawing room.

It gave Marcos a second chance to get what he'd come for, but he didn't use it.

Gerardo, the servant, hastily dressed with his nightgown stuffed into his breeches, was in a small parlour pouring wine into three thick-stemmed glasses. Alina made a fuss about removing her cloak and giggling as she drank. As Ludo sent Gerardo back to bed, she turned to Marcos, "Got them?" she mouthed. Marcos shook his head.

"What?" demanded Ludo, closing the door that Gerardo had left open.

"I was telling her we shouldn't have woken you like this," Marcos replied.

"No, you could have waited perfectly well until morning."

"Wrong!" stated Alina. "I shan't be here in the morning. I am going to Coimbra with Dom Enrique and the duchess to see a new house."

There was an awkward silence then Ludo said, "Delighted to hear it. You are taking up residence in Portugal, then? Are you taking up spying as well, *carina*? They must know of your links to Madrid, via your father."

Alina looked down. "That's silly. Whatever gave you that idea?"

Ludo cocked his head to one side and gave one of his wry grins. "Because I now know who Dom Enrique is."

Alina sighed and flopped back in a tapestry-covered chair, all pretence at tipsiness forgotten. "Who is he, Ludo? But only tell me the truth. Oh, no," she began fanning her face with a hand, "I've dropped my fan. It must have been when I opened the window. Marcos, be an angel; go and get it for me."

Marcos stared at her unseeing, his mind trying to make a connection between the mysterious white-haired marquis Dom Enrique, Ludo and Alina.

"It's probably near the window – on the floor."

Alina's voice penetrated his thoughts and he looked up. Before he could answer Ludo said, "I'll go," and went to the door. Then he turned and asked, "What do you need a fan for in the middle of the night?"

"A lady never goes anywhere without a fan in Lisbon, don't you know that? Marcos will go. You stay here and tell me the worst about the charming Dom Enrique, I'm sure you'll have a lovely time blackening his name."

Marcos left the room. Bumping between the narrow walls of the stairway he groped his way into the dark bedchamber then bumped around until he found the bed. Under the pillows were sharp-edged bundles tied in handkerchiefs and three chamois pouches, he stuffed them into his inner cloak pockets and breeches, then made some attempt to see if there really was a fan on the floor.

Going back down, he waited for a moment outside the door to the parlour, not wanting to disturb an embarrassing scene. It was too quiet.

Marcos closed his eyes and took a deep breath. This was awful: not only was he eavesdropping, he was stealing from Ludo. He coughed loudly, opened the door and entered the room. They were sitting apart. He took another deep breath and said, "I can't find it. Too dark to see anything."

"She can get it in the morning," Ludo replied. "Or when she comes back from Coimbra. *If* she comes back. Failing that, I'll send Gerardo to her lodgings, or we can stop this nonsense altogether and you can tell me what is really going on."

Marcos removed his cloak, folded it carefully to conceal the pockets in the lining and laid it across a vacant stool. Taking a chair at the table, he said, "Well, it's like this. I went back to Plymouth and ..." and out it all came – why he was in Ludo's lodging in the dead of night.

"So, to show your newfound loyalty to a country that has done its best to kill you on more than one occasion, you have come to steal from me," Ludo said.

"No!" Alina came to his rescue. "You left us in Chateau Thierry to manage as best we could, knowing we were in a very difficult situation. You did nothing to help us then. You can't criticise us now for doing what we can to secure our futures. We have to decide where our loyalties lie and follow that path."

"Your loyalties lie with me!"

Marcos had rarely seen Ludo genuinely angry. He looked at his hands.

"With you!" Alina was lighting up now. "After what you've done to us?"

"Done to you or *for* you, *milady*?" The last word was thrown at her loaded with sarcasm. "I gave you, both of you, exactly what you wanted. You, Marcos," Ludo swung round to glare at him, "you wanted to be my servant and get as far away from your mother's kitchen as you could. I gave you the skills to become a merchant and make yourself rich in the process. Now you are ignoring those skills, abandoning your enterprise to serve the empty promises of mendacious Englishmen. Hah!" He turned back to Alina. "As for you, *milady*, you did not want to die an old maid if I remember, and you needed a husband to save your good name after being captured by corsairs; I gave you a titled husband –"

"You sold me to his father and kept the money!"

"That's a very crude interpretation, *carina*, and you have an English title to disprove it. A title of your own, not just the dubious honour of being the daughter of a spendthrift grandee, thanks to me. A title that brought you to the notice of the Queen of England and you are now using to get near the Queen of Portugal."

Alina opened her mouth to speak then closed it and put a hand to her throat.

"Quite," Ludo snapped. "You must be spoilt for choice: return to the exiled Queen of England or listen to your Dom Enrique's promises and stay with the Queen of Portugal. Who would have predicted that outcome on a Santander quayside?"

Alina huffed and lifted her chin, but Ludo caught her eye and she turned her head away.

"So, where, I ask you both, should your allegiances lie?" Ludo began to pace the small room.

Marcos swigged down his wine too fast and choked. Putting his hand into a pocket for his handkerchief he touched a chamois pouch. Slowly, he pulled it out and placed it on the table. Then he removed the others and went to the cloak to collect the white linen bundles hidden there.

"No, keep them," Ludo said, his voice barely a whisper. "I'm done. I'll be leaving as soon as I can get my crew back together. I need to get to Salé as soon as possible."

"Salé? Morocco?" Marcos queried.

"Yes, Morocco. It's where my children are in hiding. I hope. I had until April to get the damned jewels to Rogelio or he would seek out my family and –"

"Ludo, that's awful," Alina gasped. "Marcos, give them back to him."

"I already have." Marcos pushed the bundles across the polished surface of the table.

Ludo lifted a hand, "It's all right. I don't need them. Not anymore." He inhaled deeply then exhaled and said, "It's an ill wind ... Irony of ironies, Leonora's last cargo has made it into Lisbon safe and sound. We set off in a convoy from Goa but they were blown off course. I feared them lost, and now discover we – I – have made a fortune with cinnamon and pepper. I was at the Casa da Índia this morning and I've decided to continue with her business after all. I'm sailing for Salé to collect my children then we'll go back to Goa. Then, depending on circumstances, we might move on. Somewhere Rogelio's spies can't find us. Here," he took a key from his robe and opened a cabinet, fumbled inside and extracted an exquisite, oriental casket. Setting it before them, he picked out a pouch and tipped smoky pearls onto the table. "They're from Hormuz via Zanzibar, and technically mine, but you can have them if you want."

"This is ridiculous," Alina announced, taking charge. "There has to be a way out of this – for each of us."

Ludo lifted the jug, "More wine?" he asked. "This could be a long night."

As his glass was refilled, Marcos said, "This Rogelio, he's the priest –"

"He's a Vatican agent and known assassin," Ludo interrupted.

"I think he's here."

"That does not surprise me in the least. You have been followed?"

Marcos had already been told that he had, but did that include the Vatican agent? He cast his mind back, starting with his arrival in Lisbon to the shadow that passed him earlier in the day. "I think so, yes."

"Could he have followed you here? Don't answer that, it's a certainty. You made enough noise. He'll be outside my door right now, I expect, or one of his henchmen will." Ludo paused.

"Your servant Gerardo is in someone's pay, he ..." Marcos started to say, but Ludo's sarcastic laugh silenced him.

"Then here is one possible solution – before Gerardo tries to rob me as well." Ludo returned to the cabinet and extracted a square, ebony box the size but not the shape of a house brick. Placing the box on the table among the other treasures, he stood back and waited.

Alina sighed. "Go on, tell us what's in the box," she said. "Take charge of our lives again, why don't you?"

Ludo gave her a sharp look then focused on opening his box. "I've seen that before," Marcos blurted. "It's one of your Portuguese bizalho boxes."

"For carrying loose gems from India – correct. But this time, my loose gems have been made into works of art. Antique jewellery in double quick time." Ludo took out a cloak clasp brooch consisting of three oblong rubies set around a pyramid-shaped diamond and adorned with four giant pearls.

"That's the Three Brethren," Alina gasped.

"Possibly," replied Ludo. He then set a heavy diamond necklace on the table, then another with a ruby pendant.

"They're fakes!"

"*Alora! Madonna!*" Ludo threw his hands up in the air. "These gems are most definitely genuine. The settings, I admit," he cocked his head on one side, "are contrived to look antique, but I hardly think this warrants the term 'fake'. Let's call them expert reproductions." He gave her a twinkling smile that lit up his sea-green eyes and took the original jewels from three tied handkerchiefs. Placing the original items – the Three Brethren, Queen Bess's diamonds and Catherine of Aragon's pendant – together, he shuffled them around the table like an amateur magician. "One set has been made here, for me. But each has high-quality gemstones, some of them, selected by serendipitous chance by my own hand, in India and Zanzibar. The stones in Bess's necklace come from the Golconda dealers in Goa; the pyramid diamond for the brooch was sourced by a distant relative of my late wife here in Lisbon. They couldn't locate a yellow one identical to the original, but they came up with a good alternative. As long as people don't look too closely, and don't know what to look for, it'll pass."

Marcos and Alina both laughed. "What?" demanded Ludo. "It is true, look carefully, my children, and tell me which is the old and which is the new." Ludo moved a candle closer to the jewels. Marcos could not tell original from new.

"They must have worked jolly fast ..." Alina started to say something else then stopped. "You arranged this the minute we landed," she said looking at Ludo. "You've been planning to cheat the queen from the beginning."

"Cheat! What a dreadful word. If you're back to criticising my actions let me ask you this: is your precious Henrietta not cheating her son, who should inherit all this? Hmm, hmm, hmm? Is she not cheating the very people of England?"

"That's why I'm here," Marcos sighed. "That's why I have to take the jewels back to the Prince of Wales."

"Well, help yourself – take what you like. Take the originals and let's be done with it," Ludo spread a hand across the table like a master merchant displaying his wares.

Marcos shook his head in despair. "This only complicates things."

"Precisely. But I was hoping it would also resolve my problem with Rogelio. He wants two of them as well, you see." Ludo's voice lost its jocular tone.

"Why?" Alina asked.

"For his cardinal, and as blackmail."

"Blackmail, I don't understand," Marcos said.

"It's the price I pay for him to leave my family in peace."

"*Dios mío*," Marcos muttered.

"Not to worry, once you have taken one set and milady has sold the other, I'll get back to Salé as fast as I possibly can. *Tulip* can out-sail a Vatican tub any day." Ludo gave Marcos the ghost of a wink in the candlelight. "Let Alina take what she needs to for the duchess and you can take this blasted casket back to the little prince, or whoever you're working for now. I've only had three things copied; it's not as if we're duplicating the entire Crown Jewels."

"We!" Marcos spluttered.

Ignoring him, Ludo turned to Alina, "Take the Brethren and Bess's diamonds and Catalina's ugly pendant, *madonna*. Sell them to the Duchess of Braganza, then take the money back to your beloved queen, or don't sell them to the duchess and keep them."

"No," Alina replied flatly.

"No?" Ludo queried.

"I can't do it. I have no idea how to begin, even if ..." Alina's voice trailed off. "I only need to be *involved* so the duchess knows I've come from the English court and that I am close to Henrietta Maria. I could say ... I could show her what Henrietta is offering – but you'll have to close the transaction, I have no idea about money. I could feed her the idea of using the jewels as her daughter's dowry for her marriage to the prince, though. If that will help – as a means of keeping Portugal close to Britain by helping King Charles's cause."

"And safeguarding Crimphele," Marcos muttered to himself.

Picking up his words, Ludo nodded. There was a brief silence, then Ludo broke it. Looking at Alina, he said, "As you wish. Either way, now we have the second set, Marcos can take what he has to back to England as instructed."

"And what happens when the duplicates arrive back in England as the princess's dowry?" Marcos asked. "Assuming this all goes according to your neat little scheme."

"Oh, we'll be long gone by then," Ludo chuckled. "And who's to know *we knew* there were duplicates? Nothing to worry about there. No, Alina can go with her fine new beau to his new house in Coimbra as planned tomorrow, and when the right moment comes, she can mention what Henrietta is selling and why ..." He looked away but addressing Alina he said, "Make the most of your time with him, *carina*, and with the duchess. Find yourself a place with them."

Alina wiped a hand across her eyes as if she were crying. Ludo's tone softened, "If you want to keep them or sell the duchess the jewels yourself, you can, I shan't mind. I've got my pepper money; it's not as if I can't pay my rent."

"That's not the point," Alina huffed.

"I don't think you know what the point is anymore, do you, *carina*? If it's so important, though, I would say it's better for the Dom to accept you for what you are – an aristocratic widow in need of a husband. That's what you said you wanted, isn't it? To be who and what you are." Ludo moved to a chair by the fireplace and sat down, his face and body in profile.

"What about your black shadow priest?" Marcos asked. "You said he wanted the jewels."

"That is why I had copies made. So he could have them. Alina was to have one set to sell to the duchess; he the other. I wasn't banking on your arriving to muddy the waters."

Marcos felt a lump rise in his throat: what had he done? Guilt turned him cold. "No," he said, "it's all right. I'll leave in the morning. I can get across country to Sanlúcar. I'll go back to the *cortijo*, like you suggested."

"As you wish." Ludo repeated from across the small drawing room: he could have been miles away. "*Tulip* and I will leave as soon as I have concluded the business with my recently arrived cargo."

The three friends sat in silence, each musing on private thoughts. Eventually, Alina said, "There is a way round this – so we each benefit. Ludo sells or gives one set to this Rogelio, then he sells the real ones to the duchess, as we planned, and I take the proceeds back to Henrietta in France. And you, Marcos, get away as fast as you can back to Spain."

Marcos felt as if she'd slapped him. Alina wasn't remotely interested in helping him receive a knighthood or obtain land in England. She couldn't care less. Then his stomach did a loop-the-loop. Here was a solution and a dilemma all in one. He could offer to take the gems to Rogelio, and take them back to England instead, or to the Portuguese marquis ... except no, that put Ludo's family in jeopardy.

Ludo stroked his fashionable black beard and turned to them with his wry, one-dimpled grin. "That's more or less what I was planning, of course."

"There we are, then," Alina drank down her wine and slammed the goblet onto the table in a most unladylike fashion.

"But Ludo, will this keep your family safe from Rogelio?" Marcos asked.

"Who knows what goes on in a snake's head? Handing them to him personally would have put me within striking distance, anyway. Have to admit, it's a risk I have been avoiding. Mostly because I may have to do something I don't want to."

"Like break his neck?" Marcos suggested.

"For example."

"Then let me take them. I'll do it," Marcos heard himself say.

"Would you?"

"I'm being followed, though."

"Doesn't matter. Rogelio will be in the monastery. *His* watchers will assume you are going to him, anyone else can assume you are in search of spiritual guidance."

"What do I tell him?" Marcos asked, leaning forward.

Ludo turned to him slowly. "Tell him that I've had a change of heart: that he can have the jewels he requested on condition he takes them directly to Rome and leaves my family in peace."

"Do you trust him to do that?"

"Not in the slightest. That is why I'm preparing to sail as soon as I possibly can."

Chapter 27

Less than an hour later, Marcos tucked two pouches into his pockets and swung his thick black cloak around his shoulders, ready to leave. "I'll see you again before you go, won't I?" he said, looking at Ludo.

"No, better not. Do what we've agreed and get away as fast as possible."

"Yes, might be better. I don't need my watchers sending messages back to England before I even cross the border."

Alina came to him and snuggled into his cloak, giving him a hug. "Are you horribly disappointed not to be an English Sir," she asked.

"No!" And Marcos suddenly knew that was true. He was going home, to be what he had planned when he and Ludo were in Amsterdam, a successful merchant of Sanlúcar, someone to be respected, someone with a sizable *cortijo* that once belonged to the Conde-Duque de Olivares into the bargain.

Alina released him and Ludo pulled him into bear hug, saying, "I'm leaving as soon as I can. Toxo and Javi are signing on crew for me. They'll go back to Vigo, though, when I go south, so you'll still be able to work with them from Sanlúcar, if you want to."

They had made their farewells on previous occasions, but Marcos knew this time would be the last. He turned and gave Ludo and Alina a wide smile, "*Adiós,*" he said, and left the warm sitting room.

Gerardo, Ludo's servant was waiting on the tiny landing. Heavy-eyed and stubble-chinned, he bowed and led the way down the stairs to open the door to the street. The door closed and Marcos stood alone in the street, taking stock of the night, pulling his cloak around him more tightly to ward off the chill. Clouds had hidden the moon and there was barely a light to be seen. He shuddered, this was no time to go anywhere; he would make the transaction with Rogelio in the morning. He was too weary and befuddled with wine to face a Vatican agent in the small hours, even assuming he gained access to the monastery.

Setting off down the street towards his lodgings, though, Marcos suddenly felt strangely elated, full of the prospects for the future. Alive, more sober and invigorated by the sharp night air, he pulled the wide collar of his new cloak up to his chin and set off at a good pace towards the harbour, then lost his way as he turned down an alley that appeared to loop back on itself. He halted at a junction where narrow balconies became looming beasts above him and tried to decide which would lead down to the water. As he stood there, trying to subdue a rising panic, he listened for footsteps.

Knowing he was almost certainly being followed by the marquis' operatives, Marcos was expecting to hear footsteps behind him the moment he left Ludo's doorstep, but there had been nothing. He walked on, moving through an alley so narrow he could touch the walls on either side. His senses were on alert now: this was no place to be caught with pockets full of jewels.

The alley came to a sudden end and he was back on a wider street. A light showed beneath a double doorway, he crossed the street and realised he was going back uphill. He turned and headed down again, passing the entrance to the alleyway he thought he'd just left, sniffing at the fish-entrail laden damp to see if he was getting nearer the harbour. He paused, listened again, then strode on, purposeful yet lost.

No footfalls; no sounds other than an occasional scavenging dog snuffling among refuse, and mules and donkeys shuffling inside closed yards. A woman called out in ecstasy or agony as he passed a low window. Apart from this, the only sounds were his feet on cobbled streets. But a prickling of the skin on the back of his neck told him he *was* being followed and he became more nervous. Grateful that Alina wasn't with him, Marcos kept his head down and hurried on.

A big man was loitering at the next corner, but the blow came from behind. Striking him across the shoulders, a cudgel sent Marcos staggering into the middle of the street. The second blow was to the nape of his neck; his knees buckled.

A voice gave orders in dockside argot. The cloak was pulled from him: his pockets raided. There was more scuffling. Strong arms lifted him upright and he was carried down to the quayside between two male torsos – like any other drunk. Lolling in and out of consciousness, Marcos was vaguely aware where they were taking him, and it was the way he wanted to go.

Chapter 28

The house in Coimbra was pleasing to the eye, wide and spacious with patterned red brickwork and dozens of tall windows framed in white stone. It was like a doll's house. Hetty would like living here: there were ponds and streams, bushes shaped into chickens and peacocks. The grounds were well-stocked, the box hedges and yew trees elaborate and mature, for this was a re-modelled house not a new one, as Alina soon learned when they went indoors.

Rooms facing onto the drive had been modernised with wooden panelling and new chimneypieces, but rooms to the rear of the building dated back over a century, and the kitchens were primitive. As the duchess's visiting party made their way down to the lake, Alina separated herself from her new, aptly named chaperone, Dona Dolores of the long-suffering countenance, and wandered along the top terrace, then went in through an open side door, deliberately aiming for the kitchens. She needed to know their conditions; it would make all the difference to her future role – if there was to be a future role, of course.

The main kitchen, judging by the cook-fire and hanging pots, was alarmingly empty given that there was to be a grand supper for a new queen, who might also demand refreshment at any moment. The fire was lit and a pot containing a muslin-covered steamed pudding was hanging over glowing embers, but the trivets and other hooks were empty. Looking up, she saw a few bunches of dried herbs but no hanging hams. It was the silence of the place that concerned her most. Where were the ever-squabbling kitchen maids? Who was feeding the party staying overnight, and with what?

Curious and critical, Alina made her way around the kitchen, finding a bucket containing what she thought might be salted cod on the floor and three skinny boiling fowl on a table. A gardener appeared, touched his forehead respectfully then dumped a pile of winter carrots, soggy and black at the tips, on the same table. A younger boy followed with an armful of wilting greens, which were also dumped next to the chickens, leaving a spray of muddy crumbs around them. The idea of gritty chicken reminded her of Agnes at Crimphele, but that was where the similarity ended. Crook-back Aggie was a terrible cook but she had a heart of gold and many other valuable skills. This kitchen was heartless and cold.

Alina walked to the back door and looked into the yard. It was all far too much like her old home near Santander; the empty yard, the bare kitchen, the meagre cook-fire ... but that had been due to lack of money. Or rather her father's lack of sense, and the fact that what little they had was spent at gaming tables in Madrid. This, she sighed, suggested wilful neglect.

She crossed to the bake-house and found a woman elbow deep in brown dough. "*Perdone,*" Alina said in Spanish, "I am trying to get something to drink."

The servant stared at her then called out something incomprehensible. A skivvy appeared at the door. Sharp words were issued and the terrified skivvy raced into the yard – presumably to an outdoor pump.

Alina followed but the skivvy disappeared altogether. Looking around her, she tried to identify what in Cornwall was called the buttery, where milk and cream were churned, then caught the nauseating smell of sour milk and followed her nose. The light was poor, but the smell told her churns hadn't been cleaned properly for a very long time. She tried to convince herself it was because the house had been unoccupied, but that was also not the case, as she was about to learn.

Returning to the front terrace along a scruffy path, without the cup of water, she was greeted by Dom Enrique. "My dear, we have been looking for you."

"I wandered away and ... then you were gone." Alina gave him a winning smile, but as she looked at him, her eyes were drawn to a small regiment in drab grey lined up along the front of the house.

Dom Enrique followed her glance, "Ah, they have arrived. Permit me to introduce my children."

Shivering with cold, four girls of varying heights and shapes were clasping their hands into the front of their skirts for warmth. Two small boys completed the line: one was red-faced and robust, and looked as if he spent all his time with a catapult, the other wizened like a little old man and coughing persistently. Their tutor, standing at the end of the row, took no notice.

Ignoring the girls, Dom Enrique waved a hand in the boys' direction saying, "Dona Maria de Los Angeles, my two younger sons: Pedro and Pablo." As he spoke, a dumpy figure in voluminous black appeared from the door and hurried towards them. "Their maiden aunt," Dom Enrique explained, turning Alina towards the terrace steps before she could reach them.

Alina turned to glance back as the aunt ushered the regiment indoors with her hands. Not a word had been spoken. She thought back to the Toxo offspring, their jostling and grins and giggles and rosy cheeks, their general good humour. There was little good humour here, from what she could see. Toxo had proudly introduced and named each of his children, girls included.

"So, these are your children," Alina tried to keep her tone light.

"I have two other sons, from my first marriage. One is married, the other soon will be. They are with the Duke's troops in the Algarve."

"But they normally live in Lisbon?"

"The elder of the two, yes, at present. I expect their wives will come here, once they are with child."

"One big, happy family – how pleasant for you." Alina gave a wan smile.

"Oh, I shan't be here. Far too much to do in Lisbon, far too much. Shall we return to the Duchess?"

The early spring sun disappeared behind a hilltop. A cloud took its place. Alina gave a slight shudder and followed Dom Enrique as he located the Duchess of Braganza's party and ushered them indoors.

A somewhat down-at-heel footman opened the double doors to a well-appointed dining room. Candelabra lit a beautiful table set with silver and crystal. Dona Luisa, Duchess of Braganza, beckoned Alina to her side. Perhaps the day would improve, Alina thought. The duchess effectively ruled Portugal while the Duke of Braganza – 'by the Grace of God, John IV, King of Portugal and the Algarves, before and beyond the sea in Africa, Lord of Guinea and of Conquest, Navigation, and Commerce of Ethiopia, Arabia, Persia, and India' – went hunting, leaving the power in his wife's more capable hands.

Alina remembered what Dom Enrique had said about having too much to do, implying he had an important post, or duties, or even – as his close relationship with his cousin the duchess suggested – acted as her right-hand man. Feeling somewhat more optimistic, Alina took the seat indicated, smoothed her skirts and waited.

Candlelight was not kind to Dona Luisa. Square-bodied and short of stature, her artfully plucked, black eyebrows did little to distract from her froggy eyes and wobbly chin. Fearing and expecting her envy, Alina was ready when Dona Luisa addressed her in their native Castilian Spanish.

"Do you favour black, Baroness, or do you observe mourning?"

Alina's gown was indigo blue, but she refrained from correction and said, "My husband was killed but a few months ago, Dona Luisa."

"But you do not forgo your fine jewellery."

"No," Alina gave an apologetic smile and put her hand to the emerald pendant at her throat, "I think he would forgive me this."

Alina lowered her shoulders, tried to her reduce her height as best she could: she needed this woman's friendship. She was aided by Dom Enrique, who also wanted her to make a good impression for reasons of his own; something Alina intended to consider later. Following Dona Luisa's opening, the marquis began with a light comparison about their respective parents' backgrounds then imparted Alina's pedigree in full, and then, to her surprise, expanded on her English title and what had been happening to the House of Stuart in England.

The duchess put down her knife and peered at her. "And I thought you had come to spy on us, Baroness. Tell me, are you more English than Spanish now?"

It was a good question. Alina was taken aback, then saw it as an opportunity. "Perhaps more English, given that my son is with the Stuart princes."

"Is he?" The duchess was impressed. "You are close to the Crown, then?"

"I am, Duchess. In fact, I came here on a mission from Queen Henrietta Maria herself – but not to spy," she added hastily. "She has trusted me with a very great enterprise ..." Alina let the words hang in the air. She had planned for this moment. All the way here from France she had been rehearsing what she would say when the time came and here was the opening she needed – and her resolve was gone. Her hands traced the contents of her skirt pockets as she recalled the instructions Ludo had given her: "Show the duchess a sample and suggest she invite me to show her the rest."

As Dona Luisa and Enrique exchanged words about England and the civil war, Alina's mind raced between her conflicting options, that Enrique should take her on for her true self, or that she instigate the sale of Henrietta's jewels and ensure that her English queen got the proceeds in person. She put a hand to the emerald pendant, she would keep this and the gems Ludo had given Hetty, though, whatever happened.

The conversation was conveniently interrupted by an elderly footman and a spotty youth in livery placing tureens on the table. A square of something baked in butter and burnt around the edges was dropped on the Queen of Portugal's plate then on Alina's. Dom Enrique scowled at the footman and was sublimely ignored. The spotty youth shoved a spoon in a bowl containing greens and stood back against the wall.

"Still having trouble with the servants, Quique?" Dona Luisa teased her cousin. The froggy eyes crinkled and Alina warmed to her, but out of politeness made no comment.

Enrique muttered something under his breath in response as, keeping her head down, Alina pushed a modern fork into the baked brick topping of her food. "What is it?" she asked.

"Cod, I expect," Dona Luisa chuckled. "It's always salted, very salted, cod in this house. The cheese on top might be all right."

"You mentioned an enterprise, Baroness," Dom Enrique said, diverting the topic back to what Alina had been saying and gazing at her with an expression she was unsure how to interpret.

"Yes – an enterprise." Alina took a deep breath then said in a rush, "I am to convey Her Majesty Queen Henrietta

Maria's warmest greetings and remind Dona Luisa of – erm – her adherence to our old religion – and that she has sons and daughters whom she would like to see married to spouses of the Catholic faith – not Protestants." A hand sneaked back into her skirts, tracing the outline of three balas rubies set around a pyramid diamond. Silently giving thanks to Ludo for his outrageous plan for the Three Brethren and the heretic queen's diamonds, Alina finished her utterance with a genuine smile of satisfaction.

Dom Enrique exchanged glances across the table with his cousin and snapped his fingers at a dozing footman, "More wine."

"How interesting," said the duchess. "Tell me, why did you not come to me directly on your arrival?"

Dom Enrique inclined his head in a knowing manner. Alina gave them a detailed version (specially adapted for the company with Ludo's guidance) of how she had fled England with Henrietta Maria and journeyed to France, then had travelled here on the queen's secret betrothal mission – and why her lack of appropriate attire – due to her escape and wanderings – meant she had feared to approach the duchess directly until the problem had been remedied. There was an element of truth in it.

Dom Enrique gave her a searching look and said, "Your life is full of adventure, Dona Alina."

"It is indeed," Alina sighed.

"And have you found a dress-maker now?" Dona Luisa spoke with a mouthful of gritty greens then picked a strand of stalk from between her teeth.

"I have, yes, thank you," Alina replied, looking away. The subject was closed.

Dom Enrique gave a meaningless smile that reached his white moustache but not his eyes and moved his attention back to the duchess, who was saying, "What do you have planned for tomorrow, Quique? I need to be back by early evening."

Confused and disappointed by the way her grand enterprise had been so quickly dismissed, Alina struggled through the rest of the meal in virtual silence. Exhaustion from two nights with barely any sleep began to catch up with her as she endeavoured to swallow the tasteless fowl that followed the cod then a dessert that barely reached Crookback Aggie's cuisine, drinking rather too much wine in the process. The conversation slipped between Portuguese and Spanish, the former obviously being used to exclude her from certain topics, and she was near to dropping when the duchess finally retired. Grateful the night was over at last, Alina followed her up a chilly staircase and went to her allotted chamber. It was freezing cold and she climbed under the linen sheets almost fully dressed.

Sometime later, Dom Enrique tapped at her door. Roused from deep sleep, Alina tried to get her bearings. The bed hangings were open; someone was knocking the door to her chamber. Her first thought was that Hetty needed her then she remembered she was with Blanca in Lisbon. Woozy with sleep and the effect of too much wine, she struggled to sit up in the high bed as the door opened. Dom Enrique entered carrying a small lamp. He was wearing a brocade gown over his night wear – making his intentions clear. Had he been wearing his day clothes, she would have stayed under the warm quilt; under the circumstances that was out of the question. Alina hastened from the bed, hopping from foot to foot on the freezing tiles, searched for her slippers and grabbed a shawl as her mind ran through ways to get rid of him.

Dom Enrique held the dented, brass lamp up to light the spartan chamber. It gave off a sour animal-fat odour. "You have no brazier," he said. "I hope they remembered Luisa." He put the lamp on the clothes press and moved towards her.

Pleased she was still clothed, Alina checked the small dagger in her right-hand pocket; the sharpened blade she'd kept in her skirts since an obsessed Scotsman had stalked her at Crimphele. Noting the movement, Dom Enrique laughed, "You are still in your evening clothes, my dear."

"It is very cold," Alina replied in an equally chilly tone.

"Then allow me to warm you." He placed his hands on her shoulders. "My dear, there is no need to sleep in your emeralds here. No one would dare take anything from you from under my roof."

He touched the stones at her throat and Alina jumped backwards, pulling her blade from her skirt. The slight flame from the lamp caught the steel.

"So you *are* a spy!" Dom Enrique was only half-joking.

"I don't think defending my honour makes me a spy." Alina smiled and edged further from the bed towards the door. "A spy, really? Who on earth gave you that idea?"

Dom Enrique shrugged and pulled the belt of his gown tighter. "Information comes to me from many sources. Lately it comes from France. May I see?" He held his hand out for the dagger.

Alina handed it to him like a naughty child caught playing with knives. He held it to the lamp then said, "Toledo work."

"I doubt it." Then a memory jogged – one of Thomas's ancestors had been in the party to collect Catherine of Aragon for her wedding, well over a hundred years ago. So, another antique. "May I have it back?"

"To defend your honour or for inconvenient necks?"

"That is silly," Alina snapped. "Where has this idea come from?"

"From a Vatican envoy, who has been with the English court in exile and made it his business to tell me what he thought I ought to know."

Alina frowned, "I don't know any Vatican envoy."

"Oh, I think you do. Your Genoese lover certainly does."

Alina bit her lip. It was bound to happen; she had been foolish to hope it wouldn't. Attack being the best form of defence, she stood tall and demanded, "If you are referring to Ludovico da Portovenere, I assure you he escorted us – my child, her nurse and I – from Le Havre on Queen Henrietta's business. He provided transport for me, and nothing more."

Dom Enrique raised an eyebrow. "The envoy from Rome tells me he is in Lisbon to ensure this Genoese character carries out the English queen's wishes – to sell Dona Luisa some rather special jewels."

"Yes, that is correct. But what has it to do with a Vatican envoy?"

"My thoughts entirely." Enrique's white beard twitched as if he might be smiling, but then he said, "Your presence appears to annoy him. Why might that be, do you think?"

"Him?"

"Father Rogelio, you do know him."

Alina gulped. "The queen's confessor? He's an envoy, too? I didn't know that." She was struggling. "I have no idea why I might annoy him. And frankly I don't care, either. He is nothing to do with me. I am here on the Queen of England's business, not his."

"Mmm," the marquis stepped nearer. "I wonder what all this is about. Something isn't right, is it?"

Alina gave an elaborate, careless shrug, masking her anxiety to know how the marquis was connected to Ludo's enemy, Rogelio. "I can't see why this man is interested in me. Don Ludovico brought us in his vessel because, as I said, he will be the one dealing with the duchess – him being a merchant and I a lady-in-waiting with no experience of any form of commerce, naturally."

"Naturally, but you have been entrusted with what is normally a diplomat's task. Is there something else I should know?"

Alina stayed very still. She had no idea how to deal with this situation and greatly feared whatever she said could only make things worse.

Dom Enrique extended a hand, "Come," he said, "let us go to my rooms where I have a log fire." Alina clasped the shawl tightly about her shoulders and shook her head. "I insist. We have matters to discuss and this chamber is freezing. You may have your dagger back if that helps."

Alina pushed the small blade back into her specially lined pocket then started to say, "Truly, Dom Enrique –"

"*Enrique*, please." He took her elbow and guided her to the door.

As if in a bad dream, Alina allowed herself to be taken to a small parlour hung with tapestries. Taking a seat on a padded chair, she accepted a cup of fortified wine hoping it would stop her trembling, and tried to get her ideas in order. *Why was Enrique in contact with Rogelio? Who must have the jewels from Marcos by now, one set of them, anyway. Thank heavens she hadn't shown them to the duchess. Or had Rogelio approached Enrique before Marcos's transaction? Was he here on another matter altogether, he was a Vatican agent after all?*

Enrique seated himself beside the fire, his body at a slight angle, and said quietly, "As I have just made you aware, Dona Alina, I now know more about you than perhaps you'd like. But we can disregard it, nay, even use it to our advantage."

Alina was completely lost. "I have nothing to be ashamed of. I am the daughter of a grandee who –"

"Is an enemy of Portugal and not well-respected; whose daughter was abducted by corsairs and re-appears with a merchant of dubious character ... Shall I continue?"

"I am the widow of an English nobleman, whose son is being educated with the heirs to the English and Scottish thrones." Alina narrowly avoided stamping her foot.

"Which is why I am willing to offer you my protection, if you will consent to be my wife."

Alina was so busy reviewing the comment about how she met Ludo that she almost didn't hear the proposal. She opened and closed her eyes, which Enrique took as encouragement. "It is wholly unorthodox, of course," he said, "not the least because you are Spanish, have children, and are in this room with me on such a short acquaintance, but we are not orthodox people, are we, my dear? Except I am sure you would like to be – and that is what I am offering: my house; my name; my family. This house requires taking in hand, and I think you have the strength of character to do it."

"It is rather a surprise. Dom Enrique –"

"*Enrique.*"

"I need to think about it, about how it will affect my children." *And*, Alina thought, whether I want to take on this house and those miserable-looking girls and their aunt. "Was there anything else? I would like to return to my room now." She got up to leave and Enrique came to her side. Taking her hand, he turned the palm upward and kissed the cushion under her thumb. Alina looked at the back of his head and her body turned to ice. She forced a polite smile, trying not to think of how her body had responded when Ludo had made the same gesture.

Leading her to her door, Enrique said, "Given your situation with the English I expect you would benefit from an allowance; your lodgings are hardly adequate for a lady of your standing. I will arrange for you to move into the palace – if you accept my offer of marriage. You will like, that won't you? But for now, let me have the jewels and I'll keep them in my strongbox."

Alina straightened her shoulders: it was a trap. "What jewels?" she asked, entering her room.

"The jewels belonging to the English Crown."

Alina widened her eyes. "I do not have them," she lied.

"You mean, you do not have them here?"

Alina nodded then shook her head. "Only those I am wearing – which are mine," she added hastily. "Except, I do have an antique clasp that belonged to – erm – a distant ancestor of King Charles. Don Ludovico suggested I show it to Dona Luisa before he ..."

Enrique held out his hand. "May I have it?"

"No! I mean, no – that is – it's not mine to give. Far from it. It belongs to Queen Henrietta until ..." Alina took a deep breath. "You must speak to Don Ludovico."

"Meaning what this Roman priest is telling me is true."

"I have no idea what he is telling you, Enrique."

"He's telling me that your Don Ludovico stole them from your English queen for his own profit."

Alina wavered, knowing that it could be true. Then knew it for a trap. "No, that cannot be the way of it. Ludovico was summoned to France by Her Majesty. I was there. Once he has concluded his business with the duchess – if she is interested in Queen Henrietta's proposal – then I am to return to France with ..." Alina stifled a genuine yawn. "I'm sorry, I'm so tired."

Enrique studied Alina's face then nodded slowly, "I see: a curious arrangement. I shall be most interested in its outcome, especially as its outcome affects our future, my dear."

Alina didn't bother to ask how or why; knowing in that moment she would never marry this man.

Enrique turned to go to his room. Alina slipped back between icy sheets and traced the shape of the Three Brethren nestled in her left-hand skirt pocket, then put a hand to the antique necklace in a draw-string pocket tied around her waist. A doubt clawed at her chest: supposing Rogelio had let Enrique know he'd got these items now – that he had told Enrique she was peddling fakes. What a mess: what a stupid mess. She had lost her chance to show the duchess the Three Brethren and she had talked herself into an appalling situation with Enrique. And it was all Ludo's fault.

Twisting and turning to find a smooth spot on a lumpy mattress, Alina gave in to tears of exhaustion and despair. She had been exceedingly foolish. Tears turned to wracking sobs as she realised how much she missed the stability and comfort of Thomas and their quiet life at Crimphele. She missed it more than she could ever have imagined.

Chapter 29

The journey back to Lisbon was interminable and uncomfortable beyond measure, for the roads were truly atrocious. It was nearly dark, as bumped and bruised from where the Three Brethren pressed into her thigh, Alina climbed the stairs to her rooms lost in the simple desire to sink into the bed and sleep until the next day. The main door to the apartment was open, but there was silence.

Alina's heart missed a beat then raced. Blanca might have left the door open behind her. Why hadn't the maid shut it? Why was it so quiet? It was the silence that bothered her. There was no sign of her maids, maids who Marcos had told her were spies ... She knew absolutely that Hetty was not there: no place was quiet when Hetty was around, except when she was asleep, and it was long after siesta time.

"Hetty!" she called, her voice croaking, her throat dry.

Dona Dolores tutted loudly behind her, making her jump, then dumped Alina's tapestry bag on the floor. Ignoring her, Alina took a few steps inside the living room. Even in the poor light from the window she could see furniture had been moved. She pushed past a chair and rushed into the chamber Hetty and Blanca shared. Both cot and truckle bed had been pulled apart. The small press where they kept Hetty's clothing was open, her little dresses pulled out and scattered on the floor. Alina turned and tripped on Hetty's padded hat. Blanca never took Hetty outdoors without her protective pudding hat.

Alina hurried into her bedchamber. It was a shambles: her new dresses torn from the press, sheets, blankets and pillows tossed to the floor. Her travelling chest had been completely over-turned.

"Hetty!" Alina screamed. "Blanca!"

No one answered.

Alina charged around the rooms looking for clues; had they taken their coats? A piece of red felt clung to a door latch. Had Hetty got her rag doll Etta with her? Or had someone taken the poppet – and Hetty?

Where would Blanca go for help – if she could?

"Ludo!" Alina shouted, and raced out of the door, knocking Dona Dolores sideways. Hiking her skirts up the way she used to when she was a girl, she pelted down the stairs then down the street, running as fast as she could in her decent shoes to Ludo's narrow house.

He wasn't in. Gerardo, the servant said he was either at the Casa da India or down at the harbour. Of course, *Tulip* was preparing to sail.

"Go and fetch him," Alina yelled. "Go and fetch him, I need him!"

Gerardo stared at her as if she had gone mad. "Oh, never mind, I'll go."

And she was off again, stitch tearing at her side, tripping on loose cobbles, dodging stray dogs, nipping between fishwives and wicker baskets, mules and donkey carts, down to the harbour. Where was *The Tulip*? More importantly, where was the pinnace that Ludo used to reach her? Why hadn't she taken any notice of these things before?

As she pushed and shoved her way through the crowd on the quayside, she fell into a huddle of Lisbon stevedores and African labourers standing around a dead body. A dead body … wearing Marcos's clothes. Alina gasped.

A man stood aside. "Make room! Make room," he shouted, "here's the wife."

Alina dropped to her knees, put a hand to the swollen, blue-tinged faced. "Marcos," she whispered. *"Cariño, despierta, por favor, despiértate."*

The men around her stepped back, embarrassed, anxious to be gone. One by one, they drifted away; it was none of their business – all except an urchin gnawing on a stick of bread. He came closer to get a better look then, catching her eye, scooted away as fast as his rag-wrapped feet would take him.

Alina knelt over Marcos's body, crooning his name. Then she untied the strings of her cloak, pulled it off and spread it over him, tucking the dark wool under his wet, wispy beard. As she did so his jerkin fell open. She pulled the cloak down and felt inside the sodden leather. The pocket containing the curious spinel clasp was empty. The other pocket was empty, too.

Alina sat back on the filthy stone paving of the quay as a new group of people gathered around her. A woman bent down and touched her arm. She spoke kindly. Alina had no idea what she was saying, but when another woman pushed a handcart next to her, she understood. Together, the women, fishwives and quayside trollops, helped Alina lift Marcos's body onto the cart.

"Para onde?" said one.

"Onde é a sua casa?" asked another.

Alina understood but couldn't reply.

The women conferred among themselves and began to push the cart slowly along the waterside. Alina followed in a daze. A few yards on she thought they might be taking him to the Jerónimos Monastery further along the sea front, and let them.

They pushed the cart into an arcade then across a stone-tiled yard to a separate building and left it at a side door. They seemed to know where to go. One kissed her cheek and pressed a sprig of rosemary into her hand.

Alina stood there in the chill afternoon light beside Marcos's cold body and could neither move nor cry, nor speak.

A novice monk took the handles of the cart and she followed him into a high-ceilinged space, the infirmary. The novice and cart disappeared through a door. An elderly monk came to her. He spoke to her in Portuguese then tried in Spanish. "*Señora*, please come with me."

She heard the words but they did not register. Two different monks accompanied her into some kind of parlour and offered her warm milk. The smell made her gag. They left and she was alone with wandering images of the only real friend she had ever had.

Sometime later, she had no idea how long, the novice came into the parlour and coughed politely. "Come," he said.

Alina followed him. She thought it was a chapel at first, although the walls were slimy and smelled of dank sea water. It was dark, save for a meagre tallow candle flickering beside a lectern. The monk lit a tin lamp. Its shadows threw up elongated shapes. They weren't in a chapel. There was a row of stone slabs. A body lay on one, covered in a rough, grey sheet. This was the morgue. Alina clamped her hands over her mouth to prevent a scream escaping.

"This was your husband?" the elderly monk enquired.

Alina moved her lips but still no sound came.

Across the echoing black space, eyes glared at her. Two red, glowing eyes. The eyes of the devil. "My daughter!" she screamed. "What have you done with my daughter?"

"Your daughter?" A monk holding two small lamps stepped forward. It wasn't Rogelio.

Alina ran out of the door, colliding with an urchin with rag-wrapped feet, who nipped around her and entered another building.

Chapter 30

Alerted by the boy, Rogelio watched the woman from across the yard as she ran from the morgue. He signalled the urchin to follow. Then, waiting until the boy had gone, he went to the elderly monk to enquire why she had been there.

Before the monk had even finished speaking, Rogelio said, "There was nothing on him; you are quite sure?"

"Nothing to identify him, no. His pockets were empty and there was no purse. His clothes are of quality, but he'd been robbed of everything he was carrying."

"And he was killed, how? Drowning?"

"He was beaten badly beforehand, I believe, then thrown to the water. The usual thing."

"Damnation!" Rogelio clenched a fist. "Hell and damnation!"

Surprised, the monk hastened back into the infirmary. Rogelio flung out of the morgue into the chilly evening, his short gown flapping around his thin legs as he strode purposefully along the sea wall towards the harbour.

The only hope now was that the man Gerardo had been wrong ... unless Ludovico had paid his servant to mislead him? Rogelio pulled a small square of paper torn from a book and re-read the bad hand-writing on it. *'The Spanish gentleman from England has the jewels.'* The note had arrived the previous morning, but the body of Marcos Alonso showed signs of having been dumped in the sea earlier, and his own men knew nothing about it.

He'd have to search the Spaniard's room at the hostel again. If the jewels weren't hidden there, three possibilities remained: they had been stolen before the Spaniard went in the water, the stupid servant was wrong and the woman had them, or Ludovico was playing games, trying to outwit him.

And if that was the case, how did Ludovico even know he was in Lisbon – except through Gerardo?

For a moment, Rogelio was tempted to abandon his chase. He'd be better buying some old-fashioned jewels and handing those over to his patrons. As long as they never consulted the stupid Henrietta, no one would be the wiser.

But that would be playing into Ludovico's hands. He'd win again, the way he had in Amsterdam; the way he'd saved the Portuguese woman's firm in Goa.

No, the cardinal had tasked him, Rogelio, with acquiring two priceless jewels, and he'd see it through. He'd get them both and *then* make a decision.

A waft of strong breeze bearing the odours of sea and dockside refuse buffeted him. Rogelio grabbed his hat and, head down, resumed his walk towards the harbour, where the urchin soon found him and gave him a message he liked. The lady was waiting further along the quay, where the pinnaces and lighters from the ships out in the estuary were tied up. It took no time to find her – taller than most women with all that hair blowing about her like a floozy – she drew attention to herself as no decent woman should.

Rogelio stood back among the hand-carts and donkeys lined up against the taverns and waited, considering his options, reviewing what his hired brutes had told him. He'd made a mistake with them; they had made a complete pig's ear of following the Spaniard and a worse mess of going through the baroness's apartment. They hadn't found the jewels and they hadn't been quick enough to get the child. A slip of a girl had outrun them and outwitted them in a labyrinth of backstreets. Anger and doubt filled Rogelio's throat with the acid taste of bile. And then he saw a way to get his revenge, and possibly the jewels at the same time.

He told the urchin to fetch his tame brutes. They'd have one final task and after that they could find their own way home: if they failed this time, they'd never see another coin from him.

As the boy ran off towards the Alfama end of the harbour, Rogelio was rewarded by the sight of Ludovico's lighter arriving at the quay. The woman noticed it at the same time and started screaming at Ludovico in Spanish before he was even out of the boat, causing a pleasing stir of amusement and vulgar interest among the labourers loitering around her for work. Ludovico took her in his arms and tried to lead her away. But she wouldn't move; she screamed at him again then pummelled at his chest and then did what all stupid, angry women did, fell against him and cried long and loud.

Rogelio sniffed with satisfaction. Her behaviour confirmed their relationship; and one of them definitely had the jewels. He should have taken the child in the first place as he'd planned, used her to get what he wanted, but there was still time. *The Tulip* was preparing to sail but it hadn't weighed anchor yet.

Rogelio watched, consumed with disgust, jealousy and hate as his Genoese cousin stroked the woman's hair, kissed her eyes and hugged her to him.

Chapter 31

Ludo put a hand on Alina's back and guided her into the nearest tavern.

"Hot brandy," he ordered. "Two, with sugar, if you have any."

A trollop with a cleavage advertising her wares nudged another. They stood up and made room for the lady to sit down. Ludo manoeuvred Alina onto the bench; she was drained of colour and had no will of her own. One of the women took her hand and patted it. The brandy arrived. Ludo handed a clay cup to Alina then tossed his back. It scalded his throat, but it was what he needed; the past week had been exhausting and now his madness had caused Marcos's death. The whole foolish commission had to be brought to a halt.

Ludo looked at the two women meaningfully and nodded his head in the direction of the door. They moved away a few paces to lounge against two sides of a splintering pillar. Ludo turned back to Alina, but she hadn't even noticed them.

Alina sipped her brandy then pushed the cup at him and said, "I can't stay here, I have to find Hetty."

"Hetty's all right, I've told you. You weren't listening. As soon as Blanca found me, I got them into your cabin on *Tulip*. It's the safest place. No one will get her there, not with Toxo and Javi on board. As soon as you feel better, we'll get your things and you can go aboard, too. It's safer if you stay with me now."

Alina stared at him. "I can't. I mustn't. Dom Enrique already thinks ..." she swallowed hard and shook her head.

Ludo crouched beside her. "Alina, listen, I need you to concentrate. We have to decide what to do about the jewels." The trollops' shuffled nearer. Realising he had let his guard slip, Ludo stood up and faced the two women, "Eh! You two, off with you."

This was no place to discuss anything. He slapped some coins on the counter for the brandy then led Alina back to his lodgings, because it was nearest.

Gerardo was slumped against the open front door, his dark jowls a mess of blood and pulp. To a passer-by he looked like an unlucky drunk. Unlucky he was: he'd been set upon with wooden clubs and meaty fists.

"*Maria Santissisma!*" Ludo muttered, propelling Alina inside before pulling Gerardo into the tiny hallway. As soon as he'd managed to close the door, he pushed Alina up the narrow staircase to the parlour.

At the door Alina came to her senses. "*Madre mía,*" she whispered, "this is worse than my rooms."

"Find a candle or light the lamp, if you can find it. We need to help that poor chap downstairs."

"There's an infirmary at the monastery."

"Good thinking." Ludo ran back to the main door and whistled up an urchin in rag-wrapped feet loitering across the street. "Find someone with a cart," he ordered, pushing a coin into a skinny hand. "Be quick about it and you'll get more of these."

The boy scooted off and within a very short time returned with an empty fishmonger's handcart and two other urchins. Ludo knew they had commandeered the cart, but didn't quibble. As soon as they had the servant balanced on the wooden planks, he gave them a handful of coins and instructions to go to the infirmary on the sea front.

Going back to the parlour, Ludo found Alina attempting to straighten chairs and tidy up. "Leave it," he said. "We can do it in the morning."

Alina looked at him blankly. "I can't stay here, Ludo. I have to go to Hetty then go back to my rooms. Everything I own is there. Was there."

"Hetty is not to leave the ship."

Alina looked at him through the gloom and nodded. "All right, but I can't stay here. Dom Enrique thinks you are my lover."

Ludo barked a scornful laugh. "He proposed then?" Alina looked away. Ludo's mouth twitched but he kept his true response to himself, saying instead, "Well, all this puts you in a pretty pickle. I can't let you out of my sight, you see."

Alina's chin shot up. He knew the warning sign and put out a hand, "*Calma, calma.* You are at risk with me, for more reasons than your reputation, but you're at far greater risk if I'm not around to protect you now."

"Because of Marcos." Alina slumped down in the nearest chair. "We have to arrange his funeral," she said.

"He was taken to the monastery. He'll get a Christian burial."

"A pauper's burial – as if he was some homeless, dockside nobody. Marcos was 'somebody' – somebody special, very special." Alina gulped back tears, "I called him a nobody once – more than once. I was wrong. We have to go to the monastery, make sure they give him a proper service. And send to his poor mother. We stopped him going home to her when we were in Spain that time. I stopped him going back to Sanlucar because I was at Crimphele when you came back from Holland. He thought I didn't know but I always knew, I just didn't – couldn't ... and now, again, and ... we ... I didn't ..." Alina came to a halt, gripping the back of a chair, fighting back tears.

Ludo shook his head, biting his lips, for he was close to tears himself. Shifting position, he noticed a beeswax candle at his feet, located the holder and tried to light it. As he fiddled with his flint box he said, "We can go to your rooms, if you really want to. I'll stay with you there. In the morning you can get what Hetty needs and take it to her while I go to the monastery and pay for a mass to be said for Marcos, if that's what you want?"

Alina jumped to her feet. "Yes, but now, not tomorrow. I'll come down with you."

Ludo grabbed her hand. "No. We are not going anywhere near the harbour until tomorrow morning, in the light of day. Hetty is safe with Toxo and Javi, I promise. But we are not."

Alina tugged away from him. "Coward."

Ludo threw up his hands. "All right, milady, off you go. The door is open, but I regret my servant cannot show you out."

Alina clenched her fists and stared at him. Ludo inclined his head, waiting. Finally, she said, "As you wish," then waited impatiently while he checked to see if any of his Hormuz pearls remained in the cabinet and if the few remaining loose gems that he'd kept in the much-travelled bizalho box were where he'd left them. The box was lying under a chair with its back broken, but there were a few scattered stones strewn across the floor.

Ludo gathered them and got to his feet, tapping his pockets to reassure himself he'd kept all the most valuable on his person – except the ones Alina and Marcos had taken, of course. The rope of pearls with the heavy pendant that had once belonged to a royal Spanish exile was still safely on his person, though. "At least they didn't get Queen Catherine's pearls," he said, pulling the pouch from his pocket.

Alina pounced on it. "Give it to the abbot at the monastery for their Virgin Mary."

Ludo blinked, "What! I think not, this is my trump card – my convincing argument with the duchess. The one thing that will tempt her above all – I hope." He gave Alina a searching look: she was being serious. "Ah, well ..." he murmured, and stuffed the pearls back into their pouch then deep into the pocket. A cabochon sapphire ring caught his eye in the lamplight, it was lying under the edge of the dusty rug. "Whoever has done this, they are amateurs," he said, picking up the ring and taking it to the flame to check for damage.

"These amateurs killed Marcos."

Ludo paused. "Not necessarily. Lisbon is a dangerous city at night – during the day even. I've been here before and never felt safe. Same in any harbour town, really. Could be coincidence. All right, that's enough for now, let's go."

Alina was so broken with unhappiness she let Ludo set her bed to rights and made no fuss when he stuffed his gems under her pillow and slipped in beside her. Holding her to his chest, he let her sob until she fell asleep and then fell asleep himself with his chin resting on her soft, golden hair.

As the first rays of a fine spring morning crawled through the grubby window, Ludo tried to ease his arm from under Alina's shoulders. She gave a deep sigh and put her arm over his chest. He kissed her brow. He kissed her nose and her eyes. They made quiet, slow, early morning, life-affirming love, and for the first time since he had left Genoa, he did not think of Leonora.

"*Cara carina*, stay with me," he said, meaning 'for the rest of our life'.

Alina rolled away from him and stared at the torn bed hangings. "The queen's Three Brethren and Bess's diamonds – or your copies – whichever they are – are on the floor in my skirts. Have them back. I don't want them."

"Because?"

"Because your Rogelio killed Marcos for them. Because whether your Rogelio does or does not have them, I don't want anything more to do with any of this."

Very quietly, Ludo replied, "Marcos could have been robbed in the street. Or ... or it could have been Dom Enrique." Alina took a deep breath but did not respond. "That doesn't surprise you?" Ludo asked.

"No," she said. "But no matter who took what Marcos had, it means someone in Lisbon has got the blasted jewels. What happens if the second set appears while we are still here? I can't have anything to do with them, Ludo, and you should leave as soon as you can."

"And you ... and Dom Enrique?"

Alina sat up and pushed her hair off her face and neck, letting it fall in a tousled cascade down her back. "Why would he be involved in what happened to Marcos? I wouldn't be surprised if he knows about it ... I mean, he did tell me he was in contact with Rogelio, and he did actually ask to see the jewels I was going to show the duchess, but . . ."

"But you didn't."

"Show him – or the duchess? Neither. I didn't have a good moment with the duchess and ... something wasn't right."

"I'll say!"

Alina ignored him and carried on voicing her thoughts: "He knows about the jewels because I told him – but I can't see why he would want them himself. Unless ..." Alina swung her long legs over the side of the tangled bed and said, "... *unless he* wants to give them to the duchess himself, as a personal gift – or to me? Wouldn't that be ironic?"

Ludo studied her profile. "What are you not telling me?"

"Oh – that he's looking for a house-keeper to live in Coimbra more than a wife to accompany him at court. And that he has a very close relationship with the duchess. He's more than just an elegant courtier, that's for sure." She slipped off the bed and started gathering her clothes, wandered out of the room and then returned. "Ludo, the bag

I took to Coimbra, which my new chaperone carried and dumped by my door, it isn't here. Dona Dolores put it down by the door, I distinctly remember." She gave a deep-felt sigh and flopped back down on the bed. "I know she's part of Enrique's private retinue, but why for heaven's sake take my bag of small clothes?"

"It's as good a place as any to secrete diamonds, *carina*." Ludo traced a brown finger down Alina's white spine, following the line of vertebrae one by one until she pulled away. She got up and went to wash at an unbroken basin with water from a salvaged jug.

"Ludo!" she cried, once her face was dried, "Get up! We have to go to Hetty. There are a dozen things to do."

"I know, I know, but a man can dream, can't he? I was just wondering how it would be if you and I –"

"You can stop that sort of wondering right now. There's too much to be done to wonder about anything."

"*Va bene*," Ludo sighed and dragged himself from the warm bed to find a jug of water for himself.

When he returned to her room, Alina was standing there fully dressed. Slowly, she handed the queen's jewels to him. "Are you still going to make the transaction with the duchess – now Marcos is gone?"

"Yes," he replied quietly, "I don't intend whoever attacked Marcos to halt my plans." He wanted to add, 'But this will be the last time. Rogelio will have no excuse to hurt me or mine ever again after this,' but he didn't because Alina had enough to worry about without reminding her of Rogelio – and the implicit danger to their daughter.

They did not speak more than a few words again until, fed on dry bread, they shut the door behind them and returned to the street.

As Ludo escorted Alina down to the harbour, she said, "You have to find him and punish him. Rogelio killed our best friend."

"We don't know that. I don't even know if he's here," Ludo replied, although that was partly a lie: he hadn't seen him with his own eyes but he had certainly sensed Rogelio was close.

"Ludo," Alina turned to him, her expression a mixture of sorrow and what he could only think of as anger, "death comes in threes. That's the saying, and look what's happened: first Thomas, now Marcos – we must prevent a third." She didn't say 'happening to us' but Ludo could see where her thoughts were taking her. "Besides, you must avenge Marcos, he was your partner and friend. We must decide what to do and you must kill him."

Death comes in threes. Not always, Ludo thought, when Death came calling, he took far more than three, in houses where there was sickness or plague, on ships boarded by corsairs – he'd seen that for himself from a young age. But the superstition Alina had voiced had lodged itself firmly in his mind: *first Leonora, now Marcos; who next?* He shook his head to shift a terrifying image of a small child with black curls and said sharply, "No, *madonna*, we must make sure we are as far from Rogelio as possible."

"What! After he has killed my best and only friend, you want him to walk away free? You are a coward!"

Ludo removed his hat, re-arranged the feathers then replaced it. Trying to erase unwelcome thoughts, he said, "I'll think of something."

They walked on in silence until Alina said, "I think I saw him at the monastery. I'm *sure* it was him. Do it tonight."

"I have to make my way to the duchess and conclude a very tricky bit of business, first. That way, depending on the lady's privy purse, you can leave on the morrow for France. Or stay with your marquis until she pays up and send a messenger with a bag of money to your little queen instead. If you have one vestige of sense, of course, you will sail with me as soon as possible." Ludo paused. "Do what?"

"Retaliate!" Alina swung round, angry then changed her tone and said in a hushed voice, "You *are* afraid of him."

"I am afraid of what he is capable of. He seems determined to harm or eliminate anyone I care for. I am afraid *for you*, but I am not afraid of him."

"Well I shan't let him escape punishment. Not for this." Alina strode on ahead, then turned back. "Why is he doing it anyway?"

"I wish I knew. Something to do with our family."

"Your family!"

Ludo opened a hand in a Latin gesture of resignation. "He's a Doria by-blow, same as me. Except he was dumped – sent off to a monastery and forgotten about, and I was – well, I wasn't. My mother was … It's a long story."

Alina stared at him, started to say something then changed her mind and marched on ahead.

Catching up with her, Ludo tried to take her hand, but she pulled away, stiff and silent. "What now?" He demanded. "You didn't think I might be a prince in disguise did you!"

"No. You are a heartless, feeble pirate with no feelings for anyone. I've always known it and have no illusions."

The way Alina tossed her head made Ludo want to laugh, but her words cut him to the quick.

When they reached the quay, he whistled up his pinnace, then spoke some quiet words to the oarsmen and tipped them a few coins. Alina scrambled into the boat and Ludo watched until he saw her climb aboard *The Tulip*. A boy followed her up the ladder with Hetty's belongings strapped to a shoulder, another followed her across the deck as instructed. They were to set up camp outside Alina and Hetty's cabin until he came aboard himself. Ludo nodded with satisfaction, but the bag set him thinking: *if only they would stay there* … they could sail on the morning tide and go … anywhere, once he'd fetched his family from Salé.

He turned and made his way towards the monastery; there was a funeral to arrange before he went to the palace, he wanted to pay his final respects to Marcos.

The coldness of the morgue chilled Ludo to the bone and turned his thoughts to ice. Unable to see clearly or think straight, he eventually left the monastery precincts to make his way back to his rented, ransacked house. As he climbed the steep street, he cursed loudly in Genoese dockside blasphemy; he had changed his mind twice since leaving Chateau Thierry and it had cost Marcos his life. Furious with himself and falling back into the despair he'd felt after Leonora died, he stopped at the top of the rise, gazing out between a gap in the rooftops at the shimmering Tagus Estuary: time to clear his head and come to a final decision.

If Rogelio had the copies taken from Marcos, he would – should – hasten to Rome, surely, to give them to his cardinal. Or whatever other devious purpose he intended. Whichever, there was no need for Rogelio to remain in Lisbon. That meant he'd soon be out of the way, if he hadn't already left.

Except that didn't explain the overlooked gems in his ransacked rooms, or, more worryingly, why he had raided Alina's ... Unless he'd been after Hetty. Ludo felt a moment of absolute panic at the thought of what Rogelio could do to Hetty. Quickly, he searched for *Tulip's* tall masts out in the water and took a deep breath: Hetty was safer there than anywhere else – until he could get her away.

So? So there was just time to visit the palace this evening and try to gain an audience with the forbidding Dona Luisa, to offer her the curious arrangement of three exquisite spinels and the diamonds once worn around the stiff neck of the late, great Virgin Queen, and the pendant ruby once gifted to Catherine of Aragon – which by some oversight had stayed in his pocket at the monastery. If the Duchess of Braganza wouldn't see him – so what – he'd take the jewels back to Genoa and give them to his mother, or leave them with the Abbott for a plaster Virgin to wear at fiestas, as Alina had suggested.

Ideally – preferably – of course, he'd get a decent price for the spinels, the ruby pendant and the diamonds, and that, hallelujah, would be an end to it. Alina could take the proceeds back to her Henrietta – because she had had the genuine ones with her in Coimbra, and Rogelio would be peddling the fakes. And he, Ludo da Portovenere, who still had more tricks up his sleeve than he himself could count, was free to move on. Free to return to his two children and start again. As long as he knew Rogelio had got a passage back to Rome. As long as he could find a way to stop Rogelio's vicious, petty vendetta.

Ludo gave himself a wry, one-dimpled grin. Decision made, time to make the deal.

Time to see the new Queen of Portugal and hope to Jehovah she didn't remember his name; time to sell the blasted jewels and get the hell out of Lisbon – this time forever.

Chapter 32

Ludo was shown into a small internal apartment. The walls appeared to have been papered or covered in a dark cloth bearing a feather design; the candlelight being so poor it was hard to tell. The Duchess of Braganza looked up from a small, three-legged table of oriental design. "Come," she said, and indicated a low, upholstered chair to her left.

Ludo removed his hat, and with a flourish and a sweep bowed from the waist. His hat set a Chinese vase on a cabinet to his right rocking. It was retrieved in the nick of time by the footman who, holding it to his chest, bowed to his queen and backed out of the tiny room. Ludo kept his head low, noting the lacquered table: he had seen one similar in Leonora's house in Goa. He wasn't sure where he had been expecting to be received, but this suggested he was in one of the duchess's private rooms, and it wasn't what he had expected at all. Nor was the fact that his line of sight told him the duchess was not just well-made, she was also with child – it would make any attempt at flattery suspicious. Not that flattery was much of an option in this case: Luisa de Guzman was no oil painting. Which was probably why she had chosen such poor illumination.

"Come," repeated the duchess, indicating the chair once more.

Ludo left his feathered head gear on the cabinet and lowered himself into the chair, aware that he was now at a lower level than the duchess. He gave an inward sigh and

298

looked around him. The apartment was claustrophobic, its smallness exacerbated by the presence of an over-ornate filigree screen placed at an angle to the right of his chair. Ludo took a quick look at the ceiling; there was room behind the screen for at least one listener. Unless it was for the royal chamber pot. He was tempted to sniff, but refrained in case he was right. Instead, he gave the square-set woman his most brilliant smile, "Thank you, Your Majesty, for allowing me this interview."

Dona Louisa's eyes crinkled as she returned his smile, briefly relieving her sallow pallor. She had tried to cover her naturally yellow complexion with white paste; it had formed crevices in the folds under her chin. Ludo controlled an involuntary shudder and focussed on arranging the hem of his brocade jacket. He tried to stretch out a leg; the chair was most uncomfortable. The woman wasn't expecting him to stay long, evidently.

Taking himself in hand, Ludo began his prepared preamble: "May I say, *madonna*, that it is most gracious of you to receive a mere merchant such as I –"

"It is." The line was cut before he'd finished casting. The duchess then pre-empted any chance of an alternative approach. "But I do know why you are here. And I do know you are no humble merchant because you are a member of the Doria family of Genoa. You have something to show me."

It was unexpected, but not unwelcome. Ludo gave her a genuine smile. "I do indeed," he said.

"Well, come along," the duchess tapped the table top, "show me."

Ludo's hand hovered over the right-hand pocket of his elegant coat. Which first, the Virgin's necklace or the brooch, or Catalina's pearls and pendant? He started with the last; it would appeal to Dona Luisa's Spanish upbringing, and remind her of how far she had come. Without a word, he spread a fine white handkerchief on the table. Then he placed the contents of a chamois pouch over it. The pearls coiled like a small snake around the ruby.

"This, *madonna*, once belonged to the daughter of Isabella *la Católica*. She who married first Arthur, then Henry Tudor of Britain, eighth of that name. It was passed down to her daughter, Mary Tudor, who married –"

"Felipe the second of Spain." Dona Luisa rapped the table again, which Ludo interpreted as haste to see his other wares, but was in fact a signal for a footman to enter. "Bring more light," she ordered.

An oil lamp was brought in and placed on the cabinet; a candle in a plain, domestic brass candleholder was placed on the table. Dona Louisa waited until the footman had closed the door then held the ruby pendant to the flame. She nodded as if purchasing a suitably plump cabbage in a market place. "Yes, all right. What else?"

Ludo set the Three Brethren on the table and gave its history. This time Dona Luisa spent more time examining the gems.

"They are spinels, also called balas rubies, *madonna*. Very rare. Very expensive."

"I could have three necklaces made with these," the woman said, matter-of-factly. "And the diamond for a brooch. Yes, as you say, very fine."

"You could do that, *madonna*, and more, but perhaps you should hear what I have to suggest before you decide. I also have a message from the Queen of England, relating to these gems. Would you like to see the most beautiful piece first, though?"

Dona Luisa's froggy eyes glinted as Ludo moved the more antique gems to one side and arranged Queen Bess's diamond necklace on the black table top. He lifted the candle and allowed the flame to make the sale.

The duchess gave a small gasp and picked them up in a swollen paw.

"Permit me," Ludo said. Getting to his feet somewhat inelegantly, he arranged the diamonds around the podgy Braganza neck. "These were made for the heretic queen Elizabeth of England. How fitting, how right, that they should come to you, *madonna*, who can return them to England with a Catholic queen."

Dona Luisa turned her head to stare at Ludo. "Sit," she said. "Explain."

Ludo resumed his seat and explained how a Spanish noblewoman who had become the Queen of Portugal could become a meaningful part of the English royal family and return that heretic nation to the one true faith. As he spoke, he wondered if this was what he and Alina had concocted or if it was the original plan he'd devised as he'd been jogged along the banks of the River Marne, months ago. Not that it mattered; the Duchess of Braganza was falling neatly into their net with the minimum of fuss.

That was, until he opened the discussion of payment. Then Ludo realised he had met his match. She haggled like a housewife in the souk, and so effectively that Ludo started to chuckle. The chuckle became genuine laughter.

Dona Luisa, Queen of Portugal, caught his amusement and joined in. They laughed and laughed until they had tears in their eyes.

Eventually, Ludo took a deep breath, wiped his face with the handkerchief from the table and said, "Please, Your Majesty, let me make a proposal. I suggest you contact Queen Henrietta Maria yourself, via an appropriate emissary. Arrangements can thus be made for a royal matrimony, without a third party merchant or agent, or whatever you choose to call me, being part of the financial transaction. Why not take these jewels into safe-keeping for your English grandchildren?"

"And your commission, Don Ludovico?"

"My commission is that you permit me to trade in Lisbon, continue to send in my spices, silk and Cathay cha free of tariffs."

"Queen Henrietta Maria is not expecting payment?"

"Oh, she is, *madonna*, and if I am honest, in serious need of financial support. But the knowledge that her son – one of her sons – will take possession of these English Crown Jewels again *with the backing of your faith* – that, I am certain will be sufficient recompense." Dona Luisa nodded again so he continued, "You and the Duke might choose to offer support of a more tangible kind, perhaps in armaments for the Royalist cause, or troops, instead of specie."

"We could." The duchess caressed the cold stones on her warm, round neck. "We shall. It is done. I will inform my husband."

"And also the officials in the Casa da Índia – regarding my shipments – may they be informed as well? Should I ask the footman to call for your secretary?"

"No need. It shall be as you request, you have my word."

"A document would be appropriate, *madonna,* so I can prove my status and our arrangement if requested at a future date."

"A document will be signed. Now, to personal matters: I wish to know how it is that I knew your name before this interview. The name Ludovico da Portovenere clanged like a bell in my ear. Why is that?"

"Really? I am most flattered, Duchess. Perhaps because of my dealings with your noble cousin, the Count-Duke Olivares in Madrid."

"With Gaspar?" Dona Luisa frowned and scrunched up her chin like a flatulent toad. Ludo looked away. "Perhaps," she said slowly. Then a lot more rapidly, "And this English baroness, it was she who was to represent Queen Henrietta Maria, not you, was it not?"

"On a different matter, a more feminine matter, yes, it was, I believe. To do with your royal children, but I'm afraid I have rather beaten her to it – if you'll excuse the expression. We have covered the topic just now. I, erm ..." For once Ludo was at a loss.

"And she will not mind that you have made her long journey and stay in Lisbon purposeless? Or does she already know?"

"Not exactly." Dona Luisa was casting a line now. Ludo shifted in his uncomfortable padded seat, "Did you know that Baroness Metherall is the daughter of the Marqués de Pamanes, grandee of Spain?" Her father was a count, as far as he knew, but a little elevation never hurt anyone.

"I did hear. Others are more interested than I." Dona Luisa – still wearing Queen Bess's diamonds – rapped the table with her knuckles a third time. The footman re-entered. "Escort Dom Ludovico out of my suite."

Ludo struggled back to his feet. He hovered a moment over the small table, wondering if the deal was actually concluded.

"Leave the jewels here with me, Dom Ludovico," the Duchess said. "You have my word as to our arrangement. You may go now."

Ludo took his hat from the cabinet, and bowed low. As he rose, the duchess rapped her knuckles on the table causing it to wobble. "Oporto!" she squeaked. "You were asked to take a shipment of goods from Lisbon to Oporto."

Ludo's heart sank. She knew: she remembered. Then to his utter surprise she said, "We thank you for that. Your action helped us greatly. Perhaps you should know however, that one of the officials in the Casa da Índia, a little man called Cabrera, tried to blame you for taking some of our gold."

"Did he!" Ludo's voice was innocent shock. "There was gold – in the cargo? I wasn't aware I had been trusted with such a valuable assignment. Cabrera told me to take some crates and whatnot and ... So, it wasn't merely a convenient transportation of cargo from one port to another – I was helping your cause. I am pleased." Ludo gave her the full force of the da Portovenere charm then murmured casually, "This Cabrera official – what happened? Not that it matters now, of course."

"He was dealt with; he was the only one who had access to the cargo – apart from you and your crew, but the crates were delivered intact. A considerable amount of specie went missing."

"I see; lamentable." Ludo schooled his features, tamping down the combined sense of satisfaction and regret that he could not tell Leonora.

"Lamentable, yes. Call at the Casa da Índia on the morrow. They will make the necessary arrangements for your continued trade with Portugal: it is in both our interests. I will send a message in my own hand."

Relief sent Ludo into such a low bow he hit his head on his right knee.

He was escorted out of the duchess's chambers, and then he was off, out through a labyrinth of ill-lit chambers, into a great hall then out into the fresher air of the ever-crowded palace courtyard, where, with a jaunty skip, he narrowly evaded a child's hoop. Then he was off again, almost at a run, to board *Tulip* and tell Alina he had made the deal, that not a single coin had been exchanged in the transaction but she could return to Henrietta to tell her that the Catholic Queen of Portugal was offering her daughter Catherine in marriage to the Prince of Wales – or one of the other princes, if he was already spoken for.

Or she could stay with him and they'd sail as soon as ever they could.

Chapter 33

Hetty was perfectly entertained on board, running Blanca ragged as she tried to wriggle in and out of the poop deck rails and played ball with besotted mariners, forgetting and remembering Etta here and there along the way. Alina tidied their cabin, tried to find out what they were eating for the next meal, then ran out of things to do and waited for Ludo to send for her. When he hadn't come by late noon on the second day, she swung her cloak around her shoulders and ordered Toxo to send the pinnace – with her in it – back to the harbour.

Toxo shook his head. "Can't do that, *señora*. Got strict orders for you to stay here."

Alina gave him the edge of her tongue and Toxo was so put out he let her go without a farewell. A boy Ludo had, apparently, ordered to watch her at all times followed her down to the main deck, begging her not to go. He had such a look of panic on his face she wanted to slap him. Instead, he got a tongue-lashing too.

As they neared the quay, Alina noticed a young urchin with rag-wrapped feet. She thought she'd seen him before somewhere, but the mist was coming down and shapes and faces were distorted by the dampness in the air. *Tulip*'s boys shipped their oars and manoeuvred the boat for her to climb out and she was so taken up with what she needed to do, and whether Dom Enrique would send for her and what she would say and do if he did, that she paid no more notice to who was on the quay. The prow scraped the green-weeded sea wall and Alina gathered her skirts. The tide was on the ebb so she would have to climb out with care.

One of the boys held the boat steady and, in what had become a practised move, Alina stepped onto the quay. As she did so, she was pushed backwards with such force that she landed back in the boat, ramming her spine on the end of an oar. Two swarthy Portuguese water rats jumped down off the quay and, before Alina could right herself, Ludo's boys had been knocked overboard. Splashing and gasping, they tried to grab the side of the boat. One of the rats pulled an oar from the rowlocks and pushed them repeatedly out into the choppy water. Whether they could swim or not, Alina had no time to determine, because a third man dropped into the boat and they pushed off from the quay.

Alina tried to move; she was half-lying across a bench with her spine arched backwards and the pain was excruciating. One of the men pushed her off his bench so he could get to an oar, leaving her in the bottom of the boat. Pain sent her into a bubble of red mist. She could hear muffled sounds, but could neither move nor make herself heard. Her only thought was that she had broken her back and would never walk again.

Gradually, Alina became aware of a regular rocking motion. They were out in the estuary, and then they were under the hull of a bigger vessel; one of the men picked her up, put her over his shoulder and the pain sent her away again.

When she came back to consciousness, Alina was lying wrapped in her cloak on a narrow bunk. She tried to speak but it sent a vicious pain charging through her body and she gave in once more to red darkness.

Waking again with a dry throat and no sense of where she could be, Alina clenched one fist then another, determined to stay alert. She tried to move her feet. Slowly, she separated them left and right. If she could stand her back wasn't broken. If she could first get her arms free. Lifting her head as high as she could, Alina tried to see what was holding her arms against her body. Strapped across her fine russet woollen cloak were what looked like two thick belts, each buckled tight; one under her bust, the other around her waist. She tried to lever her upper body to a sitting position, but her vertebrae screeched in pain and left her gasping for breath.

Lying still, waiting for the pain to subside, Alina tried to take stock of her situation. There was a gentle rolling motion, so she was no longer in the underbelly of a pinnace but in a ship of some sort. Where? Why? Tears welled in her eyes and ran unchecked down her cheeks onto the lump of cotton-covered straw that served as a pillow.

The next time she opened her eyes, Alina took a deep breath and made an effort to think straight. The air was stale but there was light from a window, so she had to be in a stern cabin. She flexed her hands under a constraining belt, then tried to move her hand over her stomach, but she was strapped too tight. Unthinking, she shifted her bottom on the narrow bunk, causing her to shriek in pain.

The noise brought a tall, thin man with a cadaverous face to her side. He'd been sitting across the narrow cabin watching her.

"Welcome back, Baroness," he said in accented English. "I am pleased to see you are still alive."

Alina knew the face, endeavoured to frame a thought and put it into words but her head swam and her mouth was dry. All that came out was "Where?"

"Where are we? Or why are we here? What are you asking, *madonna*?"

'*Madonna*' – only Ludo ever called her that. Rogelio, Father Rogelio, the Queen's confessor in London. He had been in France, too. And in Lisbon. Brain fog started to clear: Rogelio – who had almost certainly caused Marcos to die …

Alina stretched her fingers inside her damp cloak until she located her sharp little dagger. All was not lost; she still had her knife. And he had got her, not Hetty.

Rogelio loosened the straps. "Sit up, I have a warm drink for you."

Alina tried to move but a spasm of pain made her gasp out, "I can't."

Rogelio tutted and said, "Take the drink; it will help."

He tried to pour the contents of a tiny ceramic cup into her mouth. She twisted her head away and he placed a spider-crab hand over her face and held it in place. Her instinct was to grab his ear and twist it as she used to do when her brothers pinned her to the ground in their fighting games, but it was impossible. A thick, sweet concoction dribbled down her right cheek. She tried not to lick her lips, the cloying sensation was disgusting and she wanted to vomit.

The next time Alina awoke she was alone. But not for long. The door creaked open and the priest crossed to her in a single stride. Aware only that she needed to relieve herself and that her mouth was so dry she could barely swallow, Alina tried to speak.

"What?" Rogelio asked, bending down in sham solicitude. "What do you need, *madonna*, that *I* can supply?"

"The pot!" Alina blurted. "*Ahora mismo*! Now!"

The priest was out of the door before she finished speaking. Alina bit her lips, trying to control her body. A small boy rushed in with a bucket, slammed it on the floor and struggled for what seemed hours with the buckles on the two belts, then raced out of the cabin and the door was bolted from the outside.

Once the emergency was over, it took Alina a good while to stand. Gradually she got to her feet and shuffled over to the small window. The ship was still moored in the Tagus Estuary; she could make out the hulls of other vessels and in the distance the green, rolling hills of Lisbon. Above was a rare, cloudless sky. Alina returned to the bed, snatched up the belts then, not without difficulty, pulled open the thick window pane and tossed them into the blue.

The small boy returned with food and water. He said his name was Cinco because he had four older brothers.

Alina smiled, "I have four younger brothers," she said.

"*Verdad!*" Cinco replied then clammed up, went bright puce and said not another word. He had obviously been told not to speak to her.

Later, Rogelio returned. Alina was lying on the bunk wrapped in her cloak. She swung her legs over the side and sat up, not without discomfort for the bruising to her back was agony.

Rogelio leant against the wall of the narrow cabin and surveyed her, his mouth twitching as if amused.

"Why am I here?" Alina demanded.

Rogelio raised an eyebrow and cocked his head to one side. It was an action so like Ludo that Alina's eyes shot open, not because he was taunting her, but because he did not appear to have made it deliberately.

"Yes," he said, "why, why, why? It was my intention to dispose of you as we passed the bar. But I have decided on a more fitting punishment."

"Punishment? What have I ever done to offend you?"

Rogelio's long-fingered hands opened. "You are an offence to womanhood."

"How dare you! What have I ever done against you? I am a lady-in-waiting to the Queen of England, daughter of a Spanish grandee, how dare you speak to me like this!" Alina straightened her spine, regretted it and waited for a response, swallowing down her pain. When no response came, she said, "We were together in the Queen's household in London and again in Chateau Thierry; surely you know who I am. I ..." Alina's voice fell into a whine: she felt utterly vulnerable.

Rogelio shrugged. "Who you say you are, and *what* you are, are at odds. Your situation in England is meaningless. You are my cousin's whore therefore you should be punished."

"Your cousin?" 'Cousin' was a term of endearment in the English court, but she had no idea who this cousin might be. "I am nobody's whore!" she snapped.

Rogelio gave a twisted sneer. "I have watched you, Baroness," he drawled knowingly. "I have watched your manoeuvres in Lisbon to ensnare Dom Enrique. I watched you in Spain trying for a king, you ambitious, self-seeking bitch. Then with Henry Jermyn in France. Your Queen Henrietta *would not* have liked that."

Alina shook her head in despair. "How can you think that? Jermyn hated me."

"And wanted you. I know how these men behave."

"But ..."

"But this is all quite irrelevant." Rogelio's voice changed its timbre, became business-like. "I have decided what to do with you. The stews of Rome, the back lanes of the Tiber – that is where you are going."

"You can't make me do that! You're mad. I'm not going anywhere with you."

Rogelio raised his hands in mock horror. "We leave on the morning tide."

"Not with me, you don't! I have a –" Alina was about to mention Hetty but stopped herself in time. "How could you even get me into a brothel, anyway?" she scoffed.

"With the greatest of ease. You are but a poor madwoman who believes herself to be a noblewoman, daughter of some fictitious count, rejected by a fictitious husband; a woman whose only resource is her body. What alternative could I offer but a convent? And you will *never* defile a convent."

A madwoman? Alina paused. She didn't know if the threat was bluff, but the one who was mad, twisted in the mind, was this Rogelio. Alina suddenly remembered McNab at Crimphele – he'd had a similar obsession. *What was wrong with these men with snake-pits inside their heads?* What terrified Alina at that moment most was that she knew their madness gave them strength. If Rogelio intended to keep her, what could she do? Jumping overboard was not an option: she would drown. Jumping overboard when a boat came alongside was a possibility, if she stripped down to her shift. But who would take her word against a Roman priest's?

Rogelio's mouth twitched again. "That's right, think about it. At least in Rome you have the chance to make some money – following your chosen profession – who knows, you might even earn enough to get away, perhaps even raise yourself to someone's mistress like your lover's mother."

Alina's hand grabbed her knife without thinking, but Rogelio was too quick for her. Before she could make another move, he slapped her face with the back of his hand so hard that she reeled back against the wood-panelled wall and fell to the floor. The knife clattered at her side. As Rogelio bent down to pick it up, Alina grasped his hair and yanked his head back. Had it not been for the cloak and yards of skirt wrapping her legs, she would have got him onto his front and knelt on him, but dressed as she was, she was lost. Furious, Alina slammed his head against the rough boards beneath them and crawled just out of his reach, into the corner of the cabin.

Winded and very angry, Rogelio got to his feet and moved to the door. For a moment or two he passed the precious dagger from one hand to the other. Then he folded the fingers of his right hand neatly over the carved-horn handle, balanced his weight on the balls of his feet and gripped it like a practised street-fighter, ready for use. A look of genuine pleasure crossed his face and Alina felt her guts loosen. He was going to use it on her. He was going to mutilate her face at the very least. She huddled her knees up to her chin and rolled into a ball, head beneath her elbows.

Nothing happened.

He was waiting for something, or enjoying her fear. She dared not look up. Then his voice whispered close to her ear, "A pretty knife, *madonna,* what else do you have hidden in your skirts, I wonder?"

A sensation like a streak of ice ran down Alina's back as he ripped through her clothing, slit down through silk and cotton to the skin on her spine. It was not painful – it was terrifying. She stayed immobile.

A foot kicked at her stomach and she screamed out.

The door was pushed open and Cinco peered in. Seeing Rogelio, he pulled his head back and tried to close it again.

"Come in," Rogelio ordered.

The boy stayed at the door gaping. Rogelio yanked him in so fast he stumbled over Alina's body.

"Pull her clothes off her!" Rogelio's voice rose to hysteria. Cinco blinked rapidly. "Do it! Pull the clothes off her back."

The boy's fingers fumbled down Alina's spine, pushing the stiff bodice from her shoulders. Rogelio's foot hooked into her skirt, pulling it away from her. The foot pushed her sideways, so she lay half-naked, splayed out on the cabin floor. Spittle formed at Rogelio's mouth. Cinco slapped his hands over his face, stifling a scream.

"Get out!" the priest ordered.

Cinco raced through the doorway and Rogelio leaned backwards to slam it shut.

A foot in a salt-stained boot poked at Alina's breast then he stood over her and rubbed his groin with his free hand.

He was going to rape her. Alina came to life. She inched away from between his legs, sat up and pulled her knees to her chest. Something rattled on the floor.

Rogelio noticed at once.

"You've got it – them. You've had them all along."

"What? Got what?"

"The jewels. I should have guessed. Give them to me."

Alina pulled her knees tighter against her body, her mind racing. Should she pretend she had the English jewels? She cast a quick glance at what was on the floor; the emerald pendant necklace. She held it up, the beautiful green stone dangling like bait.

"Drop it there," Rogelio instructed, indicating a point on the floor with her knife.

Alina was confused: a man who was one minute intending to rape her, now wouldn't even touch her fingers. But no, she was wrong, he was never going to rape her – not physically. He was going to – still might – do something unspeakable above her. Over her. He was repelled by women. Did this give her an advantage? If so, how?

Rogelio retrieved the jewel from the floor and lifted it to the light; licking his lips, he turned and aimed another vicious blow with his boot, this time catching her under the chin. Alina reeled back and caught her head on the bulkhead.

"It's been you all along, hasn't it? You've got them!" Rogelio's voice cracked and then recovered its sinister hiss. "I should have been following you closer. Women! Bitches! Bitches in heat, and when that's done with, you turn witch and spread poison in other ways. I've seen it. I watched it from my cradle." His voice dropped and he bent down so she could hear him as he whispered, "I was born to a bawd – I *know* how you think – I was with them long enough. She was so stupid, my mother, expecting to be treated like a lady when all she was, was a common whore. She *deserved* to be left in a brothel."

Alina glanced up, Rogelio was looking directly at her but his eyes were glazed, as if imagining or seeing someone else; as if he were in another place. When he spoke his voice was a cold, choking hiss.

"She made a fuss you see, insisted I was a Doria child until my oh-so-respected grandfather accepted that it was true. But not for me his great house and name, oh no, I was something to be so ashamed of that Agostino hid me away in a monastery. It was all right for *him* to keep a girl love-child because she was his own daughter – all right to have her legitimised – all right when she in turn produced a bastard – everything was fine for pretty Gabriella because she could be married off for a convenient alliance. Not that she did. But that's where the generosity ended. I'll get my revenge, though. And now you've given me another way to do it."

Rogelio pocketed the jewel and took a deep breath. There was a moment's silence then he resumed his rant. "Let's see how much my precious, favoured cousin really cares for you. Between the two of you, you've prevented me getting a prized reward and a safe place in Paris, but I can still make the best of a bad situation. In fact, the very best of a bad situation." He paused again and licked his lips. "Shall I let your lover know what I have planned for you in Rome?" He smirked as Alina blanched. "We have to stop off on the way, of course, to pick up his brats. He thinks I don't know where they are, but I do. I have more spies than he could even dream of. Ah, but yes!" Rogelio jiggled the knife. "I can leave you there. I might even get a good price for you in the market. That hair ... Moors love it."

"He'll follow the ship. He'll stop you!" Alina's voice squeaked.

"I don't think so. He won't have time for that. But I would like to see his face when he knows who's aboard this little caravel bound for Salé."

Alina tried to make sense of what he was saying, her thoughts snagging on his reference to Salé and 'brats'. Salé meant corsairs – what had that to do with children? Were Ludo's children there? Ah, but he intended to sell her there – of course. As if sensing how her mind was working, Rogelio stuck his long nose out towards her and hissed, "And what about yours, eh, your pretty children? You sneaked your boy in with the royals, but where's the girl? With her nurse, somewhere safe, I hope – for her sake. Not that you'll be seeing her – either of them again – ever."

The nose came closer. Alina could see hairs in the flared nostrils and shuddered. Rogelio laughed at his success. "You got away from me in Spain, Baroness, but not this time." The door closed, the bolt shot home.

Alina pulled her clothes back over her trembling body then, despite the agony, rolled back into a ball, tucking her knuckles under her chin, afraid to put a hand behind her and feel the blood seeping from the slash down her spine.

Chapter 34

Rogelio paid his respects to the captain, passed him another purse and requested their departure be delayed one more day. He was then rowed back to the quay, where his two new henchmen were waiting.

"I'll need you again," he said. "Come to this place at dusk. You'll be going aboard that vessel out there," he pointed at *Tulip* in profile against a lowering sky, "not for long, but make sure you look like mariners, not farm boys."

"What are we to do?" the slightly cleaner of the two asked.

Rogelio pulled a face and led them into a stinking alley between taverns, where he gave them careful instructions on how to board the *Tulip* posing as new crew, how to find the powder kegs, how to light a long fuse using the tinder box he gave them – and then how to get away before the ship exploded. "You can both swim I suppose."

"Swim?" they said in unison.

"Ah, well," Rogelio gave them a wan smile, "you'd better be quick then."

The men responded by screwing up their eyes suspiciously, and holding out their hands. Rogelio shook his head, "Finish tonight's job first. When that's completed to my satisfaction *then* you will be paid, and handsomely."

The men shuffled off. Smiling, this time with genuine pleasure at the outcome of the day, Rogelio returned to his spacious guest room in the waterfront monastery. Once there, he stripped out of his damp, black robes, pulled on a soft, blue woollen robe and sat down to examine his prize. Pushing the accoutrements of his jade and silver toilette set to one side, he placed the emerald necklace before him and stroked the pendant into place. It was perfect. It was worth a fortune – both in money and in terms of his future – and now he had to decide what to do with it. Should he return to Rome and pass it on to Cardinal Barberini as a token of what was to come, or keep it until he located the Three Brethren and the Tudor bastard's necklace, or forget about the jewels and carry out his threats to the Spanish whore first?

He picked up the necklace and held it to the front of his robe. The room lacked a mirror but he strode around the thickly carpeted floor, imagining himself a nobleman, the first son of a noble house, heir to a wealthy merchant whose lineage dated back to the twelfth century and beyond – the sort of man who was welcomed in the finest establishments, to whom all other men touched their forelock or doffed their feathered caps. In this mood, he opened his writing casket, placed the necklace under his Bible and locked it. Then he replaced his fine robe with a fresh soutane and prepared to take a turn among the best of Portuguese company before entering the palace, where he was to sup at the Duke of Braganza's request.

The long palace dining room was lit with a thousand candles, although the acrid smell told him they were tallow, not beeswax as they should be. The table itself was another disappointment. He'd noticed it before: not all the silver service was silver, and not all the plates matched. Still, he was back in a palace, which was where he belonged, and no longer at the beck and call of a Cardinal who looked down on him, or sent him to dirty his hands in Protestant lands.

A flunky tapped the floor with a silver-topped staff and announced the duke. The new king entered, entirely overshadowed by the lady on his arm, a large florid woman with the swollen breasts of pregnancy. Rogelio gave an inward shudder of revulsion, trying to tear his eyes away from the bosom as it advanced towards him down the room. Then he froze. Candlelight glinted off a gem pinned to the front of her cleavage. Three large balas rubies with pendant pearls around a huge pyramid diamond: The Three Brethren. Ludo da Portovenere had beaten him again.

But it was the last time. The very last time.

Chapter 35

Toxo's brother-in-law Javi noticed them first. He dug Toxo in the ribs, "Are those two listed as crew?" he asked. "They're coming aboard without any gear. I thought you said no delinquents or runaways."

"I did, Patrón won't have 'em."

"Can't be trusted, can't be trained. We've got enough of that sort from Le Havre, we don't need any more aboard. Who are you talking about?" Ludo asked, joining the brothers-in-law on the quarter deck.

Toxo indicated two men standing by the starboard rail. "I haven't signed those two, and I'm not going to, either. Most they've been on is a rowing boat." He turned to Ludo, "Unless you've taken them on, Patrón?"

"No," Ludo replied, watching the two Lisbon day labourers stare about them, confusion written in every rodent feature. The men exchanged a few words then headed for the nearest hold. "Follow them, Javi," Ludo said. "Take someone with you. Toxo, go and make sure Hetty and her mother are in their cabin, will you?"

Toxo hesitated.

"What?" demanded Ludo.

Toxo swallowed. "Doña Alina, she went ashore yesterday. Took three of our boys with her. They came back on another boat with a garbled tale that a priest had taken *Tulip*'s pinnace. Seemed odd. But it was a priest so she'll be all right."

"Seemed odd! Why didn't you tell me this just now when I came aboard?"

"Haven't had a chance," Toxo countered sharply. "You just got here."

Ludo took a deep breath. "Where was she going?"

"*Yo que sé,*" Toxo shrugged, "mind of her own that one, begging your pardon. And tongue to match." he added under his breath.

"But the child is still here?"

"With Blanca, they're in their cabin, far as I know."

"Good." Ludo pushed his hair off his face. "Send me the boys that were with her."

Toxo sent a deckhand to find the boys then discovered he was urgently needed at the mizzen and headed forward.

Ludo hovered between masts until two of the boys arrived and recited what had happened to them on the quay. "Why didn't anyone come for me?" Ludo demanded. Then relented: how would they know where to find him? "So the lady Alina was taken by the priest and they went out to another ship?"

"Yes, Patrón."

"But you don't know which?"

"No, Patrón."

"Were you hurt?" Ludo's voice softened.

"They bashed us about with an oar, Patrón."

"Does that mean she has been abducted?" Ludo asked, keeping his tone even.

"Abducted? No, a priest got in the boat."

"They stole the boat, though, and we need it," the braver of the two said.

"She fell backwards, I saw it. The priest tried to help her – I think."

"He wanted our boat," the other insisted. "Pushed us away and took it there and then. Why don't you ask his men, Patrón? I seed them come aboard just now while I was scrubbing the fore deck."

"Did you! Good lad. Where did they go?"

"Down below."

Ludo looked at the open hold. "Right, you can go. No wait – you, go to my cabin and fetch my spy-glass. Run, I need it right now! And you: station yourself outside wherever the little girl is and yell blue blazes if anyone tries to get near her."

The boys raced to their tasks and Ludo hastened to the open hold just as Javi was emerging behind a dark-featured Portuguese. A well-set French mariner they'd taken on as quarter master pushed another onto the deck behind them.

"These two," Javi said. "They are not signed on as crew."

"The hell they're not! Get them over here." Ludo moved to the port rail out of the deckhands' way, and well away from the ladder for the one remaining pinnace.

The normally pacific Javi gave his buck-toothed Portuguese a mighty shove across the deck. "Trying to set light to powder kegs!" he shouted. "And this one!"

The second man stumbled forward, doubled over to ease the pain from having his arms run up his back by the Frenchman.

Ludo took a deep breath, knowing instinctively what was afoot: Rogelio was intending to blow up the *Tulip*. "Where's the priest?" he demanded. The first Portuguese mumbled something and Ludo gave him the back of his hand, drawing blood. "Speak up. *Where* is he?"

"Ow!"

It didn't take Ludo long to get the details he needed about the powder kegs, but neither of them would say a word about Alina. Taking a gamble based on experience, Ludo had them taken to the prow and held over the water. Neither of them could swim and the prospect of being dropped overboard had a rapid effect. Ludo was so angry he would have tipped them over the rail himself, but first he needed to know about Alina. What he learned turned his guts to water. One of the stooges, having been allowed to stand upright, pointed at the other ships anchored in the estuary, gabbling that the priest had stowed 'his woman' on it.

"It? Which? Which one?" Ludo stuck out a hand and, unasked, his spy-glass was slapped into it.

"Don't remember. Ow!"

"A big galleon, like this one? Or smaller? Which one?" Ludo demanded.

"We can't say," whined the buck-toothed amateur.

"Tie them to the bow sprit," Ludo ordered. "Sling them close to the water. A dunking might clear their heads."

Javi grabbed a coil of rope and the Frenchman and the boy set about getting them onto the mast over *Tulip*'s prow. Ludo called for Toxo and started to make his way aft as a sudden wave lapped the bows.

"All right!"

"We'll tell you! We'll tell you everything."

Standing on shaky legs, Rogelio's hired men recited all they'd been asked to do, then gazed about them, trying to identify the ship the lady had been taken to. It was a caravel sitting low in the water. Ludo panned his spy-glass over it. The crew were as busy as his own; obviously preparing to sail.

This meant they had to get across to the caravel and get Alina before it weighed anchor. If not, before it crossed the bar and hit the Atlantic coastline, where even Murat Reis's corsairs had avoided boarding vessels. It meant using *Tulip's* only pinnace, which was still unloading supplies.

Ludo searched his mind for the best way to get aboard the caravel and put Rogelio, if he was there, in such a position that he could neither refuse to release Alina, nor harm her. Assuming Alina was alive. He had to assume Alina was alive. Then ... then he'd have to improvise.

But when? Immediately, or wait until dark? And could he do it on his own? One of the stooges had let slip that they were to be paid that evening in a tavern. It meant assuming

Rogelio would honour his debt and would go ashore. It meant assuming a lot of things, but there'd be no rescue without risk. And he didn't want Rogelio – far from it – he only wanted Alina back with him, safe and sound.

"Tie them up below," he ordered Javi.

"What you going to do, Patrón?" Toxo asked, coming to his side.

"For now, I am going to think. Make sure Blanca and Hetty stay out of sight, will you?" Toxo nodded and went aft.

Ludo paced the rail from prow to stern and back again: he'd boarded vessels at night, and boarded them under the sail in the past – a long time ago to be sure – but it wasn't something you forget. This boarding was a rescue, not an attack, though, which made the risk analysis all the more important. It also made avoiding violence a priority.

Within a relatively short time, however, he had the outline of a plan and set off to find Toxo.

"You'll need help, Patrón," Toxo said flatly. "You can't manage all that on your own."

"You didn't want any more adventures, if I recall. This means taking risks. You said you wanted to go back to your families."

"Nah, plenty of time for that, they aren't going anywhere. We're good at taking risks, Javi and me. Had enough practice. We'll run *Tulip* nearer the caravel after sunset and you can take over from there."

Ludo stared unseeing at the wiry Galician, weighing up the advantages and disadvantages, wondering if Rogelio had the power to order his ship to fire on the *Tulip*. "Tell the crew to get us gun ready," Ludo ordered, "but not to fire unless absolutely necessary – understand?"

"Understood. What flag do you want?"

Ludo's eyes' twinkled. "French. And use our old burgundy red sails. Send me that Frenchman, Laurent; he's sharp and looks handy with a knife. I've got a couple of lads who've been with me since Genoa I can trust for the boat – they can man the oars and stay ready for Alina. Oh, and I'll need a long rope and a grappling hook, just in case my ruse fails." Ludo began pulling off his decent jacket. "Find me some scruffy gear, Javi. I don't want the priest recognising me before I get on deck."

"You're never planning to board that tub yourself?" Toxo asked, watching him.

"Of course, I am. When have I ever sent anyone to do my dirty work? Except this time, I do need the Frenchman."

"What are you planning to do, for God's sake?"

Ludo clapped a big hand over Toxo's shoulder. "For once I'm going to tell the truth, my friend. More or less. Well, less rather than more."

Toxo's mouth opened and closed.

"Don't fret," Ludo laughed. "If it works, we'll be back aboard *Tulip* with without a scratch." *I hope,* he muttered to himself. "If push comes to shove, I can shimmy aboard – I've done it before."

But that had been with a score of corsairs who fought as a group and rode the sea like Neptune. This time, there'd only be him, the Frenchman and the staunch Galician called Javi, who'd never had reason to employ the skills in demand for this job.

A strengthening westerly pushed the whish-whish of oars further behind them. Ludo listened, all senses alert, as the slow, rhythmic slap of water against *Tulip*'s pinnace betrayed their whereabouts. If there was a watch being kept aboard the caravel, no one had noticed it – yet. The boat suddenly began to bob unevenly. The oarsmen lost their stroke. Javi, sitting silent in the bow, raised the palms of his hands, and oars were held steady in the water.

The boat then suddenly listed hard to port as a thundering beast rose from the deep. A bull dolphin breeched, sending a fountain into the evening sky, terrifying the Genoese rowers and setting Ludo's heart racing. A second breeched to starboard. A third rose and fell somewhere in their wake. Then they were gone. White phosphorescence played visual tunes on their lapping wake and the occupants of the pinnace began to curse or pray.

Ludo started to laugh then stopped and peered as best he could at the rail of the caravel. Had the beasts brought the watch to the gunwale to see the display? Would they notice his boat too soon? The Frenchman, Laurent, was to call out that he had a message for the priest, but Ludo wanted the element of surprise on their side: Rogelio would suspect it was a ruse, but Rogelio was supposed to be ashore.

Javi was ahead of him. A few words to the boys and they were pulling fast to get in under the caravel's rotund keel. They stayed there until they felt sure the dolphins had lost interest in them, then stayed longer to see if they had been detected.

When he was satisfied all was quiet again, Ludo pulled a woollen hat over his head and lit a lamp. "Ready?" he asked. The Frenchman, now dressed in an assortment of Ludo's finery, gave a short salute and got to his feet.

"Ahoy," he called out to the watch on the round ship. One of them came to the rail. The Frenchman waved an elaborate hat in one hand and large square of vellum in the other. "I am a royal emissary. I have an urgent message for your captain," he shouted in French.

"*Qué?*" came the reply from above.

Laurent explained his presence in three different tongues, insisting he be allowed aboard.

The ladder was dropped and Laurent, followed by Ludo and Javi climbed aboard. Ludo wanted to laugh out loud: he was boarding the vessel on the flimsiest excuse he could think of. He was also out of breath and nowhere near ready to take on an armed deck hand, if the need arose.

As he hauled himself over the gunwale and waited behind the Frenchman, he took stock of the small ship's sea readiness: she'd be gone on the morning tide. Many of the crew were still on deck, lowering goods into the hold by lamplight. Others had set up a kitchen on the main deck and were cooking up their supper. Two officers were on the prow. One of them slipped down the companionway to see who had come aboard.

Laurent went into his prepared routine: the lady who had been brought aboard was a lady-in-waiting to Queen Henrietta Maria. She was to sail on the next tide for Le Havre. Here were his credentials. He was here to accompany her.

The officer took the vellum square and made aft for the captain's cabin.

Laurent followed directly behind him; Ludo followed as if he'd been summoned to do so.

Javi stayed at the rail as arranged, ready to help with Alina if they were lucky, ready to act as reinforcement if they weren't. Ludo tugged a rough-spun waistcoat over his crumpled seaman's blouse, keeping his head down, hoping against hope Alina was still aboard, and fearing she'd be below, locked in a hold.

The officer knocked at the stateroom door then went inside, leaving the door open and Laurent loitering, one foot on deck, one in the cabin, in case Ludo needed him. Ludo stayed where he was and cast about for other cabin doors in the gloom. There were two. The first door was set ajar to emit tobacco smoke; a gentle rumble of male voices came from inside the cabin. Behind the second door lay silence. Ludo, a prickle of tension at his neck, paused to listen. A jug was moved on a table top. A chair scraped. A woman's voice said, "No more, please, no more."

Ludo was in, knocking a lamp to the floor and taking the priest round his neck with one hand and poking a sharp dagger at his ribs with the other. Alina was trussed up on the narrow bunk in her outdoor cloak, a rope around her arms and feet. Ludo shoved the knife through the priest's black clothing, twisting it as the point met flesh and bone. Rogelio started to speak but Ludo's left hand stifled his words. A child dodged around the door from nowhere and entered the cramped cabin.

Alina's eyes focussed first on the boy at her side, then on Ludo. "Oh, thank God. Get me out of here."

Ludo grinned, "That depends on whether you consent to be rescued by a corsair again, *carina*?"

"Don't be ridiculous!" Alina's eyes opened, overly-bright and blue.

The boy looked from Ludo to Alina, his mouth gaping.

"Well?" queried Ludo, cocking his head over Rogelio's bony black shoulder.

"Yes, get on with it," Alina's voice was slurred.

"I got her knife, sir." The boy held up Alina's special little knife.

"Good, use it."

Rogelio squirmed and Ludo tightened his grip. The small cabin boy sawed at the ropes around Alina's arms. The moment her hands were free she tried to sit, but was obviously in pain. The boy tugged at the ropes around her legs then helped her to stand.

Placing a hand on the boy's shoulder Alina looked at Ludo and said, "Now what?"

"Now it depends on what you want me to do with this?" Ludo said, meaning Rogelio. "Has he hurt you – or *anything?*"

Alina opened the cloak to show the torn bodice around her shoulders. Ludo's hand gripped Rogelio's windpipe and squeezed.

"I never touched her," the reptile wheezed.

"Liar!" Alina replied, swaying. The small boy went to her aid.

"Help the lady down to the deck," Ludo said. Then he kicked open the door with a foot and called, "Laurent, she's here."

The Frenchman was there in two strides. "You're going back to your queen, Baroness," Ludo declared, "with this gentleman, who is a special envoy come to fetch you."

Alina frowned, barely able to follow his words, then managed to pull the cloak around her shoulders and said, "Are you going to kill him?" meaning Rogelio.

"Should I?"

"He killed Marcos."

"If you mean the Spanish boy, I didn't," Rogelio stuttered.

Ludo changed his grip and the priest slumped in his arms. "Alina, go with Laurent, now!"

For once Alina did as she was bid. The door opened wider, then Ludo kicked it closed and shoved the priest onto the bunk. Rogelio squirmed against the bulkhead, a hand at his ribs. "I'm bleeding," he moaned.

"Good." Ludo righted the chair and sat down at the small table. In the scuffle a small jug had also fallen to the floor. "What's in that?" he asked. "The same stuff they gave me back in Genoa?" Rogelio's silence was sufficient. "Excellent," Ludo said. "Let me pour you a cup or two. It'll help you relax while I tell you what you are going to do. Ah, but the cup is still full. Here you are, drink up." He thrust the cup at Rogelio, who squirmed again and shook his head until Ludo grabbed his hair, yanked back his head and whispered, "Take the drink, Cousin."

Rogelio drained off the cup then said, "Will you let me live?"

"*Will I?*" Ludo snorted. It was a question he needed to answer himself.

He was happy to see his adversary suffer, happy to get revenge for what had happened to Jose in Ibiza and the way the good friar Caritas had been persecuted, for causing him to be absent when Leonora went into labour, and for a dozen other more recent troubles – but he knew he could not – would not – kill in cold blood. Ludo tilted his head, "What do you offer me in exchange for your life?"

"Offer you! Offer you – you who's had everything all your life? What sort of joke is that? I'm a humble priest, abandoned in a monastery –"

"Yes, yes. You've told me all that. Your version doesn't quite fit the facts, though, does it?"

"The fact is that you were raised with the values of a cut-throat corsair and out of choice you've kept them."

Ludo snapped his fingers. "Not entirely true. I have never cut a throat in my life – maimed a few who'd have cut mine – but that's different. Ah ... but you have given me a solution, a way to put you safely out of harm's way and avoid spilling more of your so-called Doria blood, Cousin. If that bit is true?"

Rogelio shifted: one hand on the flesh wound at his ribs the other pulling him across the bunk. "How?" he asked, his voice a terrified whisper.

Ludo's attention was caught by a writing casket under the table. "Planning to write a ransom note, were you?" He pushed at it with a foot then leaned over to open it. "Key," he demanded.

Rogelio took a key from a pocket. Ludo opened the chest and extracted a Bible.

"Don't touch that! Sacrilege," Rogelio hissed.

"No, you can keep it, you'll need it where you're going. Might even help you become a martyr – if you're brave enough. What else is here, I wonder?" Ludo rattled the casket then dropped it heavily, causing the lid to break off and a fine emerald necklace to slither out. *Allora! Que magia!*"

Keeping his hand with the dagger in Rogelio's direction, Ludo picked up the necklace and stuffed it down the front of his blouse. "Now, up on your feet, we're going."

"Where? Where are you taking me?" Rogelio's face was white with fear, his words already slurred with the effect of the sleeping draught from the jug.

"Immediately – into my pinnace. And then to Africa."

"Africa!"

"Yes, Cousin, I'm going to sell you in the Salé slave market."

Chapter 36

Liguria, Italy, Summer 1645

Sitting on Gabriella's terrace overlooking the gulf of La Spezia in the rosy glow of a late-summertime dusk, Ludo looked about him, checking on his newly extended family. Hetty and Naomi were on the garden terrace below, playing some boisterous game that required pushing Vico inside a bush and squealing a good deal; Cinco and Blanca were standing nearby exchanging worried looks; Gabriella was sitting on her divan, hugging her knees to her chest in a most un-grandmotherly position; Alina was standing at the other end of the terrace, watching the children and fanning herself with a painted silk fan, occasionally snapping it shut to bat at mosquitoes.

It was as good a time as he'd get in the next twenty-four hours: Ludo eased himself nearer to his mother and said, "Tell me – you know the questions I want to ask. Just tell me, please."

Gabriella tilted her head to one side. "But you know. You found out for yourself."

"No. I learned a version that corresponded to what you told me last autumn. Now I want to know the truth – or the rest."

"Oh, Ludo, is this really necessary? You have a delightful family, a good business and a happy future ahead; why rake up the past?"

"Because I need to know. Tell me about my real father, *please*. Who was he? What was he like?"

Gabriella pushed her greying hair off her face with two hands, an identical gesture to one Ludo made himself when he was unsure what to say or do. There was a silence and then, very quietly, his mother began to speak. "He was just a boy – just a boy, really, looking back – he came as a translator's assistant on a very secret visit to my father. I used sing and dance sometimes for my father's guests after the evening meal – only not this time. This visitor came from Turkey. I was supposed to keep out of the way."

"My father was Turkish!"

"No, he was with the Turkish merchant as a sort of secretary to the translator. He'd been captured as a young boy with his mother and raised to serve – you know how it is."

Ludo knew all about that. Boys raised and trained to be useful in Constantinople or Fez, or even Salé. To be secretaries, servants – even translators.

Gabriella, lost in the past, continued her reminiscence. "He was tall, well-made, broad shoulders – for his age. He was still very young. We both were. He had your black hair, and blue-green eyes. Handsome, and as sweet as an apple on a tree."

"You were betrothed."

"If only that had been possible – no, I was promised to a cloth-merchant's son."

"Nothing wrong with cloth merchants; I still sell the odd bale of silk myself. How did you meet him?"

"He came with his master to my father's house. The Turkish merchant and my father dined together. He was sent for when the translator needed him to write down what was being said – when they negotiated goods and prices, I suppose."

"So he was Genoese?"

"No, he came from an island. He could speak all sorts of languages: French, Castilian, a sort of Catalan from his island ..."

Ludo looked at Gabriella and blinked hard, started to say something, then decided to let her finish first.

"When he wasn't needed, we walked in the gardens ... waiting for orders, he said. We were left on our own. I'd been told to keep out of sight, but we were able to meet in the gardens. Sometimes they forgot all about us and, well, we entertained each other. Then, before they left, he came to my mother's house. At night – through my window. They never knew. My mother and your grandfather were too wrapped up in each other. That's another reason my half-brothers hated me." Gabriella gave a short sigh and changed her position. Looking away from Ludo she said, "I don't think that anyone knew about us. Anyway, by the time I realised I was carrying you, he had gone and I had been taken to Salé. You know the rest."

"But what was his full name? Where was he from?"

"His name used to be Ludovico something or other – they didn't call him that, of course, but he told me what he remembered about growing up on an island."

"An island? A big island, a small island – where?"

"I thought all islands were small. How else do you know it's an island?"

"Mother! Where?"

"I don't remember. He was some local rich man's second son. He'd had schooling before they took him."

Corsairs raided all the islands in the Mediterranean, but Ludo was certain his father was from Ibiza. Words spoken by the Chueta rabbi the last time he was there filled his head: 'It is my belief you are one of us ... Return to us.'

Gabriella eyed him closely. "You've gone very quiet; have I upset you?"

"No, far from it. I was thinking about an island named Ibiza, or Eivissa. Was that what he told you?"

"Could be. I didn't take all that much notice, I suppose. Can I assume you've lost interest in your Doria connections?"

"I most certainly have. I have my illegitimate cousin Rogelio to thank for that."

Gabriella raised a perfectly arched black eyebrow. "Good."

Ludo began to chuckle, then he was serious. "If he was a rich man's son, though, on Ibiza ... would his family have been Christian converts?"

"I have no idea. Why?"

"Just curious. Something I was told by a rabbi a few years ago. It's not important. Not to me, anyway. Except," Ludo paused, "if I wanted to, would you let me find out more about him?"

"Of course. But I never saw him again after that. I hoped, when I was taken to Salé, that he would find me and pay my ransom – marry me ... Silly. I had no idea about the reality of slavery then. The moment I was pulled into that boat from the quayside I was a lost woman."

"Something I once had to explain to the lady standing over there."

"Alina was taken by corsairs!"

"Nearly. I stopped it."

Gabriella studied his face for a moment then asked, "Who is your Alina?"

"I told you – the daughter of a Spanish grandee and widow of an English baron."

Gabriella gave him a knowing look. "And that is why it is inconvenient to have non-Christian blood. Oh, dear. My mother was from a New Christian family, too, so no hope from that quarter either."

Ludo cocked his head to one side, "Was she! Actually, it doesn't matter to me one bit, but it might help the lady over there quite a lot."

Gabriella followed the direction of his gaze, "Alina, why?"

"Because she thinks that sort of thing matters."

"And that matters to you."

"Yes and no. It matters what Alina believes, but ..." Ludo shook his head, "Religion has been at the root of all my troubles in the past ten years. Since an English priest introduced himself to me on a voyage to Amsterdam I've been used, abused, and my family has suffered. Indirectly, I think Leonora lost her life because of it. So did a boy called José, although Rogelio was directly to blame for that. And there was a very good man called Marcos." He swallowed hard and was silent for a moment. "I should go and see his parents, ask them if they want to live in a *cortijo* that was given to me." He gave an ironic laugh – that's where it all started, this religion business. I knew it would lead to trouble the moment they told me what they wanted in Holland – I should have walked out there and then. I told them it would end badly, which it did. I didn't know at the time it would end badly for me, as well – or for Marcos, who deserved so much better. No, I'm not remotely interested in religion, and I never have been."

Gabriella nodded and, being wise, changed the subject. "Have you told Alina about our treasure?"

"Not yet. I'm keeping it as a surprise."

"A wedding present perhaps?"

Ludo gave her a cheeky one-dimpled grin, "Perhaps."

The next day, Ludo took Alina across the water to Portovenere. Avoiding the castle, he led the way up a steep incline to an ancient ruin on a promontory overlooking the Ligurian Sea on one side and the Gulf of La Spezia on the other.

"It's an old Roman temple to the goddess Venus – hence the name Port of Venus – Portovenere," he explained as they entered the roofless nave.

"You're making that up," Alina laughed.

"Indeed, I am not. Would I invent such a story?"

"Indeed, you would," Alina mimicked.

Smiling, Ludo gave a shrug, "Happens to be true." He moved to a tiny arched window and looked across to Lerici. "Would you believe me if I said that there is buried treasure on a hillside over there?"

Alina joined him. "I might. Do you want me to?"

"Yes."

Sensing that this was not the right moment to discuss Murat Reis's treasure, Ludo turned around and walked the full length of the ruin, his soft boots making barely a sound on the white marble floor. Passing a pillar, he noted the remains of a mosaic for the first time, then a carved design on the pillar itself: Roman nymphs and youths, lightweight, ephemeral but dancing forevermore in a springtime circle round and around the solid support. And thus it was, he supposed – life. A broken mosaic of the past and a dance to nowhere in the future, until, trapped in the act, the reel ceased. A random moment proving it made not a jot of difference where you actually stopped in the end.

Returning to the open stone window and he was reminded of the much larger natural window in the rocks below, where as a young man, he'd played hide and seek until a tragedy stopped his games. Bright sun glinted off the sea. He pushed the memory aside, part of his personal broken mosaic, and closed his eyes. For a moment he stayed at the warm stone sill, breathing in the sense of distance, so clean and good after the claustrophobia of palace intrigues and petty disputes, after the tragedies of losing Leonora and Marcos.

Behind him there was a movement, a sense of air moving, of summer sprigged cotton shifting motes of dust. Ludo did not need to turn. "Will you stay?" he asked.

"Here?"

"With me."

"Where?"

"Where? You tell me. I belong here and nowhere."

Ludo guided Alina out of the ruin to a stone bench. Together they sat and gazed at the sea and sky and Ludo let his mind wander – where to next?

Alina leant against his arm, touched his cheek with her lips. He turned to her, his sombre mood changed forever. "Come on!" he said, clapping his hands, "time to make a move."

"Where are we going now?" Alina gave a dramatic sigh of despair.

"We're taking the children on a treasure hunt."

She laughed then caught his expression. "You aren't joking, are you?"

"No, I'm not. There is a very serious cache of pirate treasure on that hill over there, waiting for us to retrieve it. I have a very good feeling about that hillside, too. We could build a house there. You'd be conveniently near your mother-in-law."

"Oh, no, no, no, no. I like her dearly – but no. One mother-in-law in a lifetime is quite sufficient. And I had the worst of the lot. Not that your Gabriella is anything like that harpy. Far from it."

"Ah, well. It was a nice idea."

Alina stayed where she was and Ludo went back to staring at the vista. They were silent again.

"That's it!" Ludo cried, flinging his arms up in a Eureka gesture. "I can run my business from anywhere, and Goa can look after itself. Neither of us really belongs to one particular place, so we'll find a place and make it our own, starting the quest at sea."

"That's what I was thinking." Alina smiled. "You still have a galleon, remember."

Ludo turned, surprised. "And where would you have *Tulip* take us, *madonna*?"

"I was wondering about the New World."

"The Americas – because?"

"Because many years ago I began writing a story about a young woman who sailed across the great sea to a place called Florida and had adventures. I would like to finish it."

"Ah, well, if that is the reason, let us set off at once. We cannot leave a tale like that unfinished."

"Actually, we can. We have to, for now. At least until we know whether my son Tomás will get his inheritance back in Cornwall."

"So – where – for now?"

"Over there will do, where your treasure is hidden. We'll build your house before we go, so we have a home to come back to."

Ludo was lost for words. Eventually he said, "Are you sure? You'll be a long way from civilised living, society and the like."

"No different than at Crimphele. Will we be safe from corsairs up there?"

"As safe as the house we choose to build. There are olive groves, and people have lived there before. There are vines and running water and it's –"

"It's what I would like, Ludo. For us and for the children, yours, mine, ours."

Ludo pulled Alina to him, nestled his face in her golden hair and whispered, "*Perfetto*."

The end

As a means of raising funds for the Royalist cause and her husband in particular, King Charles I's French-born Catholic queen, Henrietta Maria (1609-1669), tried to pawn and sell a large part of the English Crown Jewels during the 1640s. Her attitude was that they were the property of the reigning monarch, not the State. When considering Henrietta Maria's attitude, one must bear in mind that she was the youngest daughter of Henry IV of France and Marie de Medici, and that she was married to a Stuart, who believed entirely in the divine right of kings. Needless to say, her actions met with opposition from Parliament and their supporters, known as Roundheads, and quite a few Royalists themselves.

The jewel at the centre of this story, The Three Brethren, comprised of a massive pyramid-cut, wine-yellow diamond surrounded by three spinel rubies and three large pearls. The diamond weighed approximately 30 carats. In the early fifteenth century it had been described as the largest faceted diamond in Europe. The jewel was said to have been commissioned as a shoulder-clasp for John the Fearless, who was Duke of Burgundy from 1404 to his assassination in 1419. His grandson, Charles the Bold, owned it in 1467, when his inventory describes it as "Un Gros Dyamant Pointé a Fass". It was then possibly sold to or via a banker named Fugger, and came into the possession of Henry VIII in England circa 1546. In 1551, it belonged to Henry's only son, Edward VI. On Edward's death, the magnificent Three Brethren passed into the hands of his elder sister Mary then became a favourite jewel of her successor, Elizabeth I. The Three Brethren can be seen in several of the Virgin Queen's portraits, including the famous Ermine Portrait'. Subsequent portraits of James 1st of England and VI of Scotland, show him wearing The Three Brethren as well.

Catherine of Aragon's ruby pendant was given to her by her mother, Isabel *la Catolica* of Spain when she went to England as a bride. It also features in royal portraits. Queen Elizabeth's diamonds were almost certainly broken up to make new necklaces, but what happened to The Three Brethren during the Civil War is uncertain. Various theories suggest it was sold, or pawned but not retrieved in Amsterdam or Antwerp; that three more diamonds were added to it and it was renamed the Three Sisters; that Cardinal Mazarin, who collected valuable gemstones, acquired it along with the debts he purchased from Henrietta Maria. One theory says the jewel was adapted and offered for sale through Henrietta Maria's agent, a 'Monsieur Cletstex' of the Bank of Lombardy in Rotterdam. What really happened to The Three Brethren is open for speculation. It may well have arrived in Portugal with Ludo da Portovenere.

In 1644, Henrietta Maria gave birth to her last child in England then, gravely ill, returned to her homeland of France. Despite ill-health and lack of a permanent home (she was not welcome in Paris at the time and moved between various towns until finally allotted a suite in St Germaine), she continued to pawn and/or sell items considered to be part of the Crown Jewels to raise funds for the floundering Royalist army in England. Parliament maintained watchful spies, but Henrietta succeeded in raising money and credit in various European markets until her husband was imprisoned.

Much of the background to this novel comes from Henrietta Maria's letters to Charles Stuart, some of which are available on line. I also extracted details from reports to the Doge of Venice from his emissary to the Court of King Charles, the gentleman was a tremendous gossip. My other sources are too numerous to mention here.

I would like to give special thanks to author Elizabeth St. John, who checked the chapters dealing with her ancestor Lady Dalkeith and Henrietta Maria's removal to France. Finally, a note of thanks to my publisher, Michael James, for his enthusiasm and support for *The Chosen Man Trilogy*.

J.G. Harlond

Málaga, December, 2018

Originally from the south west of England, J.G Harlond (Jane) studied and worked in various different countries before finally settling down with her husband, a retired Spanish naval captain, in rural Andalucía, Spain. Despite being 'rubbish' at history at school because she wanted to turn everything into a story, she survived the History element of her B.A. and went on to get an M.A. in Social and Political Thought. Her historical fiction, set in the 17th century and the first half of the 20th century, features many of the places Jane has visited—along with flawed rogues, wicked crimes, and the more serious issues of being an outsider. Apart from fiction, Jane also writes school text books under her married name. Her favourite reading is along the Dorothy Dunnett lines: well-researched stories with compelling plots and complex characters.

If You Enjoyed This Book

Please write a review.
This is important to the author and helps to get the word out to
others
Visit

PENMORE PRESS
www.penmorepress.com

All Penmore Press books are available directly through our website,
amazon.com, Barnes and Noble and Nook,, Apple iTunes, Kobo
books and via leading bookshops across the United States, Canada,
the UK, Australia and Europe.

The Chosen Man

by

J. G Harlond

From the bulb of a rare flower bloom ambition and scandal

Rome, 1635: As Flanders braces for another long year of war, a Spanish count presents the Vatican with a means of disrupting the Dutch rebels' booming economy. His plan is brilliant. They just need the right man to implement it.

They choose Ludovico da Portovenere, a charismatic spice and silk merchant. Intrigued by the Vatican's proposal—and hungry for profit—Ludo sets off for Amsterdam to sow greed and venture capitalism for a disastrous harvest, hampered by a timid English priest sent from Rome, accompanied by a quick-witted young admirer he will use as a spy, and bothered by the memory of the beautiful young lady he refused to take with him.

Set in a world of international politics and domestic intrigue, *The Chosen Man* spins an engrossing tale about the Dutch financial scandal known as tulip mania—and how decisions made in high places can have terrible repercussions on innocent lives.

PENMORE PRESS
www.penmorepress.com

A Turning Wind

by

J. G Harlond

LUDO DA PORTOVENERE,ONE TIME CORSAIR, SOMETIME MERCHANT, SECRET AGENT OF MONARCHS, SERVANT OF NONE.

From the trading colony of Goa to the royal courts of England and Spain, Ludo da Portovenere completes difficult and dangerous secret commissions on his own terms and for his own reasons. But, as these tasks bring him closer to success, Ludo is forced to confront dangerous secrets of his own. While Ludo pursues a delicate mission for the English queen in the Spanish royal court, Alina, Baroness Metherall, faces challenges and dangers of her own as she tries to come to terms with what it means to be married to one person and love another. Ultimately, Ludo and Alina must decide who they really are, and to what extent their shared past should influence their future.

"Harlond's brilliantly realized portrait of the sea-trade in 17th century is a gem...Ludo is a great character with wit, intelligence and daring. Exploiting his position as an envoy between Charles I and the Spanish court results in a seafaring novel of danger and double-dealing. Highly recommended." Deborah Swift, author of Pleasing Mr Pepys

"Ms. Harlond details a credible, intricate world of deals and alliances, threats and opportunities, uncertainty and trust, in which her hero, the wily Genoese merchant Ludo da Portovenere, must tread with extreme caution. Let's hear yet more of him!" --Antoine Vanner, author of The Dawlish Chronicles series.

penmorepress.com

THE EMPRESS EMERALD

BY

J. G. HARLOND

Stolen: A child, a priceless jewel, and an identity

Abandoned as a child in a Bombay orphanage, Leo Kazan's life takes an unanticipated turn when he becomes the protégé of Sir Lionel Pinecoffin, the city's District Political Officer in Bombay. Under Pinecoffin's tutelage, the boy, adept at learning languages and theft, is trained as a spy and becomes immersed in international espionage, revolutionary politics, and diamond smuggling. In 1918, during a visit to London, he has a brief but memorable affair with a young English woman Davina Dymond in London before leaving for Russia.

Separated, their lives take different turns. As he matures Leo begins to question his family history, seeking to uncover the truth about his parents. A pregnant Davina is married off and exiled to Spain, where she gives birth to Leo's daughter. They are fated to meet again in Gibraltar in 1936, their love rekindled. But a new war plunges Europe into crisis, the Spanish Civil War tearing them apart, leaving, Leo and Davina in a fight to reclaim their lives and their love amid the violent storms of war.

PENMORE PRESS
www.penmorepress.com

Local Resistance

by

J. G. Harlond

WWII in England, Cornwall smugglers, Intelligence agents, detective story, locals and war in the UK, German navy operations on the coast of the UK. Murder thriller. Espionage.

On a stormy night in March 1941, Maisie Rose Hawkins leaves her drunk husband, Stan, out in the rain—and he disappears. Detective Sergeant Bob Robbins and young PC Laurie Oliver are called out to investigate and discover that Stan's small fishing boat is gone, the rope sawn through. As Bob searches for answers, it becomes apparent that in this small Cornish village where everyone knows everything about everybody, nobody quite knows the truth.

Beneath the surface of village life, a fierce battle is being waged against wartime deprivations. Shopkeepers quietly evade rationing restrictions. Food inspector Archibald Bantry, charged with enforcing those restrictions, dies in a suspicious car crash. Various leads connect a sea cave full of smuggled black-market goods to the missing Stan Hawkins. And what seems like the work of local malcontents becomes more complex and dangerous when Bob stumbles on the truth in a disused copper mine, where a much deadlier affair is underway.

"Uncanny happenings and warm characterization. . . . The realities of wartime life in this novel combine with a lovely sense of place to create a distinctly Cornish mixture of secluded charm and the unsettlingly mysterious." —Robert Wilton, prize-winning author of the Comptrollerate-General historical thrillers.

PENMORE PRESS
www.penmorepress.com

Historical fiction and nonfiction
Paperback available for order on line
and as Ebook with all major distributers

Fortune's Whelp
by
Benerson Little

Privateer, Swordsman, and Rake:

Set in the 17th century during the heyday of privateering and the decline of buccaneering, *Fortune's Whelp* is a brash, swords-out sea-going adventure. Scotsman Edward MacNaughton, a former privateer captain, twice accused and acquitted of piracy and currently seeking a commission, is ensnared in the intrigue associated with the attempt to assassinate King William III in 1696. Who plots to kill the king, who will rise in rebellion—and which of three women in his life, the dangerous smuggler, the wealthy widow with a dark past, or the former lover seeking independence—might kill to further political ends? Variously wooing and defying Fortune, Captain MacNaughton approaches life in the same way he wields a sword or commands a fighting ship: with the heart of a lion and the craft of a fox.

PENMORE PRESS
www.penmorepress.com